HIDDEN CURRENTS

Further Titles by Rowena Summers from Severn House

ANGEL OF THE EVENING
BARGAIN BRIDE
ELLIE'S ISLAND
HIGHLAND HERITAGE
KILLIGREW CLAY
SAVAGE MOON
THE SWEET RED EARTH
VELVET DAWN

Writing as Jean Saunders

GOLDEN DESTINY
THE KISSING TIME
PARTNERS IN LOVE
TO LOVE AND HONOUR
WITH THIS RING

Chapter 1

1843

Only the old men who hung around the waterfront watching the comings and goings of the busy little river tugs, the sailing barges and traders with the same unconcern, were in no hurry for the day's big event. They were frequently heard to say that it would happen all in good time, and there was no hurrying God or the vagaries of the tide. But for the young and impatient, it felt as though the nineteenth day of July would never arrive.

When it did, it seemed as if the whole city was on the move from early morning onwards, in anticipation of the celebrations. From the elegant mansions in Clifton, high above the city grime and the tavern filth, to the lowly dockside cottages, few clocks were needed to waken the inhabitants of Bristol.

The Stuckey family had no problems in tumbling out of their beds, all of them as fresh as summer larks. Sam Stuckey roused his family smartly, knowing there would hardly be a Bristol soul who wouldn't turn out for the launch of their great ship, and that laggardly stay-a-beds would miss the best of the show.

Plenty of curious out-of-town folk would be swelling their numbers too. He'd informed them so, with the air of inside information that belied his relatively humble involvement in the day. The most important fact of all

was that Bristol was to be honoured by the presence of Prince Albert, who would be arriving by special train from Paddington, with Izzy himself on the footplate.

Sam's wife had taken the news with her usual tolerance, but their daughter, Carrie, had been all of a bother when word first got around that royalty would be attending, and he'd had to put her quickly in her place.

"You just get them stars out o' your eyes, my girl. It's unlikely that we ordinary folk will get a sniff of either prince or engineer," he'd said severely. "And even if we do, 'tis a pound to a pinch of pig's swill that neither will take notice of you," he'd added for good measure.

She'd tossed her long coppery hair then, in the imperious way that was starting to needle him lately. Young girls of barely seventeen years old had no right to look so bonny and filled-out that they were beginning to attract the attention of lusty young men. There were too many foreigners and dark-eyed sailors hereabouts, forever loitering around the waterfront, and usually up to no good once they were ashore from the barges and trading vessels. Sam had expected the prospect of keeping an eye on his pretty daughter to be some time away yet . . .

But he put such uneasy thoughts out of his mind for the present, as his family all vyed for their morning space in the narrow cramped house on Jacob's Wells Hill. It was a far from fashionable area, and although it might not be right in the city's centre, anyone with sense knew that the waterfront was Bristol's throb and heartbeat.

As he collided with one of his tall sons in the crowded parlour, he mildly cursed his defensive thoughts, knowing that the house was becoming far too small for the six of them, and that he'd do better to concentrate on practical matters, however euphoric this day.

Once they had all eaten a good breakfast of thick dripping toast and tea, he looked his family over, and decided that they'd do. He'd never been one for displaying

2

private feelings, except when his anger was roused. But he couldn't deny the surge of pride that was deep in his gut for this day, knowing he'd played his part, albeit in a minor way, towards the completion of the great ship that was about to be officially named the S.S. *Great Britain.*

Iron lady she might be, and a credit to the great engineer they affectionately referred to as Izzy among themselves, but she'd still needed the skilled hands of carpenters like himself to fit out her beautiful dining room for the likes of the gentry, and fashion the huge length of her elegant promenade decking. He'd relished being part of the task more than any other job he'd undertaken. The refining of raw pieces of timber to something approaching perfection, and the sweet dry tang of sawdust, was in his bones, and in that of his older sons' bones too. By the time the craftmanship was done, and he held a fine piece of expertly planed and polished wood in his hands, Sam was as stirred as if he stroked a woman's skin . . .

"Are we all ready then?" he said sharply now, to cover the sinful feeling of pride in his own achievements, and the even more sinful stirring in his loins. His May would be more affronted with him than ever if she'd known where his thoughts were straying. And in the morning too.

"Ready as we'll ever be, Pa," his son Frank said, sprawled out on the settle as if this was a Sunday. "'Tis all set to be a good day, and too fine to be indoors."

His brother turned from fastening his necktie, older and more caustic than the other. "You find it easy to forget that the work's come to an end, don't you, bruth? We've had a good run of work on the ship, but tomorrow we start looking for new jobs. 'Tis a pity we ain't engine fitters, then we'd still have plenty to do with our hands."

Sam frowned, annoyed with Wilf for putting a sting into the day. The ship might look incongruous to some, sitting high out of the water before her engines were fitted, but it also served to emphasise her enormous size,

3

by which men and machines were dwarfed. And to see her eased carefully out of her protective dock into the floating harbour was going to be a sight to savour for years to come.

"We'll worry about that tomorrow, boy. We want no such thoughts spoiling the day. Now, if the womenfolk have finished titivating themselves, and Ma's got that basket of pies ready to take with us, let's get down to the wharf and find our viewing place."

"Do I look all right then, Pa?"

Carrie had listened impatiently to the three of them, but she couldn't be bothered with all this men's talk of finding new work tomorrow, and she twirled around, sending her thick red-gold curls flying out from beneath the poke bonnet. Her favourite gossamer-light lilac woollen shawl was draped with careless allure around her best summer frock, since Pa had said they must look their grandest for the occasion, and her own secret feelings of vanity were impossible to contain.

Her mother spoke in her usual level way, just as aware of her daughter's approaching womanhood as Sam.

"You look a treat, Carrie, but don't waste your time looking for compliments from your Pa, for you know you'll get none. Now, you just take hold of young Billy's hand, and let's get down to the dock."

"I don't need nobody holding my hand," Billy complained at once, not so excited at the prospect of spending hours down at the dockside to submit so readily. Carrie grasped his palm firmly, wincing a little at the clamminess of it, and constantly amazed to know how an eight-year-old could get so sticky without going anywhere or touching anything.

"Yes, you do, our Billy, and you're to do as I say."

"I ain't doing what you say. You're not my Ma."

His reward for his cheek was a swift clout around the head from his father.

4

"That's enough of that talk. You're to stay close to Carrie and the rest of us, and there's an end to it. Either that, or you and I will stay behind and miss the show."

Carrie knew Billy wasn't yet canny enough to know that wild horses wouldn't stop their father witnessing the great launching of the wondrous S.S. *Great Britain* from their vantage-site in Hotwell Road. It was still a miracle to all of them that Sam had managed to purchase admission tickets to the Grand Stand seating area on Ballast-wharf, right opposite the head of the ship. His gaffer, Aaron Woolley, was a close acquaintance of the builder responsible, and had been in on the ticket-issuing early, and therefore able to arrange admission for all the Stuckey family. If Sam had felt a few qualms, wondering if they might feel out of place among the nobs, he'd never let on so to the rest of his family, and they were all too eager now to worry about such things.

But the thought of having to stay home in disgrace was obviously enough to quell Billy's arguments, and he merely scowled in silence as they closed the door of the tall house behind them, and began the long processional family walk down the steep cobbled road towards the wharf.

Carrie hadn't quite known what to expect of today. For weeks now, it seemed, they had seen the erection of stands and bunting, and excited talk about the launch of the great ship had been on everyone's lips. Triumphal arches linked many of the gabled houses to one another in Bristol's main streets, and the whole city was now a mass of colour, strewn with flags and flowers and streamers. When the moment of floating the ship out of her dock arrived, there would be bells ringing, guns firing, and bands playing triumphant music. No-one in Bristol, or for miles around for that matter, could be unaware of the achievement that this day celebrated.

5

Carrie felt a swell of pride for the part her Pa and brothers had contributed to it. Even if the folk who would be jostling beside her in the Grand Stand didn't know it, *she* did. Some of them might even be important. By now, the newspapers were giving ever more garbled reports of the personages expected to be present. Lords and ladies, the posh folk from up Clifton way, and all the city dignitaries . . . but, of course, none of them could eclipse the presence of Prince Albert and the famous engineer. And as far Carrie was concerned, each was as important as the other.

As the soles of her shoes rang with a metallic sound on the cobbled hillside, she balked a little at the size of the crowds ahead of her. The Stuckeys were early, but they certainly weren't the first to take their places. The very air vibrated with noise and laughter, and for a moment, Carrie wondered how those who had never seen the building of Mr Brunel's ship must feel, seeing the enormous vessel for the first time.

Living on the steep hill above the very dock where she was built, Carrie had seen the ship take shape from its beginning, and although she didn't take quite the same proprietorial view of her as her menfolk, she couldn't help but be stirred by the sight of her. Some said it was a miracle that such a hulk could float at all, but all Bristolians had faith in the great engineer's ability to prove it.

"Sometimes, Carrie Stuckey, I think you've gone daft in the brain over your Mr Brunel," her friend Elsie had scoffed. "Your head is full of dreams these days. It ain't as if you'll ever get to meet him, and much good it'd do if you did. He's as old as your Pa for a start, and out of your class. Give me a real lively boy to cuddle up to any day."

"It's real lively boys who get you into trouble," Carrie had replied smartly.

Elsie had stared at her in derision. "Don't you ever want a boy of your own then?"

6

"'Course I do, but I'm choosey who I give my cuddles to," Carrie had said, with a toss of the curls that were the envy of her friend, and left Elsie in no doubt as to what Carrie thought of reckless flirting with the tavern lads and the market boyos from Wales at the Welsh Back quay.

But she was determined not to be goaded by any of the little barbs that frequently prickled between herself and Elsie today. It was far too glorious a day, and as they neared the Grand Stand area, she squinted her eyes to see if she could catch a glimpse of her friend. Her Pa had generously purchased a seat for Elsie too. Elsie's old granpa was too infirm to venture out of the mean little cottage the two of them shared. It was little wonder that Elsie frequently ached to get out of there . . . she had her dreams too.

Her small feeling of magnanimity swiftly fading, Carrie gave a small sigh. She knew full well that if Elsie had her way, she'd be sitting as stiflingly close to Wilf Stuckey as was possible today. And Carrie could have told her how futile it was for Elsie to be toying with the idea of setting her sights on the tallest, best-looking of her brothers.

"There's your friend now, more's the pity," Wilf said shortly.

Carrie hid a smile, as the truth of her fleeting thoughts was confirmed. Elsie Miller had a long way to go yet, if she thought her flirty eyes and flouncing ways could make Wilf partial to her. But she defended her at once.

"I wish you wouldn't always show how much you despise her, Wilf. Elsie's not a bad girl – "

"I'll wager she would be, given half the chance," Frank put in with a grin. "You want to watch your step with her, our Carrie, or you'll both end up as bad lots."

Carrie felt her cheeks flush. It was one thing to have her Pa eyeing her uneasily lately, as her shape began to blossom out in places it hadn't done before. It was

7

another thing to have her Ma looking at her quizzically, and patently wondering if there were things her daughter should be told about growing up – the things she and Elsie had already discussed in as intimate detail as possible with their scanty knowledge . . . but it was something else entirely to have her brothers being so knowing about female matters. Carrie hated that. As if to insist privately that no changes were taking place in her body or her life at all, she clutched hold of young Billy's hand so tightly that he hollered out.

"I'm sorry, lamb," she said contritely. "Come on, let's follow Pa until we find the best seats, and we'll save one for Elsie."

"Why must we? I don't like her," he said at once, clearly intending to be at his cantankerous worst today. "She always smells funny."

"That's because she works with the fish so much," Carrie told him. "She can't help the smell, and you're not to say anything about it, do you understand?"

She sympathised with Elsie about the smell. It wasn't easy, working between the various markets and handling the slippery fish all day long. The fish market at St James was held on Mondays, Wednesdays and Fridays, but Elsie had a reprieve from there on Wednesdays, when she worked the Welsh Market. Though it wasn't merely for a change of goods from the fish, as Carrie well knew. At the Welsh Market there was fresh and live produce; geese, pigs, ducks and fowls, as well as cider trading, fruit and nuts, and usually some scraps to take home for her granpa at the end of the day . . . and there were also the stocky dark-haired boyos that came across the Bristol Channel on the trows to sell their wares.

Elsie didn't seem to mind handling the fish on the other days, but Carrie shuddered, knowing she couldn't bear their cold, clammy skin, nor ever get used to the smell. And whatever other faults Elsie had, she was as fastidious about herself as Carrie. She scrubbed at her hands and changed her clothes frequently, but still the fishy smell persisted. It was enough to turn a boy right off . . . but by all accounts, it didn't do so.

Carrie's own work at the wash-tub with her mother, caring for the fine and delicate fabrics that the high-society Clifton ladies didn't care to trust to the laundries, might seem demeaning to some, but at least she wasn't at the mercy and catcalls of the flotsom that came in from the sea. And providing they hadn't had to use too much bleach or vinegar in the rinsing water, the only smell that came from her hands was that of soap.

Besides all that, there was always the dreaming thought that perhaps some day this fine chemise, or that beautiful lace-trimmed evening gown, might one day adorn her own shape. Once, Carrie had dared to try on one of the shimmering garments, the like of which she knew she would never own. She had felt the sensuality of the satin fabric against her skin, and wondered how it must feel to always wear such garments . . . and then she had felt the sting of her mother's hand when she had been discovered preening herself in front of the looking-glass in the room she shared with Billy.

She suddenly stumbled, nearly pulling Billy off his feet in the process, and blushed furiously as someone in the crowd shouted at her to be more careful. Her heart skipped a sickening beat as she recognised the man.

"Can't you control your girl, Sam Stuckey?" Mr Woolley, her father's stout-bellied gaffer, bawled at him, though his eyes were concentrated on Carrie in a way she hated. She averted her eyes quickly, knowing her Pa wouldn't care to be chastised in front of a crowd because of his daughter's clumsiness. And then her friend caught up with them, and she heard Elsie laughing.

"Lord, what a comical sight you look, Carrie Stuckey, with your bonnet tipped all over your eyes. Can't you be more careful where you put your feet, girl?" She did a fair mimicry of gaffer Woolley's voice, which started Billy giggling.

"Shut up, you ninny," Carrie told him crossly. "You'll only get Pa more riled if he thinks you're laughing at him."

She adjusted her bonnet swiftly, wondering just why she counted Elsie so much a friend, when they were so often at loggerheads. But she'd once heard someone say that that was the mark of a real friendship. Such trivial irritations made no difference to the way true friends cared for one another, and she and Elsie had known one another since infancy. Carrie's mother had comforted the small girl when her own mother had died, so soon after the father's ship had gone down with all hands lost. She gave the other girl a forgiving smile.

"Come and sit here." She patted the wooden seat behind her, as the family took up their allotted row in the Grand Stand. Elsie didn't immediately respond, gazing around her, as if looking for someone.

"Sit *down*, for pity's sake," Carrie said. "Our Wilf's gone to fetch some sweets for Billy, if that's who you're looking for."

"You can sit by me instead, if you like," Frank said encouragingly. Elsie looked at him coolly. The second son was good-looking, if not quite the spit of his brother, but he had none of Wilf's arrogant swagger. Besides, to Elsie, second son meant second best.

"No thanks, I'll sit by my friend," she said, settling herself on the far side of Carrie and Billy, and concentrated on scanning the sea of bonnets and tall hats below for anyone who could recognise her among the toffs. Not that she counted Carrie's family as toffs, but they had what she didn't. They all had each other.

Carrie's mother leaned forward to smile kindly at the girl. "How does your granpa fare, Elsie?"

She shrugged. "Fair to middling, as usual, Mrs Stuckey. The doctor says he'll not last another winter, but he's been saying that for the last three, so we don't take much notice. Granpa don't care to see him too often. He says it's a waste of money to keep on hearing the same thing, and he'll go when his time comes and not before."

Carrie felt mildly thankful that the old grandpa existed. If it wasn't for the fact that her mother respected the way Elsie dutifully cared for him in the ramshackle hovel where they lived, she wasn't sure May Stuckey would have wanted her to continue their friendship, despite all. The Stuckeys weren't snobs, but they were more than a cut above some of the cottagers on the waterfront.

But she put such thoughts out of her mind now, as a sudden shaft of sunlight seemed to strike the golden Arms of England on the bow of the great ship. To anyone of a fanciful nature, it must have seemed as if the gods themselves blessed the gleaming black hull with its six great masts bedecked with flags. When she came out of her dry dock and was sitting up so high and noble in the water, she would appear to have a divine weightlessness.

Carrie guiltily wondered if such a thought would be construed as blasphemous. But no-one could deny that the ship completely dominated the river. The dozens of small craft plying about on the water like worker bees around their queen, were totally insignificant beside her.

"Do you think you'd care to travel to America in her, Elsie?" Carrie said suddenly, as her thoughts roamed.

"Would pigs like to fly?"

"I shouldn't think so," Carrie said, thinking the remark one of Elsie's sillier ones. "But it must be wonderful to take a sea voyage and act the part of a lady."

"The only way you're likely to do that is to marry a rich man, or become a lady's maid, our Carrie," Frank said.

"She's much too good to become a rich man's toy, or to kow-tow to society ladies," her brother Wilf said, catching the end of the conversation as he returned with the sweets for Billy. He seated himself on the far side of Frank, so that the brothers and the Stuckey parents flanked the girls and the small boy.

"Don't you think I do a menial enough job already, washing their dirty linen?" Carrie said. "If that's not kow-towing to the nobs, I don't know what is."

She bit her lip, hoping her mother hadn't heard her, and thankful for the bustle and noise all around her. If she despised herself for the work she did, then she implied that she despised Ma too, and she could never do that. She felt suddenly depressed, and looked down at the roughness of the wash-tub hands in her lap. Her cotton gloves couldn't hide the shame of their redness, any more than the whiff of fish that came from Elsie every now and then, could hide the evidence of her own work.

"You do an honest job, Carrie, and there's no shame in that," Wilf told her. "At least Ma knows where you are each day, and that you're safe from harm."

It had always been a comfort to the men to be sure of that. It had been a comfort to Carrie, too, to know that her two strong brothers would come to her aid at once, if she was threatened in any way. It had never felt like a restriction before. But lately, she had been aware of a new restlessness inside her, and sometimes it seemed ready to burst in her veins. Girls far younger than herself had proper jobs outside the home. They looked after themselves and their dependent relatives – even Elsie did that – while Carrie Stuckey's world often seemed as cloistered as a nunnery.

Sometimes, it seemed that they were all closing in on her . . . her Ma and Pa, her two older brothers . . . it was as if her very growing-up had to be protected against some silent enemy, but none of them ever explained what that enemy was. Instead, they made guarded remarks that she was supposed to understand. It was as if they all shared a secret that she was still too young to be told, but which was a danger to her very self. It made her frustrated, and it made her angry.

"You're wearing your tight face, Carrie," she heard Elsie crow. "What's the matter? Are you sulking because you haven't seen your famous engineer yet?"

"Of course not, because he hasn't arrived yet," Carrie said crossly. "Pa says the nobs are having a banquet before the launch, so we've got a long time to wait yet."

"Why couldn't we have waited at home, then?" Billy howled at once.

"Because, my sweet cherub, we wouldn't have had a seat to watch the show, if we hadn't got here early," Carrie told him. "If we didn't claim our places early, other people would have sat in them, no matter whether we had tickets or not, and I didn't want to stand up all day long, thank-you!"

But she could see he was already getting bored. If it hadn't been for the bend in the steep hill that was Jacob's Wells Road, their own house would have been within sight, and he could have been at home playing with his marbles or his counters. Instead, he was starting to fidget and scuff his feet, and Carrie couldn't really blame him.

"Let's play a game," she suggested.

"What game?"

She ignored the belligerence in his voice. "Let's count the small boats on the river."

It was a harmless diversion that could take as long as it interested the boy. And for a while, Billy was quite amenable to the game. They counted boats, then they counted top hats such as Mr Brunel always wore. It was to hide his short stature, Wilf always said, to Carrie's annoyance at this criticism of her hero. Then they counted white bonnets and blue ones, until Billy got utterly fed up with counting at all, and slumped down in his seat. Elsie gave a great yawn without covering her mouth, and Carrie

13

heard her mother tut-tut at this show of bad manners in a public place.

"Should we take Billy for a walk, Ma?" she asked quickly. "The rest of you can keep our seats."

"Well, don't go too far. We don't want him getting lost. Though if he's getting too bored, you can take him home for a drink," May Stuckey said. "When you come back, we'll have our picnic. There's enough for you too, Elsie."

The girl thanked her, and Carrie knew she wouldn't have thought of such a thing for herself. To her credit, Carrie knew she would have left her old granpa well supplied with food and drink for the day, but Elsie would have gone hungry rather than bother to prepare a picnic for herself.

They each took one of Billy's hands and eased their way through the crowds on the Grand Stand and beyond, and long before they reached the edge of the waterfront, Carrie wondered if this had been such a sensible idea after all.

People were good-natured enough at waiting for the ship to be launched, but an irritating threesome, linked together and trying to get through their ranks, was more than an annoyance. Anyone who moved back was in danger of losing a precious viewing spot, and when a gentleman cursed her volubly for stepping on his toe, her face flamed with embarrassment.

"I've had enough of this," she said to Elsie. "Let's go back to the others. One of Ma's pies will keep Billy occupied for a while."

"I want to watch the boats!" Billy yelled.

They were some distance away from the others, and they couldn't see them at all because of the bend in the river. For some minutes now, Billy had been fascinated by the showmanship of a young man in a paddle tug-boat containing half a dozen well-dressed ladies and gentlemen.

The young man caught sight of Billy and waved to him, and Billy leapt up and down in delight, unable to wave back because of the two hands holding him firmly.

It was quite a smart boat, obviously having been given a new coat of paint to make it all ship-shape and Bristol fashion for the occasion. An older man was explaining to the passengers some of the finer points of the floating harbour and, no doubt, the S.S. *Great Britain* herself.

Tug-boats like this one were ten a penny on the river, many of them family-owned, and helping to pay their way by running summer excursions for folk wanting the thrill of being on the water. Some even went out into the Bristol Channel to the twin islands of Flatholm and Steepholm, with their fine views of the watering-hole of Weston-super-Mare on one side, and the Welsh coast on the other.

"Well, you can't watch them any longer," Carrie said crossly, seeing the grinning face of the young man at Billy's frustration. "Ma will be wondering where we've got to."

Before she could say anything more, Billy had slipped his hand out of her grasp, and his forceful little figure was rushing towards the bank. Carrie shouted at him to come back, but he was deaf to her voice, all his interest centred on the excitement of watching the deft movements of the boatman.

Everything happened fast after that. One minute Billy was dancing with glee at being free, and waving furiously at his new-found friend; in the next, his arms were thrashing like windmills as he over-balanced, and with a great shriek of terror he was hurtling headlong into the deep waters of the floating harbour.

The boatman didn't hesitate. To the accompanying screams of the onlookers who had seen the incident, he dived in to where Billy had disappeared beneath the water, dangerously churned up by so much river activity. It seemed like an eternity to Carrie, but within seconds the man had dragged up the dripping, bedraggled child and was dumping him beside her. He hauled himself up after Billy, to applause and cheers from those who had seen what happened. To her amazement, the man wasn't even angry. Wet through though he was, she could see the laughter in his dark eyes, and how his dark hair curled attractively into his neck and over his forehead.

"What was the little feller trying to do? Learn to swim?" the man said with a grin. The words confused Carrie for a moment, when she'd expected abuse for her carelessness at the very least.

"I'm indebted to you for your quick action, sir," she stammered, hardly knowing what else to say. What *did* you say to a man who had just saved a child from almost certain drowning? In her embarrassment, she turned angrily on Billy, shaking him hard.

"You stupid little idiot! What did I tell you about holding tight to me?"

"Don't rattle his teeth, miss. You'd best get him home and into dry clothes, or he'll miss all the fun," the young man said lazily.

Carrie glared at him now, but aware that he was going to miss it too. It was Elsie who alerted her to her manners.

"I'm Elsie Miller, and this is Carrie Stuckey," she said. "The boy's name is Billy. They only live up the hill, so we'll have time to get him changed and back down again before anybody misses us, at the rate things are happening here."

Carrie saw how the water dripped off the young man. "I'm afraid we've ruined the day for you as well. Unless – " she hesitated as a daring thought occurred to her. She knew she shouldn't even suggest it, but it would be a way of saying thank-you, and surely even her Pa couldn't object to it . . .

"If you wouldn't think I've got a cheek for saying

16

it, you're welcome to borrow some of my brother's clothes. You're about the same size, and as Elsie says, we only live up the hill." Her voice trailed away, feeling like a hussy for her daring, and aware that Elsie was gaping at her.

The man turned away as the older one in the tug-boat called to him. Carrie felt awful then, wondering if she had made a terrible mistake. The unbidden thought came to her mind that none of the young ladies whose gowns she laundered so carefully would have made such a blatant invitation to a stranger. He must think her very forward indeed. She didn't hear what he said to the other man as she hustled Billy away, while Elsie lingered behind for a moment. When she caught up to the two of them, she hissed in Carrie's ear.

"Well, you're a dark horse and no mistake. He's coming too. He called the other one Uncle and told him he's going for some dry clothes, and he'll meet him back at the passenger landing pontoon soon. I'd like to know what *your* Pa's going to say about it when he finds out you've invited a man into the house without a chaperone!"

Carrie looked behind her, feeling her heart thump with unexpected speed. And it wasn't just because of the fright Billy had given her, nor the relief that he was safe, either. It was more to do with the fact that the young man was following them through the crowds and up towards Jacob's Wells Road, and he was the handsomest young man she'd ever seen, apart from her brothers.

As for what Elsie had just said, well, she had two chaperones of sorts. She had Billy, and she had Elsie, though what good either of them would be if she was physically attacked, she couldn't think. But instinct told her the boatman wasn't the attacking kind. And it was only common courtesy to offer him a change of dry clothes after he'd saved Billy from a watery grave. It was going to be her defence later, once she faced the inevitable wrath of her Pa.

Chapter 2

His name was John Travis. He'd hurriedly changed into a set of Wilf's old working clothes, and departed from the house, promising to have the garments cleaned and returned as soon as possible.

"It's not necessary to return them," Carrie said in a fright. "They're old clothes that my brother doesn't use any more. He won't miss them."

She hoped her words carried conviction. She could just imagine the fuss if John Travis turned up at the house with a parcel of clothes. It was far better to forget all about them, and Wilf would never notice they were gone.

It was more than half an hour before the girls got back to their Grand Stand seats. By then, Carrie had scrubbed and tidied Billy, and she was flushed and excited by the time they returned to the rest of the family, and Billy was still smarting at being sworn to secrecy about his adventure.

"You're not to say anything about what happened until we get back home later, do you hear?" Carrie had said sharply, giving him a hearty shake to emphasise her words. "It will spoil Pa's day if you do, and if you dare breathe a word about it before I say you can, I promise he'll skin your hide for being so stupid as to fall into the river, and you'll get another one from me for disobeying orders."

"Good God, Carrie, you've missed your vocation. You should have been a Sunday school teacher," Elsie

19

said with grudging admiration, as they fought their way back through the crowds. "I swear you'd make a saint quake."

"It's the only way to keep him quiet," she retorted, knowing the truth of it from past experience.

"They'll probably know eventually. Your Billy won't keep quiet for ever, and Wilf won't be too pleased at passing on his clobber to a stranger. Nor taking him home."

"Oh, shut up, Elsie. It's too hot to argue," Carrie said, thankful to reach the family at last, and becoming more uneasy by the minute at the recklessness of what she'd done.

She didn't need Elsie to keep telling her so. Elsie had been surprisingly dumb all the time the stranger had been in the house, clearly still staggered at Carrie's nerve at inviting him there. Elsie's rare silence only unnerved Carrie more. Perhaps if John Travis had been older, and plainer, and less of a splendid figure, he might have been more acceptable to the older Stuckeys as a stranger to their house. But he wasn't old, nor plain, and he was all that a silly romantic young girl might dream of in a man . . .

"Where in pity's name have you been, Carrie?" Ma said at once. "And why is our Billy wearing different clothes?"

"He spilled a drink all down his others, Mrs Stuckey," Elsie said, far more glib and innocent than Carrie could have been on the spur of the moment. "We had to get him cleaned up, and it was quicker to take him back and change him. We haven't missed anything, have we?"

"Not likely," Frank said with a grin. "Though there seemed to be something going on down by the waterfront earlier. Did you see anything?"

"No," Carrie said, giving Billy a kick on the shins as he opened his mouth. "But there are some jugglers and mummers wandering about, so I expect they were giving a free show."

"Full marks," Elsie breathed to her, but Carrie didn't enjoy the deceit. She rarely had occasion to lie to her family, and she didn't care for it at all. Besides, a lie always caught you out in the end, and even though the invention was to save her Ma and Pa's enjoyment of a day they'd looked forward to so much, it didn't make a lie any less of a lie.

A sudden surge of chatter all around them stopped the need for any more questioning. They craned their necks to see if anything of importance was happening. But it was only a party of ladies and gentlemen arriving to take the seats that had been secured for them by their servants, and once they were settled the excitement subsided again.

"We might as well eat these pies now, seeing as how we carried them down here," Ma said practically. "Nothing's going to happen for a while yet, by the looks of it, and neither prince nor engineer is worth wasting good food for."

"You wouldn't agree with that, would you, Carrie?" Elsie grinned. "You'd give a week's grub to rub shoulders with 'em, and not only shoulders, neither."

"For pity's sake!" Carrie groaned. "If Ma hears such talk, she'll stop me seeing you."

Elsie looked at her with her usual defiance. "Well, it's just as well I ain't got no Ma to tell me what to do, if it keeps you in chains."

"I'm not kept in chains! You say the daftest things sometimes, Elsie."

"You might just as well be, if you can't even say what you think and do what you like."

"I took John Travis home, didn't I? I don't recall you ever taking a boy home before," she hissed, as the pies were passed along.

Although it was hardly the way it sounded, the words

effectively shut Elsie up for a while, and they munched their pies in silence. By now they were all starting to get impatient of waiting for a ceremony that seemed as far away as ever. But eventually, the whispering and rustling among the crowd heralded the fact that it was finally about to begin, and the most important personages appeared on the platform adjacent to the great ship.

"Well, I call it a bloody let-down," Elsie complained in Carrie's ear. "All that time waiting, and we couldn't hear a thing because of the cheering and jostling. All we saw was the bottle of champagne crashing against the ship, and then all hell was let loose with the guns and bands and bell-ringing. I swear I'll be deaf for a month if it goes on much longer."

They were pressed tight together amongst the crowd now, having lost sight of the rest of their party as soon as people began to disperse. Sam Stuckey had shouted that he and Ma had hold of Billy, and were taking him back home, and the others could find their own way back when they liked. There was no work for anybody for the rest of that day.

Carrie's brothers had shot off in the direction of the platform to try to catch a closer glimpse of Izzy. Carrie had wanted to do the same, but she had reluctantly agreed that it was hopeless, still fuming that neither Wilf nor Frank had thought it important enough to take her along with them.

But she couldn't help agreeing with Elsie that the day had been a bit of a let-down. The great ceremony they had all anticipated so much had been no more than opening the dry dock sluices at the moment the champagne had burst against the ship's bows. It was a fine achievement, of course, and the S.S. *Great Britain* was now sitting resplendently high in the water after being towed slowly out of the dock and into the floating harbour.

Now it was virtually all over, and there was nothing else to do but wander about among the crowds, or go back home. There was no sense of order among the crush of people, and the girls were jostled on all sides as they struggled to move out of the Grand Stand and onto the waterfront.

"I wonder what your friend's doing for the rest of the day," Elsie said, scowling as she got a dig in the ribs from a ragged urchin, and promptly kicked him back.

"What friend?" Carrie said without thinking, and then felt her face flood with colour as she realised who Elsie meant. "John Travis is hardly a friend, for pity's sake. I don't even know him."

"You knew him well enough to hand over your Wilf's clothes," Elsie sniggered. "I keep trying to imagine his face when he finds out. When are you going to tell him?"

Carrie frowned uneasily.

"Perhaps never. They were clothes he ain't worn in ages, so he won't be missing 'em. And our Billy will be too damn scared of what Pa will do to him for being so daft as to fall in the water to say anything. I wish they'd left him with us, though, so I could have made sure of it."

"Are you having second thoughts about the kid now?"

Carrie shrugged. "Well, you can never tell with our Billy. He can be a contrary little devil when he likes."

Elsie grinned. "I shouldn't worry. Your face was enough to scare the feathers off a duck's back. He'll do as you say, school-marm! Anyway, there he is."

Carrie felt her heart leap. For a moment, she thought Elsie was still referring to her little brother Billy, and she felt a brief panic. Surely he hadn't slipped away from her Ma and Pa now? Then, among the flotilla of small boats paying court to the newly named giant ship, she recognised one of the paddle-tugs being expertly steered through the water towards it. The excited passengers sat on the canvas chairs that had obviously been put on board for the temporary conversion to a pleasure-boat. John Travis stood in the bows, as magnificent as any ship's figurehead as he pointed out the detail on the *Great Britain*.

"He's certainly a fine-looking boy," Elsie breathed admiringly. The sun had dried his thick hair, and it was ruffled by the river-breeze. Dark and unkempt, it merely added to the dashing figure he made.

For a moment, Carrie thought about the grey serge shirt that John Travis was wearing now. Her brother Wilf's shirt, that Carrie had washed and ironed so many times. She thought about it caressing John Travis's skin and maybe catching on the hairs on John Travis's chest, the way Wilf used to complain that it did on his. She thought about John Travis's chest, and how broad and strong it was, and let herself dream about how it would feel to lay her head against it and hear his heartbeats . . .

Carrie was aware of her own erratic heartbeats, as John Travis caught sight of the two girls and raised his hand. Before she could even lift her hand to wave back, Elsie was waving furiously with both arms.

"For goodness' sake, stop making a spectacle of yourself," Carrie said crossly, still caught up in the dream, and embarrassed by the wanton foolishness of it. "Let's get away from here and get some fresh air. We're in danger of being pushed into the harbour ourselves by these crowds, and all these boats are churning up the stinking river mud."

Before she got too disdainful of it, remarking that the stink would get into their clothes and their hair if they weren't careful, she remembered that Elsie wouldn't be too bothered by the stench of the river, living so close to it.

"Where do you want to go, then? I don't feel like

being indoors today, and me granpa won't be expecting me back for hours yet," Elsie said, just as rattled.

"Let's go up on the Downs. There might be a fair up there, and if not we can sit on the grass above the cliffs and watch the boats on the river."

"Or watch the rich folk go by. That's what you really want to do, isn't it? Playing your old games in your head that you're one of 'em, I suppose."

Carrie reddened again. "There's nothing wrong with that. It's a harmless game."

"It's not harmless to try to get too much above yourself, Carrie Stuckey. You think yourself better than the rest of us, don't you?"

Carrie stopped walking so suddenly that the people behind cannoned into her. As they moved away, she heard them complaining loudly, but she ignored them and glared at Elsie.

"What's that supposed to mean?"

Elsie glared back. "Just because you wash the clothes of those posh Clifton folk, don't mean you're one of 'em, does it? Just because you've tried a few fine frocks on, don't mean you'd ever fit comfortably into 'em, either. You don't talk like one of 'em, and you ain't got the white hands of a lady, so don't go acting like one."

"I never do! And even if I did, I'd rather put on airs and graces than act like a tart!"

"And I know why you want to go up on the Downs, too. You're hoping one of they fancy ladies you wash for will recognise you and pass the time of day. Just as if!"

The two of them were breathing heavily now. But they had both let off enough steam, and their eyes were beginning to sparkle with the exhilaration of one of their regular bouts of hurling insults. They'd hardly noticed the small crowd of urchins that had gathered around them, egging them on to what was obviously better than a bun-fight. One of them leered encouragement at Elsie.

"You give 'er what for, duck. She ain't worth bothering about, wiv 'er 'igh and mighty airs. Come and have a jar of ale at the Old Tavern wiv us, instead."

Elsie rounded on him at once.

"Piss off, dumb-bell. When I want your help, I'll ask for it. Meanwhile, me and my friend have got better things to do than bandy words with river-scum!"

She linked arms with Carrie at once, and the two of them fought their way through the cat-calling crowd. By the time they reached Jacob's Wells Road, they were both laughing. Their arguments were often fast and furious, but they never reached breaking point in their friendship. It would take a major clash between them to do that.

Clifton Downs overlooked the city of Bristol with a benevolent air. The grass was summer-soft now, sweet and green and fragrant. It was a toiling, uphill walk from the teeming city below, but worth it once you got there. The forest of ships' masts in the docks, and the thriving river-life, appeared no more than a leisurely activity seen from the wide expanses of open grassland, and the spacious mansions of Clifton. But aesthetically, the two entities were worlds apart.

There were already swarms of people on the Downs. There was no organised fair, but the more enterprising folk had set up stalls for the sale of trinkets and goods, and the street entertainers had found their way up here early, hoping to get a good day's takings from the richer Clifton folk. And there were the usual orators who could always be relied on to gather crowds around them.

Carrie and Elsie paused by one of the soap-box orators now. He had the nerve to describe Bristol as a money-grabbing den of thieves and entrepreneurs, while Clifton was filled with elegant gentlefolk who wished to keep their village as far removed from the trade concepts of their neighbours as possible.

"Cheeky bugger," Elsie snapped, as the pompous orator urged all Clifton folk to resist any idea of further building infiltrating into their green and pleasant hillside oasis. "Me granpa says they'll never stop folk building houses, and one day the small towns will be all one big one anyway, no matter how these toffs look down on us."

"Don't you mind being looked down on?" Carrie said, almost swayed by the charm of the orator's accent, and the fine cut of his clothes. She felt Elsie poke her with her elbow.

"Nobody looks down on me, ninny, and I'd cuff the first one who did."

"They do, though. Look down on us, I mean. We're all tarred with the same brush, just because we live near the river."

Elsie tossed her head. "You take too much notice of what people think, Carrie Stuckey. What's it matter, anyway? You're as good as you think you are, and I reckon that makes me as good as anybody. You're getting to be a real snob, you know that?"

Carrie laughed uneasily. "Don't be daft. People with money and big houses are snobs, not folk like us."

Elsie shook her head. "Living in a smart house don't make you a snob. It's what's inside you that does that."

Carrie tilted her chin, deliberately ignoring the implications in her friend's remark. But sometimes, she was forced to concede, Elsie had more sense in that air-head of hers than might be credited.

She was still brooding over it when she heard a cultured female voice speak close beside her.

"Why, it's Carrie, isn't it?"

She turned quickly, and blushed scarlet as she saw one of the young ladies whose silk gowns and lace underpinnings she regularly laundered. She had a swift

27

vision of the young lady's huge stone-built mansion where she collected the soiled clothes, and later delivered them, fresh and clean. They had only ever met at the Barclay mansion, with Carrie in her servile capacity, and Carrie immediately felt all fingers and thumbs at seeing her in a different environment.

"It is, Miss Barclay," she stammered.

"And what's Carrie doing up here today?" Helen Barclay said in amusement. "I thought you'd have been watching the launch of the great ship."

"Oh I was, miss. But then me and me friend came up here for a breath of fresh air."

She bit her lip, hearing her own deferential speech. Even worse, being aware of her own shortcomings in it, with none of the beautiful rounded vowel sounds of the young lady. Helen Barclay was just little older than herself, but that was the only similarity between them. Helen had the palest gold hair, as soft as silk, and eyes of the roundest china-blue. Behind her stood a gentleman of quality, whom Carrie knew from the Barclay kitchen gossip was an admirer whom the particular and pampered Miss Barclay would soon discard like all the rest.

"Well, it's good to see you enjoying yourself, Carrie," the young lady said. "I'll see you again soon."

Elsie breathed out a snort of derision as the couple moved away.

"Well, if that don't just beat all. You acted like a puppet the minute her ladyship spoke to you. You'll never be one of 'em, and the sooner you realise it, the better."

Carrie spoke angrily. "You don't know what you're talking about. She's a very nice young lady, and at least she was gracious enough to speak to me."

"Oh yes. 'I'll see you again soon,'" Elsie mimicked. "What she means is, she'll be seeing you when she's got some more dirty clobber for you to wash."

"Sometimes, Elsie, I wonder why I ever put up with you," Carrie said deliberately.

"It's because you know you'll get the truth out of me, and I'll still be your friend. Even if you are a snob," she added, ducking the arm-lashing she knew would follow.

Immediately, Carrie wished she hadn't done it. It was common to be seen brawling, especially here, when they were as good as mingling with all sorts. Oh yes, she was a bit of a snob, she thought ruefully, but she couldn't see how a little snobbery could hurt if it meant you wanted to better yourself. And that didn't hurt either, she thought, with a touch of defiance, no matter what Elsie thought.

The two of them wandered about the Downs, pausing to listen to the hurdy-gurdy man and watch the antics of his little monkey when the toffs tossed him a copper or two. They watched several mummers performing, and marvelled at an impromptu magic act where the magician apparently swallowed a coin and then drew it from behind a sailor's ear, amid gasps and applause. After the unusual leisure of whiling away an hour with no work to do, they each bought a rosy red apple glazed with honey-coloured toffee, and lay face-down on the edge of the cliffs to watch the progress of the river craft, hundreds of feet below.

"I wonder where they're going," Carrie said dreamily, as a tall-masted ship moved majestically towards the mouth of the river into the Bristol Channel and the open sea. "I wonder if I'll ever be rich enough to take a sea voyage. Helen Barclay's parents took her to France on a ship last summer – "

Elsie's hoot of laughter stopped her in mid-sentence.

"Your head is completely turned by these Barclays and your stupid Izzy."

"He's not stupid. And my head is not turned at all. If you'd ever seen the inside of their house, you wouldn't be able to resist being envious, either."

"What's it like then? I bet you've only seen the kitchens, anyway."

"Well, that's where you're wrong. Mind you, I admit it was while the family was away from home," she said with a grin. "One of the house-maids gave me a look around the drawing-room and Miss Helen's bedroom."

Her voice grew wistful with envy. The Bible said it was wrong to covet what others had, but how could it be wrong to wonder what life might have been like, if you'd been born into different circumstances? But that was definitely wrong, because it meant denying Ma and Pa, and that was something she would never do . . .

"Go on, then. What was Miss High-and-Mighty's bedroom like?" Elsie encouraged, and Carrie knew she'd got her attention at last. She rolled over on her back, remembering.

"It was as big as our entire house. There was a white coverlet on the bed, and a thick flowered carpet on the floor, so your feet didn't make a sound when you walked. The window looked out over the Downs, and there was a writing table and chair next to it – "

"Well, that wouldn't be any good to you and me then, would it? Who would we write letters to, even if we were any good at it? Or were you thinking of writing to John Travis?"

"Why would I write to him?" she said, cross with Elsie for interrupting her reverie.

Her ability at writing wasn't that good, though she constantly strived to make it better. Her schooling had been sparse, but fluent reading and writing was something that separated the gentry from the scruffs. She knew that, even if Elsie didn't. And she had enough pride to want to do it, however laboriously.

"You don't need to write letters to him anyway, when you can just as easily talk to him, if you dare."

Elsie said it so slyly that Carrie knew he must be within

30

sight. She sat up quickly, wishing the toffee apple hadn't made her fingers and mouth feel so sticky.

There, not ten yards away from her, and wearing another change of clothes that were obviously his own, and not Wilf's working clobber, was John Travis. He looked different, away from the river environment. He looked slicked down and smarter, almost halfway between being a working man and a toff. Carrie reasoned that that's what he probably would be, if he was part-owner of a family tug-boat.

And she was suddenly petrified of him. How had she ever had the nerve to invite him to their mean little house on Jacob's Wells Road and offer him Wilf's clothes? He'd clearly discarded them fast enough, once the day's business was over.

"Go on then," Elsie urged. "Go and talk to him. He's not with anybody."

Her voice trailed away as a small group of young men and girls joined him at that moment. They were all laughing together, and Carrie turned away quickly, not wanting to be seen staring at them.

"I wish you'd mind your own business for once," she said savagely to Elsie. "What a fool I'd have looked if I'd called out to him just then."

"Why? You're as good as any of them. They're nobodies."

"They're friends of his, and I'm not. Just leave it alone, will you? Or I'm going straight back home this minute."

Elsie clamped her lips together and refused to say anything for the next few minutes. It was a situation that was too peaceful to last, and if anything, it gave Carrie too much time to think. The thought churning in her mind was that she would have dearly liked to be counted as one of John Travis's friends. She would have so liked to be as free and easy with him as those others seemed to be.

But she couldn't even pretend with him now. He knew her exactly for what she was. He'd seen the house she lived in, and knew she had a humble background . . . she hated herself for the way her thoughts were going. She should be satisfied with her lot, but somehow today her thoughts were all at sixes and sevens. In a fit of unreasonable anger, she wished she'd never seen Miss Helen Barclay's bedroom, because then she'd never have compared it with the virtual cupboard she shared with Billy . . . but she might as well wish for the moon, for it was just as unattainable.

"Hello again. I thought it was you two enjoying the sunshine."

Carrie felt as if she turned her head in slow motion as the voice she remembered spoke alongside her. She squinted up at him as he smiled down at her. His dark head was haloed against the light, and for a brief moment she was reminded of a god in one of her old Sunday-school picture-books . . . and then he moved, and the illusion was gone.

"Why don't you sit down beside us, so I don't have to keep on craning my neck?" she said, a mite ungraciously. He seated himself easily on the grass.

"I just wanted to say thank-you again for what you did earlier. It would have taken me ages to get through the crowds to Bedminster and back again in dry clothes if you hadn't come to my rescue."

"Is that where you live?" Elsie said. He nodded, but Carrie ignored the information for the moment, embarrassed by the civility of the young man after her own bad manners.

"I'm the one who should be thanking you," she said quickly. "We might not have had our Billy any more if you hadn't acted so fast."

"It just happened to be me who fished him out of the water," he said, as if it was an everyday occurrence to haul foolish children out of the river. "Somebody else would have done it if I hadn't got there first."

32

Carrie shivered. He might take it casually, but the river had been so churned up, with so many boats vying for space, and so many crowds, that a small boy could easily have been drowned and hardly noticed, and they both knew it. Her eyes met his in a frank stare.

"All the same, I owe you his life, Mr Travis, and I won't forget it."

"Then if you're so indebted to me, you can at least call me John," he said with a smile. "And if you permit it, I'll dispense with the formality and call you Carrie. It's a very pretty name."

"It's really Caroline, but that's too fussy for me," she said, even more confused now. It was the first time a young man had paid her a compliment, apart from her brothers, and the compliments she got from them were usually made tongue-in-cheek.

For a fleeting moment she wished she was still wearing gloves to cover her wash-tub hands. She wished she had the style of Miss Helen Barclay, so that she could speak to a boy without blushing, or the feeling that the whole world was laughing at her diffidence. She even wished she had Elsie's brash self-confidence.

"So what does John Travis do?" Elsie said pushily now, evidently thinking she had been silent for long enough.

"I thought you knew. My uncle owns the paddle-boat you saw us in earlier, and I work for him. Mostly we do ferrying work, but the pleasure trips are becoming more profitable now. The boat will be mine one day, but before that day comes I hope to buy a bigger boat of my own, and concentrate on pleasure trips for folk willing to pay for them. That's going to be the big thing of the future."

"I know some boys who come across from Wales in the trows for the markets. Is it one of those you're wanting?" Elsie asked, airing her knowledge.

John laughed. "Good God, no, begging your pardon. I'm after bigger fish than a sailing barge."

33

"You've got ambitions then," Carrie said, feeling as if everything he said put him farther out of reach.

His mouth was still curved in a wide smile as he looked her steadily in the eyes, and she felt her heart skip a beat. Dreams . . . ambitions . . . they were one and the same. They were something that Elsie considered of little value, but they were clearly something she and John Travis shared. The thought made her bolder and she smiled back.

"Of course. A man without ambition might as well be dead," he said.

She was still caught up in the notion that she might have found a kindred spirit, despite the fact that he was a cut above herself, when the group of people he had been with earlier, appeared again.

"Come on, John. We're all waiting for you," one of the young ladies called out.

He stood up at once, brushing the grass off his trousers.

"Time to go," he said. "But I'll be seeing you again, Carrie. I've asked the woman who does our washing to get your brother's clothes presentable as quickly as possible, then I'll return them to you."

"Oh, but I told you not to bother – "

He wasn't listening. He waved his hand and strode off to rejoin the others. Seconds later he was lost in the crowd, and Carrie felt as if she'd been hit in the pit of her stomach.

"There you are," Elsie said triumphantly. "Didn't I tell you he was goggle-eyed for you?"

"Oh yes, I'm sure he is. I'm such a bloody great catch, aren't I?"

"What's up now?" Elsie said. Even she couldn't fail to recognise the misery in Carrie's voice.

"You wouldn't see it, would you? He *pays* somebody to do his washing."

"So what? It's an honest job, isn't it? You always said it was." She stopped abruptly.

"Hooray. You've seen daylight," Carrie said, bitterly aware of a great inner hurt that had no logical reason behind it, but was nonetheless needle-sharp.

"You mean that just because you and your Ma do the washing for the toffs, and your John Travis pays somebody else to do his, he'll think you're beneath him, is that it?"

"Of course that's it," Carrie said angrily. She must be the world's biggest fool to look down on the work she and Ma did, just because a boy had smiled at her with a certain light in his eyes, but she was suddenly unable to avoid the shame of it all. Washing other folks' clothes was hardly the work of an artiste or a craftsman. And who would want to be seen walking out with such a person?

She gave a sudden laugh. When had there ever been any suggestion of John Travis wanting to walk out with her, anyway? She was making her usual mountains out of anthills. Seeing hidden meanings in things that didn't exist. Shooting at rainbows, as per bloody usual . . . she made an effort to sound quite unconcerned.

"I wish you could see your face," she told Elsie. "Do you really think I care what he thinks of me?"

"Don't you?"

"Of course not," Carrie said, with a carelessness she didn't feel, but needing to save face all the same.

Elsie gave her a mischievous grin. "Maybe there's room for me then. If you don't fancy him, I just might."

"I never said I didn't fancy him – " but she felt her face go hot, knowing she was caught out, and Elsie's chortle told her she knew it too.

"Don't worry, I won't queer your pitch," she said, already tiring of the game. "Anyway, I'd trade him for your Wilf any time."

"Elsie, I've told you before – our Wilf thinks you're too

young for him," Carrie said, treading carefully, since she knew very well Wilf didn't give a thought for her friend. "Frank likes you though."

"So you keep telling me. Oh, to blazes with them all," she said. "Look over there, Carrie. Let's go and get our fortune told."

Elsie pointed to where a gypsy fortune-teller's tent was set up some distance away from them. The aged woman seemed to have no customers for the moment. She sat outside her small canvas tent, ablaze with spangles and glitter, her skin so swarthy and dark as to suggest she was a true Romany.

As if aware that she was being watched, she turned her head slowly, her black eyes mesmerising, even from a distance. She didn't smile or wave, yet it was as though some special aura about her was drawing the girls to her. Carrie shivered.

"I don't think so."

"Oh, come on. It'll be a lark. You don't have to believe any of her nonsense, do you? Not unless she told you that John Travis was destined to be your own true love."

"I'd rather leave the fairy-tales for our Billy," Carrie snapped, wondering if Elsie had seen right inside her head at that moment.

Because just for the very briefest of moments, she had let herself dream that that was exactly what Madame gypsy-whoever-she-was was about to tell her . . . and nobody in their right minds would dare to dispute what a gypsy told them. Even her no-nonsense Ma always bought a sprig of lucky heather with a bundle of new clothes pegs, from any gypsy who knocked at the door, and never refused to cross the palm with a coin, even if it was rarely a silver one.

"Come on then," Elsie challenged.

"Oh, all right. Perhaps she'll tell us we're destined to

marry rich men and live the life of luxury and never have to dirty our hands again."

They linked arms, suddenly euphoric at the very notion, and ran laughing across the grass towards the gypsy fortune-teller.

Chapter 3

John Travis wasn't sure what the pretty girls he'd met earlier were thinking as he strode off to rejoin his party, but he knew that to this mixed university group, down from Oxford for a few days, he was merely a temporary employee. They were to be his paying customers for a pleasure cruise around the *Great Britain* tomorrow, and somehow they'd cajoled him into giving them a guided walking tour of the city this afternoon.

His city, he amended, with a swell of pride. He loved every stick and stone and unsavoury stink of it, although up here on the elegant Clifton Downs, and across the river towards Bedmister Hill where he lived, it was easy enough to forget the raggle-taggle life that also existed in it. But he didn't deny that the ant-like workers who slaved away at the docks and markets, the warehouses and glassworks, were its heart and soul. He sometimes had extravagant dreams of sailing away to explore the world, yet he cheerfully doubted that it would ever happen. And just as surely, he knew that if it did, he would always return. The city was in his bones.

He cleared his throat as the emotive thoughts threatened to invade the prosaic descriptions of the city he was telling these paying customers. He'd already had to grit his teeth as he'd been informed by one of them that he had an enchantingly poetic turn of phrase. It sounded altogether too pretty a term to describe a lusty young fellow, and certainly wasn't the way he'd want the mates on the waterfront to hear him described.

"Is is true that there are caves beneath these cliffs, John?" one of the young ladies said, using the free and easy familiarity of university students.

"It's quite true. If you'll look over there, you'll see a tower near the abutments for Mr Brunel's bridge that's to be built over the river. An artist called Mr West lives in the tower, and he's erected a camera obscura in the summit with which to spy on the surrounding countryside."

"I think my sister is more interested in caves and tunnels, than spying, sir. Isn't that right, Susannah?" one of the male students put in. She nodded.

"I was coming to that," John said. "It just so happens that a passage leads down from the inside of the tower through the cliffs to a cave, hundreds of feet below. But that's only one of the many caverns and tunnels to be found in the Avon Gorge. For many years they've been dug out to provide sandstone for the glass industry. Have you seen the conical towers of the glass works near the river in Hotwells?"

"We had them pointed out to us. I must say you're a very knowledgeable person for a boatman, John," the young lady said admiringly.

He just managed not to sound mocking. "Oh, even boatmen are capable of reading and writing and taking in knowledge, miss. The city has always been home to me, and I believe you should get to know your own city as intimately as, well, as a wife, I suppose."

He had never intended saying any such thing, but the words came out as soon as they entered his head. He was instantly embarrassed by them, but these intellectuals didn't seem to find anything odd about the simile.

"That's a very astute observation, if I may say so, sir.

But what of the city passages? We've heard something about them as well," the young man said.

John nodded. "There's a great network of underground passages beneath the city. There was a time, not so very long distant, when the evil press gangs were very prevalent in Bristol. There was many a reluctant sailor who escaped their clutches through the maze of tunnels connecting the old taverns hereabouts."

"How fascinating," Susannah said, her eyes shining. She was soft and young, and would probably stir plenty of men's hearts before she was done, but John was already intrigued by someone else he had met that day. A girl with red-gold hair and the bluest eyes, and he didn't give a damn whether or not she came from a humble background.

"Oh, there's a fortune-teller's tent," one of the other girls in the group said excitedly. "Do we dare go in?"

"We do not," Susannah's brother said sternly. "The true Romanies never shy from telling you things you'd probably rather not hear, and the rest are charlatans who will tell you anything to get their sixpences out of you."

"Rupert's right," Susannah said quickly. "Let's get away from here anyway. I want to hear more about these underground passages. Is there a tea-room somewhere, John, where we can sit comfortably?"

"Not around here. We'll have to go back to the city, and I doubt that you'd get inside one today even if they're staying open, with all the excitement going on."

"Then we must go back to our hotel, and you can take tea with us there," Susannah declared at once. "Rupert's quite right about the fortune-tellers, Amy. Let's get away from here before she comes out of the tent and puts her evil eye on us."

She gathered up her flounced skirts and walked quickly across the Downs with the rest of them. John followed, his eyes glinting with amusement at their presumption. He'd rubbed shoulders with many a gypsy at a country fair or in a smoke-filled tavern, and enjoyed their company.

This group thought themselves highly educated, but any fool knew that a gypsy with the second sight could forecast the future with deadly accuracy. And a true Romany would never tell a client any more than he wished to know.

The inside of the gypsy tent was cloying and hot, and Carrie had a job not to pinch her nostrils together as she and Elsie squeezed inside it and were bidden to sit down. There was only a narrow bench that was hardly big enough for the two of them, but it was comforting to sit close and try not to be overawed or terrified by the impressive figure of the fortune-teller.

Inside the tent, she seemed to dominate the space on the far side of the small cloth-covered table, on which a pack of cards lay face-down.

"Now then, my pretties," she said in a hoarse voice. "Which of you wants to be the first to know what destiny has in store for you?"

Carrie's mouth was so dry she could hardly speak, but Elsie gave a laugh that was full of bravado.

"I'll go first if you like. We don't have much money, mind, so it'll have to be a very short consultation."

She stumbled over the word, knowing it was the right one to use, and the gypsy's eyes flickered.

"Madame Zara is well aware that you don't have much money, girl, and that you didn't choose to come here of your own will. Madame Zara chose you, my dears, not the other way around."

Carrie swallowed. "I don't like this," she muttered beneath her breath. "I don't want to hear anything – "

Madame Zara suddenly banged her hand on the table, making them both jump.

"You've nothing to fear, my young one. You've a lucky

41

aura, and the fates will always favour you, just as they did earlier this day, when the water threatened you."

Carrie felt her heart leap. She wasn't the one who'd been in danger from the river, but if Billy had drowned, she and her whole family would have been devastated. But there was no way this crone could possibly have known about that.

"She's guessing," Elsie hissed in her ear. "Anybody in the crowd today was in danger of being pushed into the river."

The gypsy fixed her gaze on Elsie's face. "So we have a disbeliever, but it's no matter. Fate takes no account of such things, and what's to come to you will come. Shuffle the pack and divide it into three piles," she instructed.

Without thinking, Elsie did as she was told. Madame Zara turned over the top card on the first pile. It was the four of hearts.

"Do you have any troubles, girl?" she said.

Elsie snorted. "The same as most people, I daresay. Not enough money, and me poor old granpa getting worse by the day. Why? Is this a bad card?"

"Not if you've no real worries," the crone said ambiguously. "If you do, you'll be set free of any troubles within half a year."

Elsie glanced at Carrie, her expression saying what a pack of rubbish she believed she was hearing. The crone turned over the second card, the eight of diamonds.

"You can be a bit devious at times, can't you? You need to learn that you'll only prosper by telling the truth."

"Well, that's a fine thing to say to anybody," Elsie said, full of indignation. But the woman was already turning over the last card, and Elsie stopped talking as soon as she saw it.

"Don't they call that the death card?" she said thickly, seeing the black mass of the ace of spades.

"It can be," Madame Zara said, her voice crisper now.

"But the interpretation of the fortune depends on the combination of the three cards."

"So what do you see for me?" Elsie was less brash now, and Carrie could see the small film of perspiration on her forehead. The woman gave a reassuring cackle.

"Nothing too serious, my pretty. Your fortunes may change within the year, but tell the truth and keep a calm head on your shoulders, and you'll weather through."

She gathered up the cards and shuffled them several times, then handed them to Carrie.

"Shuffle the cards well and do as your friend did."

Carrie knew by now that she'd far rather not do it at all, but unless she wanted to make Elsie furious, she could hardly back down. Besides, there had been nothing very terrible in what Madame Zara had said, and the advice had been so general as to apply to anyone.

She shuffled the cards and separated them into the three piles. Madame Zara turned over the first. It was a diamond card.

"The mystic seven," she commented, with a small nod. "It comes as no surprise to me. You have the look of luck about you, dearie. Whatever surprises appear in the future, you must welcome them."

She motioned Carrie to turn over the second card. It was the six of hearts.

"The combination of two close-numbered red cards is a lucky omen," Madame Zara said. "But there's a small warning in the six of hearts. Don't take everyone on trust. There could be mischief-making in a friend, so keep your wits about you."

Carrie could hear Elsie's impatient breathing at that, and she quickly turned over her last card to reveal the knave of hearts. Madame Zara sat back with a satisfied smirk on her coarse features.

"So, I'm proved right about you, my pretty. Three red cards ending with the knave prophesies good fortune and

43

a true lover. If you haven't already met him, then you're going to meet him very soon. You're one of fortune's favoured ones."

"Thank you," Carrie muttered, feeling stupid and uncomfortable by the way the old woman seemed to be fawning over her, and very conscious of Elsie's fury beside her.

"Can we go now?" Elsie said. "Or are there any more little warnings you want to give us?"

"Nobody's keeping you here," Madame Zara said. "Just remember my words."

They stumbled out of the makeshift tent, blinking as the sunlight hit their eyes.

"What bilge," Elsie said angrily. "I don't believe a word of it!"

"Well, you're a fine one. It was your idea to go in there, and now you're mocking everything she told you."

"I didn't say I was going to believe it, did I? I thought it would be a lark, that's all."

Carrie glared at her. "Why are you so upset if you don't believe any of it? Did it really worry you to see the ace of spades?"

"Maybe it did. Granpa always said it was the death card, that's all."

Carrie just managed to stop herself saying that the most likely death to occur within the year was going to be Granpa Miller's, anyway. It was the logical and natural way of things, but Elsie was in no mood to listen to logic right now.

"Anyway," Carrie said resolutely, as they strolled on aimlessly around the Downs, "I don't think I believe it either. It's all a game, isn't it? She could say anything to suit the way she felt about her clients, and you managed to annoy her from the start."

"And it was just as obvious she thought the sun shone out of your backside!" Elsie stopped walking, so that

44

Carrie was obliged to stop as well. "I suppose you think I'm going to be your mischief-making friend!"

"We both know you're not, so don't get in such a fret about it," Carrie said, linking her arm in her friend's. She suddenly heard Elsie give a mollified laugh.

"Maybe she was right about the knave of hearts showing up your true lover, though."

"What are you talking about now? Sometimes you do talk in riddles, Elsie."

"I do not. The knave's another name for the jack, isn't it? And everybody knows that Jack's another name for John. John Travis, see?"

Carrie felt the hot colour flood her face, and she unhitched herself from Elsie's arm.

"Madame Zara was right about your devious mind too," she said. "You're as daft as they come, Elsie Miller, and I've had enough of your nonsense. My feet hurt and I'm going home."

She marched away across the springy grass with as much dignity as she could. She didn't care if Elsie followed her or not. The visit to the fortune-teller hadn't been her idea, and she hadn't wanted to go into the dingy little tent. But now that she had, the words of the old crone were filling her head and dazzling her mind, and if she wasn't careful she could almost believe she had a special angel bestowing that golden aura of good fortune around her.

"Hey, mind where you're going, can't you!"

A raucous voice bawled at her as she tripped over the feet of some rough-looking youths sprawled out on the grass, and she muttered a swift apology. As she moved on down the hill, she heard them cat-calling after her.

"No need to apologise, pretty maid. What's your hurry? Come back and take a jar of ale with we."

"How about a quick tumble in the bushes, girl?"

"Never you mind what this 'un says, lovely. I'll show 'ee such a good time, you'll be paying I for it – "

45

She didn't look back as the voices faded behind her. But the golden aura had vanished. Those louts would never have yelled so bawdily after Miss Helen Barclay or any of the elegant young Clifton ladies. Their rowdiness reminded her of who she was, and all she wanted to do now was to get home and be inside the comfort and safety of her own front door.

After the excitement of the day, and meeting John Travis, and the brief euphoria of the gypsy's words, she felt humiliated and depressed. She smarted over the argument with Elsie, despite the fact that it was no worse than usual. But somehow it was made worse because she knew they'd both be remembering the various things Madama Zara had told them. And somehow it divided them.

She knew it was foolish to take such heed of it all, but it was like her Ma always said. Words once said could never be unsaid, and the uneasy messages from the unknown stuck in her memory like little barbs.

"Ma's gone to sit with old Mrs Dewhurst up the road. She said you're to give me a bath," Billy greeted her belligerently. "She says I smell like the river."

"You didn't tell her what happened, did you?" Carrie snapped, everything else forgotten at once. "You know what I told you."

"I never told nobody," he howled. "Why are you so cross-faced?"

Immediately, she was full of compunction. It wasn't his fault that she was out of sorts with Elsie and the whole world right now. It wasn't his fault that she'd met a handsome young man that day, and she was unaccountably depressed at knowing she might never see him again. It wasn't Billy's fault that she'd listened to a fortune-telling gypsy, and wanted so much to believe that she had already met her true and future lover.

46

Her brother stood in the middle of the room, as snappy as an aggressive mongrel, and she stooped and gathered him up in a hug. She caught the strong whiff of the river in his hair. She had scrubbed him well enough earlier, but there had been no time to wash the river out of his hair, only to rub it dry.

"All right then. We'd better get you bathed before Ma comes back," she said, as he squirmed away from her. "Where's Pa and the boys?"

"Pa's gone drinking, and Ma says he'd better not come back roaring out of his skull," Billy recited, "and I ain't seen Wilf nor Frank since they left the wharf. I daresay they've gone a'whoring."

Carrie felt her mouth drop open at the careless words, and she gave him a little shake.

"Where did you hear such talk? You're not to repeat such words, do you hear? If you say 'em again, I'll scrub your mouth out with soap."

"Why shouldn't I say 'em? Our Frank does. What's it mean, anyway?" He was full of resentment, but his last words slowed Carrie's anger down.

"It's something bad, and if you don't know what it means, it's because you're not old enough to know. Just don't say it again, do you hear?"

He glowered at her sullenly, not answering at once, as he tried to digest all that she'd said. He spoke up after a minute or so. "Well, do you think that river man's doing what I ain't got to say as well?"

She went blank for a minute, and then realised Billy was referring to his hero, John Travis. She turned away, aware that her heart was beating fast. The last thing she wanted to imagine was John Travis visiting one of the waterfront inns where it was well known that a man could pick up a girl for a ten-minute fumble for the price of a meat pie.

"Mr Travis did a good thing in saving you, so I don't think he'd do anything bad," she said, knowing very well

47

that the one thing didn't exclude the other, but trusting in Billy's simple reasoning to believe it.

Quickly, she told him to get undressed, while she ran upstairs to change out of her finery into her working dress and sacking apron. Then she went into the back yard to haul in the smaller wash tub that Billy could fit into well enough by buckling up his knees. There was water heating in the copper in the scullery, and two buckets of hot and two of cold filled the tub adequately.

Billy stepped into it, and sat down cautiously with his usual grumbles. Carrie ignored them and began soaping him all over, instructing him to lean his head back while she paid particular attention to rubbing the lather into his hair to rid it of the river smell.

"What does it mean, though, our Carrie?" he said suddenly, between yells of protest that the soap was going in his eyes.

"What does what mean?" she said, concentrating on his ears now, in which Ma always said they could grow potatoes.

"Going a'whoring. I ain't really saying it," he added hastily. "I'm only asking what it means, so I don't say it when I shouldn't."

She avoided giving him a swipe with a soapy hand, knowing the question had been innocently asked. But it was difficult to explain, especially when it was something she and Elsie had only ever surmised about when they saw one of the painted women mincing along the street in her furs and feathers.

"It's when a man takes a fancy to a lady and just stays with her for an hour or so, instead of marrying her and living with her all the time," she said at last, hoping this would be enough to satisfy his curiosity.

"And is that bad?"

Carrie resorted to safety. "If the Bible says it's bad, it must be – "

"But what if our Wilf and Frank go doing it? They ain't bad, are they?"

Carrie scrubbed his back vigorously, making him holler out. It wasn't her job to tell him such things, and nor did she know whether or not her older brothers had ever paid street women for their favours. It wasn't something they'd be likely to tell her, or anybody else.

"I don't think for one minute that Wilf and Frank do any such thing. They may just have mentioned the word for some reason, but I'm sure that one day they'll find nice girls and marry them, and be as happy and Ma and Pa."

"Our Frank fancies Elsie Miller," Billy said. "He told me so."

"Well, that's just too bad, because Elsie fancies our Wilf," Carrie said smartly, and immediately wished she hadn't as his mouth opened to ask more questions. "Now, just shut up about it and stand up and let me get you dry before Ma gets back. You're clean enough to whistle through."

He stepped out onto one of the rag rugs that she and Ma had made from scraps of material from the big Clifton houses, and Carrie wrapped the towel around him.

She felt a surge of guilt about Elsie. Elsie was her friend, and she was loyal to her friend, but the truth of it was, that she wouldn't want Elsie marrying either of her brothers. Elsie was too flighty, and she'd flirted with too many boys already to stay faithful to any of them. Once she'd made a conquest, she strayed to somebody else. It was probably why she found Wilf so attractive, because he'd made it so plain that he wasn't interested.

With a foresight as good as anything Madame Zara could offer, Carrie had long seen trouble ahead for Elsie. Most of the married men around here were lusty and possessive, and viciously intolerant of flighty wives.

"You're done," Carrie said, giving Billy's backside a

final slap with the towel. "Get your clothes on again while I bale out your bath water, then you can help me peel the potatoes and carrots for supper, to save Ma a job."

"Have I got to?" he grumbled.

"Yes, you have. If Ma's good enough to go and sit with Mrs Dewhurst, then you can help me to save her a job when she gets home."

"Ma said Mrs Dewhurst's going to die soon, and probably won't last out the week," Billy said, word for word as usual. "Is Elsie's granpa going to die soon?"

"I don't know. Only God knows that," Carrie said evenly. For a fleeting moment, the words "within the year" came into her mind. Madame's Zara's words . . . but she hadn't specifically referred to a death, despite the ace of spades, and such predictions were vague and general . . . she'd only implied that Elsie's fortunes were going to change within the year, and that could apply to anybody.

She turned with some relief as Frank came into the house. Her thoughts were becoming altogether too serious and self-questioning for her peace of mind.

"Good. Now you can help me bale out," she told him. "Where's our Wilf?"

"He went to see somebody. He'll be back for supper."

He sounded evasive enough to arouse Carrie's curiosity at once.

"Who's he gone to see? Somebody about a job, do you mean? Pa will be thankful about that."

"It's not somebody about a job. It's just a person he had to see."

The conversation with Billy was still uppermost in Carrie's mind. *A person Wilf had to see* could mean anything. It could mean one of the fellows he'd been working with lately; a tavern acquaintance; a female of the lowest variety, who'd find Wilf Stuckey's tall, handsome appearance far more alluring than some of the sweaty sailors who frequented the waterfront inns . . . dear Lord, Carrie thought in alarm, wondering where her thoughts were leading her to today.

"Don't look so shocked," Frank began to laugh. "He hasn't gone to the devil, just because he didn't come home with me, Carrie. We don't have to stick to one another like glue, just because we're brothers."

She gave an embarrassed smile, thankful Frank hadn't been able to follow her thoughts. She hesitated, then said what was uppermost in her mind.

"Does our Wilf have a lady-friend, Frank?"

She expected him to pooh-pooh the idea at once. Neither of her brothers had shown more than a passing interest in girls. Pa had always been strict about such things, and in any case, the three men of the house shared such a keenness for their work, inside and outside the home, that it had always seemed enough to occupy their time.

"It shouldn't come as a surprise if he does," Frank answered. "You wouldn't expect Wilf, or me, to stay unwed for ever, would you?"

It wasn't a satisfactory answer, but before she could sort out the questions brimming in her mind at his reply, Ma came bustling indoors with an empty basket, and Carrie guessed it had gone out full for the ailing Mrs Dewhurst along the road. The Stuckeys might not have much, but there were always folk who had less.

She persuaded Ma to sit down for five minutes while she turned to the black kettle singing away on the hob. She made them both some tea before Ma returned to Mrs Dewhurst's bedside, and tried not to listen too closely to the finer details of the unfortunate woman's medical condition. But it momentarily allayed her curiosity about her brother Wilf.

*   *   *

51

Wilf Stuckey was unused to ordering afternoon refreshments in Park Street tea-houses, but nor was he used to asking out the daughter of his boss, and having her accept his invitation.

The fact that both had happened that very afternoon was in danger of making him tongue-tied. It was only the fact that the beautiful Miss Nora Woolley was going to think him a bloody buffoon if he didn't speak up to the waitress hovering alongside them with her pencil poised over her note-pad, that gave him courage.

"Tea and cakes for two, please, miss," he said, as if he was in the habit of doing this kind of thing every day.

He looked across the window-seat table of the tea-room at the hazel-eyed girl seated opposite him. "I trust that will be all right for you, Miss Woolley?"

"Oh yes. That will be lovely," she said.

The waitress in her black dress and starched white apron and cap, gave a little bob and went away. There was a small silence between the two at the table, which Wilf tried frantically to break. He was thankful there was a buzz of conversation all around them.

He cursed the fact that ever since he was a small boy, his Pa had made such a point of sternly instructing his two elder sons never to bring home disgrace to the family, that he had never really managed to cultivate any easy talk with the opposite sex. It gave him an air of aloofness that seemed to attract them, all the same.

All through the launch of the *Great Britain*, Wilf had been aware of Miss Nora Woolley's lemon yellow bonnet bobbing up and down some three rows of seats in front of him on the Grand Stand. And when gaffer Woolley had caught hold of his arm, and asked him to escort his daughter home, since he was going to be busy for the next couple of hours, Wilf had finally overcome his natural reserve and suggested they make a small detour for some refreshment.

He'd caught Frank's approving wink, and was glad his brother had made himself scarce at that moment. He'd probably be even more tongue-tied if Frank had come along with them, since Frank was a mite less repressed than himself when it came to women.

"Did you enjoy watching the waterfront festivities today, Miss Woolley?" he said finally, knowing he was on safe territory there.

"I did indeed – but please won't you call me Nora? And I know your name is Wilf, because I've heard my father call you by name so many times. He always speaks well of you and your family, you know."

"But not enough to keep us in work after today, I suspect," he couldn't resist saying.

"That's not his fault," she chided him. "If the work's not there, he can't afford to pay his men. You can surely see the sense in that."

"Oh, I see the sense in it all right. It don't help to put food in the family's bellies though, does it?"

He was horrified at his own blundering crudity. Miss Nora Woolley was a fine young woman, far more educated than himself, and his clumsy words would probably make her regret ever agreeing to be seen in this public place with him. He avoided looking at her for a moment, not wanting to see the annoyance in her eyes.

"Poor Wilf," he heard her say softly. "But truly, I do understand. Would you like me to ask Father if there's any other work available?"

He looked at her quickly. Her eyes were as expressive as his sister Carrie's, and filled with sympathy now. Her mouth was soft, and he felt his heartbeats quicken. She was obviously sincere, but he'd be damned if he'd allow a woman to beg for him. He had far too much pride for that.

"That's not necessary," he said, more easily than he felt. "Besides, I've got a couple of things in mind."

"Then I'm sorry," she said contritely. "I can see that I've offended you, and I didn't mean to do so."

The arrival of the waitress with the tray of tea and cakes, prevented him from answering immediately, and he waited while the girl poured out the tea for them both, and left them the plate of cakes for their selection.

"You choose first," Wilf said, and was oddly pleased when she chose a cream-filled pastry. He had no patience with girls who ate like sparrows. He chose his favourite ginger cake, and bit into it hungrily. A day spent more idly than normally by the river had certainly sharpened his appetite.

"You haven't offended me," he said at last. "It's just that after working on the *Great Britain* and helping to get her ship-shape, anything else is going to seem like a let-down. In a way, we've all been a part of her, no matter how menial a task we've been doing, and I need to rearrange my thoughts before I decide what to do next."

"Yes, I can see that, Wilf."

"Can you? Then you don't think I'm being noddle-headed to be talking so possessively about a ship?"

He began to relax, and he grinned at his own words. Miss Nora Woolley smiled back, and if Wilf had believed in such things, he'd have said he was halfway to being bewitched by that smile.

"I don't think you're noddle-headed at all," she said. "I've seen you around the wharf, and I've always thought – "

She stopped, and at the blush in her cheeks, Wilf thought he'd never seen such a delicate shade of pink. It emboldened him to lean forward a little.

"What did you think, Nora?" He said her name for the first time, and saw her smile widen. Little teasing lights seemed to dance in her eyes, and he was already half in love with her.

"I'm not going to tell you," she said gaily. "It will only make you swollen-headed."

"Well, at least that would be an improvement on being noddle-headed, wouldn't it?" he teased back.

Amazed, he felt as if he was standing back from himself, and watching this suddenly confident Wilf Stuckey enjoying the company of a young lady, and able to find the words that seemed to amuse her.

"But you've noticed me then?" he persisted.

And he had noticed her . . . with all the humility of a mere human worshipping a goddess from afar. Yet it had never been in his nature to be humble, except where Miss Nora Woolley had been concerned, and his feelings had been far too private to tell anyone about them. But the fact that fate – and her father – had pushed them together, was nothing short of spectacular, and was making him extra bold.

Nora laughed, her eyes sparkling. Impulsively, she reached across the table and covered his hand with her own for a moment.

"Oh Wilf, you're so funny. How could anyone miss you, when you stand head and shoulders above all the rest of them in Father's employ? And I don't just mean physically, either."

Aware that she'd said far more than a young lady should, she withdrew her hand at once, and lowered her eyes from the sudden hot gaze she glimpsed in Wilf Stuckey's eyes.

But not before someone else, on her roundabout way from Clifton, down Park Street to the city, had seen the way the two of them had seemed to lean towards one another so lovingly in the window seat of the tearoom, and the intimate way the girl had pressed Wilf's hand. For Elsie Miller, it was the biggest, and most disagreeable shock of the day, and needed considerable thought.

Chapter 4

The trouble with Elsie was that she never gave considerable thought to anything. Rushing straight into trouble, like a bull in a china shop, was the way Carrie frequently described her. Carrie was the sensible one, the caring one, while Elsie courted trouble like other girls courted their beaus.

She scowled as the thought came into her mind. Because the thing most troublesome to her right now, was that Wilf Stuckey had obviously found a belle of his own, and it wasn't *her*. Not that he'd ever given her cause to think he was remotely interested . . . but Elsie had a way of dismissing such trivialities.

She hardly noticed how she was jostled about in the crowds that still lingered in the city, as if reluctant to put this wonderful day behind them. For Elsie, the day had already gone sour, and she wondered resentfully what her friend Carrie was doing now. She'd still be up on Clifton Downs, Elsie guessed, and probably hoping to hob-nob with some of the posh young ladies like that Helen Barclay.

Elsie scowled, knowing that for all her own brash self-assurance, Carrie had an inborn kind of dignity that made the Helen Barclays of the world quite ready to stop and talk and exchange pleasantries. Carrie might be poor, but she would never be common . . .

"Elsie, I want me tea!"

She heard her granpa bawling out his instructions the

56

minute she'd crashed the door behind her. She bawled back.

"Give me a minute to get me hat off, can't you? I ain't steam-driven!"

"You've been gone all day, and I ain't seen nobody. I mighta died here all alone."

She mimed the well-used words as he spoke, and went into the room where he ate and slept, wrinkling her nose at the undoubted smells of old age and stale urine. He couldn't help himself, but nor could she help being affronted by it.

"Well, you ain't dead, are you? So what do you want for your tea? There's bread and dripping and a bit of seed cake left."

"That'll do," he said, beginning to whine. "Just so long as you stay and keep me company, girl."

She gritted her teeth and went to get the food. She could never eat in the same room as him, because of the smells, and by the time she got her own meal, the smells seemed to be a part of her, so she couldn't eat much anyway. But she supposed it was one way of keeping thin. Besides, she didn't feel like food now. She hacked at the bread viciously, remembering the fair-haired girl leaning so prettily towards Wilf Stuckey, and wished she was hacking through those golden curls instead.

In the darkness of her box-like bedroom, trying to ignore her granpa's wheezing snores in the room next door she was able to transport herself and her surroundings into one glorious romp with Wilf. She'd imagined his arms holding her so often, and his eyes darkening as they looked deep into hers, that it had come a brutal shock to see him gazing into that prissy fair-haired girl's eyes in the Park Street tea-room.

She couldn't think yet what she was going to do with the information. One side of her told her to forget it, and then it simply wouldn't exist. But the darker side of her wanted to punish Wilf, just for wanting that fancy tart, instead of wanting *her*.

Wilf whistled jauntily as he strode home an hour later. By then, he'd escorted Miss Nora Woolley to the house in Ashton Way where she lived with her father, and tried not to gulp at the size of it. A house like this should put a girl like Nora well out of his reach, but she hadn't seemed to think so. He was astute enough to know that the feelings stirring inside him for her, were being returned.

It was the first time he'd seriously thought about his future with regard to a girl. He was only twenty years old, and his Pa had instilled in all of them that a man wasn't properly ready for marriage and settling down until he was nearing thirty. But a couple of hours in the company of a certain young lady had changed all those ideas.

Even though the dreams were foolish, and Aaron Woolley would undoubtedly want something better for his daughter than marriage to a woodworking man, Wilf wasn't ready to let go of his dreams just yet.

He met up with his brother Frank just before he reached the bottom of Jacob's Wells Road. Frank was lounging about with some of the foreign sailors from one of the trading vessels in the docks, and no doubt having his head filled with tales of exotic foreign places as usual. Frank excused himself from the group as soon as he saw Wilf, and fell into step alongside him. Their boots rang and sparked on the cobbles as the two of them began the walk up the steep hill towards home.

"Well? How did it go, bruth? Did she give you any encouragement?" Frank said cheekily.

"I didn't go with her for that. It was Gaffer's idea, you know that."

"I know you've had your eye on her for some weeks past," Frank said slyly. "Every time she brought Gaffer's tucker down to the wharf, your eyes nearly popped out of your head. You might fool a lot of people with your icy looks, Wilf, but I know you too well."

Wilf gave a short laugh, and his powerful shoulders relaxed. "I guess you do. All right then. We had some tea and cakes in Park Street, and then I took her home. That's all there was to it. Have you ever seen Woolley's place?"

"I'd rather hear about the girl. Did she give you the glad eye after all that soft-soaping?"

"Maybe." He refused to give an inch, and Frank gave an irritated sigh.

"You can be as close as a bloody clam when it suits you, our Wilf. Anyway, a certain somebody will have her nose put out of joint if you start courting the Woolley girl, so there may be a chance for me yet."

Wilf looked at him blankly. His mind was too full of Nora Woolley to think of anything else, and it was only when Carrie came out of the front door of their own house that he realised what Frank meant.

"Have either of you seen Elsie? She was working up to a fine old stew when I left her on the Downs, and I wanted to make my peace with her."

"The less I see of that baggage, the better," Wilf muttered, "and I'd advise you to think the same way, Frank. She's nothing but trouble."

Carrie was near enough to hear his words, and sprang to her friend's defence as usual.

"I wish you wouldn't always be so mean to her, Wilf," she snapped. "She thinks a lot of you – "

"Oh ah, me and half the boyos who come over on the Welsh trows every Wednesday." He was brasher than usual because of his own conquest that afternoon. "If our Elsie ain't tried 'em all by night-time, she'll be thinking there's summat wrong with her."

Carrie gasped with fury. "That's a horrible thing to say, Wilf, and it's not true. Elsie's a very friendly girl, that's all, and you're not to imply that she does anything more than chat to the fellows."

She turned on her heel to go back indoors, when her mother came hurrying down from the top of the street, annoyed at finding her children squabbling on the doorstep, and flustered and upset at her afternoon's visit.

"I'd make you all get indoors and stop disgracing us, if there weren't more important things to do. Carrie, you're to go for the doctor for poor Mrs Dewhurst. He can't do nothing, as she's just passed away, but I'm not prepared to do the laying-out until he gives me his say-so. She's always paid up her weekly penny for his services, so she has a right to him seeing her out."

There was also the fact of the doctor seeing that Ma got paid for her laying-out from the weekly fund, but this was hardly the time to mention it.

She turned to her second son. "Frank, you go and see if you can find that boy of hers. He'll not be overly concerned, but it's his business, and I'll not be responsible for her send-off without him making the arrangements. And Wilf, you stay here with our Billy while I go back with Mrs Dewhurst until somebody comes. I doubt that your Pa's home yet, and if he is, he'll hardly be sensible."

They listened to her crisp words, and didn't fail to note the derision in her last comment. Pa would be roaring drunk by the end of the night, and waking tomorrow with a gale-force headache. Ma was calm, sensible, and completely in charge – and they all knew they'd get the rasp of her tongue if they didn't comply exactly with her wishes.

The three of them scattered, while she toiled back up the hill to the dead woman's cottage once more. They all knew the unpleasant fact that there were several others in the vicinity willing to be paid for the unsavoury task of laying-out, and Ma needed to guard her old lady until the doctor authorised her task.

60

Carrie followed up the hill, her feet skimming over the cobblestones, to where the doctor's house stood at the edge of the Clifton mansions. She had to pause to catch her breath before she could go inside, and it was while she was leaning on the gatepost with her hand over the painful stitch in her side, that she saw a familiar figure coming down the hill towards her.

"Are you ill, Carrie?" John Travis said, seeing the way her face was flushed, and how heavily she leaned on the gatepost of the doctor's house.

He moved forward at once and put his arm around her. It was done purely as a gesture of concern for a fellow human being. But the contact was so warm, and his appearance so unforeseen, that she was very tempted to lean against him, and feign an illness she didn't have, simply for the joy of being so unexpectedly in his arms.

"Catch your breath before you say anything," John instructed, hearing her ragged breathing. "You probably ran too quickly up the hill."

"No, it's not that."

To her own annoyance, she felt obliged not to let him go on thinking she was sick, even though her heart was racing twice as fast as normal. Elsie would have relished this kind of situation, Carrie thought, but she herself was too honest to let it continue.

"I'm not here for the doctor on my own account. An old lady along the road from us has died, and Ma needs the doctor to come to her before she sees to the laying-out."

She bit her lip, aware of how plain and ordinary they sounded. Her Ma did the laying-out as an extra bit of income, doing all the worst tasks one human being could do for another, and doing it with compassion. She felt a fierce love and respect for her Ma, but all the same, it shamed her to speak of such things to a man like John Travis.

"Would you like me to come in with you? You look

61

very hot and bothered, and maybe the doctor would want to take a look at you."

"You can come if you like," she mumbled. "I only have to inform him that Mrs Dewhurst's dead, and ask him to come straight away."

Oh, why couldn't she be coquettish like Elsie, when this nice young man was looking at her with such concern? Why couldn't she lower her eyes and brush his hand with her finger-tips the way she'd seen Elsie do it, and give an unspoken invitation that she liked him enormously? But she didn't have Elsie's flair and never could have.

"I'll wait for you," John said decisively. "Our paths seem destined to cross today, so it would be going against fate if I left you here now, wouldn't it? Or don't you believe in fate?"

She guessed he was talking to keep her from remembering the reason she was here, and the gruesome task her Ma had to perform, but she managed a brief smile at his words, as they pushed open the garden gate and walked together up the long pathway to the doctor's front door.

"I suppose everybody believes in fate, though I think people make up their own minds what they do with it."

"That's a very perceptive thought," he said, and although she wasn't sure what perceptive meant, it was obviously something good, because of the admiring way he said it. But all thoughts of self-esteem went out of her head as the door of the doctor's house opened, and the crusty medical man stood there.

"What is it, Carrie? Has young Billy crashed his head into a wall again?"

"No. I've come about Mrs Dewhurst, Doctor Flowers. Ma says she's dead, so can you please come at once?"

He gave a snort. "Trust somebody to break up my dinner party. Well, it can't be helped. Tell your mother I'll be there in half an hour, and that she can go ahead. She's a trustworthy woman and has a skill with these things. You'll maybe take up the job yourself one day, Carrie," he added, with an attempt at joviality.

"I will not!" she said, shuddering, remembering the smells that lingered on her mother's hands after such a job.

The doctor laughed, and she squirmed, presuming that being so used to life and death and everything in between, must make you this insensitive. The doctor suddenly looked more keenly at her companion.

"It's young Travis from Bedminster Hill, isn't it? How does your uncle fare these days?"

"He's very well, sir. I'll tell him you were asking after him."

It was obvious to Carrie that the doctor held John and his uncle in some regard, and she felt doubly awkward at why she was here. But she kept her head high as they left the house while the doctor went to make his apologies to his dinner guests, and Carrie didn't attempt to break the small silence between them.

"You shouldn't take Doctor Flowers' brusqueness to heart," John said at last. "When you're dealing every day with sickness and death, you have to keep a hard shell around you."

"I know. A doctor has to be impersonal, but it can't be so easy when it's a relative, can it?" She had never had to face death in a relative or friend yet, but it was something that Elsie was going to have to do sooner or later. She and her old granpa constantly scraped one another up the wrong way, but they were a family, all the same.

"You learn to face it," John said, and from his voice she knew at once that he had already done so. She was embarrassed that such intimate feelings had somehow come to the surface between them when they hardly knew one another.

A group of urchins came hurtling towards them and they

were forced to part for a moment to let them through, and then John held on to her arm firmly.

"I don't want to lose you already," he commented. "I hadn't expected to see you again so soon, but this has got to be fate. We saw each other on the Downs this afternoon, and now again."

"Oh yes, you were with your friends," she said, as if only just remembering, when in fact she felt she could recall every face of the laughing, confident crowd he had been with.

"Hardly my friends," he grinned. "They were merely paying clients who wanted a guided tour of the city. After their pleasure cruise tomorrow, they'll be returning to Oxford, and I doubt that I'll ever see them again."

"Oh, I see," Carrie said, trying not to sound too pleased at the explanation.

The road had become very congested with people making their way back up from the waterfront, or moving down towards it. Carrie was glad of the crowds as they passed Mrs Dewhurst's cottage. She thought of the poor old dab inside it, with her Ma keeping a quiet vigil alongside her, and shivered again. Suddenly she wanted to be indoors, where everything was safe and secure and familiar, and she told John quickly that she had better walk the last part alone, lest her Pa was keeping an eye out for her.

"Would he object to your walking out with a boy then?" he asked teasingly.

"He might," she said, flustered. "But we're not walking out, are we?"

The crowds divided them again, and she had no idea what he might have answered. But she was within reach of her own front door now, and she almost flew inside it, slamming it fast behind her.

"Where's the fire?" Wilf said mildly.

"Our Carrie's afraid of ghosts, afraid of ghosts," Billy

64

began to chant. "She's afraid old Mrs Dewhurst's ghost is going to get her."

"Don't be so daft," Carrie snapped. "And don't be so disrespectful, neither. If you don't shut up and behave yourself, I won't cook your tea, and you'll be going to bed without any."

He scowled. "Why are you in such a bad mood? I like Elsie better than you now. She gives me sweets from the market."

That's because Elsie doesn't pay for them, Carrie said silently beneath her breath.

"I'm not in a bad mood," she said, trying to lighten the atmosphere in the house. Wilf seemed to be a dreamworld of his own, probably worrying about finding work, she thought guiltily, and here she was, snapping and snarling at Billy for the thinnest of reasons.

"Do I have to eat my carrots then?" he said hopefully, recognising the glimmer of guilt with all the cunning of a fox-cub.

"Just a few," she compromised, knowing how he hated them. "If we have our pie and vegetables before Ma gets back, she won't know if you haven't had many, will she? But you're not to tell her, mind."

He practised the wink he couldn't quite manage. "That's two things we don't have to tell her, then."

Carrie felt her blood freeze for a second, before it surged through her veins.

"What's the other thing?" Wilf said lazily.

"It's the sweets Elsie keeps giving him from the market," Carrie said quickly. "You know Ma don't like him eating too many, or he gets the belly-ache."

And before Billy could open his mouth to say that was three things he didn't have to tell Ma, she bundled him over to the sideboard and instructed him to put the knives and forks on the table for the meal.

Not that Ma would want any, Carrie thought. She never

had the stomach for it after a laying-out. And Pa would be too full of beer to eat, and spend the night belching and snoring and keeping the rest of them awake. Wilf seemed preoccupied, and she didn't really feel like food. That left only Frank and Billy, who never lost their appetites, and probably never would, whatever disaster befell them.

It didn't matter. Whatever didn't get eaten today would be served up tomorrow, and the day after, and the day after that, until it was gone. They couldn't afford to waste food, especially now that the men's jobs on the *Great Britain* had finished. Once the vegetables were simmering on the hob, and the pie browning nicely in the oven, she glanced at her oldest brother.

"What will you do tomorrow, Wilf? Does Gaffer Woolley have anything to offer you?"

Wilf's head was full of Gaffer Woolley's daughter at that moment, and he shook his head.

"I ain't asked him yet. Tomorrow will be soon enough."

He was more abrupt than usual, remembering how Miss Nora Woolley had said she'd put in a good word for him with her father, if he liked. He hadn't liked. It was a man's duty to find his own work, and not have a woman doing it for him.

Carrie saw his tight lips, and didn't pursue the question, though she thought that tomorrow was long overdue for finding new jobs. She sometimes thought her menfolk buried their heads too deep in the sand, believing in their own craftsmanship, and thinking the work would come to them. It didn't happen that way as she and Ma knew only too well.

Once long ago, when jobs were scarce and they'd been barely surviving, her Ma had walked the Clifton streets asking for work, taking the then tiny Carrie with her. It had been the beginning of the work for which Ma prided herself now, the laundering of the fine silks and laces of the rich Clifton folk. But it had all begun by literally walking the streets and knocking on doors, and almost begging for work.

Perhaps a woman was better suited to beg, Carrie thought now, or more prepared to lose face for her family's survival. A man had too much pride, while a woman was prepared to sink her pride when needs demanded it, knowing that it could always be restored. They called men the superior sex, but sometimes she wondered.

"Do I have a smut on my nose or something?" Wilf asked, and she realised how intently she had been staring, without really seeing him at all.

"I was only thinking," she said lightly.

"You don't want to do too much of that. Too much thinking in a woman stretches the brain."

"How does too much thinking stretch the brain?" Billy said curiously, before she could draw enough breath to explode at Wilf's remark. "Will it bulge out of our Carrie's head if she thinks too much?"

Carrie laughed. "Of course it won't, you goose. And Wilf shouldn't say such daft things."

It said a lot about the way he thought of her, though, she thought uneasily. He, and Frank, and especially Pa. They didn't really like their womenfolk to think too much. They wanted all the thinking in the household to be left to the men. But none of them had been canny enough to see that they should have got tomorrow's jobs sorted out long before now, when they'd be just a handful of carpenters looking for work in a city full of men as skilled as themselves.

A week later it was obvious that there were few jobs to be had for men preferring to work together as a team if they could. It was also obvious they should have seen this work shortage coming, and not relied on the good nature of Gaffer Woolley to find them something. Gaffer Woolley was hard-pressed to pay the wages of the men he still had on his books, without finding jobs that didn't exist for the rest.

"What are we, if we ain't been loyal workers all these months?" Pa scowled, after another fruitless walk around the city looking for work. "They want us quick enough when they need an urgent job done, and they'm just as quick to lay us off when it goes slack."

Ma paused in her rhythmic swishing of the Swiss embroidered lawn shifts through the cold blue rinse, and handing them over to Carrie for their final rinsing and careful light starching in an isinglass dip. They worked outside in the yard, for the day was a hot one, and Ma's face glowed as red as the proverbial turkey-cock's.

"We're all right for the time being," Ma said as patiently as she could. "Me and Carrie ain't short of work, and the kitchen servants at the mansions are always generous with any food left over."

"Bloody charity!" Pa bellowed. "Since when did we ever have to rely on charity, woman?"

"When we don't have anything else, I'd say," she said smartly. "There's no use you getting on your high horse and complaining, Sam. If we want to eat, then we have to accept what we can get."

"Well, I ain't staying here and listening to this." He leapt up from his wooden yard chair, sending it spinning. "And I ain't prepared to see my women working while I'm idle. It ain't right."

"What you going to do about it then?" Ma said patiently, knowing what was coming.

"I'm going down the waterfront to think things over. I may meet somebody down there who's got some ideas. Anything's better than sitting here watching you two getting up to your arm-pits in lather."

He stormed out of the house, and Ma carried on

swishing and twisting without a word for a minute, and then she paused to wipe the sweat from her brow.

"He'll be back, roaring and cheerful, and ready to take on the world," she said calmly to Carrie. "But he still won't have a job to go to in the morning."

"Don't you hate it, Ma?" Carrie burst out. "You know he's not going to see a man about a job. He's just going to drink himself out of his wits again."

"It's his way, girl. I've known him too long to try to change him. You can't change a proud man's habits by threats and tears, and it's a foolish woman who thinks she can. He'll come to terms with what's happening in his own good time. And by then, there may well be more jobs around."

As she bent to her task more furiously, Carrie thought she was either very brave or very foolish, and couldn't decide which. But it was a fact that her Pa was coming home drunk every night now. Frank was usually with him, and he was more than tipsy too. Wilf was going the Lord knew where of an evening, and was becoming more secretive than usual.

She had seen nothing more of John Travis. He hadn't really wanted to know her, she thought bitterly. It was all in her imagination, and the gypsy's fortune-telling had merely been to excite a gullible young girl.

Ma stood up, easing her aching back. The washing lines in the yard were filled with shimmering fabrics, and the fine shawls and undergarments of the gentry billowed like gossamer sails in the wind. Carrie envied the young ladies who wore them, but envy was a sin, and she tried to smother the feeling as much as possible.

"Nearly done," Ma remarked in the late afternoon. "You and Billy can take a walk up to the Barclay house now, Carrie, and deliver the work that was ironed this morning. Miss Barclay particularly wanted the ivory afternoon-gown, so mind you don't crease it too much when you fold it."

Carrie didn't need a second telling. The yard had become progressively hotter, and the air had stilled until there was barely a breeze now to ruffle the lines of washing. It would be a relief to be up on the grassy Downs where you didn't feel stifled by the city.

"Come on, Billy. Help me with the baskets," she told him, when he lay lethargically on the rug in the parlour. He knew he'd get some tit-bits from the kitchens, where the Barclay cook always made a pet of him, so he moved reasonably quickly. Carrie packed the garments carefully between tissue paper and laid them gently in the wicker baskets she put onto the handcart. It took the two of them to push the loaded cart up the steep hill, and the two of them to hold it back empty on the return journey.

Nowadays it wasn't usually empty. After they had left the baskets to be taken upstairs to Miss Barclay, they would go down to the kitchens where Cook was generous in passing on a fruit cake or two, or some meat from the Barclay pantry, and sometimes fruit as well.

There was a message for Carrie that Miss Barclay wanted to see her that day, and she left Billy eating his fill of chocolate pudding at the scrubbed kitchen work-table, praying that he wouldn't be sick.

She was shown into Helen Barclay's bedroom, half-dreading that she may have marked one of the recent laundry garments, and was being called to task, when the other girl turned with a smile.

"Carrie, I've been turning out my wardrobe, and there are a few things here that I don't wear any more, and I wondered if you'd like them," she said. "If they're no use to you, then you can do what you like with them. Pass them on to the poor house, or whatever you do," she finished vaguely.

Carrie ignored the fact that Miss Helen Barclay wouldn't have the faintest idea what lesser folk did with passed-on clothes, such as shortening them or cutting them down, or making homely rag rugs for their comfort. She was too enthralled with the pile of clothes that lay on Miss Barclay's bed. They were far too good for Sunday best for the likes of Carrie Stuckey, and all given to her as a gift from heaven. Such a thing had never happened before, and if it was an act of charity, made out of sympathy because the Stuckey menfolk were out of work, then she didn't care one jot.

"It's very kind of you, miss," she stuttered.

"Nonsense. It's better than throwing them away. I'll have them put into your baskets when my clean laundry has been put away, and you can take it all away when you leave."

Carrie sailed down the servants' stairs of the mansion as if she walked on air. It would have been far too rude to inspect the clothes she had been given, but she knew they would all be beautiful. She had quickly recognised one or two items, though these cast-offs weren't Miss Barclay's finest things, and understandably so. When in the world would Carrie Stuckey have worn satin and lace!

By the time she and Billy were ready to leave, she was feeling cock-a-hoop. Ma would be pleased with the parcels of food Cook had given them, and she was going to have a wonderful evening trying on all her new clothes. And how Elsie was going to envy her! She hadn't seen her for a couple of days, and they'd been scratchy the last time they met, but this new clobber was going to give her a boost of confidence she sorely needed. What with the men of the house looking so gloomy, and not seeing John Travis since the day of the ship's launch . . .

They pushed the handcart around the back of the house and into the shed in the yard. Billy raced indoors ahead of her with a box containing a precious fruit cake in his arms, yelling to Ma that they were home. Carrie smiled at the excitement in his voice, and then was aware that he quickly became quiet. She piled the baskets on

71

top of one another and lugged them awkwardly into the house.

She prayed that Pa wasn't back yet. In his present mood, he'd only complain loudly over receiving more charity. She prayed too, that he didn't have a particularly bad head so early in the evening. She dumped the baskets on the floor of the parlour, and stood up with a sigh of relief from the exertion. And then her heart stopped.

Her Ma was sitting primly upright, with Frank and Wilf stiffly flanking her like matching book-ends. Pa stood glowering by the fireplace, swaying more than slightly, and standing near the front door was John Travis. On the table was an opened brown paper parcel, in which there was a serge working shirt and a pair of neatly pressed trousers. Pa rounded on Carrie at once, slurring his words in the slow, loud deliberation of the very drunk.

"I'd like to know just how long my daughter has been in the habit of inviting strangers into the house, and offering him her brother's clothes to wear. Do we have a harlot in the house now, and are we going to have to hang a red light in the window for all to see?"

Carrie gasped at the unfairness of it all, and cringed even more at the shock on John Travis's face. He must have thought he'd come into a mad-house to hear a man speak to his daughter in such a way.

"Sir, I assure you it wasn't like that at all, and your daughter behaved with the utmost propriety," John began, but Sam waved his aside, looking dangerously near to falling over until he clung to the mantelpiece once more.

"I'd like to hear my daughter's side of it, if you don't mind, *sir*," he replied. "Well, girl? How long have you known this man, and what does he mean to you?"

Carrie was so humiliated, she could hardly breathe. She would dearly have loved to say he was everything to her – or could be, given the chance. But she doubted that such a chance would ever come now. Her dream was all spoiled,

72

and John would be regretting the day he'd ever set eyes on her.

"It was my fault!" Billy suddenly said shrilly. "It wasn't our Carrie's fault, and she's not a harlot. What's a harlot, Ma? Anyway, she's not, and if I hadn't fallen in the river – "

"You did *what?*" Pa turned on his son now, his furious eyes daring him to tell any lies. Billy cowered, but he clung to Carrie's skirt for security, and began to sob.

"It was my fault. It was when the ship got launched. I fell in the river, and the man jumped in and fished me out. We were all wet, and he had to get back on his boat with the people, and Carrie said there was some of Wilf's old clobber here that he could wear. We came back home, me and Carrie and Elsie and the man. It weren't her fault, Pa! It was mine."

He buried his face in Carrie's skirt, and Wilf spoke up harshly.

"I heard something about a child being rescued from the river, but nobody knew the name of the boatman involved, and he refused to be interviewed." He turned to John Travis in some disbelief. "Are you saying that was you and our Billy?"

John gave a brief nod. "I'm afraid it was. It might have been better if we'd come clean from the beginning, Carrie," he said, trying to lighten the atmosphere. Then they heard Ma give a choking sob as she realised the implications of what he was saying.

"Then we owe you our Billy's life," she gasped. "And there's no way we can ever repay you for that."

In the silence that followed, John spoke evenly.

"There's one way," he said. "You can allow me to walk out with your daughter."

Chapter 5

For a moment, Carrie thought Pa was going to have a seizure. The veins stood out on his forehead like purple cords, and she heard Ma's pull of breath as she put a restraining hand on his arm. He shook her off as if she were an irritating insect.

"You insolent young whelp!" Pa bellowed. "The girl's no more than a child, and I'll not have some fresh-faced fellow sniffing at her skirts just because he thinks I owe him summat."

May asserted herself at that, despite Sam's fury.

"Of course we owe Mr Travis summat. We owe him our Billy's life, and we can't forget that. You should remember summat else too, Sam. Our Carrie's no longer a child, and the time's right for her to be courting."

Her voice thinned as Sam glowered at her. She didn't often go against him so blatantly in the midst of her family, and never with a stranger listening. Though, like all women she was adept at subtle handling when she wanted her own way, as he very well knew.

His scowling gaze moved towards his daughter. Of course he'd noted her in her finery on the day of the launch, in the same way he'd noted the rest of his family, spruced and oiled, and doing him proud in the Grand Stand along with the nobs. But he'd preferred not to notice Carrie too much as a growing-up female, with all the problems such a state was likely to bring into the home. He wanted to go on thinking of Carrie as his one ewe-lamb, even though he rarely let such sentiments into his mind, let alone pass his lips.

But he was being pushed into seeing her differently now, and he didn't thank this Travis fellow for it. He was obliged to see his girl's shining eyes and full red mouth. He saw how her shape filled out her work-dress now, and was no longer board-flat from neck to hem. He was obliged to know that she had womanly feelings inside her, wanting him to let her go walking out with this stranger. Wanting to be free of childish restraints, before he was ready to let her go . . . but he knew too, that you could no more hold back a child who was straining to be free, than you could capture a breeze.

"I'd need to know summat more about you before I felt willing to agree to any such thing," he almost roared at John.

Ma spoke at once, seeing the threat of more than one temper exploding. "Sit you down, Mr Travis, and I'll make us all some tea."

"If Mr Stuckey has no objection," John said, still addressing him, and hardly looking at Carrie.

"How the hell else am I going to find out the whys and wherefores about you? For God's sake, sit down, boy, and tell us about yourself," Sam spoke testily now, annoyed at realising that his wife and the stranger were being far more gracious and dignified than himself.

John sat on the carved wooden settle, and Billy curled up beside him, clearly besotted by his hero, and enchanted by the idea that it seemed he'd be seeing him again, even if he had no idea what "walking out" meant.

Quickly, Carrie followed Ma out to the scullery to help prepare the tea, closing the connecting door behind her. She leaned against it, her heart beating sickeningly fast.

Everything had happened with such speed, and she didn't know whether excitement or fright was uppermost in her mind. She had never walked out with a boy before, and she wouldn't know how to behave when she was alone with him – or just how often they would be allowed to be alone together without a chaperone.

And nobody had actually asked *her* what she thought about it, she thought. It was all the business of the men, as if she had no say, or no feelings in the matter at all. But she had a mind of her own, and it was going to be her decision in the end.

Besides which, she felt good and angry at John. She'd seen the way her Pa had glanced at her, and guessed that her eyes were sparkling. But they'd been sparkling with rage, as much as anything else, for hadn't she expressly asked John not to bring the clobber back to the house? She'd known there would be uproar about it, and she was certain it wasn't over yet. Nor was she going to give in meekly to the flattery of going out with a boy, without letting him know exactly what she thought!

Her hands felt clammy, for she certainly did have feelings for John Travis, although they weren't too clear in her mind. She didn't really know him at all, and he could be after more than just innocent courting. Elsie had put those ideas in her head . . . and as her thoughts flitted towards Elsie, she knew she must ask her for advice. Elsie had been with boys, and she'd know what to do.

She realised that Ma was clattering cups and plates about, the way she did when she was out of sorts. Guilt surged through Carrie now, over the deceit that had brought about this situation.

"I'm sorry, Ma," she said uneasily. "I should have told you about bringing John – Mr Travis here, and giving him our Wilf's old clothes. I told him not to bother returning 'em, as Wilf never wears 'em now, but I suppose he forgot."

"And how long did you think our Billy was going to keep the secret all to himself? I've known since the day of the launch that he had summat bursting to be told.

You did wrong not to tell us he'd fallen in the river, Carrie. What if he'd been drowned?"

"Well, he wasn't, and I didn't want to spoil the day for you. He was only in the water for a few minutes before John jumped in after him and hauled him out." She was becoming belligerent, thinking that it was a fine old thing if meeting a boy could bring about all this fuss.

But she saw her mother shiver. The river had claimed many lives before, and although the huge floating harbour was relatively calm when boats weren't churning up its waters, it was still deep. And further downstream, in the Cumberland Basin and into the river itself, there were hidden currents and thick sucking mud that meant constant danger to those living and working in and around it.

"We won't talk about it any more for the present, but I'm displeased with you, and I'm sure your Pa's not done with you yet," Ma said. "You've got his say-so on walking out, providing he thinks well enough of the young man, but from now on you'll have to mind yourself."

"Mind myself? How do you mean?"

May Stuckey gave an embarrassed little cough.

"I mean there are certain things we need to discuss, when the men are out of the house, and our Billy's in bed. It's women's talk, Carrie."

She would say no more as the kettle began to sing, and Carrie hurriedly attended to the tea-making, her face as flushed as Ma's, knowing that she didn't want to hear this "women's talk". They worked in silence, until the tea had brewed, and there was a platter piled high with buttered buns and plum jam. It was all taken into the parlour, where the men sat in even stiffer silence. Even Billy was unusually subdued for once. Carrie glanced at John and saw his uneasy smile.

From her Pa's red neck, she thought she could guess only too well what had happened. Pa had suddenly discovered that John Travis was no fly-by-night sniffing around

77

his daughter, but the nephew of a respectable boat-owning man, who had aspirations of being the same.

And Sam Stuckey was temporarily an out-of-work carpenter, together with his elder sons, and with a wife and daughter who took in laundry for the nobs. After his first angry reaction to John's arrival, Sam's pride would have taken a severe knocking.

Far from crowing over her Pa's discomfiture, Carrie felt a rush of love for him. It wasn't his fault he had no work at present, nor that he felt fiercely defensive towards his family, and frequently showed it in his aggressive manner. And far from being excited at the thought of walking out with a boy, she was fast becoming resentful of John Travis, in coming here with Wilf's working clobber, when it had been the last thing she'd wanted.

She offered round the plate of buns, and caught sight of her workaday hands. She was reminded at once of the contrast between her own and Miss Helen Barclay's soft white hands, and in so doing, she remembered her manners, even if the rest of her stubborn family seemed to have temporarily forgotten them. John would undoubtedly be regretting the day he'd become involved with the difficult and insular Stuckey family, Carrie thought. She tried to speak naturally through her sudden misery, by bringing her Pa's expertise to his notice.

"Do you notice the craftsmanship of the settle you're sitting on, John? Pa made it for Ma as a wedding gift."

He seemed thankful to examine the deep-grained wood of the settle, highly polished over the years now, despite the many scratches and nicks made by the nails from childish boots.

"It's a very fine piece of work," John agreed. "In fact, I'd think it a great honour if Mr Stuckey would make us a similar one when the time comes for us to be wed. It would be a good family tradition to continue."

Sam's cup banged onto his saucer, the compliment on

his craft dismissed in the rest of John's words, and clearly seeing himself patronised by this young upstart.

"You're thinking away too far ahead of yourself, boy. I gave my permission for you to court our Carrie, but she's far too young to be thinking of getting wed yet. There's many a long day between the one and the other."

"Perhaps you could keep the idea in mind for which of us gets wed first, Pa," Carrie said nervously, involving her brothers as well as herself. "It could be the start of a family tradition, with the same rose and leaf design on it that you made for Ma."

"Mebbe," Sam snapped, but it was obvious that he refused to give any thought to weddings in the family at all. And truth to tell, Carrie was too flustered with all that was happening to think of it either. Her thoughts hadn't gone that far ahead. One part of her was flattered and excited that John had made an offer for her, and another part was furious that he'd come unannounced and put all sorts of cats among the pigeons.

She sat tensely on the settle, with Billy separating herself and John. He was far calmer than herself, she realised, even though he could scarcely be impressed with his reception. In her heart, Carrie was deeply humiliated, thinking how differently a young man would have been received at the home of Miss Helen Barclay, whose golden image seemed to be more prominent in her mind these days than she wanted it to be.

But John Travis certainly had more self-assurance than anyone here, and even her easy-going brother, Frank, said little, while she was astute enough to see that Wilf's usual aloof manner hid his own anger at what she had done.

"I've asked Mr Stuckey if you can come to meet my uncle on Saturday week, Carrie. You're invited for tea, so I'll collect you at about four o'clock," John said, when the silence stretched into awkwardness.

Carrie felt her skin prickle. She was in a unique

situation that had never happened before. A young man was asking her out, with her family listening, and nobody was really objecting. She was aware of a freedom she had never known before, yet it didn't please her the way it should.

For a brief instant, she mourned the passing of the old Carrie with something like a physical pain, and told herself severely not to be so foolish. The one thing you couldn't stop, according to Ma, was the passing of time. Things moved on, and so did folk.

"Thank you," she said, in a scratchy voice. "I shall look forward to meeting your uncle."

But it wasn't strictly true. Meeting new people always made her feel all fingers and thumbs, and she didn't know enough about John Travis yet to feel totally at ease with him. There had to be more to a person than good looks and a sound background, and going courting meant a certain amount of time alone with a boy. Now that it was about to happen, Carrie wasn't sure that she was ready for it. But at least he was giving her a little time to get used to it, she thought in relief. It wasn't for another ten days or so.

Elsie was as snappy as a floundering crab when Carrie told her the news. Elsie was still seething over the fact of seeing Wilf Stuckey making eyes at that Woolley girl in a Park Street tea-room, and her temper wasn't improved by the necessity of sitting up for the last three nights with her granpa heaving and hawking and swearing his time had come – which it hadn't.

Carrie found her sitting on the wharf a few evenings after John's visit, throwing stones into the harbour with a viciousness that should have been warning enough. The huge dark mass of the floating and tethered *Great Britain* threw this side of the wharf in shadow, as if to emphasise Elsie's black mood. But by now, Carrie's head was too full of the fluster of having a boy of her own to notice it.

"Where have you been hiding yourself all this time?" Elsie greeted her irritably. "I ain't seen hide nor hair of you lately. Been busy drooling over Miss Helen Barclay's lace frills, have you?"

"No, I have not," Carrie said, wondering why she'd never noticed before quite how vindictive Elsie could be, nor how Elsie's accent was so drearily common. Elsie would never try to better herself in a million years . . . she caught herself up sharply, knowing what snobbish thoughts they were. But the thought that if – or when – she and John were married, she'd eventually be the wife of a boat-owning man, was enough to turn any girl's head.

If they were married. She was aware that her own dark thoughts couldn't make such a certainty of it, even now. Even though he'd come to the house and braved Pa to ask for her.

"Well, what have you been doing then?" Elsie said, glaring at her.

Carrie folded her arms, as if to put a barrier between herself and the taunts she knew were to come.

"If you must know, John Travis has been to see Pa, and asked if we can start walking out," she said grandly.

It was a slight stretching of the truth, but only slight. John's request had only come about as a result of taking back Wilf's clothes, and seizing an opportunity. She knew that but for fate, they wouldn't be in this situation now. If it hadn't been for Billy's accident, she and John would probably never have met. It gave her a creepy feeling, to know how small an incident could change the course of a person's future. She immediately chided herself, for thinking of poor Billy's accident as a small incident.

She saw Elsie's mouth drop open. "I bet your Pa had summat to say about that, then! He still thinks of you as a bab in arms. Did he clap you around the ears?"

Elsie's derision was enough to make Carrie's eyes flash. "No. He agreed to it, and at the end of next week I'm going to meet John's uncle for tea."

Elsie's mouth clamped shut in a straight line. "Well, that's it then. I shan't be seeing you no more if you're hobnobbing for Saturday tea with the likes of the Bedminster Hill folk."

"Don't be daft. What difference will it make to you and me? It's only one Saturday."

"That's how it starts, dummy. Once a boy takes a fancy to you, he'll want to see you all the time, not just once now and then. Any fool knows that."

"And I know Pa won't allow that," Carrie said, feeling totally deflated by this reaction. "Anyway, I wanted to ask your advice."

"You don't need advice from me. You can catch a boy without even trying," Elsie said rudely.

"Well, look who's talking! The girl who's got half the boyos at the Welsh Market mooning over her!" Carrie didn't know whether to laugh or snarl, until she saw that Elsie was deadly serious. "What's wrong with you, anyway? Is it to do with your granpa?"

"Yeah," Elsie lied. "I ain't had no sleep with him these past three nights. But never mind me. What's this advice you're wanting?"

Carrie took a deep breath. They had begun walking along the waterfront in the direction of the Hotwell Spa, where various small craft bobbed gently on the swell of the silvery full tide, and a tall-masted trading ship made its way majestically to tie up at one of the lower wharves for unloading. They sat on a wooden seat to watch the seamen and dockers unloading and stacking the crates, idly wondering what they contained. French brandy, perhaps, or tobacco for the manufactories, or something far more mundane, like sand for the glassworks.

"*Well?*" Elsie said.

Now that she had the opportunity, Carrie was almost dumb, especially when Elsie was in this unforthcoming mood. She wished she'd never mentioned it, but Elsie was like a dog with a ferret when she wanted something, the way she was over her unlikely obsession with Wilf.

"I ain't been out with a boy before," she said stiffly. "And I was wondering – "

Elsie gave a hoot of laughter.

"You want to know how to pucker up your lips to kiss 'im, I suppose, and whether your noses will crash together in the process? You don't need to worry about that, ninny! Just close your eyes, and he'll see to it all."

Carrie was more than irritated by her superior smile.

"I'm not talking about the way you carry on with the Welsh boyos at the Market," she snapped. "I'm talking about me and John Travis, whose intentions are honourable."

Elsie's smile vanished. "And that puts you a cut above me, does it? Well, I thought you wanted to know about kissing, and I told you. And now I'm going home before I say summat I'll really regret. Let me know when you want to know about anything else, and I might just tell you a few more secrets."

She marched off, and Carrie didn't miss the whistles from some of the unloaders at the dock as she flounced past them. Being Elsie, she couldn't resist giving them a cheeky wave, which produced more whistling and cheering. Carrie turned to go back home, smarting at how everything seemed to be going wrong between herself and Elsie, just when she needed a friend the most. She'd really wanted to know more, especially after her awkward talk with Ma the other night. She still wanted to crawl away from the memory.

"Now then, Carrie," Ma had begun when the men had gone out, and Billy was tucked up in bed. "We'll have that talk. There are things you need to know to keep yourself clean for your wedding-day."

"I ain't thinking about a wedding-day for years yet, Ma," she'd said in a fright. "You know Pa wouldn't hear of it, and I'm sure John won't want to rush into anything. We hardly know each other yet."

"But he'll want to know you, girl. It's in a man's nature, and it's up to a woman to make sure he respects her at all times."

"But he does respect me. He did the right thing in asking Pa, didn't he?"

She heard Ma sigh. "I'm talking about the lustier side of a man's nature, Carrie. It's when he's alone with you that it's most likely to happen, and that's when you must be at your most watchful. Do you understand me?"

"I think so," Carrie mumbled. Lord knew that Elsie had hinted at it enough times, but she'd always thought Elsie had been exaggerating at the way a boyo tried to fumble at her chest, and how she'd fought him off with much giggling and teasing. Elsie had made it all sound like a lark, while her Ma was so earnest that she cringed with embarrassment.

"If he wants you to do anything that you don't want to do, then you're to say no," Ma instructed. "If he wants to touch your person, other than in the most respected way, you must resist, Carrie. Otherwise, the way is open to damnation."

Once her mother resorted to the scriptures, Carrie knew she was being very serious indeed.

Eventually the conversation had ended, and they had each gone thankfully to their beds. But Carrie had tossed and turned, unable to sleep, unable to think of anything but that John Travis might want to touch her person in an intimate way, where she never even touched herself if she could help it, except for washing and drying herself. And she began to wish she'd never agreed to go courting at all.

A couple of nights later, she was still thinking the same way after the talk with Elsie, which hadn't really helped at all. And she couldn't sleep for thinking about it. She heard Frank come to bed, and then Ma. By then, her mouth was dry, and she crept downstairs for a drink of water. The lamp was still burning low, so she guessed Wilf and Pa weren't home yet. The dull yellow glow threw soft shadows around the parlour, filling the room with its rich, oily aroma. And then her heart leapt in alarm as she saw a figure slumped on the settle.

"Wilf!" she croaked. "You gave me a fright – what's happened to you?"

She suddenly realised that his face was bloodied, his clothes torn. His handsome face was contorted with rage. He was far more complex than Frank, and rarely confided his thoughts to the family. But she saw how his hands were clenched together, and although his knuckles looked raw, he ignored any pain.

"It seems that your fancy boatman is a bit of a bare-knuckle fighter," he scowled.

Carrie felt her heart begin to beat painfully fast. She certainly hadn't expected this.

"You've been fighting with John Travis?" she whispered. "For pity's sake, why?"

His voice was harsh. "For one thing, I assured him that if he hurt you, he'd have to answer to me. And for another, I told him what I thought of him for coming here and taking my clobber. You did wrong to ask him, Carrie, but he was more at fault to accept. Anything might have happened, and I wanted to make sure he understood me."

"You had no right to do that! And he wasn't wrong.

He was soaked through, and he had a boatload of people to look after," she said, incensed now.

"Oh, I know all about that. Blokes like him take their chance and cash in on whatever feeble job's going," Wilf said, the weight of his own unemployment clearly adding to whatever other frustrations he felt.

"Why are you being so hateful?" Carrie said, close to tears. "Don't you want me to have a boy of my own? Don't you want to have a young lady yourself someday?"

The minute she said it, she saw his face darken even more, and one hand crashed into the other. Blood oozed out, and without another word, Carrie fetched the medicine box from the scullery, and dabbed some soothing salve on each of the raw knuckles. Instinct told her at once that Wilf was in some kind of trouble with a young lady, and her own association with John Travis was somehow underlining it. She didn't know how, or who, but she knew her brother well enough to know when he was suffering.

"You haven't answered my questions," she said eventually. "John hasn't said or done one thing out of place, so why did you fight with him?"

"I didn't pick the fight. He did. Your fancy man is clever with the fisticuffs, and has a temper to match anything Pa doles out. You should beware of it, Carrie."

She felt a shiver of unease. Not that she believed John had picked the fight or sought Wilf out, and she knew only too well how her sharp-tongued brother could goad another person into an argument.

"Do you have a young lady, Wilf?" she said, hoping to take him off guard. For a second, he said nothing, and then he gave a short grunt.

"I thought so, or at least, I thought I had her father's approval to see her. But it seems I was mistaken. Our late lord and master don't think me a fit person to court his lovely daughter, now that I'm out of a job. Ironic, isn't it, when he was the one who fired me?"

"You don't mean Nora Woolley?" Carrie said, unable to believe it. Since she'd had no idea Wilf had been seeing the girl, she couldn't hide her astonishment.

"You see? Even you don't think me a suitable chap for Gaffer Woolley's daughter."

"Don't be stupid, Wilf. You'd be good enough for the Queen, as far as I'm concerned."

But she was highly embarrassed now. She'd never been invited to discuss either of her older brothers' *amours*, and she felt awkward at seeing Wilf's dejection. This was her strongest brother, and John Travis had clearly done nothing to ease his self-esteem, she thought resentfully. John was powerfully built, with large, capable hands, and she had a vivid image of the fight that had taken place between them.

Loyalty to her brother made her almost decide not to go to tea with him when the time came . . . but since she didn't know where John lived, she couldn't send a message to that effect. It would be even more embarrassing to let him come to the house in Jacob's Wells Road and then refuse to go out. Wilf might be able to find him, and pass on the message that she didn't want to see him again, but she doubted that he'd believe Wilf, and it would probably cause another fist-fight.

Besides, what good would it do? And she *did* want to see him again, despite all . . . for one thing, she wanted to get to the bottom of the antagonism between John and Wilf, which didn't bode well for the future. The prospect of having a young man, and being invited to Saturday tea, should be so lovely, and so genteel. Yet it was filling her with all sorts of doubts and unease.

"Never mind about me," Wilf said now. "You just mind yourself, that's all. And get on back to bed before Pa comes home, or that'll be wrong."

For a second, she wished she dared give him a hug and a kiss, hating to leave him bruised like this. But they weren't a kissing family, and he'd probably think she'd gone soft in the head if she did any such thing.

So she went back to bed, and brooded even more about John Travis, and how she had to mind herself, and wished even more heartily that she'd never met him at all.

The Saturday of the visit was fine and sunny and warm, the way a midsummer day should be. By then, Carrie had rubbed so much lanolin into her hands to soften them, that two of her finger-nails had succumbed to it and split. She had to cut them almost down to the quick to stop them catching on the best blue frock she was wearing for the occasion.

Its silk frills and folds that sat so gracefully over the hooped petticoat had once adorned the slender figure of Miss Helen Barclay, and had been adapted and shortened by Ma, until it fitted her snugly. She adored the feel of it against her skin, and waited in a mixture of dread and anticipation for the arrival of John Travis that afteroon.

"You look too fine to be our Carrie," Billy complained, when she refused to play with him in the yard for fear of soiling the frock. "I don't like you being posh."

"I'm not posh, you goose."

"Yes you are, and I don't like it when you try and talk all funny, like that Miss Barclay."

Carrie tried not to look at Ma, busily cutting strips out of some of the other discarded Barclay garments to stitch into a new rag rug. With the heavy amount of foot traffic in the small house, the rugs wore out fairly quickly, and constantly needed renewing, so they were fortunate in being supplied with plenty of bags of cast-off clothing from the toffs' houses for the task.

"Carrie wants to look her best, because she's invited

out for tea," Ma said evenly. "But she's still the same Carrie inside, no matter what she's wearing."

"Why aren't I invited out to tea?" Billy said at once. "John Travis is my friend too."

"I'm not sure he should be anybody's friend any more," Ma said, more severely than usual. Carrie felt her skin prickle again, the way it did whenever she felt defensive.

"I thought you were on our side, Ma."

"Your Pa's taken umbrage at the fighting between him and Wilf, and I don't blame him. We ain't got much, but we've got our pride, Carrie, and street fighting's shameful."

"I might have guessed that Wilf would lay all the blame on John," Carrie said bitterly. "But it seemed to me that they each provoked the other."

Ma seemed more prickly than usual, and she had a pinched, tight look on her face that invited no arguments. At the look, Carrie wisely knew when to desist, and of course, Ma knew nothing about Wilf's own problems. Wilf had his pride too, as fierce as Pa's, and Carrie guessed that no-one but herself knew how Wilf smarted over Gaffer Woolley's slight.

He certainly wouldn't have confided in Frank, who would have blabbed it everywhere. Carrie couldn't really see why her own walking-out with John Travis so offended Wilf, but she supposed that in his present state of mind, he was ready to resent any other couple who had a sunny relationship.

She wasn't sure yet that that description could be applied to herself and John Travis. John had fought with Wilf, and they were at loggerheads. And what affected one member of their family, affected all of them. It was their way.

"Just be thankful your Pa's snoring the afternoon away as usual, or you'd be getting even more instructions, girl,"

Ma said sharply. "And don't be home later than eight o'clock."

"Oh, Ma! Eight o'clock's for children!" she spluttered, seeing the humiliation in announcing such a curfew to a young man.

"It's late enough this first time. Stick by the rules, Carrie. Your Pa was all for sending Wilf or Frank with you to meet these fine folk, so be thankful I persuaded him to change his mind on that." Her voice softened a mite. "I know you'll want to be alone with your young man, Carrie, but just mind everything I've said."

Carrie's heart beat sickeningly. Did she want to be alone with her young man? How would she know what to say, how to behave, how to react if he wanted to hold her hand or kiss her? How far was she supposed to accept his advances? For a wild moment she ached to retreat straight back into childhood, playing with marbles and wooden spinning tops, the way Billy was doing in the backyard now. She didn't want to venture into this realm of adulthood, where everything was fraught with dangers and unknown delights.

"That'll be him now," Ma said, as they both heard a knocking on the front door. And Carrie knew it was far too late to change her mind.

She stepped into the sunlight, feeling as if she was going to her execution, rather than a *tête-à-tête* with a young man. But it wouldn't be like that for the whole day, she remembered with a rush of relief. She was meeting his uncle, the older man she had glimpsed in the boat on the day of the *Great Britain*'s launch. The two men had seemed as working-class as themselves then, but now . . .

She was tongue-tied from the moment she saw John. He was Saturday-spruced in his gentleman's clothes, as fine as herself in her hand-me-down frock, but there was also an unmistakeable air about him. It wasn't the inborn breeding and self-confidence of the Clifton folk, but it wasn't far off. It diminished her dwindling self-confidence, especially when he offered her his arm in the way the gentry did. She felt a bit silly at taking it, as if she were an invalid or something.

"It's a fine afternoon for walking," he said, when she didn't seem to offer any conversation at all. "Have you ever been to Bedminster Hill before, Carrie?"

"No. I stay on our own side of the river, though I've been into the city often enough, and up the hill to Clifton many times," she said. She immediately bit her lip, for he'd know why she went there by now. She didn't consort with Clifton folk, except to collect their soiled laundry, and deliver it again when she and Ma had washed it.

"It's a different world on the other side of the river," he commented. He probably hadn't meant anything by the remark, but to Carrie, it seemed to emphasise the status of the Bedminster Hill folk. They walked in silence, and Carrie wondered if they were ever going to regain the easy friendship of their first meeting. The time between had been too long.

How had she ever dared to ask this fine young man to borrow her brother's clothes? How had she dared to invite him into their narrow little house? And how dared she demean herself and her family by thinking themselves so much less than he?

By the time they reached the foot of the steep climb, she was wishing herself miles away from here. John must surely be wondering why he'd asked out such a dummy, and she couldn't help remembering those eloquent university students with whom he'd chatted so easily on Clifton Downs. He was the type who could talk with anyone – except her, it seemed.

She was very conscious of the dark swelling on his cheek, and the cut above his eye, for which she assumed

Wilf was responsible. Wilf disapproved of her seeing John, and however much she thought she had a right to choose her own friends, she had always respected Wilf's judgement, and felt a sense of disloyalty to him. And however stupid or misguided that was, it was a feeling she couldn't ignore, and it put an invisible barrier between herself and John Travis.

Chapter 6

Wilf Stuckey wasn't used to deception. He didn't have the open nature of his aptly named brother, Frank, but he wasn't one for intrigue eithcr. He'd never taken more than a passing interest in girls, and he'd often thought that if his sister's irritating and flirtatious friend, Elsie, was anything to go by, he'd as soon steer clear of them. But all that was before he met Miss Nora Woolley.

He'd seen her around the wharf occasionally, of course, when she'd come there with a message for her Pa. And like many of the other dock-workers, he'd touched his forehead or tipped his cap to the golden-haired girl, and watched her elegant progress through the maze of ropes, wood and metal on the wharf, and wondered how a bull of a man like Aaron Woolley could have fathered such a delicate maid.

But he'd never expected to fall hook, line and sinker, as the saying went. He'd thought he had too steady a head on his shoulders to be so stunned by the mere sight of a girl. His heart felt as if it was alternately in his boots or bouncing about in his chest like river flotsam. He was both amused and amazed at the change that this situation had brought about in him.

He found himself thinking of every line of poetry he'd ever heard – which didn't amount to many – every ditty that was ever sung in praise of a pretty face – and applying them all to the love of his heart. And the glory of it was, that the enchanting Miss Nora Woolley seemed just as enamoured of himself as he was of her. Which meant that everything should have been plain sailing.

Wilf scowled as he strode along the waterfront in the direction of the city on that Saturday afternoon, having got out of the house long before John Travis was due to take his sister off to Bedminster Hill. Everything was ship-shape for the two of them, he thought resentfully.

Even his Pa hadn't raised any long-lasting objections to Carrie walking out with the fellow, despite the dubious start to their acquaintance. Wilf didn't normally take an instant dislike to a man, but there was something about John Travis that had stuck in his gullet.

He was big enough to know it was more than half envy, because Travis seemed the sort who would always get what he wanted, while Wilf had always had to strive for every bloody thing. Even now, after the magnificence of the occasion just a few weeks ago, when their great ship was safely launched, it had thrown him and his menfolk into the doldrums, while Travis and others like him were picking up even more trade with their summer boating excursions.

But he bloody well wasn't going to let thoughts of Travis blight this day, he thought resolutely. Nor was he going to let the memory of the other evening spoil it. He was off to meet Nora Woolley in one of the secluded copses in Ashton Park. It was a very recent turn of events that not even his sister Carrie knew about, and he already regretted even mentioning Nora to her at all.

He felt a lift of his heart, just thinking of her name, and refused to heed the unwelcome memory of Gaffer Woolley's most recent barring of his entrance outside the wrought iron gates of the Woolley residence. His belligerent appearance had startled Wilf. He'd smarted enough when Gaffer Woolley had ticked him off for idly chattering with his daughter, but this had looked more like a confrontation, Wilf thought uneasily.

"That's far enough, my fine young cock-bird," the man had said in his guttural manner.

"I wanted to have words with you, Gaffer," Wilf had said. The man had always upheld the workmanship of the Stuckey men, as well as being affable to good workers, so this attitude was alien and unexpected.

"I suspect that you're about to seek my permission to court my daughter, since she's been singing your praises at every opportunity," Aaron Woolley said baldly. "But I'm telling you now that the answer's no. The fact that I asked you to escort her home on the day of the launch don't give you any rights, so you needn't go getting any ideas above your station, boy."

Wilf had felt a deep humiliation and fury at being stopped so ignominiously, and with such a response.

"As a matter of fact, I had no such intentions, Gaffer. I came to see you on another matter," he'd said stiffly. "It's work that my Pa and my brother and myself are wanting, and nothing else."

"You and half the city, Stuckey, but I ain't got nothing to offer you for the present," Woolley said, his eyes glinting. "Nor do I take kindly to young upstarts coming to my home and begging."

"I've never begged for anything in my life, man," Wilf felt his temper beginning to erupt. "My family needs work, and you ain't denying that we've always given you good service."

"You've got spunk, I'll say that for you. But what makes you think I owe you summat?"

"You owe us some consideration for the years we've given you. It's folk like us who've enabled you to live in a fine house and have good food in your bellies. If it weren't for the craftsmanship of people like the Stuckeys, there'd be no businesses for the gaffers to own."

By now, Wilf knew he was losing control, but he believed in what he was saying. He saw the mockery in standing here arguing with a man who could be as implacable as a solid wall when he chose. He was never going to win this argument, but the fact just made him the more determined to have his say now. He was very conscious of being on the outside of these tall filigree iron gates, while Gaffer Woolley – and his daughter Nora – were on the other side, where the velvet lawns stretched away towards the large stone-built house he could just glimpse beyond them.

Aaron Woolley thrust out his massive arms, his hands on his hips. His gold watch-chain quivered on his great stomach, and his expression was even more bull-like as he glowered at the tall young man in front of him, who'd dared to confront him like this.

"And that's cooked your goose for once and all," he bellowed. "Don't let me see you or any of your family in my boatyard again, you hear? Carpenters are ten a penny in the city now, and when I want to employ one, I'll not be looking for one named Stuckey!"

"They may be ten a penny, but you'll not find any as good, so just you remember that," Wilf bellowed back.

He turned away in a red rage, but not before he'd glimpsed the silk skirts of Nora and her mother, hurrying across the lawns to see what all the rumpus was about. Wilf had been sick to his stomach, thinking his goose was truly cooked in all directions now. He'd done for his folks, and he'd done for himself. No job, no prospects, no girl . . .

But he'd reckoned without the determination of Nora. He'd marched off to the nearby Ashton Park, in the blackest mood of his life, and a short while later, he'd seen the same cream-coloured silk skirts he'd glimpsed earlier as Nora had sat down on the wooden seat beside him. She had put a tentative hand on his arm.

"Don't be too distressed, Wilf. Pa will come round in

time, I know he will. It's well known that his bark's always worse than his bite."

"That may be so, but I hardly expected you to speak to me again after my show of temper, nor to seek me out," he said after a pause. "I thought that was the end of whatever small friendship we had, Nora."

"Is that what you want?"

"Of course it's not what I bloody well want," he said, forgetting he was talking to a lady in his frustration.

"It's not what I want either," Nora said quietly. "So what are we going to do about it, Wilf?"

He heard the tremulous note in her voice. He looked into her soft hazel eyes, and saw in them all that he wanted to see. The man in him surged to the fore, blinding him to anything else but the fact that this lovely girl was his for the asking. Her father was forgotten as he took her waiting hands in his, and felt their trembling. And he was lost.

And now here he was, on his way to another of the almost daily clandestine meetings that had taken place since then, and hating more and more the secrecy of it all. He'd always been a private person, but for the first time in his life, he wanted to share his feelings with the world. He wanted everyone to know that he adored Miss Nora Woolley, and that she loved him in return. And it was the very last thing he was able to do.

If her father knew, Nora would be forbidden to leave the house at all, and she had begged him not to do anything foolish. So he kept his frustration under control as best he could, while they made the most of their time together in the shrubbery of the their favourite silent copse in Ashton Park, where the song of the birds in the foliage high above them created a melodic accompaniment to their loving.

And very loving it had become. By now, he knew every

contour of her soft womanly shape, and the taste of her kisses. He had whispered words of love he'd hardly known were invented, and amazed himself at the ease with which he said them. And Nora responded with all the ardour he could wish for. But sometimes, the frustration of his situation came through, no matter how much he tried to suppress it when he was with her.

"I wish I had more to offer you than these hole-and-corner meetings, sweetheart," he said, as she lay in the crook of his arm. "If only I could find work so that your father would have more respect for me."

"Shush, Wilf," Nora said, her finger against his mouth. "You know I respect you, and that's all that matters."

"But it's not. Not if I want to obtain my dream."

"And what might that dream be, may I ask?"

His troubled face relaxed as he looked down into her teasing face. "You know well enough, you minx. But if I were to ask your father for your hand, he'd expire on the spot. My only hope would be to run away with you and make you my slave."

Nora laughed, enjoying the dreams they both shared. "I suspect that he'd expire mainly because we haven't known one another long enough to know our own minds."

"Haven't we?" Wilf said.

She drew in her breath as he looked deep into her eyes, and knew that nothing and no-one could make her change from wanting Wilf Stuckey, no matter who or what he was. He was right for her, and although she daren't mention Wilf's name at home just yet, somehow her father must be made to see it, no matter how long it took.

She didn't answer the question with words. Instead, she drew Wilf's face down to hers, oblivious to everything but the fact that she loved him beyond all reason.

Carrie paused for breath at the top of Bedminster Hill,

accepting the fact that John's helping hand had been very necessary for the climb. It was odd how she and Billy could struggle up the steep hill to Clifton with their laundry cart and hardly feel winded, yet over these grassy slopes on the opposite side of the river, she had almost had the breath knocked out of her.

"Are you all right?" John said now, as she pressed her hand to her chest.

"I think so. I don't know why I should feel so out of breath when I'm so used to walking."

"It's probably because the hills on your side are hemmed in by buildings, so you don't get the same feeling of space as we do over here," he said.

She wasn't sure if he was being complacent or patronising, or just plain telling it as it was. She was still nervous at being alone with him, and therefore she was starting to see hidden meanings in all that he said. It was unreasonable and annoying, when she wanted to be as carefree as Elsie would be on such a glorious day. She turned to look behind her, and felt a great dizziness wash over her.

"Steady on, there. I don't want you rolling back down the hill," John said.

But she hardly heard him. She was still saucer-eyed at the panorama spread out before her. In all her years, she had never climbed this hill. Why should she, when there was no reason for crossing over to the other side of the river? And she was awed to discover there was truth in what John had said. There was so much more space up here. So much green beneath their feet, and so much blue sky above them.

It was a different feeling to being on the Clifton Downs, which undulated very gradually in places, and in others were quite flat. Here, the great sweep of the hillside stretched from the heights where they stood now, down to the great winding river that had made generations of Bristol merchants rich. The river throbbed with life now, with the forest of masts of the larger ships, and the ever-moving busy little river-boats, forming a basin between the twin hills of Clifton and Bedminster.

"Now I see just why it was named the Cumberland Basin," she said suddenly. "It truly is a basin, isn't it?"

"It truly is," John said, smiling, "and it was worth every bit of the climb to see how your eyes shine, Carrie. Your eyes are as blue as the sky today, and just as fathomless."

Her heart jolted at the words, and she spoke awkwardly. "I'm not used to such compliments, John, so you must forgive me if I don't respond to them in the way you would wish."

"Has no-one ever paid you compliments before? No other young man? I can hardly believe that."

He dropped down on to the grass, holding out his hand to her, and after a moment's indecision, she sank down beside him. She was thankful for the brief rest, despite the ridiculous arranging of her hooped petticoats that made such a performance out of a simple act.

"You've met my Pa," she said wryly in answer to his question. "You'll know by now that he doesn't take easily to outsiders, let alone young men who want to come courting."

"I hope there's only going to be one young man coming courting from now on," John said, turning to half-lean over her. His body blotted out the sun for a moment, and Carrie was sure he was about to kiss her.

She could feel his warm breath on her cheek, and the weight of him was beginning to press down on her. And she simply took fright. She turned her face away quickly, aware that he was breathing more heavily than before. The exertion of the climb had stilled her own

100

breathing a little by now, so she knew that wasn't the reason for it.

"Why are you afraid of me, Carrie?" she heard him say.

He wasn't making any attempt to force her into a kiss, she thought suddenly, feeling very foolish now. Elsie would have enjoyed this, teasing and inviting, and pouting her lips, no matter what the consequences, Carrie thought. She was being so very naive.

"I'm not afraid of you."

"Are you afraid of yourself, then?"

"I don't know what you mean by that. How can I be afraid of myself?"

"A person can be afraid of their own emotions, Carrie. You could be afraid that if I were to kiss you, or touch you, you might suddenly discover there's no longer a nervous little girl inside that pretty gown, but a woman, with all a woman's desires."

She realised he had suddenly become very intense. She could hear it in his voice, and see it in the darkening of his eyes.

"I'm not nervous," she said, the quickness of her voice belying the words. "I'm older than Elsie, and nobody could call her a nervous anything."

"Don't even compare yourself with Elsie," John said, his voice rougher now. Without warning he covered her breast with his hand. "Elsie would probably squirm and squeal if I did this, while I wager that you have no idea of the pleasure it can bring to a man, and a woman too."

She lay perfectly still. She didn't deny that it felt very pleasant to have his hand covering her breast, but she couldn't see what excitement it was supposed to evoke. It was just warm and comforting, and it was only when his hand began to move, in so gentle a caressing movement that she hardly noticed it, that she was aware of feelings inside her that she didn't know existed. There were deep

101

stirrings of the mind as well as the body, and a sudden sweet arousal in the part of her that he was kneading rather more urgently now.

"John, please, I'm sure there are other folk on the hill," she gasped. But there were none that could see them. They were isolated in a small pocket of sweet-smelling grass, and he gave a sort of strangled sound in his throat as he pulled her to him and kissed her on the mouth.

It was just as Elsie had said. She didn't need any instruction. Her arms moved around his back and held him as close as he held her, her fingers entwining in the hair at the back of his neck. Her mouth was warm and fast against his, her breasts flattened against the hardness of his chest, and she knew the first sensations of erotic need for another human being. She never wanted the kiss to end, and her face was feverish when it did, knowing she had clung to him so madly.

He traced his fingers around her lips, and she was tongue-tied all over again. John's voice was still thicker than usual.

"You see, my love? You may have the looks of an angel, but there's all the fire of the devil in you."

She didn't know how to answer him. His words charmed her, but they alarmed her too. They alerted in her all the warnings her Ma had tried to tell her in her clumsy, embarrassed way. A girl could arouse a man without even knowing it, and there was no knowing where such wickedness could lead. She pushed John's hands away from her body, and got to her feet.

As he stood beside her, she almost lost her balance, and she swayed against him for a moment. If she was truly in love, it was such a topsy-turvy emotion that she didn't know whether she liked it or hated it. The euphoria of the discovery was somehow slipping away from her. She saw John grimace as her hands gripped his for support, and she saw his recently broken knuckles, the same as her brother's.

She was brought back to reality with a rude little shock, knowing it was something she'd meant to get clear in her mind.

"Why were you fighting with our Wilf the other day?" she said, the words tumbling out before she could stop them.

He didn't answer as they completed the climb to the top of the long, steep hill, and he let go of her hand as they reached the very top. It seemed ominous to Carrie, as if he was mentally ridding himself of anyone who was associated with the aggressive Wilf Stuckey. But that couldn't be, she thought, pushing the unwelcome thought aside. No-one who had kissed her as John had done, could reject her so readily.

"Your brother needed teaching a lesson," he said, in a voice several degrees cooler than before.

"And what made you think you were the one to teach him anything?" Carrie said, instantly defensive. The arrogance of his statement took her by surprise. Who did John Travis think he was, anyway?

"I don't like being accused of taking advantage of a young girl and wheedling my way into her house," he said shortly.

"Oh?" she said, smarting at the words "young girl", which were so much less attractive to her ears than the woman he'd so lately thought her. "And what were you doing minutes ago, may I ask, if you weren't taking advantage?"

She hadn't meant to say such a thing. She knew she had been willing and pliant in his arms, and she was surprised at how fervently she longed to be there again. But they might have been two strangers again, from the cold and distant way they faced one another now. His voice oozed sarcasm.

"I apologise if I offended you, Carrie. I thought I'd found a kindred spirit in you, and not a little girl who would take fright the first time a man touches her."

She ignored his implication that of course it was the first time a man had touched her or got close to her. It must have been so obvious . . . but wasn't that what every man wanted in a woman? It was what Ma had said. Her words had been solemn, and almost biblical. Every man wanted his woman to be pure and untouched by another when he brought her to the marriage bed . . . Carrie flinched, wondering if she had already sullied her own bright image by allowing John Travis to caress her so intimately.

"Please don't look so downcast," he said, less sternly now. "And I'd prefer to forget what happened between your brother and me. I'm sure he's forgotten it by now."

Carrie was quite sure he had not. Wilf rarely forgot an insult, and sometimes he bore a grudge for far too long . . . but she knew she had the choice now of brooding on it and letting it spoil the day, or putting it to the back of her mind – at least for now.

"It's already forgotten," she lied. "Do we have much farther to go?"

"We're almost there. Do you see the house across the street with the white fence around the garden?"

Carrie gaped. The house was larger than she had imagined, and beyond the low fence she could see that there was a big garden with outside chairs and a sun canopy for idling. A house with a garden was something Carrie yearned for above all. Their own backyard was so small, and constantly filled with the billowing lines of other folks' washing which blocked out the daylight. Up here on Bedminster Hill, she thought again that there was more sky than she had ever seen in her life before.

She felt the dampness in her palms as John pushed open

the gate in the white fence, and stood aside for her to enter the garden. The scents of roses and honeysuckle drifted into her nostrils, and the hum of bees busy about their work mingled with the lively sounds of crickets and other insects in the flower borders. To Carrie, starved of such perfection in the crowded cottages of the city dwellings, it was idyllic.

"Are you a gardener as well?" she asked.

"Not me. I can just about tell one plant from another, but it's my uncle's passion. He and Mrs Ryan spend as many hours in the garden as they can."

"You haven't mentioned Mrs Ryan before," Carrie said.

"She's my uncle's friend. I'd say she was intended, but it's more like the other way around. Uncle Oswald's resisting like the very devil, but Mrs Ryan is tired of being a widow-woman, and has every intention of getting my uncle to the altar. You'll find her interesting, Carrie."

"Is she going to be here today then?" The prospect of another woman was moderately reassuring, and the idea of two old people fencing around one another, the one determined on marriage, and the other just as determined to avoid it, tickled her imagination.

"She wouldn't miss meeting you. She'll dispense tea, and try to find out everything about you, but she means well."

They had reached the front door by now, and John pushed it open, calling out that they had arrived. The elderly man whom Carrie had last seen in shabby boat-man's gear came out of the parlour to greet her, and she had a job not to show her surprise. He was every bit as dapper as his nephew now, his grey hair smooth and unruffled by any river breeze, and he wore neat, smart clothes.

The house was no riverfront house either . . . there were Axminster carpets on the floor, and good solid mahogany furniture, and glass and china ornaments adorned every surface. Carrie felt her heart sink, remembering how she had invited John home on that first day, thinking him as lowly as herself. And lending him Wilf's clobber too . . . he must have thought he'd gone down in the world.

She lifted her chin as Oswald Travis shook her hand, and tried not to show how awkward she felt. The woman behind him looked her over, and nodded as if she approved of what she saw. Though Carrie had no idea of knowing whether the approval was at the sight of herself, or of Miss Helen Barclay's silk frock that she wore. She despised herself for feeling so class-aware, but she couldn't seem to help it.

John should have warned her, she thought, in a fit of pique, though quite what she would have expected him to say, she didn't know. All this would be normal and natural to him. He'd take for granted all the elegant chinaware and cutlery laid out on the table for tea, the dainty cut sandwiches, and the fruit cake topped with cream that had a hint of brandy to flavour it.

"You must tell us all about yourself, Carrie," Mrs Ryan said grandly, an hour or so later. By then, they had all eaten their fill and were sitting out in the garden, where the balmy summer breezes wafted the lovely evening scents of the roses all around them. It was all so *genteel*, Carrie thought, unable to get the wretched word out of her head for more than minutes at a time.

And there was nothing more guaranteed to set her thoughts in a spin than responding to Mrs Ryan's request.

"There's nothing much to tell. I live with Ma – with my parents and my two older brothers, and my small brother Billy."

"Is that the little rascal who fell into the river?"

"That's right."

She stopped. She had summed up their lives in the briefest of sentences, and a right boring mess she had made of it. Why couldn't she have said something lively, about her brother Frank always having had a yen to go to sea . . .? Or about her own fascination with Mr Brunel and his great works . . .? Or even about Billy being so good with his letters already . . .?

"And what does your family do? John has said hardly anything about you at all, which makes you something of a mystery to his uncle and me."

Carrie didn't think Uncle Oswald could have cared a jot about what she or her family did, and it was only Mrs Ryan's sharp eyes that wanted to bore right into her soul.

"Pa and my brothers are carpenters, and real craftsmen at that," she said quickly. "They did some of the work on the *Great Britain* while she was in dry dock, and they made every stick of furniture in our house."

"Fancy!" Mrs Ryan said.

Carrie gritted her teeth, hoping it didn't sound as if they couldn't afford to have someone else make their furniture for them. It wasn't that at all. There was no need, when the Stuckey men turned out as fine a piece of work as could be bought in any workshop.

"Carrie's father should start up his own workshop," John said, unconsciously echoing her thoughts. "He'd do a brisk trade with his sons to assist him."

"I daresay he would, but you need money to set up such a place," Carrie said smartly. "And Pa's never been a man to save his money."

She blushed, wishing the talk would move away from her family. Nor did she want to convey the fact that once the meagre housekeeping money was put away, whatever money Pa had left went out just as quickly into one of the riverside taverns. But Mrs Ryan wasn't done with her yet.

"And what about you, my dear? What work do you do?"

It was obvious to anyone that Carrie wasn't a lady who sat around all day and did nothing. She had never been ashamed of the work she did before these last weeks, and she wasn't ashamed now, she thought defiantly. But the sparky little devil inside her made her refuse to give a direct answer.

"I have a special arrangement with Miss Helen Barclay of Clifton as a lady's helper," she said.

It was stretching the truth considerably, yet she persuaded herself that it wasn't quite a lie either. She definitely helped Miss Barclay to look her best on all occasions, and her well-lanolined hands still felt squidgy and damp, but at least for the moment they didn't bear the reddened marks of the washer-woman.

"A lady's helper, indeed. The young lady in question must think very highly of you, Carrie," Mrs Ryan said in some admiration.

"I believe she does, ma'am," Carrie said demurely.

The ordeal was finally over, and an ordeal it had been. If there had just been John and his uncle in the house, Carrie thought she would have felt more relaxed. But the widowed Mrs Ryan was keeping a very proprietorial eye on the house on Bedminster Hill, and Carrie thought she knew very well why. When John married, he would presumably bring his wife to live there, and the matronly lady already had her sights set on ruling it.

She let out her breath in a long sigh of relief as they left the house at last, and began the walk back down the hill. The grass was already damp with the evening dew settling on it with a diamond-bright sheen, but she didn't worry about the dampness seeping through her thin shoes. She felt like a child let out of charity school, or a bird set free from a cage, and it showed.

"Was it so bad?" John said in amusement.

"In some ways, yes!" she burst out, unable to hide her

feelings. "But only because of that awful woman! I liked your uncle, but if he marries her, he'll be under petticoat rule quicker than blinking."

"I always thought they were well-matched."

Carrie shook her head decisively. "That's probably because you want to see your uncle settled," she said, with insight. "I'm sure a man doesn't always want a woman fussing around him, and clearing up after him before he's even had time to enjoy making a mess in his own home."

"You're quite the little philosopher, aren't you?"

He had taken her arm to stop her sliding on the damp grass. It was very slippery in places, and she was glad of his support, but she didn't miss the edge in his voice.

"Well, I'm sorry if I'm speaking out of turn," she said. "I didn't mean to imply that your uncle hasn't got a mind of his own. But you did ask!"

"I'm sorry I did, now, if it's got you so riled up. It doesn't take much, does it?"

"And what about you? Now that I've seen you at home, I'd have thought you were far too *genteel* to be brawling in the street with my brother."

She bit her lip as that damnable word slipped out of her lips again. Truth to tell, she hated fighting, and she hated street fighting above all, since it invariably involved a crowd and the constables.

"I'm not too keen on it myself," John said. "I much prefer to keep my pugilistic activities confined to the ring."

For a second, Carrie couldn't follow the long words. When she did, she stopped abruptly, but as John strode on down the slippery hill, she found her feet sliding after him. Eventually they both managed to stop, and she faced him furiously.

"Are you telling me you fight for money?"

His eyes flashed ominously at the accusation in her voice. "It's an honest sport when it's properly organised."

"*Sport!* You might have killed our Wilf, and you call that sport!"

He was gripping her arms now, as she bristled like a fire-cracker with rage.

"Come on now, Carrie, you're getting this out of all proportion. It was your brother who started it, and I didn't really hurt him. Believe me, if I'd wanted to, he'd have come off far worse than he did."

The sheer arrogance of the statement left her gasping. She shook him off, and stepped back a pace.

"I don't think I want to know you any more. And you needn't escort me any farther. I'm quite capable of finding my own way home," she said in a freezing tone.

She slid on down the hill, praying that she wouldn't fall head over backside and look a complete fool. She thought he would follow her, but he didn't, and her eyes stung when she glanced back and saw him still standing there, his arms folded implacably. His uncle may be the sort to be manipulated by a woman's wiles, but John Travis clearly was not.

When she reached the bottom of the hill, she turned to the right with her head in the air, and hurried along the cobbled road until she could cross the river by one of the city bridges.

This lovely day had all turned sour, and she couldn't help thinking bitterly that it wouldn't have mattered a tuppenny toss to Elsie that a man earned extra money as a bare-knuckle fighter – which was also about as far from being genteel as she could imagine. But then, Elsie didn't have her standards – or her bloody saintly sense of pride, either.

Chapter 7

For long moments, John Travis remained standing quite still with his arms folded. An onlooker might have thought he was contemplating the spectacular scarlet glory of the sunset on the river, but instead, he was watching the stiff-shouldered figure of Carrie Stuckey diminish from sight as she marched along the waterfront towards the city bridges.

Women! John thought savagely. They were a breed apart, and this one in particular, as sweet to look at as a rose in bloom, was as hot-headed as they came. Never giving him a chance to explain . . . just going off half-cocked at the mere mention of bare-knuckle fighting, as if it was akin to doing bloody murder.

He swore aloud, vehemently and satisfactorily, as the arrogant Miss Carrie Stuckey's reaction sent his thoughts right back to the days when it had been a desperate necessity for him to learn to fight, or go under.

"It was your grandpa's dying wish to send you to be eddicated, John, and it'll make a man of you," his Uncle Oswald had said on that gloomy winter's day long ago, when the boy had done his unmanly crying over the burying of the old man he'd adored. "There's nobody left but we two now, and I'm to see that his wishes are carried out with what he saved for you."

"I never knew he had any money," John had mumbled, shocked at the thought. "He never acted rich."

"Ah well, that's because he never made no fuss about it. And he weren't rich like they toffs up Clifton, mind, but what he had was always meant for you, so there's to be no arguing, now. You're to go to this here decent school, like your grandpa wanted, and make summat of yourself. You don't want to end up ferrying folk about on the river like me."

"But that's just what I *do* want," John had almost sobbed then. "I love the river, and I don't want to go away. Don't send me, Uncle – *please*."

But his pleading had been futile, and he'd gone away to the all-boys school to be educated. In the end, he had cause to be thankful for his education, because it enabled him to be completely at ease with all kinds of folk now, including the university students who came down to the river for a day's excursion.

But there were other things he had learned that weren't so savoury. He discovered that for those who wanted it, there was more than the basics of reading and writing, and the higher advantages of a foreign language and the sciences on offer. In that cloistered school world, John had been rudely initiated into the dark side of human nature by boys who were older than he, who wanted far more than he was prepared to give, and who took an instant fancy to the sturdy new boy with the handsome dark eyes and the interestingly earthy accent.

He was revolted by their lewd suggestions, and it was then that he took up the optional lessons of boxing, its name elevated to that of noble art by the muscular and totally masculine tutor. He had discovered a natural talent for the sport, and when one or another of the nancy boys had slyly approached him, he was smartly put in his place with a bloodied nose and bruised ribs. Word quickly got around, until the small obnoxious clique had finally got his message, and from then on, he was left strictly alone.

So, Miss Purity Stuckey, he thought viciously now, *if*

you had been prepared to listen, and I'd been prepared to relate the details of such practices into your delicate ears, you might have learned that it had been no lust for violence that had led me into fighting, but to keep off the unwanted attentions of the bum boys.

When his schooldays were over, he'd been tempted by the occasional advertising posters inviting contestants to try their bare-knuckle skills against a professional opponent, either up on Clifton Downs, or in one of the hastily erected arenas in one of the city parks. It kept his hand in, should he ever need it, and it was a useful way of earning a bit of extra money towards that boat he intended buying one day. But he certainly wasn't any lover of fighting for fighting's sake, and he did it strictly as a sideline.

He was satisfied that he had lived out his grandpa's dream of educating him, and the rough edges of his accent had been moderately smoothed out. But it did more for his self-respect than all the schooling he received, to know he could fend off anyone he chose, especially the likes of the pansies he could spot a mile off by their scents and postures.

In the end, it was still the river that he chose for his livelihood, just as he had always promised himself. In the end, a man had to follow his own dream . . . He had no wish to be known as a bare-knuckle fighter, and he was still cursing himself for letting the words slip out when he was walking out with Carrie Stuckey. But maybe it was as well he'd seen the prim side of her before it was too late. As her Pa had said, there was a long way to go between walking out and the marriage stakes.

"Well, you look in a fine old state. What bee's got into your bonnet?" Elsie Miller puffed, running inelegantly across the bridge to catch up with the friend she'd glimpsed in the distance. "Weren't you supposed to be having tea with your young man today?"

Carrie stopped stalking along with her head in the air, causing Elsie to cannon right into her. Elsie looked decidedly flushed, and Carrie guessed she'd been up to no good, and probably with some boy. It didn't make her own scratchy feelings towards John any more agreeable.

"I was, and I did," she said crossly.

Elsie stared at her. "Why didn't he walk you home then? You haven't fallen out with him already, have you? Did he try something on? I bet he did, and you got all tight-arsed about it!"

Carrie gave her a freezing look. Even for Elsie, this was going too far. "Sometimes you can be so coarse!"

She got a sudden whiff of something coming from the other girl, and she spoke suspiciously. "Have you been drinking?"

Elsie tossed her head. "What if I have? 'S'no crime, is it? And it helps me sleep at night, instead of listening to me granpa moaning and spitting."

She lurched against Carrie as a lady and gentleman went to pass them on the bridge, and Carrie held her firmly, flashing an apologetic smile at the disapproving pair. It was clear that in their eyes she was tarred with the same unsavoury brush as Elsie at that moment.

"Come on, I'll walk you home," she said sharply.

"Not before you tell me what happened between you and the lovely John," she slurred. "Did he kiss you?"

Already, to Carrie, it seemed like a very long time ago, and the memory of those sweet, intoxicating moments on the hillside were frighteningly fading. And it was all her fault. All her own bloody, stupid, self-righteous fault! Just because she'd got up on her high horse about John's interest in fighting . . . she shivered, because if she had lost him because of it, that was her own fault too.

And now that she'd had time to cool down a little,

she knew that it wasn't even so much the actual fighting that had offended her. It was the shock of knowing that someone she'd thought so far above herself, could be capable of enjoying such a sweaty, disgusting, and downright cruel pursuit. If he'd said he indulged in cock-fighting, she couldn't have been more shocked, and that was the truth of it.

But it hadn't been anything like so repugnant, and some folk even called it an honourable and masculine sport.

She was already regretting her hasty retorts . . .

"*Well?*" Elsie demanded, still swaying dreamily back and forth.

Carrie's self-righteousness suddenly vanished, and she felt her face crumple. "Oh Elsie, I've been such a fool!"

"Good God, what have you done?" Elsie squealed. "You ain't let him do it to you already, have you? You could have made 'im wait a coupla weeks, girl, and you're a bloody dark horse if you haven't, that's all I can say!"

For a moment, Carrie looked at her blankly, and then her face went a fiery red, as she realised what her friend meant. More than that, she realised there was a look of excited admiration on Elsie's face, and she knew Elsie was waiting to relish every lascivious little detail of what she imagined had happened.

"You've got it all wrong as usual," she snapped. "But I'm not going to say another word, so you can either take my arm and try to walk upright, or I'll go on without you. And if you end up in the river, just see if I care!"

For a moment, the two of them glared at one another, and then Elsie capitulated, clinging to Carrie's arm as if she was a very old woman. If Carrie had needed to clear her head before she went home and faced her family with news of John's home and his uncle, and the fine tea they'd had, then so did Elsie need to clear her head before she

115

went to bed that night. She'd have a roaring headache tomorrow.

But since neither Elsie nor her granpa spent Sunday mornings regularly in church like the Stuckeys did, it probably wouldn't matter. Elsie would just sleep the morning away, and her granpa would wait patiently until she was fit to grope around and get him some soup, which was all he seemed to eat nowadays.

For a moment, Carrie's mouth watered at the thought. The Stuckeys never ate hot food on Sundays, not even soup. Sunday was a day of rest and contemplation, and no cooking was done in the house. Carrie had often thought irreverently that God surely wouldn't object to folk putting a bit of hot nourishment in their bellies on His special day, but Ma's word on the subject was law, and there was no changing it.

"Oh, all right," Elsie gave in, grumbling. "I ain't never going to get there by meself, but I'd still like to know what you and John Travis have been up to."

"We haven't been up to anything, and never likely to, if you must know," Carrie muttered, completely forgetting her vow to say nothing at all about it.

"Don't tell me you've finished with him already! If you have, I'd be more than willing to take him on," Elsie giggled as if she'd said something very clever, and stumbled as Carrie pulled at her arm.

"Come on, I haven't got all day. I'm supposed to be home by eight o'clock, and it's nearly that already."

She suddenly realised that she was never going to be indoors inside her curfew if she took Elsie all the way home. But Elsie was in no fit state to get there by herself . . . silly little idiot that she was, Carrie simply couldn't abandon her.

She almost pelted her down the winding Hotwells Road towards the hovel where she lived. Once there, they were both winded, and Elsie's face was flushed and sweating.

116

"Will you be all right? I'll have to go, or Pa will skin my hide for me," she said desperately, as Elsie swayed against the door, fumbling for the latch.

"Good God, where's the fire?" she said nastily. "Don't worry 'bout me. You look after number one, as usual."

As she got the door open she almost fell inside, and Carrie got a swift whiff of the dingy interior. It was a mixture of old age and stale urine, allied with the pungent aromas of Elsie's cheap scents with which she lavishly splashed herself.

"I've got to go," Carrie gasped, almost retching at the thought of putting one foot inside that door. "I'll see you when I see you."

She fled back along the waterfront, dodging the lounging sailors and tavern boys who whistled and called after her. She tore up Jacob's Wells Road, holding her skirts above her ankle so she could run faster. She felt undignified and dishevelled, and it flashed through her mind that never in a million years would Miss Helen Barclay be arriving home like this after an outing with a young man.

Not that John Travis would care a jot about how she arrived home by now! The disastrous ending to the afternoon made her eyes smart, and then she forgot all about John Travis and the likes of Miss Helen Barclay as she saw what was ahead of her. Her Pa was standing outside their door, waiting for her, and his dark brows were drawn together until they met in the middle of his forehead. It didn't bode well.

"I'm sorry, Pa. I met Elsie and she'd been taken ill, so I walked her home," she began stuttering at once.

"Get in the house, girl, and don't stand on the doorstep blabbing your excuses," he thundered. "What kind of a state is this to be coming home in, and showing off your body to all and sundry?"

Carrie dropped her skirt at once, forgetting she'd been

117

holding it aloft. Her face flamed. She had hardly been showing off her body, just the merest sliver of ankle to help her running. She felt the flat of Pa's hand on her back as he pushed her inside. To be punished now was the final straw after this terrible day . . . and then she saw why he was more aggressive than usual.

"Ma! What's happened?" she croaked, everything else forgotten as she saw her mother lying prostrate on the settle, a cushion beneath her head. It was so unusual to see her mother lying down, or even sitting for more than minutes at a time, that Carrie was sure something must be terribly wrong. She felt a great fear in her heart. Ma was their mainstay, and if she was really ill . . .

She ran to her side, kneeling down and taking her mother's cold hands in her own. She had been so hot after her racing home, and then her Pa's censure, and now she was sure she must be as deathly white as Ma, with the fear tying her stomach up in knots.

"There's nothing wrong, Carrie, leastways, nothing that's going to kill me," Ma said testily. "Don't take on so, girl. Our Wilf's gone for the doctor, though he had no business doing so. There's no money to spare for night visits. I know what ails me, and it was just a bout of faintness, that's all, but your Pa wouldn't listen to me."

She was talking much faster than usual, and Carrie looked uncertainly from her to her Pa. She was struggling to sit up now, and the colour was starting to come back to her face. Carrie ran her tongue around her dry lips.

"What do you think it is then, Ma?" she said huskily. All kinds of wild ideas ran around her mind. The tuberculosis, or scarlet fever . . . or even some fever of an alien nature that Frank might be unknowingly carrying from his sorties with the foreign sailors at the docks.

"I think 'tis another babby," Ma said calmly. "And the Lord only knows how we're going to keep it."

*   *   *

Wilf's arrival with Doctor Flowers was convenient enough for Carrie to hide the total shock she felt at the words. She glanced at Pa, and couldn't begin to read his expression. She thought she could guess at the way his thoughts were going. Another mouth to feed was the very last thing that was wanted in the house, however much a babby was thought of as a cause for rejoicing.

She was quite sure Pa wouldn't reject his own child, even though the men were already relying on the women-folk for the bulk of their needs. But Ma would be growing bigger every day and unable to attend to much of the Clifton wash . . . and at the whirling thoughts inside her head, Carrie began to feel as though the entire weight of the family survival was going to sit squarely on her own slim shoulders, and wondered if she was going to faint off herself . . . and a fat lot of good that would do, she thought angrily.

She and the men stayed back in the room as Doctor Flowers say down beside her Ma. He looked deep into her eyes and asked a few questions before he nodded. It didn't seem like much of a consultation, but Carrie presumed that a woman who'd borne four children already, and helped to birth quite a few more, knew the signs well enough. But Ma wasn't a young woman now, and things could go wrong . . . Carrie felt panic wash over her again, and then the doctor was getting to his feet and brushing aside Ma's murmurs about payment for his visit.

"You've done enough good turns in your time, mis-sus, so we'll forget all about payment this time. I had business in this part of town anyway, so just rest up as much as you can and send your girl to arrange for the midwife when your time comes. If anything untoward should happen between now and then, you know where to find me."

"Thank you, Doctor," Carrie heard Ma say faintly, far

119

less vocal than usual. It was true then. There was going to be another babby in the house, and the Lord knew where they were going to put him. Pa had fashioned Billy's crib, but it had been passed on to needier folk long ago. Now they were the needy ones, but at least crib-making would give Pa something to do with his idle hands.

Carrie suddenly avoided looking at her Pa, thankful that he was showing the doctor out of the door. She'd never thought about her Ma and Pa doing the kind of things Ma had been warning herself against. She wasn't daft enough not to know that married folk did it, but you never wanted to think of it in connection with your own parents.

Wilf wasn't looking at Pa either, she realised, and was offering to go and look for Frank to tell him the news, now he was sure she was all right.

"You go, Wilf, but don't you be worrying him about any of this, mind. I'm as strong as a dray-horse, so you remember that as well."

Carrie crossed her fingers as she heard the words. Ma was . . . she had to think quickly. Ma was nearly forty-five years old, and it was too old to be having another babby. She had been too old for childbirth when she'd had Billy, and although that was eight years ago now, Carrie could still remember the screams and moans through the paper-thin walls of Ma's bedroom, and how she'd hid her head beneath the bedclothes to shut out the sound. She didn't want Ma to have to go through that again.

She went across to her quickly, and sat down beside her on the settle, taking her cold hands in hers.

"I'll help you all I can, Ma," she said huskily. "You're to do as the doctor says, and rest up as much as possible."

May removed her hands from her daughter's. She couldn't abide sentiment, even though Carrie would have thought this was the perfect moment for the special bonds between them to be strengthened. Carrie longed for Ma to see her as another woman, to embrace her and rely on her for once. But it didn't happen. As always, Ma had to be the strong one, and Carrie felt herself pushed aside, relegated once more to the dutiful daughter.

"I'll rest up for a day or so when I'm confined and not before, so I don't want no fuss about this, Carrie," she almost snapped. "The babby won't come until it's ready, and I ain't sitting on my backside doing nothing until that day. So you can come and talk to me while I make some cocoa if you've a mind, and tell me about your day."

Her day was all but forgotten in the more momentous happenings in the Stuckey household. It seemed of little importance now, and when they were in the scullery together, she blurted out that the tea had been quite pleasant, but that she wasn't sure that she and John Travis were altogether suited after all.

"Why not?" Ma said, pausing in lifting the heavy kettle onto the stove, and ignoring Carrie's quick remark that she shouldn't be doing it at all. "He didn't do any of the things I warned you against, did he?"

"No Ma, he was a perfect gentleman," she said wearily, wondering just why relationships between men and women had to be so complicated. She and Elsie could have the most blistering rows, and it made not the slightest difference to their friendship. While she and John had had the merest of brushes, and already they seemed to be poles apart.

Suddenly, she felt her face go as hot as fire. Her Ma was expecting another babby, and while the news was kept inside this house, they had only themselves to consider. But now she wondered how other folk would see it. Elsie and her hooting, incredulous laughter; Gaffer Woolley and Pa's old mates at the wharf, who would no doubt be sniggering behind their hands at the thought, or else calling Pa a sly old dog and lifting their ale jugs at the waterfront tavern and sending him home rolling drunk.

And John Travis, who would raise his fine eyebrows at the news and hide his real feelings behind those handsome features . . . and Miss Helen Barclay, whose cook had once told Carrie grandly that the Barclay family issue had ended after the arrival of their one beautiful child, since it was deemed *infra dig* to flood the county with children. Carrie hadn't understood the words any more than cook did, but in any case, she could never imagine the snooty-nosed Barclay parents performing *it* more than once in their lives.

"Have you gone into a trance, girl? I've asked you twice about your young man's uncle and what his home was like," she heard Ma saying.

Carrie couldn't think for a moment. What the Jack Jones did any of that matter, compared with the fact that her Ma was having another babby? A fact that folk might snigger about, or sneer at, or simply avoid mentioning, knowing the dire straits in which the Stuckeys were finding themselves? She felt fiercely protective of Ma, and without thinking, she rushed to her and put her arms around her.

"What's all this about?" Ma said crossly, pushing her away and eyeing her keenly. "You ain't answered me properly yet, Carrie. Did that young man do summat he shouldn't? Was that your reason for bein' in late?"

Carrie felt her throat thicken. "Oh Ma, there was nothing like that! I'm just worried about you, that's all."

Her mother looked genuinely astonished. "What ever for? There's nothing for you to be worrying about on my account. A babby's just nature's way of saying the family ain't yet complete, that's all."

"But you always said it was," Carrie heard herself say, as the ghosts of past whispered conversations between her Ma and Pa nagged away at her. "You always said our Billy was an afterthought, and that enough was enough."

"I don't want to hear no more of that talk," Ma said briskly. "Our Billy don't know yet, and there's no reason for telling him for a while yet."

"When will it be, do you think?"

The painful mysteries of child-bearing were an alien part of life that Carrie didn't want to think about, but now she was being forced to think about it. And she guessed that Ma would already have it all worked out, without the doctor's or the midwife's say-so.

"Soon after Christmas, I'd say. Maybe even on the Lord's day itself. That 'ould give it His blessing and no mistake. He'd never allow things to go wrong on His day."

She turned away to attend to the singing kettle. She was talking almost to herself by then, but Carrie was able to catch the last muttered words well enough. And she knew then, that it wasn't only herself who was afraid. Ma was afraid too.

On Sundays the Stuckeys went to church, as ship-shape and tidy as any other family. The prided themselves on that, though it had always been down to Ma to insist on it. Pa would undoubtedly have preferred to spend the day idling, but since that was mostly all he did these days, going to church was something of a welcome outing instead. And it was the same church that many of his old workmates, and the dockside bosses attended, and that included Gaffer Woolley and his pretty daughter.

Carrie sang the last hymn from the hymn sheet on that brisk August morning, with already a hint of autumn tinging the air, and smiled to herself at Billy's lusty, but slightly off-key notes beside her. But at least he could read the words, which was more than many another child of his age, or even older. Billy was as keen to learn his letters as all the Stuckey children had been, and Ma and Pa should be proud of that too. And then she caught the minister's eye on her, and hastily pushed down all thoughts of sinful pride that were so out of place in this House of God.

Afterwards, as they all spilled out into the morning sunshine, the minister was there to shake each hand, and the finer folk among them stopped to chat to one another, while the lesser ones stood farther back to admire or envy them.

"How go things for you, Sam?" the minister said to Carrie's father. "Do you have work yet?"

"We do not, and there's nothing on offer as far as I can see," Pa said, more curtly than usual at the pious question. The minister pressed his hand more firmly.

"Have faith, man, and the good Lord will provide."

"Well, you might tell Him to provide it soon, Mr Pritchard," Pa said, his patience running out. "For there's hardly enough food to put in our bellies as it is, without – "

"*Sam*, that's no way to speak to Mr Pritchard," Ma said, before he could blab to all and sundry about the coming baby. She turned to the minster apologetically. "Please excuse his manners, sir. The times don't make for pleasantries."

"I understand, dear lady, and I take no offence. I shall pray for you," he said, adding more oil to Pa's explosive fury.

"Come on, Pa, let's get home." Wilf almost pushed him ahead of them. He was already aware of Gaffer Woolley and Nora talking with their friends. Nora had glanced his way, and even managed a secret smile at him, but he was too humiliated by his Pa's little outburst to do anything other than pretend he hadn't seen her. Then, to his horror, Pa noticed them too, and strode right across to the little group.

"'Tis a pity you can't carry out some of the Lord's work and provide summat for good workers, Gaffer, instead of chucking 'em on the scrap heap," he said loudly. "Ten years of my life I gave you, and my sons followed on, thinking we had a secure future with Woolleys – "

"Go home, man. You're drunk, and you're a disgrace to your family," Gaffer Woolley said coldly.

"I ain't drunk, and I'll kill the first man who says I am," Pa suddenly yelled. "And it's my family I'm thinking about, same as the rest of 'em around here, if only they'd up and say so."

But it was obvious to him, as to everyone else, that most were subservient to the bosses, and unlikely to uphold anything Sam Stuckey was saying without due warning and sufficient rebel-rousing.

Carrie wished the ground would open up and swallow her. She'd heard the saying, and thought it melodramatic, but now she knew the absolute truth of it. Frank was almost grinning, impervious to Gaffer's insults, and Billy was huddled close to Ma's skirts. But Wilf . . . she realised that Wilf was as tense as herself, and that Miss Nora Woolley had gone a fiery red and looked as though she'd like to make herself invisible too. And then the minister intervened, speaking in his most condemning pulpit voice.

"May I remind you both that this is still God's House? Please continue your discussions outside the church grounds, and I suggest you each make a private examination of your anger and resolve your differences before you set foot in this place again." He turned on his heel to continue greeting the rest of his flock, clearly dismissing this unruly element in his church.

The slight to his own character, allied with Sam Stuckey's, made Aaron Woolley's florid neck seem to inflate like a bull-frog's, Carrie thought, in sudden awful fascination. She wondered if it would inflate sufficiently to explode right here and now.

"I shan't forget this, Stuckey," Gaffer grated. "You and

your brood will never find work with me again, and you can tell that lusty sprog of yours to stop sniffing around my daughter."

Before any of them could take all of it in, he had bundled Nora away to his waiting carriage. It was Wilf who hustled his family away in the same manner. But not before Sam had looked at him in a fury, seeing the truth of Gaffer's statement in every brittle movement his son made.

He had never guessed . . . but why should he, when Wilf was the most secretive, more sensitive of his sons? Not like Frank, who was grinning openly now, and ragging Wilf unmercifully all the way down to Jacob's Wells Road. Wilf stuck it out in cold silence for most of the way, and Pa was too busy getting tongue-pie from Ma for the shameful show outside the church, but Wilf reached the limit of his patience at Frank's final taunt.

"Anyway, I doubt that you'd get anywhere with the lovely Nora, bruth. They say she don't look kindly at any man earning less than five hundred a year."

To Carrie's horror, she saw Wilf go for his brother's throat, and Pa had the devil's job to prise them apart. She could be thankful that the Woolleys and most others had gone on their way now, and that they were virtually outside their own front door.

"I'll not have my boys fighting over a piece of skirt," Pa roared, banging their heads together to their mutual howls of pain and rage. "You may think yourselves men, but I'm still your father, and while you're under my roof, you'll behave accordingly, do you understand?"

"Does that include threatening to kill a man outside the church?" Wilf snapped, and ducked again as Sam took a swipe at him.

"I've had enough of this, so get inside, all of you," Ma suddenly said, her voice alarmingly shaky.

She was the most stoical of women, but Carrie could

126

see that her eyes were large in her pinched, white face, and she suddenly remembered Ma's condition. Ma might be scornful about letting it upset her normal working life, but emotional upsets were different. She couldn't predict how family squabbles were going to affect her now.

"Ma's right," Carrie said shrilly. "You should all be ashamed of yourselves for upsetting her so, and with the babby to think about and all." She clamped her hands to her mouth at once, as Billy turned his round, inquisitive eyes on her.

Pa pushed them all inside, but it was too late. Billy began his shrieking questions at once.

"What babby? There ain't no babby in this house, only me. You always said I was the babby, Ma."

"And you always hated me saying it, didn't you?"

He conveniently ignored that. "I don't want no other babby," he howled. "I shall hate it and I shan't speak to it, nor let it play with my things. I shall hide my top and my marbles away from it."

Frank's laughter stopped him in full flood. "And a good thing too, squirt. We don't want the babby to be swallowing marbles and choking itself, do we?"

Billy glared at him. Somehow Frank's words made the babby more of a loving, breathing certainty than anything else. His stocky little figure was as taut as a statue, and Ma made a rare gesture of affection towards him and tried to gather him into her arms. His reply was to pummel her in the stomach in his frustration. She was taken completely off-balance and she staggered backwards, grasping at the settle to save herself from the blows.

"Billy, no!" Carrie gasped, pulling the unwitting child away from her mother.

"I'm all right, and he didn't know what he was doing," Ma said, breathing quickly. "But I suppose that's summat else that'll need to be explained soon." And it was obvious that she didn't relish the thought of doing so.

Before any of them could stop him, Pa had boxed Billy's ears, which started the boy screeching indignantly.

"I ain't done nothing!" he yelled. "And I don't want no whining babby in this house, neither. I'll go and live at the orphanage if you bring it here, so there."

Carrie could have laughed at his comical little face, if it hadn't been so obvious that the situation was so tragic to him. He stood defiantly, rubbing his sore ears, his shoulders stiff and hunched, his face blotchy with trying to hold back the tears.

She went to take him in her arms, but he wrenched away from her, wanting nobody. He went stomping up the stairs, crashing the bedroom door behind him. As Pa made to go after him, Ma put out a hand and stopped him.

"Let him be, Sam. He's put out at the thought of not being the babby any more, but he'll come round to it."

She was calmer than the lot of them, Carrie thought. Calmer than Pa, who looked thunderous again.

"Seems like none of us have got much choice about that," he said savagely, and turned on his heel to go out the front door and away down the street.

He had impressed on them all their lives that it was only the low-life who went wandering aimlessly on a Sunday, and such activities were frowned on by respectable folk, which made his action all the more damning.

In the silence that followed, they could hear his Sunday boots striking on the cobbles before the sounds finally died away. Then, Carrie was only too aware of her heart's pounding, and the way her Ma's breath had caught. She heard Wilf clear his throat and Frank give a nervous laugh, but it was fast dawning on them all that Billy wasn't the only one resenting the coming baby.

Pa didn't want it either, and it was so unbelievable, even in their present circumstances, that Carrie couldn't even imagine how Ma would feel about that. The Stuckeys were a close-knit family, and had always defended one another, no matter what . . . and all of a sudden, it seemed that anything and everything was conspiring to tear them apart.

Chapter 8

By the time August had slid into September, an occasional morning frost was already glazing the streets and
reddening the noses of the early risers. Those who
had work went about their business and ignored the
changing of the season. Those who didn't, but who
were accustomed to rising at dawn, gave an habitual
small shiver at the smell of autumn in the air, and tried
to ignore the dread thought of the idle winter that was
just around the corner.

Then they mostly snuggled back beneath the bedclothes, pretending to themselves and their families that
they were making the most of the inactivity while it
lasted, while sending up a fervent prayer that it couldn't
last for ever.

Those who never got up early were completely unaware
of such inconveniences as belt-tightening due to the lack
of money to buy food. Or of sending small boys to the
docks to collect any coal bits or wood shavings to use on
the stove for cooking what meagre fare they had, and
to store up in sheds and lean-tos and bunkers for the
winter fires.

Helen Barclay never rose before the hour of ten o'clock.
Her father was one of Bristol's rich financiers, and it was
only when she heard the wheels of his carriage leave the
house for his splendid offices in the city, that she decided
it was time enough for her to leave her luxuriously warm

bed. She had become accustomed to eating her breakfast in her room, and it was a little ritual in which she was indulged by her Mama and everyone else in the Barclay's Clifton mansion.

That September morning Helen was putting the finishing touches to her toilet. Her irritating maid had helped her through the ritual of dressing in her shifts and the hooped wire underskirt, and then into the new morning gown of soft lilac voile. Sophie had teased wisps of her golden hair into becoming little trails around her face and piled the rest of it into a rich thick knot on the top of her head.

"You look a real picture and no mistake, Miss Helen," Sophie said, in the sycophantic way that was beginning to heartily grate on Helen's ears.

"Sometimes I wonder what it's all for," she said to herself, and not expecting any comment.

The pudgy-faced girl sniffed.

"I'm sure I don't know why you should be so discontented, miss. Seems to me you're a young lady who can have anything she wants, so you've no reason for sounding so out of sorts, begging your pardon, of course."

Helen swivelled round on the velvet-covered dressing-table stool. The girl took far too many liberties for someone only here on a probationary basis. She would be given her month's grace, but after that, Helen would shed no tears to see her go.

"I don't expect you to understand!" she said, unable to keep the annoyance out of her voice. "How would you know how pointless it feels to be dressed up like a peacock at ten in the morning, with nowhere to go and no-one to see, and then having to take it all off again after lunch to be on my best behaviour when Mama's friends come for afternoon tea?"

She paused for breath, furious with herself for even deigning to discuss such matters with this gossipy girl.

131

Sophie sniffed, having been in service for various young ladies long enough to recognise the signs when she saw them, and pert enough to speak her mind when she felt like it.

"You're just peaky, that's all. 'Tis what we common folk call the time of the month, and the gypsy's curse. You fine folk like to pretend it don't happen to you, but it's no respecter of persons."

Helen went a delicate pink. It was certainly something her elegant mother never referred to, and would never do so in front of servants! The temptation to tell the girl to leave the room at once was tempered by knowing the truth of her own irritability, and she gave a grimace.

"You're impertinent to say such things, but I shan't deny that the sooner the next few days are over, the better. Why do you call it the gypsy's curse anyway?"

"Just because I'm one o' they common folk who talks common, miss," the girl said, tongue in cheek.

Her inverted snobbery made Helen all the more annoyed.

"And do all common folk have such interesting topics of conversation?" she said sarcastically. She knew very well that they were fencing with each other, but it was a mite less irksome to spark with her maid than to wander about the house, reading or embroidering or picking at the pianoforte, or any one of the other little amusements a young lady was supposed to enjoy during the tedious hours of the morning.

"I dunno about the rest of 'em, but some do, I daresay. Even the girl who comes to collect the laundry fineries ain't above a bit o' morning gossip," Sophie said, wondering how long it would be before Miss Barclay tired of all this chit-chat.

"What girl? Oh, you mean Carrie Stuckey. Well, what does she have to say, ninny?" Helen said, wondering why she was bothering with all this, but caught now by the chatter of this plain-faced doll.

She leaned back against her dressing-table, while the girl stood fidgeting. She really was a sketch, Helen thought, with her brown hair wild and unruly, and a decidedly shifty look. The girl, Carrie Stuckey, for all her humble background, had far more of an air about her than this thin scarecrow!

"I dunno much about her," Sophie said with a shrug. "Though there's always rumours below stairs, o' course."

Helen sat up straighter. Her Mama would be furious at her for probing for kitchen gossip, but her Mama was quite content to while away her morning hours doing little or nothing, while Helen was not.

"What rumours? Is she in some kind of trouble?"

To her surprise, she didn't want to think so. She remembered the girl who brought back her exquisitely laundered finery, accompanied by her small scallywag of a brother. She remembered her more clearly from the day she'd seen her on Clifton Downs, flushed and sparkling beside a more common-looking girl. And a handsome young man had clearly found Miss Carrie Stuckey as attractive as any society lady.

Sophie snorted. "'Tain't her that's in trouble, but her whole family, be all accounts. Out of work, the lot of 'em, so Cook says, and only the mother and Carrie doin' any work at all. Cook says she heard as how the mother's expecting another babby an' all."

"Oh, I see."

Helen was startled by such intimate details, and wondered just how Cook seemed to collect so many tit-bits of information. Those below-stairs had all the best luck in such respects, she thought in annoyance, and then scolded herself for not giving due sympathy to all that Sophie had said. Poor Carrie.

But even though she might feel sympathy for the girl and her family, she had no real notion of what a disaster a new baby was going to be for them if the men continued

133

to be out of work. A small baby didn't eat much, did it? And she was sure the other rich Clifton families beside themselves, for whom the Stuckey women worked, would gladly donate some baby clothes when the infant arrived. It never even occurred to Helen that such generosity would be seen as charity.

Sophie finished picking up clothes and tidying them away in closets, and asked Helen if she could take an hour off to visit that sick friend of hers in the city.

"I suppose so, but your friends do seem to have very frequent illnesses," Helen commented.

"'Tis the damp that gets 'em every time," Sophie said glibly. "You wouldn't know about that, miss, living in such warm surroundings."

"Oh, all right, off you go," Helen said, before she had to listen to another whining session about how lucky the likes of the Barclays were, compared with the peasants who lived in damp miserable hovels. Sometimes she wondered why Sophie didn't just stand with her hand held out for alms and be done with it.

She was still sitting by her window, gazing out across the Downs where a group of urchins teased a dog with a stick, when her mother came bustling into her bedroom. For a heavily built, well-proportioned lady, Gertrude Barclay normally managed to retain an air of enviable serenity and coolness, but today she was unusually flushed. As usual, she came straight to the point of her visit.

"Have you borrowed my jade ear-rings, Helen?"

"Of course not. I wouldn't take them without asking, Mama," she said mildly. "You were wearing them at dinner last evening, I remember."

Helen didn't particularly want to remember last evening's dinner party, with several young men paraded for her approval in so clumsy a fashion by her father. She was in no hurry to be married, unless it was to a man of her own choice. So far, one hadn't appeared on her horizon who was remotely interesting enough for her to want to spend the rest of her life with him.

"I know I was wearing them last evening, and I removed them in my bathroom because they were pinching my ears," her Mama said testily. "I should have replaced them in my jewel case, but I can't have done so, because they're not there. I especially wanted to wear them this afternoon, since Lady Wetherby admired them so much."

And you would naturally want to flaunt them in front of her again, Helen thought, with a glimmer of amusement. But the amusement faded as she saw the genuine distress in her mother's eyes. The ear-rings had been a birthday gift from her father, and were really rather fine.

"You can't have lost them, Mama," she protested. "Perhaps Papa put them away somewhere for safe keeping."

"Don't be ridiculous. He wouldn't have noticed them, and no-one else has been in the bathroom except for that stupid temporary maid. I can't imagine she'd have been bright enough to put them away in a safe place. If she did, she hasn't had the sense to tell me."

She paused, and Helen knew a sharp frisson of anxiety. The ear-rings weren't outrageously valuable, but valuable enough to fetch a good price at a pawn-broker's. And they weren't the only things to go missing from the house lately.

Other things had disappeared, a silver cigarette box, a crystal vase that had been supposedly smashed but never seen again, an opal brooch, a set of tortoise-shell hairbrushes with silver rims . . . Until now, the items had been assumed to be inadvertently mislaid, and would eventually turn up . . . Just as sharply now, Helen couldn't help remembering the maid's slick way of filtering such ideas into the mind. And the jade

135

ear-rings were certainly the most valuable of all the items.

"You surely don't think that Sophie – " Helen began, jumping up from her window seat with her hands clenched tightly at her sides.

"I most certainly do think," Gertrude snapped. "Where is the girl? I want her brought here at once."

Helen ran her tongue around her dry lips. "She's not here. I gave her an hour's grace to go and visit her sick friend. She must have been gone almost that long already."

She felt sick to her stomach. If Sophie was indeed the thief, then she might never return, especially if the jade ear-rings had been her most-valuable prize, and most likely to begin a hue and cry. Helen hated to think they had been so betrayed, but it was obvious that there were no such doubts in her mother's mind. She had never cared for the bumptious girl the domestic employment agency had recommended, and Helen guessed they would never get her patronage again.

"Come with me, Helen, and we'll get to the bottom of this right now."

There were those who compared Gertrude Barclay with an outrigger in full sail when she stormed out of a room with all guns blazing. Helen followed quickly, her heart pounding, knowing there was bound to be a scene if Sophie had returned, and her mother accused her outright of stealing. And what if they were wrong? She tried to remonstrate with her mother.

"Please don't go rushing in and accusing her, Mama," she begged. "Give her a chance to defend herself."

"She'll need to defend herself in a courtroom if she's a common thief," was the reply. She picked up her skirts and climbed the uncarpeted stairs to the servants' quarters, to pause, breathing heavily, outside Sophie's shared room.

Gertrude opened the door without knocking. The room was as empty as it should be, with the servants about their work. Helen wrinkled her nose at the smell of stale cheap scent and sweat that permeated it. She had hardly ever visited the servants' rooms, which were horrid little places with tiny windows, and with the beds all squashed together. But she did know that the girls kept their boxes of belongings on top of their wall closets. There was one missing, and there was only one explanation for that.

"She's gone," she said hoarsely. "But she couldn't have known she was under suspicion."

"You're far too gullible, my dear. She had obviously decided that with the theft of my ear-rings it was time to move on. No doubt it was all planned, and this so-called visit to a sick friend was just a ploy. Has she asked for time off to visit this sick friend before?"

Helen nodded dumbly. Three or four times recently . . . how *could* she have been so foolish as to be taken in?

"And I daresay these other visits were to pass on the things she had taken as well, so that nothing could be found in her room. I'll have the law on her for this!" Gertrude snapped, clearly incensed.

"But you don't have any real proof, Mama."

She didn't know why she was bothering to defend the girl, except that she felt so badly let down, and so very stupid . . . But she found that she was talking to the air, as her Mama turned and clattered back down the stairs with far less decorum than usual. Perhaps the proof would be in Sophie's box, when and if the law caught up with her, but more likely, the items would have been quickly pawned or sold.

Helen wondered if they would ever find her again. Bristol had a maze of hiding-places, from the tunnels that ran beneath the city, to the caves in the rocks, to any number of thieves' dens where Sophie might well be known and looked after. She had often boasted of her

137

many friends and acquaintances in the city, and hinted that she didn't really need to do this kind of work.

At the time, Helen had thought it was mere bravado, but now she wondered if working in the Bristol mansions was a means to an end, after all. As the suspicions mounted, she doubted that they would ever see her or any of their belongings again. And, aside from her mother's distress at losing the jade ear-rings, and the feeling of humiliation she felt, they were nothing but baubles after all. None of them had been physically hurt.

With a glimmer of wry understanding, Helen knew there would eventually be a positive side to it. Once the constables had been alerted, and an inventory taken of all the missing things, her mother would have a choice bit of upstairs gossip to relate to her autocratic friends at the tea-table. And there was nothing like upstairs gossip to brighten a dull tea-table.

By the time Helen went downstairs to find her mother, a messenger had already been sent for the constables to come to the house for the thefts to be reported. And she was finding it hard to hold back the tears now.

"What is it?" Gertrude said sharply.

Helen held out one of her lovely lace shifts. It was torn and filthy, and the sight of it had shaken her more badly than she would have believed.

"It was at the bottom of my closet. It's been worn, Mama. That awful girl must have worn it! I feel so dirty, knowing it had been next to her skin."

"Pull yourself together, my love. It can be mended, and the young washer-girl can get rid of the stains. She may even be downstairs right now."

"No!" Helen flung the garment away from her, and rubbed her hands together as if she had been touched by a leper. "I never want to see it again. Please dispose of it, Mama – and – and if Carrie has arrived, then please send her to me. I shall be in my room."

She turned and fled while her mother was still tut-tutting at such an unseemly display of emotion. Nor did she see any reason why the washer-girl should be required to visit her daughter in her bedroom. But Gertrude gave a sigh. Helen was highly strung, and if she wanted to give special instructions to the washer-girl she supposed it was best to humour her. She rang a bell for a servant, and requested that when the washer-girl arrived, she was to be shown to Miss Helen's room at once.

"She's here now, ma'am," the maid replied uneasily, clearly thinking something was amiss. "Shall I send her up?"

"That's what I said, didn't I? Or have you suddenly gone deaf?" Gertrude snapped, and once the maid had scuttled away she took several long deep breaths. It was so lowering to lose one's temper in front of servants, but the whole world was making her scratchy today. She still had the constable to see regarding the thefts, and she had to be serene and composed by this afternoon's soiree. She tried to calm her features, and to think sweet thoughts, before the tell-tale lines of stress creased her otherwise smooth forehead.

"Miss Helen wants to see me in her room?" Carrie said in a fright as the maid called Daisy spoke tersely to her. "What do you suppose I've done wrong?"

For the life of her, she couldn't think of anything. She'd never put too much starch in the underpinnings to irritate Miss Helen's tender skin. She'd never faded or bleached any of the delicate colours of her gowns. She'd never charged her a penny more than was necessary . . . with her Ma's growing indisposition, Carrie had taken on more and more of the work lately, and her hands were showing the truth of it.

She hid them behind her involuntarily as the maid looked at her with impatience. The short tempers in the household were having a building-block effect now, and the maid snapped back at her.

"How would I know? I'm just passing on the message, so if you want me to show you the way, you'd best come now. I've enough work to do without wasting my time while you stand gawping."

Carrie felt Billy's hand creep into hers. "We ain't getting sacked, are we, Carrie?" he mumbled.

She prayed that they weren't. She didn't know what they would do if they lost the only income they had. She felt the beads of sweat on her forehead, and quickly dashed them away, not wanting to look a sight in front of Miss Helen.

"Of course not," she whispered back. "You just wait here with Cook, and I'll be back soon."

"He'll be all right wi' me," Cook said comfortably. "Another slice of seed cake will soon wipe that furrow from his brow, won't it, me lad?"

Carrie didn't wait to hear his reply. She followed the stiff-backed Daisy through the house, up the deep-carpeted staircase where her feet never made a sound, and where she was almost afraid to put her hand on the highly polished banister for fear of marking it. Along the wide corridor with its fine paintings in their gilt-edged frames, and the mahogany chests with the flower arrangements and porcelain ornaments adorning them, until they reached the room she'd glimpsed once before.

Had someone told on her? she thought in sudden panic. Did Miss Helen know she'd already sneaked up here when the family was away, and seen the splendour of her bedroom, and was about to chastise her for it?

"She won't eat you," Daisy said more kindly now. "Everyone's in a bit of a tizzy for some reason today, and Jackson's had to send out for the constable."

140

If there was anything to make Carrie more nervous than ever, it was this last piece of news. Dear Lord, what did any of this have to do with her? But there was no going back now. With a brief knock on Miss Helen's door, Daisy turned the handle, and pushed Carrie inside. She felt how a lamb must feel, going to the slaughter.

"You – you wanted to see me, Miss Helen?"

Her voice was so thin, it didn't even sound like hers. She was angry at herself for sounding so feeble, when she was sure she had done nothing wrong. She tried to drag some of her personal pride to the fore, and squared her shoulders as she moved further into the room.

Helen was sitting in her favourite window-seat, and she looked so tense and strained that Carrie felt a moment of sympathy. And then she thought how ludicrous it was to feel sympathy for a young lady who had everything. Helen turned towards her, and Carrie was startled to see that her face was blotchy as if she'd been crying.

"Come here, Carrie," she said quietly. She held out a hand towards her. Carrie walked quickly across the soft carpet, and as the hand was still extended, Carrie put her own into it.

Nothing could have made a bigger contrast between them. She was horrified at her own unthinking action, and as she glanced down at the joined hands, the one so soft and white, and the other so rough and red, she made to snatch her own away at once.

"No, please don't be embarrassed," Helen said, as if quite unaware of the reason for the embarrassment. "I want to talk to you as a friend. I feel that I can trust you. Can I trust you, Carrie?"

"I hope so," Carrie muttered, feeling more stupid by the second to be standing here holding Miss Helen Barclay's hand for no good reason at all that she could think of.

"I hope so too, because I've got a proposition to put

141

to you," Helen said calmly. She had been thinking of it ever since that dreadful girl had gone out of their lives. Perhaps even before that. Perhaps Sophie herself had unwittingly put the idea into her head.

And now that she took a good look at Carrie, she could see the difference in her since the day she'd seen her with her friend on the day of the *Great Britain*'s launch. Then, Carrie Stuckey had been happy and laughing, enjoying the blissfully sunny day, and not averse to the admiring glances of a handsome young man.

Her cheeks had been full and rosy then, and although they were flushed now, Helen could see the pallor underneath, and the hollows that hadn't been there before. And Helen, who never had to bother her head about meat on the table, or clothes on her back, was suddenly starting to concern herrself with how a family like the Stuckeys were managing with all their menfolk out of work.

"I don't know what you mean, miss," Carrie mumbled. "I don't know what you mean by 'proposition'. I don't know the word."

It dawned on her that she was feeling and acting humbly and it enraged her to know it. She pulled her hand away now, hoping that it didn't scratch Miss Barclay, and suddenly uncaring if it bloody well did. If there was going to be trouble, then the sooner it was out in the open, the better. She stared into Miss Barclay's china blue eyes, and saw the swift sympathy there. That didn't help her pride either. She lifted her chin and stuck it out – like a dog sniffing a bone, as Pa would say.

"Carrie, I mean I want to offer you a job," Helen said more gently. "A real job, here, with me. Not just doing my laundry, although I'd be enormously pleased if you would still take care of that. But I want you to be my personal helper. My own personal maid. I have a feeling that you'd suit me very well, and of course, you would be paid accordingly. The only thing is, I'd want you to live in, Carrie. It would be a full-time arrangement, but I'd see that you had sufficient time off to see your family. I understand that your mother is temporarily unwell, and I know you would want time to visit her and it's not as though it's too far away, is it?"

Helen was aware that she was prattling in a quite undignified manner, and that her mother would be very annoyed at the way she was almost pleading with this girl to come and work for her. But the idea had come swiftly, and had to be acted upon. She was sure that Carrie Stuckey was trustworthy. Hadn't she entrusted her with some of her costliest garments in the past, and had them returned beautifully cared for?

Carrie was still gaping, open-mouthed, and wondering if she was dreaming. The gypsy fortune-teller had prophesied good fortune for her, and she herself had grandly informed John Travis's uncle's lady-friend that she was a personal helper to a Clifton lady . . . her thoughts whirled, wondering if she was in the grip of some kind of witchcraft, of wishing too hard for something, then making it happen . . . she swallowed, as she realised Miss Helen was expecting an answer.

"I – I don't know what to say," she gasped, as the implications of all that this could mean to her family began to flood into her mind.

Helen laughed, as if relaxing for the first time that day.

"Then say yes, Carrie! Just say yes!"

Helen would never beg, but she badly wanted to get the thing settled before her mother began fussing over finding someone else, and having to go through the dreary business of interviewing and reading references that may or may not be genuine. Many were faked, as the gentry very well knew, and as all the lower orders glibly believed they did not.

143

With this girl, none of it need happen. Helen already knew her worth, and her stability, and she wanted her.

"I s'pose I'd better say yes then," she heard Carrie say prosaically. "And just to put you right, miss, me Ma's not properly unwell. She's just expecting a babby, that's all, and it's taking her badly, but once it's born, I'm sure she'll be her usual self again."

But she crossed her fingers as she spoke. Charmed by witchcraft or not, she was taking no chances.

"Well, thank you for telling me," Helen said, taken aback at this frank disclosure. "I'm sure my Mama will agree that she's to be sent some nourishing food from the kitchen on a regular basis, Carrie. I'm very pleased we've come to an arrangement, and naturally I'd like you to start right away."

"I can't start until I've been home and told my folks, and I'm not too sure what Pa's going to say about it," she spoke in sudden fright now that it all seemed so imminent. "And besides, I don't know nothing about being a personal maid to a young lady, miss. Are you sure it's me that you want?"

"I'm quite sure. And I shall only require you to be of direct help to me. Making my bed and changing my linen and helping me dress – that sort of thing," she said vaguely. "And of course you must inform your parents. Shall we say that you'll be here by eight-thirty tomorrow morning? That will be time for Cook to give you your uniform and show you where you will sleep, and help you prepare my breakfast tray. You will bring it to my room at nine-thirty exactly."

The atmosphere between them had subtly changed. Carrie was now the servant, being given instructions as to her duties, where minutes before she'd felt that Miss Helen was almost desperate to employ her. And she had been airily thinking it over, and cheekily implying that

144

she couldn't possibly begin work until she'd thought it all over and got her Pa's approval.

"Very well, Miss Helen," she said, more meekly than Carrie Stuckey normally spoke. But this was turning out to be no normal day, and she was only just beginning to realise that she would be leaving home for the first time in her life. Even though there were no more than a couple of miles between them, the elegance of the Clifton mansions and the crowded cottages of Jacob's Wells Road might have been a continent apart.

"And when you leave, you may tell Cook she may give you a basket of eggs and anything else that's suitable for your mother," Helen said graciously. "I'm sure she'll know the kind of thing."

Miss Helen Barclay had her pride too. The disgraced maid, Sophie, would never know that it had taken such little time and effort to replace her, but Helen would know. And that had been part of her impulsive move towards hiring Carrie Stuckey. But the more she thought about it, the more she was sure that it was going to be the right move.

As Carrie hurriedly went back below stairs she wondered if she was still dreaming. Her thoughts were still whirling as she saw her small brother in the kitchen, his face still being stuffed with seed cake as if there was no tomorrow. But tomorrow he could drink milk and eat eggs . . . she felt her face crack into a smile as several faces looked at her anxiously.

"I'm going to work here," she announced, still awed by her own words. "I'm going to be Miss Helen's personal maid! And she says we're to take some milk and eggs and whatever else you think suitable for Ma's condition, Cook. What do you think of that!"

Cook's mouth fell open, and the kitchen-maids crowded around, sensing something more behind the obvious.

"Well, I never," Cook said at last. "I daresay you'll make a good job of it, if you mind your Ps and Qs. But what's happened to the hoity-toity miss who's been here for the last three weeks?"

"I bet that's what all the fuss was about," one of the young kitchen-maids said excitedly. "When I was taking the rubbish outside I overheard Mrs Barclay talking ever so sharply to Jackson, and then he went off at a rate, and I don't know as he's come back yet neither."

"You hear too much for your own good, Nellie," Cook told her smartly. "Still, 'tis a pity you didn't hear no more, if there's summat going on."

"Well, it's none of my business," Carrie said, itching to be away now and tell Ma her news. "I've left the basket of Miss Helen's things in the usual place, and I'll see you all again tomorrow. I'm to be here at eight-thirty and collect my uniform from you, Cook, and you're to show me where I'm to sleep and all."

She gulped, suddenly realising the enormity of what she was saying. There would be no more gossipy chit-chat with Ma late at night; no more checking on Billy's regular, snuffly breathing, as gentle as that of a young fawn; no more scent of the river rising from the docks in the eerie, fog-bound mornings; no more familiarity . . .

"Ain't you going to be livin' at home no more, our Carrie?" Billy's face came into focus, wide-eyed and fearful. He wasn't yet old enough to welcome changes in his life.

"I shan't be far away, you goose," she said quickly. "And you'll be coming up to Clifton most days with Ma's wash loads, just the same, and I'll be going home to visit whenever I can."

But she felt an undoubted surge of anxiety now. She'd be leaving home just when Ma most needed her. The extra money she'd be earning would be such a help – but she realised she didn't even know what her wages were

146

going to be. She was such a ninny, because she'd never even thought to ask! But she supposed that would be left to Mr Barclay to decide, and she had never even seen the gentleman. She shivered. There were a good many changes and adjustments to be made, but she'd given her agreement now, and there was no going back on it.

Billy was unusually quiet as they went back down the steep hill towards home. Carrie tried to cajole him into his usual chatter, but he was filled with gloom at her going away.

"It's not as if you see me all day long," she said. "In the afternoons you go to school, and it's only in the mornings when we're really together."

"I hate school," he scowled, and she sighed as he scuffed his shoes against the cobblestones, knowing that everything she said was going to be met with objections. After a while she simply gave up coaxing.

"You can run on down to the waterfront to play if you like," she said. "I'll take the cart on home by myself."

He brightened at that. "I'll look out for John Travis then. We ain't seen him around the house lately. Have you and him had a falling-out, our Carrie?"

He experimented with the grown-up sounding words, and was encouraged by seeing his sister's face go scarlet.

"I bet you have! I bet he don't fancy sparking with you no more!"

"Where did you hear such talk! You just mind what you say, do you hear me?" Carrie yelled after him as he raced on down the hill, cat-calling behind him at a safe distance.

Her footsteps slowed down, knowing there was too much truth in Billy's childish jeers for comfort. John's visits to the house had become increasingly rare since that first Saturday outing when she'd gone with him up Bedminster Hill.

They were still officially "walking out", but there wasn't much walking or talking being done lately, she thought miserably. It was as though he'd taken note of her sharp tongue, and even sharper reactions to his love of fisticuffs, and decided he wanted little to do with it.

He was what Elsie had astutely called "letting her down gently". And she strongly suspected that as usual, Elsie was probably right.

John would undoubtedly be pleased to hear of her new position as Miss Helen Barclay's personal maid. It meant he wouldn't have to pretend to enjoy calling on the irritating Carrie Stuckey any more, because she'd be too well occupied to go courting whenever she pleased. And just when she had started to feel on top of the world, it was the most depressing thought of all to cloud this sunny day.

Chapter 9

"I won't allow it," Pa thundered, as soon as Carrie had gabbled out her news.

She felt total shock at this reaction. His face was florid and sweating from drink, and he swayed on his feet, even though it was barely the middle of the day. It had become a habitual thing now for him to frequent the waterfront inns, morning and evening. It was ostensibly to enquire for work, and to take any drink that was offered.

There was no money to spare for such luxuries, but Pa had always been a story-teller, and somehow he always managed to find a fellow willing to stand him a jug of ale in return for a salty tale or two. If Ma had strongly disapproved at first, she held her tongue now, rather than encourage his frequent frustrated rages, and merely commented that a man needed to forget his troubles whatever way he could.

"Why won't you allow it?" Carrie stuttered, starting to feel as if the ground was reeling beneath her own feet, as well as her Pa's.

"Because you'll end up getting up above yourself, miss, that's why. And besides that, your Ma needs you here!"

"I ain't being put out to grass yet, just because I'm expecting," Ma said crossly. "I can still manage a day's load of washing, and our Billy can do the hauling in two cartloads if need be. Our Carrie should be given her chance, Sam."

"I'll say what's to do here, woman, and I say 'tain't right for the family to be split at this time," he ranted on, crashing his hand down on the parlour table to add weight to his words. He leaned there heavily, and for a moment Carrie wondered if he was going to have a seizure.

"I've already told Miss Barclay I'll take the job," she muttered. Her disappointment was acute, and all her pleasure was fizzling out by the minute at this furore. She'd thought they would all be so pleased

"It'd be good for her, Pa." Frank had been lounging on the settle all this time, but he spoke up lazily now. "It would also help her get the likes of John Travis out of her system."

Carrie reddened furiously. She needed no reminders from her brother that John hadn't come calling much recently, and didn't seem inclined to do so again. But before she could say anything, Pa rounded on Frank at once.

"When I want any spineless opinions from you, boy, I'll ask for 'em. If I say Carrie ain't to go working for they toffs, then there's an end to it."

Frank was slow to anger, but when he did, his rages equalled those of Sam's. He leapt to his feet now, his eyes blazing.

"And I say the girl's got a right to take any job she can, seeing as how the rest of us ain't managing to bring tuppence into the house. I ain't proud of leaning on my womenfolk, but if Carrie's got this chance, and wants to do it, then I say we should all be thankful."

He got no farther before his father had cuffed him a stinging blow on the side of his head. Frank rocked on his heels for a moment, then, before anyone could guess what he was about, his hands were around Sam's throat, and he was near to throttling him.

"Frank, you're killing him," Ma screamed. "Leave him be, for God's sake!"

For a moment, it seemed as if Frank wasn't even hearing her. He was almost demented as he rattled Sam to and fro like a rag doll, and Sam's fire seemed to be dissolving in front of their eyes. Ma dug her finger-nails into her son's rigid hands, still screaming into his face.

At last, with Carrie's help, she managed to prise his hands away from her husband. Sam's eyes were bulging now, and he glowered murderously at his son. He coughed and hawked, and swore volubly. He leaned heavily against the table.

"I should have you horse-whipped for that, but I suppose I should be grateful at least that you've got some spunk in you," he said hoarsely, rubbing at his neck. "There were times when I wondered just what I'd spawned."

Frank snapped a reply, his voice as hard as iron.

"I know you never thought as much of me as you did of our Wilf. And where do you suppose he is now? And where does he go of a night-time? Maybe your fine fellow's gone soft-eyed over a few petticoats."

"Frank, *don't!*" Carrie moved swiftly in front of him, pleading silently for him to say nothing about Wilf's association with Nora Woolley. They both knew about it now. They also knew that Gaffer Woolley had become Sam's number one enemy ever since the man refused to employ any of the Stuckey men. Unemployment in the carpentry trade was general, but Sam took everything personally, and was slighted beyond measure at what he saw as Gaffer's snub to a craftsman.

Thankfully, Sam saw nothing significant in Frank's words, and instead of probing for more information, he continued sneering at his second son.

"Showing an interest in petticoats is normal, at least. 'Tis better than hanging around they seamen at the docks, and filling your head with tales of foreign places you're never likely to see."

Frank took an angry breath. "That's just where you're wrong then. I wasn't going to say nothing yet, and I hadn't really made up my mind, but you've just made it up for me."

"What the hell are you talking about now?"

"I'm talking about going to sea."

"Frank, no," Ma beseeched. Her eyes had a rare shine of tears in them, and her hands strayed to her rounded belly as if the unborn child could give her comfort.

"I'd be obliged if everybody could stop saying 'Frank, no', and 'Frank, don't'." He spoke with sudden calm, seeing that he'd got all their attention now. "I've got the chance and I'm taking it, the same as our Carrie should. With two of us gone from the house, there'll be fewer mouths to feed come the winter."

Carrie saw that Ma's face had gone ashen. She wouldn't want the family to be split up like this. Ma's whole aim in life was to keep the family together. But it couldn't always be, and surely she must see that. All chicks had to leave their nests at some time in their lives, but Carrie wasn't sure that Frank's decision was helping her a great deal.

"Good riddance to 'ee then," Pa snarled, and stumped out of the house, crashing the door behind him.

When he'd gone, there was complete silence in the parlour, and then Carrie realised that Ma was quietly sobbing. She went to her at once. It was practically unheard of to see Ma like this, and she felt helpless and inadequate. She put her arms around her mother, but in seconds she was brushed away. Ma hated sentiment, and as she recovered her usual stoical composure she spoke quickly to Frank.

"You know your Pa didn't really mean what he just said. It was the drink and the temper talking, that's all."

"When a man's the worse for drink, he frequently says what's really in his heart," Frank said bitterly. "You know that as well as I do, Ma."

She ignored that for the moment. "But is this what you really want, my son? Or are you just doing it to give us fewer mouths to feed this winter? Because if that's the case, then you're wrong. I would never show a child of mine the door, no matter how poor we became, and you shame me by thinking so."

Frank came to sit beside her, taking her cold hands in his. She didn't push him away, Carrie noted. Ma had always favoured Frank, perhaps because Pa was so down on him. The idea entered her head that Pa might even be jealous of the attention Ma had always given to Frank. He always appeared to be so carefree, but now he seemed to have an inner strength none of them had suspected.

"I never thought that, and it was only his bullying that made me say so. I really do want to see faraway places and make my own way in the world. There's sure to be carpentering jobs on the ships, so with luck I'll still be following my trade, and I promise I'll write letters to you from whatever place the ship takes me."

Ma spoke more slowly, hearing the determination in his voice. "'Tis right for you to follow your own needs, and I'll not deny that. But I shall miss you badly."

"I'm not going for ever, Ma. They say the bad penny always turns up again."

"Don't say that about yourself! There's nothing bad about you."

The silence between them all became a little strained, and Carrie knelt down on the rag rug beside the other two.

"I shall miss you too, Frank," she said softly, and he squeezed her shoulder gently without answering.

She felt her eyes misting over. But she knew that Frank's going must make no difference to her own plans.

153

If anything, his stand against Pa made her all the more determined to take her own chance. As if Ma was reading her thoughts, she gave a small nod.

"And tomorrow morning, our Carrie will be leaving for Clifton. You just leave your Pa to me, lamb, but say no more about it this day. He'll come round to it in his own good time, but the less he actually hears about it, the better."

They all knew it was the way things had worked in the past, and they remained where they were for a while. They were a silent trio, who had always been so close, and whose paths were so soon to part.

"You won't exactly be *living* there, will you?" Elsie had said sarcastically, when she sought her out during the afternoon.

"Of course I will. It's a living-in job."

"But you'll still be a skivvy. You won't have the run of the house and be living the gracious life, the same as your snooty Miss Helen, will you? I bet you'll be stuck up in some miserable attic room with six others. I've heard that's what it's like when you're in service."

"You're determined to spoil things for me, aren't you, Elsie?" Carrie said. "Why can't anyone be pleased for me?"

Elsie shrugged. She looked at Carrie slyly. "What about your young man then? Is he pleased for you?"

"I haven't told him yet. I'm going down to the ferry to see him later."

"So what do you think he'll have to say about it?" She wouldn't leave it alone, stirring the pot as usual.

"How do I know? I'm not inside his mind, am I?" Carrie was getting rattled now, as the questioning went on.

"You ain't seen much of him lately, have you? I've seen him a couple of times, walking into the city on his own. I stopped to talk to him once."

"Well then, you probably know as much about his movements as I do," Carrie snapped, smarting even more at the thought of Elsie poking her nose into her affairs. They had once shared all their secrets, but since John Travis had come on the scene, there were things Carrie didn't want to share with anyone.

Most of all was the fact that she was no longer sure whether or not she loved him. She was dazzled by him, attracted to him, and she knew they owed him their Billy's life, but was that enough to be called love? She sometimes ached to be with him, and to experience again all the sensations his caresses had awoken in her. But was that love, or something else? At night, alone in her bed in the darkness, she sometimes imagined she could feel his kisses on her mouth, and sometimes she turned restlessly, reaching out and longing for someone who wasn't there . . . was that love?

Late in the afternoon, when she had parted company with Elsie, it was with a vague feeling of defensiveness that she walked down to the ferry landing-stage. She knew she had to see John to tell him about her new job. It would never do for him to call at the Stuckey house to find her gone, but she didn't look forward to the telling.

So far, everyone who knew about it – except Frank – had managed to make her feel that she was doing the wrong thing. Even Wilf, when he'd heard, had seemed disinterested to the point of saying gruffly that if she thought it was the right thing to do, then it probably was. Which was just about as unhelpful as it could be.

Carrie waited at the water's edge where the slipway ran down to the river. It was choppy, with the breeze rippling across its surface like a giant's hand, and she could see the swell of the tide lifting John's boat and then sending it plunging slightly down again. It could make a body feel sea-sick just by watching it. She deliberately raised her eyes above the glittering undulations of the river to wave out to the man standing in the bow of his boat as it neared the landing-stage to discharge its group of passengers.

John waved back, and Carrie suddenly felt her spirits glow in the same way as on that first day, when she'd seen him dripping wet and shaking his hair like a frisky puppy, as he hauled her small brother out of the churning water. Without warning, everything in the world seemed to turn the right way up again, and she waited with her heart beating fast as John stepped out of the boat and tied up, after helping the last of his passengers ashore.

"This is a very welcome surprise," he said, smiling down at her. He took her hand in his and squeezed it hard, and then he ran one finger around her cheek in a way that made her shiver. "I've missed you lately, Carrie."

"Have you?" she said huskily. *And whose fault is that?* she wanted to ask. *It's not my place to come calling for you.*

He glanced around quickly. Several ladies and gentlemen were taking an evening stroll along the waterfront, and may well be wanting the ferry to take them across to the other side. There was little else along this way to take their interest, unless they were looking at the trading ships, or merely slumming it.

"Get in the boat and I'll take you on a special trip," he said. "It's the best way of being alone together."

She supposed it was. No-one could reach them once they were out in the river, and to all intents and purposes she would seem to be a paying passenger. She stepped into the boat gingerly, and waited until John steered it away from the landing-stage. After a few moments she realised they were heading well down-river and across to where the trees and shrubby undergrowth of Leigh Woods lay on the opposite side to the Hotwell Spa.

"If we're going to be alone, we might as well make the most of it," John said with a grin. "I'll tie up at one of the stakes, and we'll be quite secluded in the woods."

The shiver that ran through her then was a mixture of excitement and apprehension. She realised that John saw her appearance as an invitation, as well as a mute apology for all the times they had been so stiff and awkward together recently. It was the first time she had sought him out, but he didn't know yet that what she had to tell him was going to push them farther apart. But perhaps it could wait just a little while longer.

"God, but I didn't realise just how much I had missed you," he breathed, when they had made a short climb through the undergrowth to one of the grassy little copses in the lower part of the woods.

They lay full-length on the grass now, and Carrie ignored the fact that it was probably damp, and that she'd be in danger of catching pneumonia and never get to work for Miss Helen Barclay in her luxurious surroundings after all.

It was easy to ignore such trivialities when John Travis was covering her body with his own, and pressing kisses onto her mouth, just as he did in her dreaming moments. And there was never a single doubt in her mind then, that she loved him.

"I've missed you too, John," she said in a slightly strangled voice as his hand reached down and covered her breast. The fabric of her dress was between them, but even so, the touch of his fingers was as hot as fire against her flesh.

"I want to touch you and hold you, and never let you go," he whispered the words against her mouth. "Do you know what I mean, my darling girl?"

"I – I think so," she said vaguely.

He gave a soft laugh. "I don't think you do, love. I

157

don't think you have any idea of how potent you are to a man."

"Potent?" she echoed, not understanding his meaning.

"As potent as fuel to a flame. And you set me on fire just as rapidly. I've dreamed of holding you like this, sweet Carrie."

"Pinning me beneath you, you mean," she said, finding it hard to breathe, and needing to lighten the undeniably charged atmosphere between them.

She wasn't sure she could deal with his intensity. Yet she longed to discover all the secrets between a man and a woman. Elsie knew . . . or pretended that she did . . . and there was no-one in the world she would want to learn them from, other than John Travis.

She gave a small breathless sigh, and he looked deep into her eyes.

"Do I frighten you, Carrie? You know I would never hurt you."

"You don't frighten me," she answered slowly. "But I don't know what you expect of me."

She felt his hand leave her breast and move downwards. She felt him lift her skirts and the sensation of the balmy autumn air on her skin was unexpected and heady. His touch on her thigh moved so gently inwards she hardly realised what was happening until it reached its goal. She closed her eyes, frozen with indecision, knowing she should stop this now, but somehow quite unable to. She needed to know about this mysterious sensation that she had felt once before, but never so exquisitely as this.

"You're so beautiful, Carrie," she heard him say huskily. "And too damned innocent for your own good."

She was shocked as he finished speaking almost accusingly. Her eyes flew open, as she realised he was pulling her skirts down again, and rolling away from her.

"Have I done something to offend you, or have I hurt

you in some way?" she said in a small voice, hearing how raggedly he was breathing.

He gave a short laugh. "I could say yes, but I'd be lying. There was no man yet who died of an affliction like mine as far as I know."

"What affliction do you have, for pity's sake?" she said in a fright.

He said nothing, and then he took her hand and placed it firmly over his breeches. As she felt the rock hardness there, she flinched as if she'd been stung before she snatched her hand away.

"You see, sweetheart?" he said in amusement. "Your innocence is the best protection of all. One frightened look from those damnably expressive eyes of yours, and I shall dwindle fast enough."

Carrie felt the fiery colour filling her cheeks again.

"Am I such a disappointment to you, then? Is that why you haven't been calling on me so often recently?"

She felt a genuine distress. Girls like Elsie were the clever ones after all, she thought miserably. They knew how to interest a man, and how to keep him interested, while she was as naive as the day she was born.

"You could never disappoint me," he said, but she knew the mood between them had already changed, and that he must be remembering again the way they had almost come to blows once before. It was an ironic thought, because fighting was the thing that had caused them to spark against one another then.

She sat up, brushing the grass and bracken out of her hair. She looked down at her hands, lacing her fingers together, and took a deep breath.

"I wanted to see you for a special reason today," she said, remembering her purpose in seeking him out.

"Oh? And what was that?" he said, not looking at her now, but preferring to watch the stately progress of a sailing boat move up the river.

"I've been offered a living-in job with Miss Helen Barclay of Clifton, instead of being an – an outworker."

Not for the world could she say a washer-woman.

"I see," John said. "And are you going to take it?"

For a moment she stared at him stupidly, and then resentment took hold of her. Did he think such opportunities came along every day, when the Stuckeys needed every penny they could scratch? Such desperate straits had clearly never affected him. Even his working clobber was tidier than anything her Pa wore, and she'd been a fool not to see it before now. He said he wanted her, but not enough to ravish her, apparently.

And Carrie, who had never even let such a word into her thoughts before, now felt unreasonably insulted because John Travis hadn't wanted her enough to continue what he had begun. He'd left her restless and wanting . . .

"Of course I'm bloody well taking it," she snapped, and bit her lip at letting herself down so swiftly.

"I only asked," John snapped back. "It means I'm unlikely to see much of you at all from now on then."

"That hasn't seemed to bother you much recently."

"I've wanted to see you far more often, but I've been working my guts out to save up for my new boat."

"Oh yes. By fighting every Tom, Dick and Harry who'll put a wager on you, I suppose?"

The accusation spilled out of her before she could stop it, and as she saw how angry it made him, she felt a shiver of fear. He was a big man, used to fighting his way out of trouble, presumably, and ready to take on the best of the travelling bare-knuckle fighters to earn his keep. What chance would she have against him if he turned rough?

Even as the thought shot into her mind, Carrie didn't believe it would happen. For all his disreputable sideline, she knew he was still a gentleman.

"You don't think too highly of me, do you, Carrie?" he said finally.

"It's not you – it's what you do," she muttered.

As he stood up, he put out his hand and pulled her to her feet. She might have expected him to pull her into his arms, and for this *tête-à-tête* to have ended as romantically as it had begun, but he let go of her at once.

"Someday I may tell you the reason for the need to prove myself, but it can wait until you've grown up a bit more," he said.

Her cheeks burned. It was one thing to call her an innocent in the loving way he'd done previously, but this last remark was a bigger insult to her self-esteem.

In silence, they began the walk back through Leigh Woods to where the boat was tied up, and he helped her into it carefully. She was consumed with misery. Not only was she leaving all that was dear and familiar to her tomorrow, but it seemed certain that now she'd lost John as well.

But she drew a tiny hope for the future from the fact that he'd said someday he might tell her why he had begun bare-knuckle fighting. Surely that meant he intended seeing her again . . . it wasn't her place to suggest it, but her pride was so badly dented by now, that a little more humility hardly seemed worth bothering about.

"I shall be allowed some time off, John. I don't know any details yet, but if I let Ma know, perhaps you could call there sometime and then we can arrange to see one another." Her voice trailed away. "If you want to, that is."

"Are you sure it's what you want?"

At such an evasive answer, she wondered briefly if she should act up like Elsie, toss her head in the air, and tell him he could please himself or piss off. But she wasn't Elsie, and this was too important to her.

161

"I'm sure," she whispered.

"And so am I," he said.

The following morning, Carrie had her belongings packed, and made her farewells to Ma and Frank and Billy. The others were still sleeping, and she decided it was best to leave quietly without any fuss.

"When I know about my duties, I'll get back to see you as soon as I can, Ma," she said, almost in desperation, and feeling like a rat deserting a sinking ship. "And our Billy knows he can call and see me whenever he comes up to Clifton to the other houses."

"I shan't go there no more," Billy said stubbornly. "I don't like you no more."

"Well, I still like you," Carrie said evenly. "And Cook still likes you, and she'll want you to call in for Ma's basket every few days in any case."

She saw him wrestling with his pride, and then he flung himself into her arms for a kiss. He still smelled of sleep, and she hugged him tightly, reluctant to let him go.

Frank kissed her too, which was a rarity, but this was a real good-bye for him, as he intended signing onto a ship that very day. Pa was totally ignoring him now, and Frank said there was no point in letting the grass grow beneath his feet, or more accurately, letting the tide go out without him.

Wilf had given his approval of his brother's plans, but by now, they all knew that Frank had a mind of his own, and it would have made no difference what anybody else said.

Carrie gave Ma a hug, being careful not to press on Ma's belly. She wasn't having an easy time, with the babby lying awkwardly on her side, and sending the bile welling up in her when she least expected it.

"I'll see you very soon, Ma," she whispered.

"Just you do all that Miss Barclay wants of you, and mind your manners," Ma said briskly.

There was nothing left to say or do, so Carrie slipped out of the house before she couldn't leave after all, before she betrayed the fact that she felt she was apprehensive of the changes this new life was going to bring, and was beginning to wish she'd never even heard of Miss Helen Barclay.

And then she stood upright and told herself angrily not to be such a milksop. This was the opportunity of a lifetime, and there were plenty of girls who'd give their souls to be living in a mansion like the Barclays'.

She hadn't expected to be summoned to the drawing-room at ten o'clock precisely. By then, she was wearing a plain brown dress with a neat white collar and oversleeves to keep her clean and tidy, and a lacy white apron and cap. Jackson, the butler, told her quickly to remove her oversleeves before presenting herself, and she felt all fingers and thumbs as she knocked on the drawing-room door and was told to enter.

She wished Miss Helen had been there to smooth over these moments. But Miss Helen was still in bed, having smiled vaguely as Carrie took her breakfast tray up to her as her first duty. Carrie had wistfully compared the young lady's beautifully spacious bedroom with the poky, uncarpeted attic room Carrie was to share with two others. It was only right and proper, but it certainly put her in her place as she had quickly unpacked her belongings and stuffed her bags on top of the narrow closet allotted to her.

And now here she was, fidgeting awkwardly, as she faced her new master and mistress for the first time. It dawned on her that Mr Barclay was looking anything but pleased, even though the lady of the house gave her a slight, encouraging smile.

"Don't you know enough to give a bob in front of your betters, girl?" Giles Barclay said testily.

163

"I'm sorry, sir. I ain't – haven't – been in service before," Carrie said, painfully remembering the correct term. She bobbed awkwardly, and was so nervous that she nearly fell over in the process.

Giles Barclay sighed heavily. The previous day's events had left a sour taste in his mouth, to say nothing of his wife's hysterics the minute he'd arrived home to find a constable in attendance. The sooner he could get back to the comparative calm of his business premises today, the better he was going to be pleased.

"After the rumpus with the last servant, I'd have thought my daughter had more sense than to employ someone straight off the street," he said. "But I'm told you're a good outside laundress and have proved to be trustworthy. I hope we may count on that situation inside the house as well as out of it, miss."

Carrie opened her mouth to speak indignantly, and then caught the smallest shake of Mrs Barclay's head, and clamped her mouth closed again. She nodded silently instead.

"Don't you have a tongue in your head?" Giles said, more kindly now.

"Yes, sir," Carrie said, not sure just what she was supposed to say. "I shall do my very best to suit Miss Helen. Will that do for you – sir?"

To her surprise his face relaxed, and he gave a short laugh.

"'Pon my word, but I don't know whether to take that as insolence or not, but I'll give you the benefit of the doubt. Now then, Jackson will give you details of your wages, and your time off will be at my daughter's discretion. You'll be directly answerable to her – as long as things go smoothly. When they don't, I shall see you in my study."

From the way his voice sharpened, Carrie was in no doubt that a visit to his study meant a very strong reprimand. She murmured her understanding, and was dismissed.

She stood outside the drawing-room door, thinking him a real tartar, and still not knowing what he meant by all the rumpus of yesterday. It wasn't until she was called to Miss Helen's room again, that she ventured to ask.

"I don't see why you shouldn't know. In fact, it's best that all the servants know, so that they're in no doubt of the consequences, if and when the thief is caught."

Carrie gasped. It was obvious that something very serious had taken place, and her eyes widened as Helen proceeded to tell her.

"I believe I can trust you, Carrie, which is why I offered you this job," she said. "You've always taken great care of my clothes, and I think you'll continue to do so."

"Of course I will, Miss Helen!"

She prayed that no tell-tale flush was going to betray the few times she'd tried on some of those beautiful garments in her room at home, and imagined that she was a lady.

Helen smiled at her. "And how is your mother?" she said, in the way a young lady graciously enquired after a servant's relative.

"Poorly, miss. I worry about her, though she insists she's as strong as an ox, but 'tis eight years since she had our Billy, and she's not a young woman no more."

"My goodness, I didn't want her complete medical history, you goose," Helen interrupted. "But I daresay you'd like to know when you may have time off to visit her?"

"Yes please, miss," Carrie said, chastened. She was away from home, and tied to an employer for the first time in her life, and she was only just realising the restrictions it put on her. It depended on Helen Barclay's say-so whether she could go out of doors, or blow her nose, or wipe her backside, as Elsie would say.

165

"Do you have a young man?" Helen said, as if she had instantly forgotten the importance of Carrie's time off. "There was a good-looking fellow with you on the day of the Downs fair, I recall. Is he your beau, Carrie?"

"Sort of," Carrie said, and now the blush was definitely staining her face. She felt it right down in her neck, and she heard Helen laugh.

"You don't have to be so coy about it! I only ask because I daresay you'll be wanting to see him sometimes as well, won't you?"

"Well – yes!" she stammered.

"Then you may have an hour off every afternoon between three and four o'clock, and you may take two hours in the evenings while the family is at dinner, unless we go out for dinner, and I especially require you. You will be on duty at all other times, either helping me personally, or attending to my laundry as before, or accompanying me into the city for calling. Is that quite clear?"

"Yes – thank you, Miss Helen."

"Good. I suggest you write it all down – that is, if you're able to write," she said, pausing. "I'm sorry, I didn't think to ask."

"I can read and write very well," she said with some pride. "Even our Billy can do so, and he's – "

"I know. He's only eight," Helen said with a smile. "Well, I think that's all for now, so I suggest you find the laundry room and get on with your duties."

Carrie hesitated at the door. "Does that mean I can have an hour off this very afternoon, Miss?"

"Of course." Helen was already becoming bored with all the trivial explanations.

It was better than Carrie had expected. A whole hour off this very afternoon! Ma would be surprised to see her back already, and it would be as if she'd hardly gone away!

Carrie hurried down the back stairs to the kitchen, and found her way to the laundry room, where the usual pile of Helen Barclay's soiled clothes awaited her. The room was warm and thick with steam, and there were several stone sinks, buckets and bowls awaiting the wash load. The copper was already humming as the water came to the boil with its addition of softening soap.

There was a heavy sacking apron hanging behind the door, and Carrie pushed up her sleeves and tied the apron around her. She felt a sudden lift to her spirits. This was familiar territory, and it never even dawned on her that in effect she was right back where she started.

Chapter 10

Wilf could stand the inactivity no longer. His brother had gone to sea, and his sister had quickly settled into her new life in Clifton, even though it seemed that she was back home nearly as much as she was away. But it eased his anxiety over Ma, who was looking more pinched as the weeks went on. She insisted on carrying on with her wash-days for her other regulars, saying that nothing as normal as an expectant babby had ever interfered with her energy before now, and she didn't see why this one should be any different. And Billy still staggered up and down the steep hill with the loads, nearly smothered beneath the piled up cart.

Pa still ranted on about not taking on any work but what he was skilled at, and that was as a craftsman carpenter. It was futile, for word had now got about that he was drinking heavily, and his hands were so unsteady, he'd as likely carve through his fingers as look at them. He brought no money into the house except for the occasional odd job he did, one of which was to fashion coffins for the poor at a cut-price rate.

"The poor dabs can't afford to pay me much more'n the price of the wood, and that'll do me," he'd growled when Wilf had remonstrated with him. "'Tis little enough a man can do for his fellows, so let me be."

So Wilf had let him be, and confided in his lady-love that unless something happened to improve their lot soon, they'd be facing a bleak winter. Nora sympathised, but her sympathy was tinged by guilt, knowing it was her own father who'd put the Stuckeys out of work and put the word about that they were an unstable family.

"What will you do, Wilf?" she asked him, when they were ensconced in a tea-room one afternoon, well away from the docks area where her father had his warehouse and yard.

"I'm going after a railway navvy's job," he said steadily.

She gasped. Such menial work would hardly raise Wilf's status in her father's eyes. She smothered the quick burst of snobbery and tried to look interested, when in truth she was extremely shaken.

"Is that what you want?" she asked, trying to keep any intonation out of her voice. It was all too easy for Wilf to seize on any suggestion of censure these days. He was as brittle as glass, the way she guessed were all the rest of the Stuckey family in these hard times.

Out of consideration to what he saw as Nora's more refined upbringing, Wilf rarely mentioned his mother's condition. But by now she knew how deeply he resented his father for giving her another child when things were so bad. Though how it could have been prevented, short of abstaining from the natural and normal in marriage, Nora didn't know, and was too inhibited to enquire.

"No, it's not what I want," Wilf said in a low, savage voice. "But I see no other option if we're to keep our heads above water."

"But where will you be working? You won't be going away, will you, Wilf?" she said in sudden alarm.

His stormy eyes softened as he looked across the tea-room table at his girl.

"I hope not. I intend to apply at Temple Meads station and sign on for any work that's offered. The lines are constantly needing attention already. Some reckon they was put together so fast that the ground beneath 'em was

169

never properly stabilised. Any sign of sinking could be a disaster."

He saw Nora shiver, envisaging one of the great snorting steam trains from London swerving off a sinking track, and spilling out its load of screaming passengers. He wished he'd never mentioned such a thing, especially when Nora took up the fancying.

"How terrible such a happening would be, Wilf. It might even have happened in July when Prince Albert arrived by train to launch the great ship!"

He spoke more sharply now. "Don't take what I'm saying as fact, Nora! I'm only repeating what folk surmise, but it benefits the out-of-workers. The bosses have to do all they can to let the public see that safety is of prime importance, and prevent any outcry. So they probably take on more navvies than they need. But it never happened, so there's no point in playing guessing-games."

"All the same, such a disaster on the launch day would have thrown the whole city into confusion," Nora said.

"Aye, and it would certainly have upset my sister's applecart, if her dear Izzy had been involved as well," Wilf said, determined to change the conversation, and knowing that mention of Carrie would do it.

"How does she fare? Does she like her new position?"

Wilf shrugged. "I daresay. She comes to see Ma most afternoons, and seems cheerful enough."

"Is she still courting?"

"I don't know. I don't ask," he said vaguely.

Nora's blue eyes flashed. "Sometimes, Wilf Stuckey, you can be the most infuriating of men!"

"Why? I'm not interested in other folks' courting, only my own," he said with a grin that disarmed her at once. "And by my reckoning, it's time I did some."

Nora's cheeks went a delicate pink. "It's much too cold to sit in the park today, Wilf. Parker has our carriage at the mews nearby. He's very discreet and we would be very cosy inside while he drove us about. We could ride around Clifton Downs for an hour or so before I had to return home. And I would so like a change from sitting on a damp stone seat in the park!"

She had never suggested such a thing before, and she wasn't sure how he would take it. The carriage belonged to her father, of course, and it signified just how much money the Woolleys had compared to the Stuckeys. And Wilf had such stuffy pride, just like all the lower classes.

Nora bit her lip, hating herself for letting the phrase slip into her mind. But in her opinion, just because you had little money shouldn't mean a person also had to have a lower class mentality. A person should be able to rise above all that, the way some of the unfortunate aristocrats did when they fell on hard times.

In her safe little world, never having had to go without a single thing she desired in the whole of her pampered life, she found it easy to think so. And it was one of the few areas where she and Wilf were scratchy with one another.

"All right," he said carelessly. "I can point out the mansion where our Carrie is living now. At least one of the Stuckeys has come up in the world, even if it's only as far as the servants' quarters."

And Nora knew he hadn't been fooled at all by her carefully worded suggestion.

But she forgot all about that as their driver helped her into the carriage. She leaned back against the velvet squabs, and felt Wilf's arm slide around her. They were enclosed in their own little world as Parker clicked the horses into motion and Wilf felt the warm and instant response of his lady.

Carrie barely glanced at the fine carriage bowling along the Downs as she hurried towards the hill leading home.

If the thought flitted through her mind that the drawn curtains of the carriage indicated some clandestine meeting, she could only feel envy for the lovers inside.

Maybe it would be today . . . the thought whirled around in her head as her feet clattered on the cobbles. Maybe today John would have left a message about seeing her again . . . Maybe today . . . she had been at the Barclay mansion for a month now, and so far there had been no message at all. At first she had been bewildered, and then hurt, and finally angry. But the treacherous feelings in her heart wouldn't let her stop thinking and hoping all the same.

"I'm home, Ma," she called out, when she arrived at the house. She never wasted time in getting there, because the hour went by all too quickly before she had to report back to Cook again. But Cook was indulgent and prepared to overlook it if she was a few minutes late. Everyone knew by now that she was anxious about Ma, and how much she needed to reassure herself on Ma's health by these afternoon visits home.

Her heart leapt now, because the house was so quiet. It was never this silent, because one or other of them was always doing something or other. Pa with his carpentering, Wilf sometimes giving a hand, or cleaning out the chickens in the back yard, or Billy playing with his toys, or Ma, endlessly making rag rugs, or sewing, or washing, or cooking, or cleaning . . .

"Ma, where are you?" Carrie called out nervously. She went through the parlour and scullery into the yard, but there was only the washing billowing on the lines, and the two remaining scrawny chickens. The rest had been eaten. Once these two were gone, there'd be no more eggs either, save for those provided by the Barclay kitchen. God bless the Barclays, Carrie thought fervently.

She turned and ran up the stairs, but there was no-one

in the house at all. It was strange not to find Ma here, but at least she wasn't lying prostrate somewhere. As she let out her breath in a sigh of relief Carrie realised how tight with fear she had been until that moment. And then she heard a door bang downstairs, and she ran down again to see Ma come wearily inside and sit down heavily.

"I'm sorry, duck, but there was no time to get word to you, and our Billy's running an errand for your Pa, or I'd have sent him to tell you not to come today."

"What's happened, Ma?" She was even more alarmed at the whiteness of Ma's face, and the way she pressed her side where the baby lay. "Is it summat to do with Pa?"

He hadn't done much to help the family coffers lately, but it was only a temporary thing, she thought loyally. For all that, he was the family's pivot, and without Pa . . .

Ma shook her head quickly. "It's nothing to do with us, but she came to us for help, so naturally we gave it."

"*Who* did, Ma?"

May looked a little vacant, then took a deep breath, wincing as the pain in her side stabbed at her.

"I'm all at sixes and sevens, Carrie. It was your friend, Elsie. She came here all of a tizzy this morning, saying her granpa had died in the night. He'd fallen out of bed, and he was still stiff with the rigor and she couldn't move him. She was nearly out of her wits, poor thing."

"Oh!" Carrie hadn't expected this, even though it had seemed likely for years that the old man would go at any minute. But such folk seemed to go on for ever.

"Poor Elsie. How was she when you left, Ma?"

"Still all of a shake. Pa's gone down there with a rough-made coffin he thinks will fit, and I said Elsie could stop here a day or two if she liked. She said no, as long as the coffin's all right, and her granpa's got out of the cottage. She can't abide the thought of sleeping in the house tonight with him still there."

"But she'd be all alone," Carrie said, horrified.

173

Ma shrugged. "'Tis what she wanted, girl, and the dead can't hurt you none when they'm gone."

A thought struck Carrie. "Ma, you didn't – you didn't lay him out, did you?"

That disgusting old man, who couldn't help being smelly and disgusting, but who had always revolted her. And with her Ma in her condition . . .

"Somebody had to do it, and they couldn't pay for doctors' fees. Besides, there was no need. I'm still capable of doing what's needed," she said briskly.

Carrie felt a surge of admiration for her, even while she was sure now that she could smell Granpa Miller on her mother, and she edged away as discreetly as she could.

"I'll make you some strong tea, Ma," she said, excusing herself. "Where will they take him when Pa's done?"

"Billy's gone for the corpse carrier. He'll take him to the store-house until the burying tomorrow."

Carrie was thankful her Ma couldn't see how she shuddered at that moment. The store-house was what they called the wooden structure near the church where the coffins of the poor were housed until the ground could be dug for burial. Everyone knew that coffins placed in the store-house belonged to those who relied on the parishioners' charity for their last resting-place. Poor Elsie.

"What time will the burial be, Ma?"

"Twelve noon as usual."

Of course. The usual time for paupers' plantings.

"I shall beg an extra hour off from Miss Helen to attend," she said huskily. "Elsie will want me to be there."

"Don't go risking your position for the likes of that one," Ma was sharper now. "She'll rebound soon enough."

It was so unlike Ma to be uncharitable at such a time, that Carrie went back to the parlour while the kettle was still halfway to boiling. She surprised Ma by catching sight

174

of the suffering on her pinched face as she clutched at her belly. She ran to her side, all thoughts of Elsie fleeing from her mind.

"Ma, you're ill! Shall I go for Doctor Flowers?"

She shook her head decisively. "It's nobbut a stitch from hurrying too much. It'll pass soon enough. Don't fuss me, for pity's sake."

Even though she was rebuffed, Carrie knew her mother well enough to know that the sharper she got, the more pain she was in, and the more angry she got at her own weakness.

"I'll get the tea then," she said instead, and went back to the scullery to prepare it with shaking hands, hardly noticing how the boiling water spat and scalded her.

"Where's our Wilf today?" she asked, once her mother had got some colour back in her cheeks.

Ma sniffed. "Who knows where he gets to nowadays? He's talking about taking up with they railway navvies. Your Pa don't approve, but I'm too weary to argue against it."

"If it'll bring in some wages, I shouldn't think he would object to it."

"He objects to everything these days. He don't feel like a man no more. He thinks he drove our Frank away by his taunts, and now you're the only one bringing money in, apart from my bits. If Wilf finds work, your Pa will feel even more useless."

"Would he rather Wilf hung about the house idling?"

"I believe he would," Ma said, with the ghost of a smile. "But that's enough gloomy talk for one day. Are things still going well for you up at Clifton?"

"Mostly," Carrie said cautiously. "Miss Barclay is more of a stickler than I expected, and I have to put everything away just so. If anything's out of place she almost takes a fit. Cook says it's because that other maid stole from her and her Ma, and shc's para-summat about it now."

"Well, I hope she don't think you're going to steal from her," Ma said indignantly.

"I dunno what she thinks. Cook reckons she's been crossed in love and she's taking it out on the rest of us."

"This Cook seems to know a lot," Ma said, but Carrie was less interested in Cook's gossip than in something else that she was burning to know.

"Ma, has John been here since I left? It's a whole month now, and I expected a message from him."

Her voice trailed away as Ma shook her head.

"Our Billy's seen him a coupla times, Carrie, and he asked after you, but said to say he was very busy, and he'd see you when he could. That's all I can tell you."

Carrie bit her lip, smarting at the way John seemed to be snubbing her. If he didn't want her, why didn't he tell her so? The way he'd held her and caressed her in Leigh Woods had left her in no doubt that he'd wanted her then. He'd got permission from her Pa for walking-out, but they'd done precious little of it. She felt misery wash over her, and then, as she heard Billy's running footsteps, and remembered where he'd been, she chided herself for being so self-centred, when poor Elsie must be in such a turmoil.

"Do you think I should go and see Elsie now, Ma?" she said reluctantly.

Ma nodded. "Pa should be nicely finished by now, and have the old fellow nailed down. What did the corpse carrier say, Billy?"

"He's fetching him directly. Can I come back to Elsie's with you, Carrie, to see it go?"

"No, you cannot," she said crossly. "It's not a peep-show."

But she knew that it would be, for anyone of a curious disposition. She'd seen it all before. When the corpse carrier had put the loaded coffin on his cart, he'd be escorted

176

all the way back to the store-house by a gaggle of urchins, wagering their farthings on whether or not the coffin-lid was going to pop open and the shrouded occupant chase after them. She shuddered again, wondering how they could find such fascination in these ghoulish games.

She had no real wish to go and visit Elsie, but she knew she should. If the boot was on the other foot, and it was one of her family, Elsie would be the first to offer her rough comfort. It would make her late back at Clifton, she thought anxiously, but these were special times, and surely Miss Helen would understand.

"You should have been back here more than half an hour ago!" Helen screamed at her. Her normally pretty face was contorted with rage, and her eyes flashed blue fire at Carrie. "Do you think I'm paying you to dawdle about making fancy eyes at every Tom, Dick and Harry?"

It was so far from the truth it took away the shock at meeting such a tirade. Cook was probably right, Carrie thought. Miss Helen had definitely been crossed in love to make her act so unlike herself.

"I'm very sorry, miss," she said nervously. "But me friend's granpa just died, and I went to console her."

"I don't want to hear your feeble excuses," Helen raged. "And if you mean the common tart I saw you with on the Downs in the summer, then I doubt that she'll need much consoling from you. She'll soon find consolation elsewhere."

Carrie gasped, all her swift sympathy for the young lady vanishing in a trice. By now, she knew that the gentry could resort to coarseness as good as any servant could give, and the so-correct Miss Barclay had a ripe turn of phrase on her when it suited. But this was too much.

Carrie had just spent a tearful time with Elsie, and persuaded her at last to go home to Jacob's Wells Road with her and spend a couple of nights in Carrie's old room. She didn't deserve these insults. She snapped out a response.

"Elsie's in a real old state, miss, and I didn't think it right to leave her."

She yelped as she got a stinging slap across her cheek for her insolence.

"And didn't you think it right to come back here where you're paid good money for the little that you do, and have generous time off? I'm beginning to think I made a mistake in taking pity on you and your wretched family."

Carrie forced back the scalding tears. Her face stung as if a dozen bees had attacked it, but however much she hated lowering herself in front of this haughty bitch, she daren't risk losing this job. If it meant eating every crumb of humble pie, she had to do it.

"Please don't say that, Miss Helen. You know how grateful I am to be working for you, and I do try my very best to please you, truly I do. This was the first lapse I've made, and it won't happen again."

She hung her head and crossed her fingers behind her back as she spoke, feeling a hypocrite at acting so abjectly. It wasn't Carrie Stuckey's style at all, but there were times when it was necessary, and this was one of them.

She might look humble, but inside she was seething at the pain in her face, and wondering how the dickens she was going to ask for an extra hour off tomorrow to attend Granpa Miller's burying. She'd promised Elsie she'd be there, and there would be few enough mourners at the graveside.

To her astonishment, she suddenly heard Helen give a tinkling laugh. She had become quite unpredictable lately, giving more weight to Cook's suspicions that there was an unrequited love lurking in the background. But if it was so, then she hadn't confided in her personal maid.

178

"Oh Carrie, I fear that my temper is not at its best at present. Does your poor cheek pain you very much?"

"I'll live," Carrie muttered, not sure how to take this sudden show of concern. She took a pace back as Helen moved towards her, as if afraid she was going to receive another whack to send her reeling.

"Then I shall try to make amends to you," Helen announced. "What shall it be? A trinket, perhaps? A bauble for your hair?"

"If I could change my time off tomorrow to the morning for my friend's granpa's burying, that'd be enough, if it's all the same to you, miss," Carrie said quickly.

She ducked as she spoke, wondering if she'd gone too far. If Miss Helen was going to go off half-cocked again, she'd be in for another slapping. But to her wild relief, the young lady gave a shrug of her elegant shoulders, her voice careless.

"Oh, take the extra time and be done with it. I daresay your mother will want to see you again in the afternoon as usual. I trust she's thriving?"

"She's reasonable," Carrie said, knowing there was no real concern behind the question, and longing to be out of there to bathe her face with witchhazel before it bruised.

Helen nodded. "Good. Then perhaps you could attend to your duties now. Take these items away and get them back to me as soon as possible, and take especial care with the lace. I don't want to see a speck of yellowing on it."

She indicated the basket of frills, which needed hardly any laundering at all, and which Carrie guessed had been put out just for the pleasure of giving her extra work to do. She didn't care. While she attended to the task, the lace laundry room was her domain, where she could escape Miss Helen's irascible tongue for a while.

But first she must attend to her face. She sought out

179

Cook in the kitchen and asked for the witchhazel. Cook tut-tutted, full of concern as she inspected the damage.

"The young madam," she said indignantly. "Her Mama would never have struck a servant like that one does. Did you explain why you were late, dearie?"

"Oh yes, but it made no difference. Still, she's let me have time off for the burying tomorrow, so I suppose I must be grateful for that."

She listened to herself, so accepting of her betters' treatment, and it angered her to be so subservient. And to be so tied to someone that she had to ask permission to be with a friend in need, when she had always been as free as a bird. But until her menfolk found decent jobs, she had no choice.

If only John Travis could make his fortune and marry her . . . if only they could live in a fine house, and Wilf and Pa could be set up in their own workshop and have people begging for their craftsmanship . . . if only pigs could fly . . .

"Do you really think Miss Helen has a gentleman-friend who's causing her bother?" she asked Cook, when the witchhazel had been dabbed onto her cheek and she had shivered at its refreshing chill.

"So it seems. Daisy said there were all sorts of discussions going on above stairs a day or two ago. As soon as she took the tea-tray in, it all stopped, of course. And Mr Jackson forbade her to listen at the drawing-room door."

"What a shame," Carrie grinned. "Perhaps we could persuade him to do the listening and report back to us?"

She giggled at the thought of the po-faced butler doing any such thing. He was every bit as stiff and starchy as one of the penguins strutting around at the zoological gardens nearby.

"Perhaps you'd best get on with your work, Carrie,"

Cook said, suddenly businesslike, and as Carrie glimpsed a dark shape entering the outer door she knew Mr Jackson had returned from whatever mission he'd been on.

It was interesting though, she thought later, up to her elbows in hot soapy water and squeezing it through the delicate lace of Miss Helen's underpinnings. She wondered if she dared ask the young lady if anything was amiss, and hope to get a reply. It would be even more interesting to hear the details of Miss Helen's love-life, always presuming she had such a thing. She must be about twenty years old, Carrie surmised, so it was high time she was thinking about getting wed.

Her eyes went soft for a few moments, letting dreams of love and romance replace the memory of Elsie's sadness that morning, and the ugliness of death . . . until the clatter of the delivery wagons at the kitchen entrance, and the scampering of the kitchen maids to do Cook's bidding in hauling in the heavy crates and sacks, reminded her that she had a task to do.

That evening, she was fiddling with Miss Helen's hair in readiness for a country dinner party that the family was attending. Finding that none of her attentions was pleasing her ladyship, she could stand the biting censure no longer. She stood with her hands on her hips, and said the first thing that came into her head.

"I'm sure I don't know what ails you, Miss Helen, but perhaps if you cared to confide in me, we'd all get a bit o' peace. If there's a young gentleman on the horizon, then I'm sure he'd rather see a smiling face that that scowling one!"

She gave a final tug at the unruly lock of hair that refused to stay in its proper place inside the pearl and silver hair clip, and stepped back defiantly as she saw the mixture of astonishment and rage on Helen Barclay's face.

"You insolent young wretch. I should send you packing immediately for that!"

Without warning the rage fizzled out, and she was suddenly laughing, amusement dancing in her blue eyes. Carrie backed away uneasily, wondering if her mistress was losing control of her senses, and if she could call someone.

"Oh Carrie, don't look so worried. I'm not heading for the asylum, I promise you!" Helen said, almost gasping as she tried to contain her mirth. She stretched out an elegant arm towards her maid and beckoned her forward. She looked a picture of beauty and sweetness in her bronze foulard evening gown, but Carrie knew how quickly that mood could change.

"Come here – if you want to know just why I'm so out of sorts. I suppose I've been the source of kitchen gossip lately, which is a necessary evil of the gentry, but as usual the servants have got it all wrong," she finished mirthfully.

"I assure you we don't spend all day discussing you, Miss Helen," Carrie said indignantly. That much was true, at least. They didn't have time to speculate every minute of the day, when there was so much work to be done, especially the poor little kitchen maids with their endless scrubbing and polishing and servitude to Cook and Mr Jackson.

"Never mind all that," Helen said impatiently. "Now then. You think I have a beau, do you? And that I'm pining for his affections, the way you're presumably pining for your own young man?"

"Well, something like that," Carrie said uneasily, not sure how much agreement Helen wanted from her, nor if she really meant to compare her own situation with Carrie's.

"Well, you're completely wrong," Helen said. "There is a gentleman, a Mr Victor Thornton, but I've no possible desire to marry him, or even to be sociable with him. He's perfectly eligible, but he's old, and he's my father's choice, not mine. And I simply refuse to be married off to an elderly and bumptious country squire on my father's whim."

"I see," Carrie said, taken aback by her vehemence. "And is it Mr Victor Thornton's home where you're going tonight, miss?"

"It is," Helen said, her lips tightening. "And I have to smile and be pleasant and accept the old fool's arm to go into dinner – and if you dare to breathe a word of this below stairs, I shall have your hide!"

"I wouldn't dream of it. No-one will hear of it from me, I promise you."

Helen gave a faint smile. "I haven't always been fortunate in my choice of maids, but somehow I believe you. Well then. You are now my confidante, and you may wait up for me in my dressing-room until I return home and I shall tell you all that happened. It will be a relief to confide in someone." She was becoming more charmed by the minute at the thought of sharing the secret that had been such an unwanted burden until now.

"Very well, miss," Carrie said dutifully, hardly knowing how to take this change of mood. She'd half expected to be thrown out on her ear for her cheek, and here she was, being taken into the young lady's confidence. And Miss Helen could trust her. She had vowed not to reveal below stairs a single word of what was said.

Cook glared at her. "Well, I never. You're more of a sly one than you look, ain't you, young Carrie?"

"What do you mean?"

Cook sniffed. "Neither that baggage whose place you took, nor the maid who was here before her was ever invited to wait up in Miss Helen's dressing-room. They was always summoned down from their beds in the early hours to remove the young lady's finery, or whatever. Privileged you are, and no mistake."

"Well, I didn't ask for it! And I don't particularly want to wait up, neither. It will give me too much time to think about tomorrow."

She couldn't help thinking about Elsie, alone in that miserable hovel, with the smell of her granpa still lingering, and the fear of death still hovering. She prayed Elsie hadn't changed her mind about staying with the Stuckeys.

And here was Cook, and the rest of the below stairs staff, scowling at her as if she'd somehow stolen a march on the rest of them, and wheedled her way into Miss Helen's good books. It wasn't fair, when they were the ones who'd started all the gossip about Helen being thwarted in love, as the penny dreadfuls called it.

"Well, I hope it won't be too late. I need my beauty sleep," she said, hoping to provoke a mocking remark in response. Instead, she got a snappy reply from Mr Jackson.

"There's not much hope of that, miss. The Thornton estate is twenty-five miles from here, and these dinner parties go on very late. They say Mr Victor Thornton is a keen gambling man, and will almost certainly cajole Mr Barclay into a card-playing session while the ladies twiddle their thumbs. I doubt that the family will return much before three o'clock in the morning."

From Cook's furious face, Carrie saw that she realised, like the rest of them, that Mr Jackson had known far more about things than he'd let on. Carrie hid a secret smile, as some of the heat was taken away from her. All the same . . . three o'clock in the morning . . .

It was all that and more, when she heard the click of Helen's bedroom door. She struggled up from the sofa in the dressing-room where she had been dozing, prepared to help the young lady undress for bed, and hoping she didn't look too muzzy from sleep.

"Goodness, are you still awake, Carrie?" the unpredictable Miss Barclay said. "I thought you'd have been chasing sheep long ago. Anyway, I don't need you. I'm almost dead with fatigue and I shall sleep the sleep of the just tonight."

Carrie looked at her furiously. All this time, and now the bitch didn't want her services at all. Nor was she going to tell her any juicy little tid-bits of gossip, she thought indignantly . . . it was too much.

"But what about Mr Thornton's unwelcome attentions, miss?" She dared to speak his name, her eyes unblinking as she faced her mistress. If her curiosity got her a cuff around the ear, so be it. She heard Helen laugh gaily, and to her complete amazement, she was suddenly caught by both hands and swung around the room.

"He cooked his goose tonight, the old fool," she said inelegantly, when they were both out of breath and breathing heavily. "He drank too much at dinner, and when they went into the gaming room, Papa caught him cheating at cards. He tried to bluff his way out of it, of course, and said it had been a misunderstanding, but Papa's such a stickler about that sort of thing, that he's severed all connection with the Thorntons. Isn't it wonderful?"

"Wonderful," Carrie echoed. She couldn't dash the excitement in Helen's eyes, but she couldn't help wondering who her father would have lined up for her next. It must be hell to be rich, and have to have every suitor inspected like a piece of meat on a slab, she thought suddenly. As Helen moved away from her, she wondered if she could decently retire now, when she realised Helen was foraging in her jewel-box.

Thoughts of that other maid's dismissal, and the fact that no trace had been found of her or the missing items, surged into her mind. Surely she wasn't about to be accused of theft, since she had been alone in these rooms for so long.

Helen turned, a string of gleaming jet beads draped over her fingers. She held it out to Carrie.

"I want you to have this. Wear it tomorrow at your friend's funeral. I've been perfectly beastly to you lately, Carrie, and I don't usually apologise to servants, so this is my way of making it up to you. Take it and go, before I get too humble and disgrace myself. Go on – take it!"

She pushed the beads into Carrie's unwilling hands. She mumbled her thanks and stumbled out of the room, clutching the gift. And all she could think about, was the hope that by tomorrow, Miss Helen wouldn't have forgotten giving it to her.

Chapter 11

Carrie had once witnessed a far posher funeral than Granpa Miller's, and seen how the gentry decked themselves out in black furs and jewels and the blackest of jet beads and ornaments as if trying to outdo each other.

It wasn't the time nor the place to be so done up to the nines, according to Ma. She had always averred that if Christ had seen fit to go to his Maker with his followers unadorned, then there was no need for lesser folk to make such a poppy show of the occasion.

Carrie remembered that now, and seeing Elsie's plain apparel at her granpa's burying, was more than thankful she hadn't flaunted the jet beads that Helen Barclay had given her.

She glanced surreptitiously at the pitifully few mourners around the pauper's grave in the corner of the churchyard. Elsie was snivelling into a torn handkerchief, as befitted the chief mourner, garbed in her usual clothes that Ma had washed and ironed for her. She'd decided to stay in Carrie's old room after all, and Carrie had found it oddly disturbing to go home that morning, to find Elsie's things strewn about in a haphazard way.

But this wasn't the time to be thinking of such things. To swell the crowd, all the Stuckey family was in attendance, apart from Frank. Wilf was working as a railway navvy now, to Pa's intense disapproval, and had begged to change shifts with another man to attend the burying. There was the usual group of city urchins lurking about to watch the goings-on. Aside from those, there were a few old stalwarts of Granpa Miller's ilk, who didn't look as if they'd last out the day in the keen wind.

Ma too, looked paler than usual as she dragged her thin coat around her body. If it wasn't for the promiment lump beneath it, Carrie would swear she was nought but skin and bones, and she felt a stab of alarm. The birth was only a couple of months away, and she should be looking far more robust by now, since Cook sent down as much food as was reasonable from the Barclay kitchen.

Carrie caught the disapproving eye of the minister. She bent her head quickly, as the words were said over the coffin before it was lowered into the ground. Seconds later, Elsie threw a handful of dirt into the grave. She shuddered at the hollow sound as it hit the coffin Pa had made. A slanting rain had begun to fall, making the day even more dismal.

"We'll go back to the house now for a bite," Ma said briskly. Billy lingered behind in a kind of fearful fascination, alongside the city urchins peering down into the hole that was already being filled in by the gravedigger.

"Will 'e stay down there for ever, boss?" one of the raggamuffins asked in awe. The gravedigger gave a raucous laugh and scratched his head as if pondering on the question.

"Well, I ain't seen one that came up again yet, young feller. Though there's them that reckon they hear a bit o' nightly moaning from these 'ere graves. I ain't never put it to the test, mind, and I don't aim to be startin' now, but if you've a mind to come back around midnight – "

"Come away, Billy," Wilf snapped, seeing the boy's eyes grow rounder and his face whiten, as the gravedigger warmed to his tale.

He glared at the man, who merely shrugged and continued with his task, while the urchins crowded around him, clearly hoping for more gruesome stories. Wilf pulled Billy along to rejoin the rest of the family.

Truth to tell, Wilf was none too pleased that the irritating Elsie Miller was going to spend a couple of nights under their roof, and he was glad he'd be out of it for most of the time. But it was hardly right to object when the girl was mourning her granpa. He was cynical enough to suspect that she wouldn't be mourning for long. Such girls had their own ways of getting over grief.

His suspicions were confirmed when Elsie sidled across to him as they made the slow procession back to Jacob's Wells Road, and she slipped her cold hand into his for a moment.

"If you've an hour or two to spare, Wilf, I'd be glad of a hand in getting rid of some of me granpa's old stuff," she said huskily. "I can't pay you nothing – leastways, not in money – but you're welcome to taking the bed and the old wardrobe, if the wood will be of any use to you. You can take anything else that takes your fancy."

He extricated his hand from hers. He'd never been in the least charmed by Elsie's flirtatious posturings and come-hither eyes. It disgusted him that even now she couldn't help putting it into effect, whether it was done knowingly or not. He'd never be tempted by her in a million years, even if he didn't already have a sweet girl of his own.

"Pa and me will come back to the house with you and see what's to be done," he said firmly. "'Tis no task for a girl, and I doubt that you'll want any of the bedding and clothes left behind, will you?"

He saw her shudder, and regretted his harshness. But she obviously realised she wasn't going to get Wilf back to her cottage alone, and perhaps his curtness had done her a service, because her voice hardened.

"I will not! I'll be glad to get the smell of 'em out of the house."

"Then we'll take 'em away and get 'em burnt," he told her more mildly.

Carrie caught up with them then, and he left the two girls together while he went to take hold of the dawdling Billy's hand. They wanted no more tripping into the river on this damp and miserable day.

"Your Wilf don't like me, Carrie, and that's a fact," Elsie said sullenly to her friend.

Carrie squeezed her hand, and tried to be tactful on this day of all days. "It's not just you, Elsie. He's already got a girl, though I'm not supposed to talk about it, so don't go letting on while you're in the house, mind. Pa wouldn't take kindly to it."

She stopped, wishing she hadn't started on this tack. It seemed ludicrous to think that her Pa would object to a healthy young man like Wilf having a girl. It would seem odder if he showed no interest in girls at all. But it would be a different matter if Pa knew it was Nora Woolley who held the key to Wilf's heart. And as long as Elsie didn't know that, she couldn't innocently give the game away.

It didn't occur to her to wonder why Elsie didn't pursue the subject. Nor to notice how Elsie's eyes flashed, as she remembered the cosy scene of Wilf Stuckey and that Woolley girl in a tea-room. Then Elsie's eyes got suddenly calculating. Carrie was too concerned over the way Ma kept stopping and holding her side, and how Pa was looking anxious. She ran to Ma's side.

"Do you want the doctor, Ma?"

"Of course not," Ma said. "'Tis only the stitch, that's all. It'll pass once I'm indoors out of this cold wind and get some hot tea inside me."

Carrie knew she hated any fuss, but there were times when she needed to be fussed over, and times when she shut out her own family because of her very self-control. It angered and frustrated Carrie, and as she dropped back

190

to fall into step with Elsie, she turned her anger onto the weather, as a steady drizzle began to seep through their clothes and into their bones.

"This damn awful weather," she muttered savagely. "Our Frank's in the best place, somewhere where it's warm and sunny all the time."

"Oh ah, and where's that?" Elsie said, pulling her shawl around her more tightly. "I bet you ain't even heard from him since he went away."

"No, we ain't, but he'd signed up on a trading ship bound for the south of France, so he won't be having this miserable wet weather, that's for sure."

"Pity he couldn't have taken us all with him," Elsie scowled as they headed up the steep hill towards the house.

"I wouldn't want to go," Carrie said, shivering.

"That's because you ain't got no adventure in your soul. There's more to life than a piddling little tripping boat like your John Travis has got!" she crowed.

Carrie felt her heart lurch. She'd tried to keep Elsie's mind off the old man they'd just buried, and somehow they'd reverted to their usual arguments, even if it was more subdued than some. But mention of John had been sudden and unexpected, and she felt her face flush.

"I suppose he thinks you've gone up in the world now you're at your new place," Elsie said cattily. "Does he come calling there?"

Carrie was saved the embarrassment of answering by Ma's sudden cry of pain, and the sight of her leaning against their front door. She rushed to help her, and was immediately brushed away by Pa.

"I'm all right, all of you! It was just a twinge, no more, and it caught me off-balance, but I'll be mighty thankful when this babby decides to make its appearance."

It was almost the first time she'd said any such thing, and Carrie resolved to call on Doctor Flowers herself and

191

ask his opinion of the too-frequent occurrences of what her mother called her twinges. She'd been a small girl when her Ma was expecting Billy, but she could never remember anything like this. She only remembered Ma sunny and smiling and telling her she was soon going to have a brother or sister to play with.

"You girls see to the tea-making," Pa ordered as soon as they were all inside. "It will do Elsie good to keep her hands occupied, and I'll see that Ma gets out of these wet clothes and has a lie down."

"I'm not having a lie down in the middle of the day," she said at once, but she was outnumbered by the rest of them and went protestingly up the stairs with Pa following.

Carrie and Elsie looked at one another. They were damp too, but the house was warm with the stove that was kept burning constantly, and they went into the scullery together. Wilf saw to pulling off Billy's boots and rubbing him down with a towel.

"It wasn't much of a send-off for your granpa, was it, Elsie?" Carrie said, awkwardly remembering why they were all together, and guiltily wishing the time would pass so she could get back to the comparative calm of Clifton.

Elsie shrugged. "He wouldn't have expected nothing more," she said. "And at least he's planted now, so there's nothing else to be done for him."

"You did your best while he was alive, anyway," Carrie said. "He'd have been in a sorry state without you to look after him."

She turned to pour the simmering water from the big black kettle into the tea-pot and swirl it round before adding some of the precious tea. To her astonishment she heard Elsie give a harsh laugh.

"He was always in a sorry state, whether I was there or not! I don't want to talk about him no more, Carrie, so don't go thinking you've got to dredge up the good

192

old times we had, because there weren't none to speak of. He's dead and gone now, and that's the end of it."

Carrie was shocked at this callous statement, even from Elsie. "But don't you want to talk about him at all? Most folk do, after a burying."

"Well, I don't." Elsie reached for the crockery from the cupboard and slapped the cups and saucers down on the scrubbed table. "He's gone, and that's that. I've done me cryin', and I've got to think of meself from now on."

Carrie looked at her, uncertain what to make of this defiance. It could be genuine and unfeeling, or it could hide real grief . . . with Elsie, you never quite knew . . . but when she spoke again she was almost glib.

"The best thing I can do is find meself a fellow to take care of me now, wouldn't you say? I'm quite a catch now, with me own cottage and no dependants."

"I suppose so," Carrie said slowly, though how anybody could call Elsie's miserable little hovel a "catch", she couldn't imagine.

"And if I don't have a cup of this bleedin' tea soon, I'm going to be as parched as a desert," Elsie went on brightly. "I'll take one in for your Wilf, shall I?"

She gave a brilliant smile, and Carrie caught her breath. If Elsie thought the fellow who was going to take care of her was Wilf Stuckey, she had another think coming. It would send Elsie into deep depression to be rejected as thoroughly as Carrie knew only Wilf could, and she prayed that Elsie wouldn't be too blatant while she stayed here.

"I'll take one up to Ma," she said quickly, knowing the time was going on, and she'd have to leave soon. She poured out the tea and hurried upstairs, leaving the rest of them to sort themselves out.

Ma looked somewhat better now, lying on the bed she shared with Pa, and with him rubbing her hands to get some life back into them. She had removed her outer clothes, and had the coverlet over her, and she struggled to sit up when she saw the welcome cup of tea. Pa left them to it, to go stumping down the stairs, awkward at any show of illness.

"This is just what the doctor ordered," Ma said. "You're a good girl, Carrie, but don't you go staying too long and upset Miss Barclay, now."

"You're more important to me than Miss Barclay."

"But your wages are important to all of us," Ma said quietly, now that Pa was out of the room. "These little upsets happen now and then, but 'tis nothing to be alarmed about. Ten minutes' rest, and I'll be right as rain again."

"Do you take ten minutes' rest now and again, Ma?" Carrie said carefully.

"Of course I do. I know it's necessary, and when you've gone downstairs I'm just going to shut my eyes. Elsie's here now, and I daresay she'll give a hand now and then. It'll give the girl summat to do to take her mind off her troubles."

Carrie was too anxious about Ma to feel any jealousy at her words. But she didn't hold out too much hope for Elsie's home-making capabilities. She'd never done much for her granpa in the way of cooking nourishing meals or keeping the place clean and tidy.

Elsie was too slap-dash by half, but if Ma thought she was going to be a help, she wouldn't disillusion her. And why shouldn't she pay her way while she was here? She tried to put it tactfully to the girl before she left.

"You'll be better for not being alone just now, Elsie, and I'm glad to know Ma has another female in the house. I know she'll be thankful for any help you can give her."

"Oh ah, though I can't say I relish the idea of being a skivvy like you."

"I didn't mean – "

194

"I know what you meant, and I promise I'll not see her slaving on my account while I'm here," Elsie said crossly. "But I'm not staying above a day or two. I've got me own place, and me job to pay the rent, so don't go thinking I'm prepared to take on your place here, Carrie."

"I'm glad to know it," Carrie was stung to retort. "There's only one daughter in this family."

She bit her lip. It was an insensitive thing to say, but Elsie always managed to bring out the worst in her, and she didn't seem to notice the barb. She gave a faint smile.

"There's daughters-in-law though," she said, without any more comment. Carrie felt the habitual irritation she felt for her friend returning.

"Elsie, I've told you Wilf already has a girl, and you're wasting your time."

"We'll see," she said airily. "Hadn't you better be getting back to your young lady?"

Carrie looked at her in frustration. She had been prepared to be gentle and considerate for Elsie's feelings on this sad day, but sometimes she doubted that Elsie had any feelings for anyone but herself at all, and all her sympathy seemed totally wasted. Instead of hugging Elsie, as anyone might feel encouraged to do on a day such as this, she bent down to hug Billy.

"I'll see you soon then," she said to anyone who was listening. But Billy had squirmed away, Elsie had gone back to the scullery to find something to eat, Pa was in his little shed, and Wilf was in the back yard throwing scraps to the chickens. Carrie shrugged. Ma was dozing upstairs, and it seemed that nobody needed her here right now, so she might just as well get back to those who did.

She resisted the urge to bang the door behind her, and went up the hill in the rain towards Clifton, feeling unaccountably resentful against the whole world.

* * *

195

"There's somebody here to see you, Carrie," Cook said, the minute she got inside the kitchen door, shaking the rain from her dishevelled hair.

Carrie looked up quickly. The only visitor she normally got was Billy, but there was something in Cook's smug voice that alerted her at once. The kitchen was warm and steamy and comfortable, and she heard the kitchen maids giggling as John Travis seemed to unfold his long legs from a wooden chair near the stove and turn to smile at her.

"What – what on earth are you doing here?" she stammered, taken completely off-balance by this unexpected appearance.

"Well, that's a nice way to greet your young man and no mistake," she heard Cook say.

Carrie ignored her as John came towards her and took her damp hands in his own.

"I seem to have chosen a bad day to come calling. I'm sorry about your friend, Carrie. She must be very upset."

"Elsie's being – just Elsie," she muttered. "She's staying with Ma for a day or two while she gets over it."

"That's kind of your mother."

She felt all kinds of a fool, standing here making small talk while her wet clothes steamed, and the skivvies were hanging on their every word as if it was something out of a bad play. Cook took charge.

"Miss Helen gave you time off for the funeral, Carrie, and you're back sooner than expected, so why don't you go and get into some dry clothes, then you and your young man can talk together in the laundry room."

It was about the only bit of privacy she could offer, since Carrie obviously couldn't take him up to her room. She felt so embarrassed, thinking it must underline her lowly position here, but John didn't seem to notice anything odd, and nodded at once.

196

"I'll wait," he said, "providing Cook keeps me topped up with another cup of her delicious hot chocolate."

As Carrie escaped up the servants' stairs, she saw Cook's gratified smile, and guessed that she was probably wondering how the very ordinary Carrie Stuckey had got hold of such a presentable and well-mannered young man.

When she reached her room, and scrambled out of her funeral clothes into her everyday working attire, it dawned on her that John was more tidily dressed than in his usual boating clothes, as if he'd been in the city on business.

Such magnificence was in danger of making her even more tongue-tied – and if that happened, it was going to make his arrival here quite pointless. Annoyed at her own confusion, she went flying back down the stairs, to arrive breathless in the kitchen. As John stood up, she led the way to the laundry room with her chin high, aware that she'd be the subject of plenty of tittle-tattle among the young skivvies for the rest of the day.

As soon as she closed the door behind then, John caught her close. She was held so fast against his chest that she could hardly breathe, and she struggled to free herself. The joy of being in his arms again was quite lost in her resentment of his taking so long to contact her, and in the recklessness of such an uninhibited embrace.

"Are you mad?" she gasped. "What if anyone should come in? I'd get the sack at once!"

Besides which, she was still unsettled from the occasion that morning, and it didn't seem right to be canoodling so soon after . . . she stepped back a pace to lean against the cold stone sink, her eyes stormy, her arms stiff at her sides. She saw his face turn a dull, angry red, and he spoke without thinking.

197

"My God, no matter where you go, you still have a Jacob's Wells Road mentality, don't you?"

Carrie felt her skin burn with a shocked resentment at that. He had a nerve, coming here and insulting her.

"There's nothing wrong with Jacob's Wells Road," she hissed. "But I know when somebody's looking down on me for living there – "

"You're not living there now, and it's time you took a pride in yourself, that's all I mean."

She stared at him. "You mean just because I'm living among the nobs, I should be nobby like 'em? Well, I could tell you a thing or two about the high and mighty young madams who live here!" She seethed, remembering the indignity of Miss Helen Barclay's ringing slap across her cheek.

And then she stopped her tirade as she heard the distinct sound of mutterings and gigglings outside the laundry door. She turned and wrenched it open, and the two skivvies nearly fell inside.

"Get about your work and mind your own business," Carrie yelled like a fishwife.

She caught hold of them by their gawky shoulders and bundled them back to the kitchen, where Cook tut-tutted at such goings-on, but she boxed their ears just the same. The last thing Carrie heard as she slammed the laundry room door shut to enclose herself and John once more, was the sound of their yelping. The next thing she heard was the sound of John's slow handclap.

"I'll say this for you, love. There's no lack of entertainment when you're around. What are you going to do for an encore?"

She glared into his face, not even sure what the word meant. And then she saw his eyes soften and his hand reached out for hers.

"Dear God, Carrie, I didn't come all this way just to fight with you."

198

"What did you come for then?" she muttered, beginning to realise what a fool she must seem to him, and wondering why he bothered with her at all.

"To tell you what's been happening lately, and why it's been impossible for me to see you."

"Our Billy told me you were far too busy," she said, unable to hide the sarcasm. "A big man like you – "

"Stop it, you little fool," he said, almost angrily. "You must have known it was something important to stop me from seeing you."

"How was I supposed to know? You could have sent me a note, even if you couldn't see me. I *can* read!"

For a moment, she seemed to stand outside herself, and see what a defensive little madam she was being. There were more ways than one of being a snob, and she was acting the part brilliantly . . .

"My uncle was taken to hospital a couple of weeks ago," John said abruptly. "We thought he was going to die, but he didn't, though he's slightly paralysed down one side of his body, and his speech is affected."

Carrie was so shocked that she couldn't speak for a moment, and then the words came out in a rush. She realised John was still holding her hand, but it was gripping hers now, and she remembered the love he had for his uncle. She felt a surge of compassion and remorse, and moved nearer to him.

"Oh John, I'm so sorry. If only you'd let me know."

"I should have done, but everything seemed to happen so fast. He recovered from the stroke quite well, and we got him home again after a week, but then Mrs Ryan started her tricks."

"Mrs Ryan?" Carrie recalled the lady-friend with such a proprietary eye on the Travis household. "What does she have to do with it?"

"Everything," John said grimly. "She's been doing her best to persuade Uncle Oswald to change his Will in her

199

favour for all the companionship and attention she's given him in recent months. She wanted everything, the house, the boat, what money he had."

Carrie's eyes were round with outrage. "But it should all be yours when he – "

"Yes. When he dies," John retorted. "But hopefully, he's not going to die, and neither has he lost his senses. In fact, she's done him quite a good turn, and opened his eyes to the grasping woman she really is."

He seemed to be talking almost to himself now, and Carrie could see all this had been a shock to him. She spoke tentatively.

"But as long as he saw sense and didn't change his Will – " she began.

"That's just it. It turned out he never made a Will at all. He never thought it necessary, since there were only the two of us, and I was his natural nephew. But Mrs Ryan also has a nephew who's a lawyer, and says she has certain rights, since the two of them have been occasionally co-habiting. He'll contest any claim I make when the time comes, to be sure she gets a share at least."

Carrie blushed to the roots of her hair, as she realised what John meant.

"So what's happened now?"

"What's happened now is that the lady is away visiting friends for a few days, and a lawyer has been to the house today to draw up Uncle Oswald's Will. It's watertight, and everything will come to me as he always intended, and she won't get her greedy little hands on anything but the rose bush in the front garden that he's left to her. And I shall take great pleasure in digging it up when the time comes."

"But that won't be for a very long time, I hope," Carrie murmured.

He looked blank for a moment, and then nodded.

"Of course, because such an event will mean that Uncle Oswald's dead. I hope that day is far away too, but I fear he'll never be the same as he was."

"What a sad day this is turning out to be," Carrie said quietly. "First, Elsie's granpa's burying, and now this. I'm so very sorry, John."

"So am I forgiven?" he asked, his eyes slowly focusing on her again.

She moved into his arms, and he breathed in the scent of her wet hair as if it was nectar.

"Of course."

She leaned her head against him, feeling the strength of his arms around her, and wishing they could stay like this for ever. But their closeness was interrupted by a quick rap on the door, and then Cook poking her head around it.

"You'd best say good-bye to your young man, Carrie. Miss Helen's bell has been ringing for this past five minutes."

She struggled out of John's arms at once. She had vaguely heard a bell ringing from the panel in the kitchen wall, but assumed that someone else would be answering it. Naturally, if it was Miss Helen's bell, it would be summoning her. She felt her nerves jump.

"Come and see me again when you can," she whispered hurriedly. "And give your uncle my best wishes."

"I will. I haven't told you everything yet, and I wanted to warn you," he said. "But it's not important, and you'd better get upstairs and see what Miss Barclay wants."

There was no time to be curious and demand to know what he needed to warn her about. She tore up the stairs to Miss Barclay's room, knowing she'd be in for an ear-wigging at the very least. By the time she got there, she had a stitch in her side to rival Ma's. She held on to it, willing the stinging to subside, as she rushed inside the luxurious room.

*   *   *

201

"Where have you been all this time, girl?" Helen raged at once. "I was considerate enough to give you extra time off, and you abuse my kindness by taking half the day. You'll forfeit your free times for the rest of the week to make up for it."

"Oh, but I'll need to see that Ma's all right, Miss Helen," Carrie gasped.

Helen moved across the room towards her, and Carrie flinched, anticipating the slap of that surprisingly strong white hand. But it didn't come. Instead, to her surprise, she saw Helen's hands twist around the delicate lace hanky she held, and her face crumpled.

"I needed you, Carrie," she said, her voice suddenly vulnerable. "I needed a sounding-board, and you weren't here."

It was a dubious compliment, and Carrie gulped, tucking a stray lock of hair behind her ear before she was reprimanded for her untidiness. Helen's moods were so changeable, she never knew what to expect. It was true that you had to live in the same house with somebody before you really knew them, she thought. She had never expected the outwardly serene Miss Barclay to be every bit as up and down as her friend Elsie.

"I'm here now, Miss Helen," she said quickly. "Just tell me what I can do for you."

Helen's pretty face grew more sullen. "You can tell me how to get it into my father's head that I don't wish to be married to a gentleman I have no feelings for, that's what you can do! Well? Do you have any bright ideas about that?"

"Is that what he's got arranged for you now?"

"Well, of course it is, ninny," Helen snapped, and then she brushed a hand across her forehead and sat down heavily on her dressing-table stool.

"Oh Lord, I'm sorry, Carrie. I'm completely out of sorts because Papa's given me an ultimatum now. He

202

wants to see me settled, and since the Thornton fiasco, he's decided on a safe and dreary oaf for my future husband. Mr Humphrey de Vere is one of Papa's most important clients, and very well set up, so my future will be assured. He's made an offer for me, and we're to receive him at dinner this evening. If I don't accept his hand, Papa refuses to fund me for the entire season next year. I shall be obliged to wear this year's frocks at balls and soirées and I shall be a figure of fun." Her voice had risen despairingly, but she stopped sharply. "Are you laughing at me, you insolent girl?"

"Of course not," Carrie said, trying to compose her face. But what a fuss it was, over having to wear last year's frocks . . . some folk never knew when they were well off. New frocks of any sort would be a bonus for the likes of Miss Carrie Stuckey!

And how dare the haughty miss be so concerned over a few bolts of material, when other folk were going hungry . . . her mirth changed to anger, and then dissipated as she saw the genuine distress in Helen's eyes.

"The awful de Vere simply repulses me, Carrie, with his great fat stomach and the stench of those horrid cigars he smokes. And the thought of having to endure the intimacies of the marriage bed with such a man fills me with horror."

"Well, haven't you told your father how you feel?" Carrie asked, quite able to understand and sympathise with such feelings.

"He won't listen. He thinks it's a good match, and I should be very grateful for the chance to live the gracious country life. He lives even farther afield than the horrid Mr Thornton, miles from anywhere. But I shall hate it! I love the town, and I shall positively *loathe* living in the country with all those beastly insects and animals and nothing to look at but trees. And so will you," she added in passing.

Carrie's heart leapt. *"Me?"*

"Yes, parrot, *you*," Helen said irritably. "You don't think I would contemplate leaving here without you by my side, do you? As my personal maid, of course you would accompany me. So if you hate the idea as much as I do, you must think of a way of helping me to change Papa's mind. Now, you may leave me while I lie down and rid myself of my miserable head-ache. Draw the curtains and go away and put your thinking-cap on. You people are far more devious than we are, so I shall be relying on you."

Carrie tightened her lips. Young ladies had such pretty manners when they were at their social best, she thought savagely, but could be as rude as old Harry when it suited them. And most of the time they never even noticed it.

She swished the curtains across the bedroom windows and went out of the room noiselessly. She had plenty to think about, and the most important was to find a way of changing Mr Barclay's mind from marrying off his daughter to the oafish Mr Humphrey de Vere.

Carrie remembered him, and she didn't like him either. On the several occasions she had seen him at the house, he had looked her over in a way that seemed to have stripped her of her clothes. She shivered, knowing she wouldn't trust him as far as she could throw him . . . and she certainly had no intention of moving out of the city to live in a country house where any young servant girl would be at his mercy.

She slipped upstairs to her attic room to drag a comb through her still-bedraggled hair. But by then, there was a gleam in her eyes, and a daring plan was beginning to take shape in her mind. Not that she was at all sure if she would risk trying to pull it off, but if it worked, it would put Miss Helen Barclay into her debt once and for all.

Chapter 12

Carrie timed her plan carefully. She knew exactly when dinner would be over that evening, and when the gentlemen retired to the den to drink their port and smoke their horrible cigars, while the ladies sat drinking coffee in the drawing-room awaiting their reappearance.

It was a ritual that the gentry rigidly observed, Carrie had once told Elsie grandly. And Elsie had snorted and said it was no wonder the upper classes got so bored with one another if they hardly ever got together, and it explained why they were so stiff and starchy when they did.

The ritual would be followed as usual that evening, and when the group met once again, the Barclay parents would tactfully leave Mr Humphrey de Vere and their daughter alone at the far side of the long drawing-room room while he made his marriage proposal. And they fully expected their dutiful daughter to accept.

By now, Carrie knew that Helen had raged a tearful protest in her mother's boudoir, but all to no avail.

"She won't hear of my turning him down," Helen almost wept as Carrie tried vainly to keep her still long enough to do up the row of buttons at the back of her evening gown. "If I do, she'll wash her hands of me, I know she will."

Carrie was becoming exasperated by now. "Why don't you find somebody you fancy yourself then? It ain't impossible to find some fellow who ain't a chinless wonder, is it?"

"It's all right for you." Helen scowled in a way that would have her Mama throwing up her hands in despair. "It makes little difference what kind of fellow you find to take care of you, but things are different in our circle."

"Yes, ma'am," Carrie said woodenly, trying to keep her face straight at the sheer snobbishness of the remark.

Helen didn't even notice, which just went to show something or other, Carrie thought vaguely, too wrapped up in her own plan to waste too much time on the complaints of her silly young mistress. She had always envied and admired Helen Barclay so much, but sometimes she wondered just what she had in her noddle for brains. But the plan was necessary, for herself, as well as for Helen.

"How do I look?" Helen said finally, twirling around for compliments. "I wish I dared go down looking as plain as a pikestaff, and that might put Mr de Vere off for good!"

"You know you could never look plain," Carrie said, knowing that this was the expected answer, and being rewarded by the quick flash of a smile.

She was so transparent, Carrie thought. How could any gent with eyes halfway open not know she was repulsed by him? And how could any gent with any gumption at all still want such a reluctant bride? And how could any so-called caring parent keep trying to force her into such an arrangement? Respectability seemed to be all as far as the Barclay parents were concerned, and providing a suitor had no breath of scandal attached to him, he would do.

Indignation on Helen's behalf overcame the growing derision she felt far too frequently for the girl these days. Even if her own eyes were opened to the ways of the gentry now, and she admitted that she despised more than one of them, she still felt a sense of loyalty towards Helen, and not for the world would she see her condemned to a loveless marriage. Her resolve hardened.

Although she was under curfew not to leave the house for a week, she could still find out how Ma fared through Billy, and she had reconciled herself to that fact. And tonight it was useful to eat the evening meal in the kitchen with the rest of the servants, and to drop in the necessary bits of poison during the usual kitchen gossip.

Cook piled her plate with sliced mutton and cabbage, and Jackson relayed the fact that Mr de Vere had arrived in his carriage, looking every bit the swell, and that they would probably be hearing a special announcement very soon. Carrie gave a snort that was worthy of Elsie.

"I'm sorry for the poor young lady then," she said, more coolly than she felt as all eyes turned towards her. Cook almost dropped the serving spoon and Jackson spoke sharply.

"It's not your place to feel sorry for your betters, miss, and you had better explain yourself."

"You had too," Cook said. "Bless my soul, how could anyone feel sorry for that lovely young lady, with her Ma and Pa doting on her the way they do?"

"Well, so they might, but I wouldn't want my Pa pressing me to marry a gent with an eye for the servants, and a ready hand for a quick fumble whenever he gets the chance."

She knew she had gone too far when she heard the scrape of Mr Jackson's chair as he got to his feet and came around the table towards her. As he yanked her up by the scruff of her neck, she gave a screech of protest.

"We don't want any of that talk here, my girl," he shouted, as the skivvies and the other maids looked on in astonishment. The younger ones giggled nervously, not sure what to make of it all.

"Why not, if it's true?" Carrie yelled back. Her face

had gone a fiery red, because as far as she knew, none of it was true – but she'd wager a pound to a lump of manure that it was so. She'd seen the gleam in old de Vere's eyes too often to doubt it.

Cook spoke up indignantly. "Has he been trying it on with you, duck?"

"I'm not saying no more," Carrie muttered, keeping her eyes downcast as befitted a shame-faced servant. "I just wish Miss Helen wasn't being pushed into marriage with him, that's all. And I wish more than anything that she didn't expect me to go with her when she goes."

There was silence in the kitchen while they all digested her words and put their own interpretation on them. After a moment, Jackson patted her back awkwardly.

"I daresay you'll feel differently about things if you're offered a position with the new Mrs de Vere, Carrie. I'm afraid young servants do sometimes have to put up with a modicum of – uh – unwanted attention, but it's a secure post and you'd do well to look after it and do your best to ignore the rest. Now I suggest that we all forget the last few minutes and get on with our meal."

Carrie bent over her plate, her face flushed in triumph. If there were ever questions asked about the lecherous Humphrey de Vere, then everyone here would back her up . . . she hardly knew why she was going to these lengths, but it seemed like a good piece of insurance.

Much later, she went to the den where Helen's father was preparing to entertain his guest with port and cigars after a sumptuous dinner. Her heart pounding, she tapped gently on the door and went inside, and Mr Barclay looked around in some surprise.

"Yes? What is it?"

"Sir, I'm told to say there's a message for you downstairs."

"Well, why couldn't you have brought it with you?

Oh, never mind," he said irritably, when she stood in apparently dumb confusion. "Out of my way, girl, and I'll be back directly, de Vere," he threw over his shoulder.

Carrie stood where she was, her heart thudding madly now. The large man blew smoke rings into the air, where they hung in blue circles above his head. In no way could they be compared to angels' haloes, Carrie thought darkly, as she saw his oily smile.

"What do they call you, my pretty?" de Vere asked.

"I'm called Carrie, sir. I'm Miss Helen's maid," she said with a perky bob, the way she had been taught to do. Instead of leaving, she moved into the room, and for such a large man it seemed to take no time at all for him to be beside her.

"Miss Helen's maid, eh?" he said, his eyes calculating. "And should Miss Helen marry, will Miss Helen's maid be accompanying her to her new abode?"

Carrie gritted her teeth at his ingratiating manner. But she had to see this through now, and prayed that Giles Barclay would return soon . . . she simpered and smiled and flirted with her eyes, and saw the instant response. He moved even closer, and she could smell the mixture of cigar smoke and hair oil and scented body lotions on him. It was nearly enough to make her sick.

"I might," she said sweetly.

De Vere gave a sudden laugh, and swung his arm around her waist. She was pulled close to him before she could think what was happening, and it was all so exactly as she had planned it in her mind that it all but stunned her. She could see the sweat on the man's brow now, and hear the quickening of his breathing, and she suddenly panicked, because Mr Barclay must surely return at any second now, ready to denounce him for playing with his daughter's affections, and showing him the door.

*   *   *

"What the devil's going on here?" Helen's father suddenly roared from the doorway.

De Vere dropped his hold on Carrie as if she was a red-hot poker, and she almost fell. She turned tearfully towards Mr Barclay, and rushed towards him.

"Sir, thank goodness you've come. He – he –"

"Good God, man, what kind of riff-raff are you employing here?" she heard de Vere snap, as cold as ice. "The scruff threw herself at me, promising that if things go according to plan between us, and she accompanies your daughter to my home, she'll give me her favours."

Carrie felt as if her heart plummeted to her boots as she gaped in horror at the man. She should have known such an oaf would be up to this. It probably wouldn't be the first time he'd had to get himself out of a sticky situation. She spoke shrilly.

"*No!* It wasn't like that at all! It was all his doing – "

Giles didn't even look at her. "Don't be ridiculous, girl. No gentleman of Mr de Vere's stature would associate with the likes of you, especially not in my house. You're dismissed. Get out of my sight and back to your hovel."

"Oh, please *no!* You can't do that!" she said in a panic.

She had thought this plan to help Miss Helen out of a jam was so clever, and all she had done was to get herself dismissed, losing the wages her family so badly needed, and probably doing herself out of any other position among the Clifton families, since word would certainly get amongst them all as fast as lightning.

"May I put in a plea for mercy on the girl's behalf, Giles?" To her utter humiliation, she heard Humphrey de Vere speak up. "Perhaps I was a little hasty about her intentions, and it could be that she merely stumbled against me, and my arm naturally went out to save her from falling. If Helen is quite satisfied with her services, then let's give the girl the benefit of the doubt. It will be strange enough for Helen to enter her new life, without having to find a new maid to suit."

He was smooth and plausible, but it was as clear as daylight to Carrie that he'd got an eye to the main chance now, and thought there was a fine bit of kitchen sport to be had with his new wife's personal maid in the future. She looked down at the floor, wondering how the devil she had ever got herself into such a fix.

"Are you quite sure about this, sir?" Giles Barclay said, frowning.

"Quite sure. Shall we say no more about it?"

Carrie looked from one to the other. "Can I go then?" she said in a cracked voice.

"For now," Giles said coldly. "Though, since the message you mentioned seems to have miraculously disappeared, I intend getting to the bottom of this later."

She fled from the room, her cheeks scarlet, and furious with herself for ever thinking she could outwit someone of de Vere's type. And how anybody could ever think Giles Barclay a doting father for wanting his daughter to marry such a man, she couldn't think. Money overcame every other consideration, apparently.

She reached her own room, still shaking at making such a mess of things. She hadn't done a single thing to help Helen, and she had put herself under dire suspicion in Giles Barclay's mind, and left herself wide open to the unwelcome attentions of Humphrey de Vere. She had one other option, of course. She could simply quit the job of her own accord . . . but that would be another disaster.

A long while later, she jumped as the bell above her bed rang out imperiously. She leapt up too soon, feeling her head spin. Helen required her, and her nerves were at fever pitch, knowing only too well now what the outcome of this evening's dinner had been. The gent would have

211

made his proposal, and Helen would have felt bound to accept, because of her father's ultimatum. And Carrie was probably in for a blistering tirade now.

She hadn't bothered to undress yet, and she tidied herself quickly and ran down the stairs to her mistress's bedroom. To her astonishment, Helen was waltzing around the room with a satin cushion held to her chest, and laughing out loud before she flopped onto the bed.

"Is everything all right, miss?" Carrie said uneasily, wondering if she'd lost her senses.

"Everything's wonderful, you clever girl! How on earth did you do it?"

"I don't know what you mean." Carrie hedged.

Helen sat up again, her eyes sparkling.

"Of course you know. You made him lark about, and roused Papa's suspicions, didn't you? I know it was you, so don't deny it. In fact, rumours of his little philanderings were the only things Papa was doubtful about, but he chose to ignore it because of de Vere's wealth and connections."

"I see," Carrie said, wondering if all the gentry were so obsessed with money that they'd sell their souls as well as their daughters for it.

"Anyway, apparently the old fool started drinking far too much port after you left them, and began bragging about the way the little servant girls couldn't keep their hands off him. Papa simply *hates* such talk, and asked him point-blank if there had ever been any previous trouble on that score. And can you *imagine* what he said?"

Carrie suspected she was a little tipsy herself to be putting such vulgar emphasis on her words. But perhaps in the circumstances, it was understandable. She shook her head, but Helen didn't seem to expect an answer and went on, almost hysterically.

"He said there had once been an incident, when a little *peccadillo* was involved, but no-one could ever prove

212

anything. Since he and my father were both men of the world, he was sure Papa would understand, and he couldn't see that it could make any difference to his intentions regarding myself. The *arrogance* of the man! He was so stiff with drink he hardly knew he was saying the very thing to damn himself in Papa's eyes! And Papa was incensed enough to relate it all to Mama and me when he'd sent him packing."

"I take it the wedding's off then?" Carrie said mildly.

Helen looked at her blankly, and then went off into peals of laughter.

"Oh Carrie, you're rich, you really are! Of *course* the wedding's off, and both Mama and I have persuaded my father that it's not the end of the world if I don't marry immediately. I'm not exactly on the shelf, am I?"

Carrie felt her face break into a smile for the first time during that terrible evening, seeing the glowing beauty of the girl.

"I should say not, Miss Helen. And I'm ever so glad, I really am. He was never the one for you, and I'm sure you'll find the right one some day."

She stopped in embarrassment, realising she was playing the maiden aunt, and not too sure how her unpredictable mistress was going to take it. But it seemed that nothing could upset Miss Barclay tonight.

"And you'll also be glad we're not going to live in that appallingly isolated country estate he calls home," she said gaily. "I couldn't make Papa tell me everything that happened, but I strongly suspect I've got you to thank for it all, Carrie, and I shan't forget it."

"That's all right. Just as long as nobody thinks I was trying to lead him on on my own account." She shuddered as she spoke, and Helen gave an understanding nod.

"I know you didn't, and I told Papa so. Anyway, why would you want to flirt with an old *roue*, when you've got such a nice young man of your own?" she said smilingly.

"I hope you'll find one just as nice," Carrie said at once, assuming that an old *roue* was a term of disrespect.

"So do I. Now then, while you're here, you may unfasten these wretched buttons at the back of my gown, since I've no idea where my button-hook has gone." She stretched luxuriously as she spoke, twisting around on the bed so that Carrie could attend to the long row of buttons.

"Oh, it's going to be such a lovely day tomorrow, and you may consider your curfew over, Carrie. And next week you may change your time off to the mornings, because you and I are going onto the Downs during the afternoons for the duration of the Christmas Fair," she announced next.

"It surely can't be setting up already," Carrie exclaimed. "It's still three weeks until Christmas."

"I daresay the stallholders want to take our money," Helen said, her spirits suddenly beginning to flag after the heady events of the evening. "There's a poster somewhere here that you may take with you if you like. Leave me now, for if I don't get into bed soon I shall fall asleep right where I am."

She waved a slender hand towards her little desk beneath the window as she spoke, and Carrie picked up the rolled-up poster advertising the thrills and excitements of the Christmas Fair. It would be something to read aloud to the other maids if they'd finished their own tasks, and since she didn't intend gossiping on any other topic, it might help her to unwind from this extraordinary day.

She was glad to find her room still empty. She liked solitude, and she didn't get a lot of it. She undressed with

214

a shiver in the chilly December evening, relieved beyond measure that she was still employed, that Giles Barclay had been canny enough to get rid of the unsuitable old rogue, and that he had finally seen sense regarding his daughter's future.

Carrie gave an enormous sigh of relief on all counts as she pulled her nightgown over her head and slid inside the cold bedcovers. She wrapped them around her as tightly as possible up to her chin, while still managing to keep her arms outside to unroll the advertising poster.

She glanced down the usual enticements. There would be stalls selling produce and privately made toys of high quality; there would be fowls and geese on offer to the highest bidder to be kept cool in ice-boxes or cold stores for the Christmas period; there would be the usual fair travellers and gypsies, and perhaps the fortune-teller who had told her she was one of fortune's favoured ones, and that Elsie's fortunes would change within the year.

She had also made Elsie shiver when she had turned up the death card . . . Carrie shuddered. Elsie's predictions had already come true, even though she had said herself it was highly likely that old Granpa Miller was going to expire at any minute. The wonder was that he had ever managed to survive so long.

She tried to recall the more pleasant things from the fortune-telling, and her mouth curved into a smile, as she remembered turning up the three red cards ending with the Knave, who could be interpreted as Jack, her true lover . . .

Her eyes had blurred a little, remembering that heady summer day, and then they came sharply into focus again as she read the important announcement at the foot of the poster.

ADDED ATTRACTION.

We are honoured to welcome BIG LOUIE, the CEL-EBRATED INTERNATIONAL BARE-KNUCKLE FIGHTER, who has proved his SUPERIORITY in all parts of the country and France. BIG LOUIE will demonstrate his SKILLS with his sparring part-ner, and WILL THEN TAKE ON ALL-COMERS. If anyone can beat THE SHINING STAR OF PRIZE-FIGHTING, there will be a PURSE OF FIVE GUINEAS. All contestants to make them-selves known at the ringside.

Carrie knew then exactly what John Travis had wanted to warn her about that day. He knew she would be going to the fair some time, and he was going to set himself up to fight with this Big Louie. She felt a swift sharp fury from somewhere deep in her gut. He knew how she felt about fighting, but it seemed that her wishes and feelings didn't come into it.

From the size of the purse, she guessed that Big Louie and his promoters were pretty confident that no-one was going to get the better of him. John would definitely end up bloodied and hurt, and it would be his own fault. Her eyes smarted at the sheer lunacy of it, and she cursed her vivid imagination that had him practically dead and buried already.

Minutes later she heard the clatter of footsteps on the stairs, and she hastily blew out her candle and stuffed the poster beneath her pillow, feigning sleep. The last thing she wanted to do now was listen to idle prattle. She was just too angry.

By the following afternoon she had made up her mind. Now that her curfew was over, she would call in and see Ma and check on Elsie, and then walk up Bedminster Hill to see how Uncle Oswald fared. In reality, she was going to tackle John about his intentions.

"It's no business of yours, girl," Ma reminded her, when she explained why she couldn't stay long. "If a man's of a fighting inclination, you'll not be the one to change him. Our Wilf's the same, more's the pity, but I'd rather that than have a primrose around the house."

"It's not the same," Carrie said, scowling. "Our Wilf fights in self-defence. Fighting for money's shameful."

Elsie hooted, well-established in the house now, Carrie saw, with a stab of jealousy.

"You won't be saying that if he earns enough to buy you things, will you? Like those beads around your neck – they didn't grow on a tree, did they?

Ma looked at her sharply, and Carrie coloured, forgetting she had worn the beads to brighten up her plain working frock a little. Even though they were black, they glittered attractively.

"Miss Helen gave them to me," she said. "Don't worry, I didn't take them! I'm not that daft, and anyway, now that I can see you're better Ma, I'm off up Bedminster Hill. If there's time, I'll call in again on my way back."

"There's no need. I'm going to take a walk with Elsie this afternoon. The doctor says I should be getting more fresh air," Ma said.

So she had seen the doctor again, and Carrie was overcome with guilt because she'd fully intended seeing him herself, and she'd completely forgotten it. But Elsie seemed to be well in control now.

"Don't you have to get back to work to pay the rent on your own place?" she asked her pointedly.

Elsie shrugged. "In a day or two. Your Billy's gone with Wilf to clear out Granpa's stuff for me, so your Ma and me are going down to supervise."

"A fat lot of fresh air you'll get down by the river," Carrie retorted.

She knew she must be out of sorts to be reacting so badly. She should be glad that Ma and Elsie were there to bolster up one another, and that her menfolk were doing all they could for Elsie in her time of trouble. But it still seemed to shut her out.

By the time she paused for breath as she toiled towards the top of Bedminster Hill, she was telling herself she was a miserable pig to think that way. Elsie would soon get tired of playing the dutiful daughter in somebody else's house and long for her freedom again, and she shouldn't begrudge her these comfort days.

She paid attention to her footing as she reached the top of the steep hill. This morning's sharp frost still glazed the grass underfoot, and she didn't want to go head over heels back down again. But once on firm roadway, she walked more energetically towards the Travis house, knowing there wouldn't be too much time to spare. She had no idea whether or not John would be there, but there had been no sign of his boat at the top end of the river when she had scanned the waterway.

She paused at the gate of the house, suddenly nervous. It was only the second time she had been here, and the first time she had come unannounced and unchaperoned. In Helen Barclay's circle, such a thing would be frowned upon, but in the freer world of the lower classes, it hardly raised an eyebrow. It seemed to put them all into a different kind of setting, Carrie thought, and she knew which she preferred after all.

There was a welcome curl of smoke rising from the chimney of the house, and she pushed open the gate more cheerfully. There was no backing out now. She'd come this far, and once she'd seen how his Uncle Oswald fared, she was going to have it out with John.

He opened the door himself, his eyes widening as he saw her standing there. She was struck as dumb as he for a second, just as if he was an apparition she had never expected to see. And then she recovered herself.

"I've come calling on your uncle," she said abruptly. "It's permitted, I suppose?"

"Of course it is," John said, opening the door wider to admit her. "It's so good to see you, Carrie. I've been thinking about you all day."

I bet you have, she thought cynically. *Wondering how best to tell me you're going to fight BIG LOUIE . . .* as the ludicrous name flashed into her mind she gave him a crooked smile. He took both her hands in his and kissed her on the cheek as she went inside the house. She felt herself flush at the sensation of his skin against hers. His slightest touch could send her senses reeling . . . but she intended keeping a tight hold on them today.

"Has your uncle taken to his bed?" she said in a husky voice.

"That he has not, my dear," she heard a voice call out from the parlour. "And if that boy don't bring you to see me instead of keeping you standing on the doorstep, I shall come and fetch you myself."

John gave a short laugh. "As you can hear, he's lost none of his spirit, Carrie. Come and see him, while I make some tea."

"Are you acting as nursemaid then?" she said in some surprise.

"Only for today. We have a daily woman to take care of things and clean the house," he tactfully avoided saying it was to take care of his uncle, Carrie noted, and wished she hadn't used the word nursemaid. "She's had to go to a family wedding today, so I'm in charge."

"Then Mrs Ryan has gone for good?" she murmured low enough so that Uncle Oswald wouldn't hear.

"Thankfully, yes," John said.

She followed him into the parlour, where the older man sat in a high-backed chair, a stick at his side. He didn't

219

look ill, and it was only when he began to speak that Carrie could see how his face was twisted to one side a little, and how some of his words were slurred. She bent to kiss him, hoping it was the correct thing to do in the circumstances.

"I'm so glad to see you're not bed-bound," she said, to cover her embarrassment. "I didn't know what to expect."

He chuckled, with only the smallest trickle of spittle at the corner of his mouth.

"I'm not ready for my wooden box yet, girl, but it does my old eyes a power of good to see you. That boy of mine should have informed you earlier, but he took to worrying about me and my one-time lady-friend – I daresay you know all about that by now, so I don't need to explain it all, do I?"

"No," she said, a little taken aback by his frankness. "And I'm sorry."

"You needn't be. There's better men than me that's been taken in by a pretty woman, my duck. I'm not the first, and I won't be the last, but there's no harm done, that's the main thing."

By that, Carrie assumed that John had got everything sorted out with the lawyers, and that the greedy Mrs Ryan didn't have a chance of getting her hands on any Travis money or property.

He came back into the parlour with a tray of tea and biscuits then, and Carrie jumped up and took it from him. It was obvious that she couldn't expect him to leave his uncle alone for the length of time it would take to escort her home today, and she knew she couldn't start a heated argument in front of the old man. It would be enough to start off another stroke.

But Uncle Oswald was cannier than she supposed, and when he'd slurped his biscuits into his tea and noisily finished off the rest of it, he gave an artificial yawn.

"I was about to take a little rest when you came, my dear," he said glibly. "If you don't mind, I'll take myself off to my bed and leave you two to talk together. I get tired easily these days."

"Of course I don't mind," she said. "But I'll come and see you again."

"I hope you will, especially at Christmastime. I miss my dear old Annie most of all then, and it'll be good to have a female voice about the place again."

She watched as John helped him to his feet, and saw how heavily he leaned on his nephew. Through an open door, she glimpsed a narrow bed, and guessed that the old man slept downstairs now, to save him climbing the stairs. She felt a lump in her throat, remembering how active Oswald Travis had seemed on that first day she had seen him, strong and upright . . . and she shivered, thinking how quickly a person could be changed by circumstances.

When John came back to the parlour, he shut the door firmly behind him and came to sit beside her on the settle. Her hands were clenched tightly in her lap, and she saw that he was grim and unsmiling. Perhaps his uncle was worse than she thought, and if so, this seemed hardly the time for griping . . . but John said it all for her.

"It was kind of you to come and see him, Carrie, but I suspect that wasn't the only reason for this visit."

"Oh?" she said, suddenly perverse. "And what other reason could there be, I wonder? Aside from the fact that we *are* supposed to be walking out, so it might just occur to you that I'd like your company now and then."

"And you'd also like to hog-tie me to your petticoats and tell me not to attend the Christmas Fair on the Downs, wouldn't you? And in particular, not to set myself up as a target for Big Louie."

"Perhaps you could set yourself up as a clairvoyant instead," she said sarcastically.

"Are you going to tell me that's not the reason you

came here today?" he demanded. "You'll have seen the posters by now, and you're here to warn me off."

"Just like you tried to warn me that you intended contesting this big oaf, whether I liked it or not!"

"And you don't like it," he stated.

"How perceptive of you."

"Not at all. It's written all over you in petty little narrow-minded letters."

She gasped. Things weren't going at all the way she had expected. She didn't expect him to be a lap-dog, and nor would she want him that way, but a little respect for her feelings wouldn't come amiss.

"It's degrading – " she began.

"It's necessary," he snapped. "There's little money coming in from the boat trippers at this time of year, but I can still act the ferryman, since folk will always be wanting to cross the river from one side to the other. And now there's a daily woman to be paid for to look after Uncle Oswald. I don't begrudge a penny of it, but the money's got to be found, and if I can earn five pounds by my fists, then I shall damn well do it, and no piece of skirt is going to tell me otherwise."

Carrie was outraged and insulted by his words. But at the same time she was shamed by his reasoning. She bit back the furious reply that as far as she was concerned she was never going to tell him anything ever again.

"Well?" John said. "Has the cat got your tongue?"

That did it.

"You're impossible!" she raged. "The next time I come to see your uncle, I hope you're somewhere on the water like the rest of the river scum."

She slammed out of the house, knowing she was acting like a hoyden, and fully aware that she'd as good as told him she had every intention of coming here again. But it would be to see his uncle, not *him*.

222

She went back down Bedminster Hill, slipping and sliding on the glassy surface, thinking it highly unlikely that he would ever want to see her again. Their relationship had been damned from the start. And a good riddance too, she thought defiantly, dashing the furious tears out of her eyes.

Chapter 13

Wilf was developing muscles he never knew he had since starting his job on the railway. Being part of a navvy's gang was boring and tedious. His section consisted mainly of keeping a constant check on sleepers and rails, hauling the heavy stones away from the track and shoring up the banks to ensure that nothing endangered the smooth running of the trains to and from Paddington.

There was the added chore of signal-greasing to attend to now that the colder weather was here. It was also important to see that the points didn't seize up to cause a train to remain in a siding, while the fare-paying passengers slowly froze inside.

He didn't find it a rewarding job, and it had none of the thrill of fashioning a raw piece of wood into an article of perfection for people to admire and cherish. But he had managed to find his own outlet on that score. It had come about quite accidentally, when one of the table legs in the foreman's office had splintered and collapsed.

Wilf had offered to make a new leg, and had shaped it and stained it so well that nobody could tell the difference between the new and the old.

The foreman had been impressed and wanted to know how Wilf came to be so adept with his hands. The outcome was that he'd asked Wilf to make a doll's house for his young daughter for Christmas, providing him with wood and tools, and giving him after-hours access to a small workshop at the back of the station.

It was a task that was saving his sanity, he told Nora on their next clandestine meeting.

"I never knew how much I was missing being a craftsman," he said, flexing his fingers as if he held the polished wood between them. Nora gave an indulgent laugh, snuggling up to him in complete privacy behind the drawn curtains of her father's carriage.

"I do believe you think more of caressing that old wood than me," she teased him.

He immediately assured her by words and action that it wasn't the case, and when she leaned back, flushed from the ardour of his kisses, he spoke ruefully.

"Nothing could compare to the softness of your skin, my love, but I don't deny that there can be something quite erotic in the satiny curves and scents of the wood. I think my Pa feels the same, though he wouldn't have the words to say so," he commented.

"But you do," she said.

Wilf grinned. "Only since knowing you. 'Tis my brother Frank who's gifted with the gab, not me. Maybe you bring out a bit of the poet in me, though it would be as well not to let the navvy gang hear me say so."

"Do you hate it so much, Wilf?" Nora asked.

"Not so much, especially with the work the foreman's put my way. The doll's house is coming on a treat, and with the bits of wood left over, I aim to make some small furniture for the little maid as well." He found it hard to keep the enthusiasm out of his voice.

Nora spoke almost wistfully. "You know, I had everything a child could want in my nursery, except the one thing that seemed to be overlooked. I never had a doll's house. Strange, isn't it?"

Wilf ran an expert hand over the planed and polished roof of the small house. It was almost completed now. The foreman's daughter would have it by Christmas, and

225

he could just imagine a small girl's delight at playing with it.

He eased his back, deciding to call it a day. It was long after his working shift, and the day on the tracks had been hard, with the points frozen and the rails starting to be iced up. Chipping away at long lengths of rail for the trains to steam safely in and out of the station had seemed the most futile, though necessary of jobs. It had been a relief to come inside the relatively wind-free interior of the small workshop when the rest of the gang had gone home.

The candlelight threw soft shadows onto the almost-finished doll's house, and with a feeling of satisfaction, Wilf covered it with a cloth, and turned to his second project. This one was being fashioned with all the love and expertise he could put into it. He eyed it dispassionately, trying to see it through Nora's eyes, and had no doubt that she would adore it. How could she not, since it was a tiny replica of her own home?

There hadn't been the time nor the wood available to make a fancy affair like the first one. But this was a labour of love, not a toy for a child, and he was sure his Nora would know the difference. Besides, it would be easier for her to keep his gift away from her father's prying eyes. This one would fit easily into Ma's bread bin.

He longed to do a little more to it, but he knew Ma got anxious if he was away too long after his shift had finished. It was as if she feared that one of the great iron monsters that steamed down from Paddington was going to mow him down on the tracks. Besides, he'd done enough for one day. He put Nora's house carefully on a high shelf and covered it, blew out the candle and locked the workshop securely before going home.

He realised he was whistling, and that he was walking with a surprisingly jaunty air, considering he was nearly dead on his feet. But doing the job you really wanted to do gave you more incentive than all the repetitive jobs

226

in the world. Frank had clearly discovered that, from the cheerful scrappy notes they had received from him. *Some day*, Wilf thought, *some day . . .*

"I suppose you'll want some time to yourself for Christmas," Helen Barclay said carelessly.

Carrie was cautious how she answered. Things had improved enormously since the day she had virtually saved her mistress from what she still referred to as a fate worse than death. But Helen could still be unpredictable at times, and Carrie was getting to know her moods by now.

"Well, I'd like to help Ma with the cooking," she said. Though what kind of a Christmas they were going to have, she couldn't think. Frank wouldn't be there, but Elsie had been invited for the mid-day meal, so they'd be the same as usual in numbers.

The food wouldn't be up to much, though, and there'd be no gift-giving this year. Not that they ever made too much of it, since Ma always reminded them that it was Jesus Christ's birthday, not everybody else's, and they'd all do better to attend church and give thanks for His birth, rather than making merry and filling their bellies with food and ale.

"You're to have the whole day to yourself, Carrie," Helen suddenly said grandly. "You can help your mother in the morning and spend some time with your young man in the afternoon, or whatever you wish. I shan't require you until six o'clock, since we're all invited out for dinner and entertainment at Egerton Hall. I daresay the servants will be having a small evening celebration in the kitchen as usual, so you'll be able to join them once I've finished with you."

Carrie had a job not to stop her mouth from falling open. It was far more than she had dared to hope for. A whole day to herself . . . Ma would be so relieved, and with both herself and Elsie to give a hand, there would still be time to attend morning service.

"I'm very grateful, Miss Helen," she began, but Helen waved her thanks aside.

"Don't get humble, Carrie, it doesn't suit you," she said with a mischievous smile. "You'll pay for the extra time off, of course. And you may begin by forfeiting tomorrow afternoon and accompanying me onto the Downs to see something of the Christmas Fair."

"Yes miss," Carrie said, trying to keep poker-faced.

She might have known there would be strings attached to the generosity. But fairs held as much fascination for her as for everyone else, and she had already slipped across the Downs one morning to see the stalls being set up, and the huge posters announcing the attraction of BIG LOUIE.

She knew that tomorrow was the first of the days when all-comers were invited to pit their wits against the big man. A contestant could challenge BIG LOUIE as often as he dared, and five pounds would be the purse for each and any win. The promoters were clearly confident that there would be none.

And it was only the thought of catching sight of John in action against the fighter and witnessing the indignity and the humiliation of it, that had decided her against going there in the afternoons. That decision was taken out of her hands now.

But at least she had time to tell Ma she wouldn't be going home the next day. Ma was looking bloated in the face now, but it wasn't a healthy look. The doctor had said she was progressing normally, and she was merely having an uncomfortable pregnancy because of her age and the position of the baby. It seemed to satisfy Ma, but Carrie couldn't help being uneasy.

Pa still spent far too much time with his drinking cronies, she thought indignantly, when he should be giving Ma

228

support. But he could never express himself in words, and it wasn't in him to show outward affection. She supposed they had been married too long for Ma to find anything objectionable in his ways.

She was surprised and relieved to find Ma quite perky that afternoon. Elsie had returned home again and was back at work in the markets, and acting wilder than ever, according to Ma.

"Folk have to get over grief in their own way," she said mildly, seeing Carrie's frown.

"I doubt that she's grieving overmuch for Granpa Miller, but she could show a bit of respect. And I don't want to see her ending up in trouble, neither."

She avoided Ma's eyes. If Elsie landed up in the worst kind of trouble that could come to a vulnerable and flighty young girl, then it would be to the Stuckeys that she would inevitably turn for help. The Stuckeys would always be loyal to a friend in need, but Carrie wasn't sure that such a foolish friend qualified for help.

She knew she was being churlish, and more than a mite jealous of the way Ma had seemed to forget her old objections to Elsie, and taken her under her wing. Yes, she *was* jealous, she thought abjectly, and the sooner she rid herself of the feeling, the better.

"I'll try to have a talk with the girl," Ma was saying thoughtfully. "You're quite right, Carrie. There's been no woman to counsel her, so a bit of guidance probably won't come amiss."

Carrie bit her lips, guessing that Elsie could probably tell Ma a thing or two about the ways of men, and particularly those stocky dark young Welshmen. They were the ones who could always put an extra sparkle into Elsie's flirty eyes. And the name of a certain Dewi Griffiths from Cardiff had cropped up more than once in her airy ramblings about the Welsh boyos.

She pushed thoughts of Elsie out of her mind for

229

the present. There were more important things to discuss.

"I shan't be here tomorrow, Ma," she informed her. "But I've got the whole of Christmas Day free until six o'clock, so I'll be here early in the morning to give you a hand. And I've got a surprise for you. Cook says we can have one of the geese hanging in the cold store for our Christmas dinner. I can bring it down the day before."

She'd thought Ma would be so pleased, but she was horrified to see the shine of tears in her eyes. Ma never cried, and she wouldn't give a thank-you for daring to suggest that she was about to cry now. But her voice was full of sadness all the same.

"That's very good of her, Carrie. But 'tis a sad day when a family can't afford to buy their own Christmas bird."

"It's the first time, Ma," Carrie said huskily. "And I promise it will be the last. Things will improve by next year, you'll see."

She had no way of knowing it, and she crossed her fingers behind her back as she spoke. But things must surely improve. Pa would find proper work again, and Wilf's temper would improve. Maybe Frank would come home from the sea a millionaire, and the babby would be fat and healthy and strong, and put a smile on all their faces.

Billy came hurtling indoors, his face red and blotchy. There was a smear of blood on his cheek, his shirt was torn, and his small fists were tight-clenched.

"Have you been fighting, our Billy?" Ma said, her wistful mood vanishing at once.

"I had to," he said shrilly. "They was sayin' bad things about Pa, and about our Frank, and I had to let 'em know they weren't true."

Carrie caught hold of his fiercely stiff shoulders and gave them a shake.

"Slow down, ninny, and tell us what's happened. Who was saying bad things to you?"

230

"Some big boys," he said, wilting now and starting to sniff. "They said our Pa was a drunk, and that our Frank went away to sea to get away from him."

"Oh? And what about me? Didn't they have any ideas on why I left home, seeing as how they seem to know our business so well?" Carrie said mildly, seeing how Ma's face was tightening up, and trying to lessen the tension in the parlour. Billy scowled.

"You're only a girl," he said, implying that she didn't count. Carrie resisted the urge to snap back that until recently, she'd been the only one bringing money into the house. None of that mattered. What mattered was Billy's hurt pride, and the way his tirade seemed to have taken all the stuffing out of Ma.

"So I am," she agreed. "So I'll act the nurse and bathe that poor old cheek of yours."

She hustled him into the scullery where he submitted with squealing protests to her bathing the cheek with cold water, then dabbing it dry. It was only a scratch and had looked worse than it was.

"You'll live," she said dryly.

When they returned to the parlour, Ma was stabbing furiously at one of her rag rugs.

"Miss Barclay's got another bag of old clothes almost ready for me to bring down some time, Ma. At the rate you're working, we'll have more rugs than floors."

She thought Ma was going to snap her head off at that, but thankfully the needle stopped its relentless prodding, and she was rewarded with a weak smile.

"I was half wishing it was your Pa's neck I had under my fingers," she said. "But a fat lot of good that would do to ease things."

"And you don't really mean it," Carrie said quickly. She felt alarmed though. They had always been such a close-knit family, so supportive of each other, yet in recent weeks all the family closeness seemed to be disintegrating.

231

It wasn't only the departure of Frank and herself, and the change of job for Wilf. It was everything.

And it all boiled down to her Pa's pride. It didn't matter how well the rest of them did, if the man of the house couldn't support his family by his own efforts, then he would no longer consider himself a man. She knew it just as surely as if she could hear him bellowing out the words.

"'Course I don't mean it," she heard Ma say with some of her old spirit. "It's just me letting off steam, that's all. And as for they big boys, our Billy, you just tell 'em your Pa's the finest man that ever lived, and our Frank's going to be the world's best sailor."

Carrie saw Billy grin at the boastful words, and wished she could have the same belief in the impossible that she had had when she was eight years old.

She had toyed with the idea of visiting John's uncle again that day. But she had lingered so long at home, hoping Pa would return and that she could give him a hint of what had been happening, that she didn't dare spend any more time away from Clifton. She wondered how Ma would handle it. She'd always found a way around Pa, but when he had the drink in him, he was as surly as any waterfront drunk.

She felt a sliver of fear. The taunts of those boys surely hadn't been true. She didn't see Pa very often now, but she knew he was generally unshaven and unkempt, and he'd always taken a reasonable pride in his appearance.

She remembered how he'd looked on the day of the *Great Britain* launch. So upright and dapper, his pride in his family plain for all to see. He'd been Somebody then. He'd been Sam Stuckey, the master craftsman.

And what did he do now? Menial jobs when he could get them and making cheap coffins for those who couldn't afford to pay for anything better. It was enough to make Carrie want to weep.

232

She tried to push them all out of her mind as she went back up the hill towards Clifton. The roads were frosty underfoot nearly all the time now, and she had to concentrate to keep her footing.

It made a fine old downhill slide when the snow came, and all the Stuckey young 'uns had had their share of hurtling down the slippery curving slopes of Jacob's Wells Hill on their tin trays when it was six inches deep in snow.

She wondered if John Travis had done the same, down Bedminster Hill. It was funny to think of them on opposite sides of the river, probably doing the same things when they were children, and never knowing it.

Carrie paused for breath once she reached the top of the hill. Ahead of her on the Downs, the Christmas Fair stalls were already set up and many of the dealings were under way. She usually loved the fairs, but she viewed tomorrow's visit with Helen Barclay with some anxiety. How embarrassing it would be if John was actually there, and they witnessed his contest with BIG LOUIE . . . in her mind she could still only think of him as if his name was writ large, which only seemed to emphasise the implacability of the man.

She wondered if she should mention John's possible involvement to Helen, and decided against it. If John wasn't on the Downs tomorrow, there would be no need of it. And if he was, perhaps Miss Barclay's delicate sensibilities would keep her well away from such a vulgar display.

To Carrie's horror, she discovered that the prize-fighter's tent was like a mecca for the curious gentry, and it was almost the first place Helen wanted to visit.

"These showmen are such a laugh, Carrie, strutting about their arenas like Roman gladiators. We simply must go and be entertained by this one with the ridiculous name."

Carrie wasn't even sure just what Roman gladiators did, but she took Helen's word for it that BIG LOUIE was going to resemble one. And what about John? Would Helen think he was ridiculous as well . . .? She prayed that he wouldn't be there to humiliate her.

She took her seat beside Helen, sitting as small as she could while the young lady waved and nodded to various friends and acquaintances who were there to witness the spectacle of two men knocking hell out of one another, as Pa would say. It amazed Carrie to see so many well-dressed people there, and it seemed as if this bare-knuckle fighting appealed to their baser instincts.

She remembered Wilf's sneering comments once, when an acquaintance had persuaded him against his better judgement to attend a cock-fight.

"You should have seen the dandies, dressed up to the nines in their velvets and fancy weskits, their eyes glittering with greed as they put their wagers on the poor damn birds. Anything for a bet, it seemed, and the dirtier the fighting the better. And in the evening, they'd all be sitting around their tables, gorging on roast chicken, and never giving a thought to what they'd seen earlier."

Wilf's vehemence had touched her then, and it touched her now, because there was no difference between putting two cock-birds or animals into a ring, and two men. It was all the same, and those who cheered and baited the fighters were every bit as bad as those who performed it.

"For heaven's sake, must you sit there looking so dreary?" Helen said testily. "Put a happier look on your face, or I'll stop your wages for a week."

"I'm sorry, but I'm not sure that I'm going to enjoy this," Carrie muttered.

"You're not afraid of the sight of blood, are you?" Helen said in amusement. "It doesn't really hurt them, you know. These people can withstand any amount of pain."

She was so *stupid*, Carrie thought, in a sudden rage. It

234

was the typical upper-class mentality. If they preferred to look on cruelty as a sport, and chose to pretend that it hurt no-one, then it was perfectly acceptable to enjoy it.

It was exactly how they viewed fox-hunting, with never a moment's thought for the poor hunted fox; and that dreadful Spanish bull-fighting she'd heard tell about. She wondered if Frank would ever go to see such a thing on his travels, and fervently hoped he would not.

She heard Helen's voice sharpen. "Isn't that – yes, I'm sure it is, Carrie! Over there, look, waiting at the ring-side."

"I can't see anybody."

"You must be blind then, for you were looking at him adoringly enough a while back. It's your young man, isn't it? Do you want to go and speak to him for a moment?"

Carrie bit her lip. She'd caught sight of John almost at the same moment as Helen. He was in the front row, at right angles to themselves, in a prime position to leap onto the stage the minute the promoter asked for volunteers to test their skill against BIG LOUIE.

"I don't think so," she said slowly.

Helen stared at her, and then shrugged. "Oh well, you know your own business best. But if some rift between you is the cause of all these sour looks, then the sooner you resolve it, the better. I've no wish to have such a grouch accompanying me."

Carrie seethed at her pompous tone. What would she know of the rifts between lesser folk, and the struggle to simply survive, let alone enjoy life? Even if Helen's worst prospect had happened, and she had been obliged to marry the odious Humphrey de Vere, she'd have lived a life of luxury and ease, and pampered young ladies could usually make do with far less . . .

But she stopped pondering on the selfishness of her betters as the promoter came into the ring to thunderous applause, and announced the first appearance in

Bristol of the much-acclaimed BIG LOUIE, of international fame.

Then the man himself appeared in the ring, a huge handsome giant of a man, clad in a silver cloak, which he discarded at once to reveal a broad bare chest and bulging muscles over knee-length shorts.

"My goodness," Helen breathed. "He's a fine figure of a man and no mistake."

Carrie glanced around and saw than most of the other young ladies were leaning forward in their seats at the spectacle of a man stripped to the waist in honest pursuit of his trade. Those who were less genteel were openly whistling and cheering, including several young maids that Carrie recognised from the Clifton mansions. She grinned, wondering just how Elsie would respond to such blatant male physique, and guessed that she'd probably be here every minute she could get away from her market stalls.

The sparring partner appeared in the ring next. He was somewhat smaller in stature than the star, but worthy of whistles and foot-stamping for all that. Then the fighting began, and it was pretty obvious to anyone with half an ounce of gumption that it was fairly well rigged. No way was the sparring partner going to mar BIG LOUIE's handsome looks.

All the weaving and diving looked very effective, and drew jeers and applause in equal measure from the crowd. But as entertainment it was well worth the entrance fee, and apart from slightly skinned knuckles, it was hardly going to draw any blood. Carrie didn't know whether to feel relieved or cheated.

By the time the sparring partner finally staggered and fell to his knees with BIG LOUIE standing lightly over him, honour was done and the main attraction was all over. The two of them retired to the back of the tent for some minutes to take refreshment, and the promoter took the opportunity of waving a five pound note under the noses of the spectators from the safety of the raised ring.

"Now's your chance, me fine gents, to earn yourselves a fiver, if you've the nerve to step inside the ring with the chap. BIG LOUIE has demonstrated his skills and you've already seen the size of 'im."

At these words, he was obliged to pause for a moment for renewed lewd catcalls and foot-stamping. When the noise had died down, he went on with a smirk.

"I can see BIG LOUIE's attributes ain't been lost on the young ladies in our audience, and I can't say I blame 'em. If I was of the female persuasion, I'm sure I'd be real taken with 'im as well. But as I was sayin', folks – "

"Get on wiv it, you bloody pansy!" came the yells from all corners of the tent. "Let's see if some real fisticuffs can mark that pretty face of his!"

The promoter tried to quieten the sudden hullabaloo by waving his hands about frantically.

"All right, folks! As I was sayin', if there's any challenger here who wants to pit his skills against BIG LOUIE, there'll be a fiver for any man who can beat him."

His confident smile told its own tale of how unlikely a prospect he believed it to be. In seconds, a scuffle at the side of the crowd produced a brawny fellow, pushed forward by his cronies. They shoved him into the ring, where he stripped off his shirt to the roars of approval from the onlookers.

The thick covering of hair on his chest was already glistening with sweat, and Carrie felt sick as she watched him leering at his mates. But at least if he beat BIG LOUIE, that would be the end of it for the day, and there would be no opportunity for John Travis to make his challenge.

But she quickly realised that when the star of the show fought with a challenger, there was no holding back. This was the real thing, and in a very short time the challenger

237

groped his way through the ropes with a bloodied nose and a split cheek, and another had leapt onto the stage to take his place.

There were four of them altogether, and all emerged the loser in a very short time, while BIG LOUIE flexed his muscles and grinned down in triumph at his audience, and hardly looked ruffled at all.

"Good Lord in all His glory!" Helen suddenly exclaimed. "I do believe your young man is going to take up the challenge, Carrie!"

As far as she knew, John hadn't known she was there. But even if he had, she doubted that it would have stopped him. By now, she knew he had a mind of his own, and besides, he had a good reason for wanting that five pounds purse. She bit down her snappy reply, and nodded her head.

"He told me he might," she said hoarsely.

"Well, why didn't you say so? This is even more exciting!" Helen said, sitting up straighter.

Carrie had expected her to look down her nose at actually knowing anyone who would step into a ring and fight with his bare knuckles. But she couldn't miss noting the attentive way Helen watched as John slowly took off his jacket and then his shirt, and revealed his own fine physique, while never taking his own eyes off his opponent.

Carrie saw BIG LOUIE's eyes narrow, as if sensing that this was a different kind of opponent. But how could John possibly win? she thought, realising how desperately she wanted him to.

"Aren't you proud of your young man, Carrie?" she heard Helen say.

Carrie shrugged her shoulders. "I've never thought prize-fighting was anything to be proud of," she muttered. "And I'm surprised that you take such an interest in it, miss. I'd have thought it was far too – too beneath

your idea of amusements, if you'll pardon me for saying so."

She had almost said lower-class, and just managed to
stop herself in time, knowing it might have implied that
she thought Helen's own standards were lowering. She
heard the other girl laugh more indulgently than of late.

"What a child you are, Carrie. Don't you know that
most healthy young ladies find it intriguing to watch a man
flex his muscles and prove his strength? Especially when
one knows the challenger and is urging him on to win!"

She spoke now as though John Travis was her own
special *protégé*, Carrie thought resentfully. Or her own
property . . . at the thought, her heart jumped. The
elegant Helen Barclay surely couldn't be having her lovely
head turned by the sight of a boatman about to do battle
with a bare-knuckle fighter? She simply wouldn't let such
a stupid idea enter her head.

And yet . . . wasn't there something in the way Helen
was admiring John, with her mouth slightly open and her
eyes shining, that reminded Carrie all too well of someone
else? For a second longer she couldn't think who it was.
And then she knew. It was just the way she had seen
Elsie Miller drooling over the boyos at the Welsh Back
Market.

She pushed such unwelcome thoughts out of her mind
at once. But she realised her own mouth was dry too,
because she had never witnessed John's broad chest with
its sprinkling of hair, and the well-developed muscles on
his back and arms. She had been clasped in those arms
and felt the beat of his heart, but she had never seen him
partially unclothed before, and she didn't miss the ripple
of approval from the less inhibited skivvies near the front
of the arena. John was no weakling, that much was certain,
and was attracting a fair amount of female approval. But
as for being a match for BIG LOUIE . . .

"I don't know if I can bear to watch this," she gasped,

239

as a sudden panic overtook her. It had been bad enough when strangers were hurt and bloodied in the ring, but this was her love . . . she felt Helen's vice-like grip on her arm as she made to turn and flee.

"Stay where you are, ninny," Helen snapped. "I've said you'll accompany me this afternoon, and so you shall, unless you want to be sent packing."

So the sunny nature wasn't to be relied on, Carrie thought with a scowl of her own. She had no option but to stay until the fight was over. But she didn't have to watch it. She closed her eyes so tightly they hurt, but she was damned if she was going to witness John's humiliation. She knew it was about to begin by the sudden hush among the crowd as the promoter called for silence, and then rang the starting bell. After that the noise was deafening as they all shouted for their favourite to win, and even Helen Barclay had leapt to her feet along with the rest. And still Carrie sat with hands clenched and eyes closed, until she was yanked to her feet by the other girl.

"You've got to watch him, Carrie! Do you know if he's been trained in the art or is it a natural ability?"

"I've no idea," she muttered, and opened her eyes a fraction, so that the bloodied face wouldn't look so awful through the slits of her vision. But it wasn't John's face that was bloodied . . .

"Kick 'im where it hurts!" the skivvies screamed out to their local hero. "Go on, duck! Give 'im the works!"

"Kick 'im in the bollocks!" roared the less inhibited yokels egging on their man.

As Carrie became fully aware of the proceedings now, she realised it was nearly all over. The champion was staggering, doubled over and visibly almost senseless, while John stood over him like a predator from the jungle.

He was grinning down at his admirers, clearly not averse to such encouragement. One or two of the skivvies threw ribbons into the arena, followed by coins from some of the men as soon as they realised the fight was over. The champ was on his knees and was counted out, and the promoter was holding up John's arm and pronouncing him the winner.

As soon as BIG LOUIE swayed to his feet, the promoter had a hurriedly whispered consultation with the two fighters, and then there was an announcement.

"Ladies and gentleman, BIG LOUIE challenges this here fine opponent to a similar bout each day of the fair, and he's accepted the challenge at a purse of ten pounds if he wins, and nothing if he loses. All other challengers will fight at the usual rate of a fiver a win, which is fair, since no other challenger has ever beaten BIG LOUIE before."

On and on he prattled, but now that the thrill of the fight was over, most of the onlookers were already struggling to get out of the tent. On all sides, Carrie could hear the excited chatter of coming to watch the dashing challenger fight again tomorrow . . . and it wasn't until she was outside in the keen fresh air, that she let out her breath. She hadn't realised how tightly she had been holding it in until she felt how her ribs ached from the effort.

"We must wait and congratulate your young man," Helen said at once.

"Must we?"

"Well, of course! In fact, we shall invite him to take tea with us in the refreshment tent," she went on gaily. "It's my duty to know more about this handsome young man you've set your sights on, and to make sure that I think he's suitable for you!"

Savagely, Carrie knew it was only the thinnest of reasons for wanting to talk to John. And when did Miss Barclay care a fig about her maid's affairs? But since Helen was her employer, and Carrie really needed this job, there wasn't a single thing she could do about it, except rage inside.

Chapter 14

"So when are you and Carrie going to be married, or is that an indelicate question?" Helen asked in a forthright manner, once the three of them were seated in the musty interior of the refreshment tent.

Carrie felt her face blush to the edge of her hair. She and John had hardly discussed the actual question of marriage, and she frequently wondered if it would ever happen, since they were so often at loggerheads.

"As soon as the time is right," he said evenly, not losing his composure for a moment at sitting here with his lady-love and her grand employer. All the while he was attracting every whispered and smiling attention from those who now recognised him as the victor of the famed BIG LOUIE.

"What kind of an answer is that, my dear sir?" Helen laughed. "Tell me just how you expect to know when the time is right!"

"It will be right when Carrie and I decide on it," he said, his smile taking away the sting of his reply.

"*Touché*, and bravo to such gallantry!" Helen said, the smile still on her own lips, but a faint blush stained her own cheeks now.

He was a match for her, Carrie thought suddenly. If she thought to wheedle herself into his affections by her winning ways, she was doomed from the start. He was quite able to converse with those above his station, and while she had felt decidedly awkward at sitting here in her plain brown dress and being so obviously the little maid, she began to hold her chin up high.

He belonged to *her*, not to Miss Barclay, and the haughty young lady had better be fully aware of it! Money didn't buy everything, and it would certainly never buy John Travis. It was as clear as the nose on Helen Barclay's pretty face, and she sat back and watched the other two play out their little charade as if she were no more than an interested observer.

But Helen was soon tiring of this irritating young man who had an answer to all her questions, and not always the subservient answer a young lady might expect, either. She had no time for feeble male creatures, but neither did she care for working-class men who didn't pay her the respect she was due, according to her station in life. And she had a growing suspicion that John Travis was merely indulging her, and curbing his impatience to be alone with his lady-friend.

"I understand that Carrie disapproves of your little hobby, Mr Travis," Helen said sweetly, reducing his expertise to nothing. Carrie's eyes blazed in fury at the insult.

"I'd hardly call it a little hobby, miss. And I never said I disapproved, anyway. Especially after seeing John today, and knowing his reasons for doing it." Her voice trailed away. She still didn't like it, but the other girl had goaded her into denying it, and now John would think she approved of it after all.

She hated the whole mess that she was so innocently getting into, and she hated Miss Helen Barclay most of all.

"True to form, I see. It's easy to change one's mind when one senses a winner, isn't it?" Helen said, still in that sugary tone.

Helen finished her tea daintily, apparently unaware of the way her maid was seething, and ignoring the common noisy draining of the cups all around them in the refreshment tent. Helen had had enough slumming, and got to her feet. She looked directly at Carrie.

"You may accompany me home now, and if your young man wishes, he may come too, and you may then take the rest of the afternoon off. My head is buzzing with all this noise, and I shall spend an hour or so in the quiet of my room."

"Yes, Miss Helen," Carrie murmured, keeping her feelings well under control at that moment.

But she was just as thankful to be away from the raucous clamouring going on all around. She was surprised Helen had stayed so long, among what she would undoubtedly refer to as the riff-raff. The three of them made their way across the normally springy turf of the Downs, well crushed underfoot now by carriage wheels and horses' hooves, and by the boots of the visitors.

Carrie was conscious of the odd trio they made as they walked across the Downs towards the Barclay mansion. They attracted more than a few glances, especially from those who recognised John from his recent show of prowess. They could find little to say to one another once they were away from the fair, and each was secretly glad when they could part company.

"Come upstairs with me a moment, Carrie," Helen ordered. "Your young man can wait for you in the kitchen."

She did as she was asked, knowing she would be expected to unhook buttons and stays, and pull the curtains across the windows so that Helen could rest in a darkened room. The gentry had far less stamina than those who worked for a living, Carrie thought ironically, when she finally ran down the stairs to rejoin John in the kitchen.

She heard his deep laughter before she got there, and when she went inside, it was to see him flexing his arms to make the hard muscles stand out. On either side of him, two of the young kitchen maids were pressing their fingers to the taut flesh in admiration.

"I see it didn't take you very long to establish your credentials," she snapped before she could stop herself.

There was a giggle from Nellie, the youngest skivvy.

"We was only testing his strength, Carrie. 'Tain't every day you meet a prize-fighting gent who's beaten one of the best. We ain't doing no harm, so there's no cause to be jealous."

At these words, John grinned openly at them, seeing Carrie's flashing eyes and her reddened cheeks.

"Carrie knows I only have eyes for her, anyway," he said casually, "but if it upsets her, perhaps in future it's best if you just look but don't touch, girls."

"Don't be ridiculous. I'm certainly not jealous of anyone," Carrie snapped again. "And please don't talk about me as if I'm not here."

He rolled down his shirt sleeves, still with that teasing look in his eyes, but with a firmer line around his mouth now.

"Then please don't treat me as a piece of property. I talk to whom I please, and it makes no difference to me whether it's one of these kitchen girls, or your fancy mistress."

"I daresay it doesn't. They all make up to you anyway, especially after today," she said.

She was behaving badly, and she knew it, but as the black waves of jealousy washed over her, she couldn't seem to stop herself. There was a momentary awkward silence, and then the skivvies were banished from the kitchen by the cook and sent off to buy provisions. The kettle began to sing on the hob, and John was asked directly if he'd like a piece of fruit pie and custard.

"That would be very welcome," he said crisply. "Then Carrie and me had better decide what we're going to do with the rest of the day."

"What do you have in mind?" she asked, thankful that at least he still wanted to spend time with her.

"Do you want to visit your mother?"

It was what she should do, of course. Ma wasn't too good these days, and it was her duty to visit her whenever possible and take a bit of the load off her shoulders. But she did it so often. She seemed to be always tearing between the one place and the other, and hardly knew where her prime duty lay any more, here or at home . . . and she seemed to have hardly any time for herself.

"I'd love to get right away from everybody," she said longingly, not really expecting him to take her seriously. "I'd like to walk to the end of the earth and back again and never see another living soul, just for the experience."

"Well, I can't promise you any such thing," John said, starting to smile at her eloquence. "But we'll go to the far edge of the Downs, if you like, well away from the fairground noise, and just keep walking as far as the road takes us. It's a bit cold for sitting and dreaming in the open air, and I don't suppose you're going to invite me to your room."

"I don't suppose she is, young feller-me-lad," Cook put in smartly. "What do you suppose Mr Barclay would say if he heard of such a goings-on under his roof?"

Carrie's first thought had been along the same lines and she knew John hadn't expected to be taken seriously. But such opposition to a perfectly above-board and innocent suggestion managed to rile her.

"It wouldn't be a goings-on, Cook! John is a respectable young man, and after all, we are walking out, and almost as good as engaged!" She avoided looking at him at that moment, hoping she wasn't going too far. She was more interested in the principle of the thing than in actually taking up his suggestion if the truth were told.

"And it's not as if I would invite just any male person to

my room," she went on, as breezily as if this conversation went on every day. "We could leave the door open at all times, and you could put your head in whenever you liked, and I assure you that everything would be quite in order. And I'm blowed if I know how people are expected to go courting if they can't even have a minute or two alone together!"

As she finished, aghast at her own daring, Cook slapped the plate of fruit pie and custard down in front of John, and poured them both a cup of strong tea.

"I suppose there's summat in what you say, young Carrie, and I daresay you've a sensible enough head on your shoulders. So if that's what you've a mind to do, it's not my place to stop you. Take your refreshments with you when my back's turned, so I don't see the going of you, then 'tis nothing to do with me."

She stumped off to the pantry to fetch the vegetables that were to be prepared for the family evening meal, while Carrie looked at John. She really hadn't intended putting any such idea in his mind, or in Cook's, but it had been said now, and it soon became clear that John wasn't averse to it.

"Well? Are you going to show me this room of yours, so that I can picture you in it when I'm away from here? I've never seen the inside of a young lady's room before, especially in a house like this one."

"It's nothing special. And if you're expecting to see something like my lady's fancy room, then you'll be sorely disappointed in mine," she said, putting their cups of tea and his plate of pie onto a tray with suddenly nervous hands.

Why on earth had she ever started this daft conversation? But he'd think her really feeble-minded if she backed out of showing him around now.

And they needn't stay very long . . . they *mustn't* stay very long . . . such close proximity would try the patience of the saintliest of gents, and John was too red-blooded a man to be called anything like that.

"Why would I be interested in seeing Miss Barclay's room, when the only girl I'm interested in is you?" he said. He went to take the tray from her hands, but she held on to it, preferring to carry it up to her room herself. She needed it as a prop, although from the way her hands were shaking, it was a wonder the tea remained in the cups until they reached the attic room she shared.

She deliberately left the door open wide, and ignored John's small grin at her obvious attention to such detail. She put the tray down on the small dressing table, and crossed her arms defiantly as she turned and looked at him. It was such a mean little room, cramped and plain, and with an aura of stale clothes from the girls who weren't always as fussy as herself over cleanliness. It was only when seen through someone else's eyes that the shabbiness of it really struck home. And apart from the uncertainty of the wisdom of being alone in such circumstances with a young man, she felt sudden shame at bringing him here. It seemed to underline her status in life only too well. What was she, after all? Nothing but a servant in a rich man's house.

"Which is your bed?" John said softly.

Her nerves jumped. Without saying anything, her head automatically turned to the neatly made bed at one side of the room. On it was the patchwork quilt she'd brought from home to make it seem more personally hers. John sat down on the bed and ran his hand over the cotton-covered pillow.

For such an innocent movement it was oddly sensual, and Carrie felt a shiver run through her. For a second she imagined her head being on that pillow, her hair loosened and spread out all around her, and that John's sensitive fingers were stroking her cheeks and her mouth.

"Don't you want your pie and tea? It will get cold," she said in a dry little voice.

"Let it," he said. "Come here, woman."

"John, I'm not sure that this is such a good idea."

He stopped her in mid-sentence, catching hold of her around the waist and pulling her towards him. They tumbled onto the bed together in a flurry of arms and legs and Carrie's laughing protestations.

This was definitely *not* such a good idea, she thought in a panic, but before her thoughts could manifest themselves into words, she felt the touch of his mouth on hers, and then she was pinned beneath him in a passionate kiss.

The bedsprings creaked in noisy protest, but neither heeded them. It seemed so long since they had been properly alone . . . and never like this, in the warm, cloying atmosphere of a tiny attic room with no-one to hear them or disturb them, at least until Cook came labouring up the stairs, and they would surely hear her heavy footsteps.

"God, I've missed you, Carrie," John murmured against her mouth. She could feel his warm breath on her face, and the way her breasts were flattened beneath his weight. She could see the texture of his skin, and the reddened places where the fists of BIG LOUIE had struck him. She felt an urge to kiss those places, to make them better, the way she used to kiss young Billy's hurts away before he got too big to accept such attentions.

But the feelings growing inside her as she felt the heaviness of John Travis's body over hers, were not remotely like the feelings she had felt for a small brother. These were far more vibrant, adult feelings, winging through every part of her now. And they scared her.

"John, please," she said faintly.

"Please what? Please, kind sir, don't take advantage of me?" he said in a teasing, theatrical voice. "Or please, John, make love to me?"

She pushed against him, trying to twist from beneath him, and causing the bedsprings to jangle even more. Dear God, she thought in panic, anyone hearing the noises coming from this room would think the worst even when nothing was actually happening!

"You know it's not right. You know I can't." She didn't really know what she wanted to say, because deep inside she so desperately wanted to know what it was that Elsie knew.

She wanted to know about this mysterious thing called love, and having a man's body become part of hers, so that no-one could have said where one ended and the other began . . . the very eroticism of the thought made her bite her lips and close her eyes, for fear that John might read such thoughts in her face. It was unseemly for a woman to have the same lustful thoughts as a man, except the lowest kind of woman.

"When shall we be wed, sweetheart?" she heard John groan in her ear. "For I swear I don't know how much longer I can hold myself in check from wanting you, and I know you well enough to know you'll insist on a legal paper to say there's no more barriers between us."

That showed how little he really knew her, Carrie thought, because she felt an overpowering need for him too. It was no different for a woman than for a man, only it was just never supposed to be so. The biggest caution in a woman's mind at such a time was that if anything came of a coupling out of wedlock, it was always the woman who paid, and bore the shame . . . it was no wonder that men thought so many women frigid, when that coldness was more the fear of the shame than the inability to show passion.

"What is it, Carrie?" John whispered now, as his hand strayed to the sweetness of her breast, and he heard her indrawn breath. "Do I hurt you? Or is it that you're afraid of hurting me where this afternoon's opponent struck me? I assure you my ribs can stand any strain from my darling."

It was all the off-putting Carrie needed. Until he had mentioned BIG LOUIE, she had been so tempted to abandon all her principles and let him go just a little way further . . . certain that she could stop him when need be . . . but now he'd brought the image of the fighter into her mind, and her own passion vanished. She twisted out from beneath him, and the bedsprings protested in a series of squeaks.

"I can't do this, John," she said in a cracked voice. "It's not right. Cook could appear at any minute, or one of the other girls, and I'd be compromised at once."

"You're right," he said, leaning back on his elbows as she straightened her clothes, and he saw her fiery cheeks. "A hole and corner affair may be good enough for the likes of your cheap friend, but not for my girl."

It wasn't what Carrie had meant to imply at all, but she bit back her reply and sat down hastily on one of the other beds as she heard Cook's clumping footsteps on the stairs, quickly handing John his plate of pie.

"Is everything all right, Carrie?" Cook called out, clearly not wanting to climb the entire flight of steep stairs to the maids' quarters.

"Quite all right, Cook. I shall be down directly to pay a call on my mother," she called back.

"Then I'll have a bit of fruit pie ready for you to take to her, duck. Not too long, now. The day's going cold."

They heard her go back downstairs again, and Carrie realised John hadn't touched his food. He put it back on the tray with the cups of congealing tea, and took Carrie's hands in his.

"You haven't answered my question yet."

"What question was that?" she said, her knees beginning to shake.

"When are we going to be wed? I see no reason for

251

us to wait, Carrie. You can move in with my uncle and me."

"You mean you want me to skivvy for the two of you instead of for Miss Helen, is that it?"

The flippant words tripped out, not intended to be taken seriously. She was almost tongue-tied at the glorious thought, of being wed to this handsome man – even though she knew full well her Pa would never allow it until she reached eighteen years old, and that time was still six months away yet. But to her horror, John took her very seriously. He dropped her hands at once, and his voice had gone several degrees colder.

"Good God, is that really what you think of me? That I want you to marry me so you can take over the care of a semi-invalid old man and dispense with the nurse's fees?"

"John, no, I didn't mean that."

"It's what you said."

She was angry with him now. "Why must you always take everything so literally? It was said on the spur of the moment, that's all, because I was shy of answering directly. Of *course* I want to marry you. You know I do. But you get me so flummoxed at times that I hardly know what I'm saying."

"Say that you love me," he instructed, still with that hard edge to his voice.

"I do."

He was relentless now. "That's not good enough. You have to say it. Say the words, Carrie. They won't bite you."

"I love you," she said in a muffled voice. Even as the embarrassment swept over her, she wondered why it was so difficult to say those particular words. Ma always said that feelings were more important than words, but apparently it wasn't always so. Words were important too.

Folk who were more educated knew that. It was one of

the things that separated the toffs from the rest of them. John leaned forward and pressed his lips to hers.

"And I love you. Why else would I want to marry you? If I just wanted a nurse and a housekeeper I'd find some old biddy to do those chores, not the most delicious and infuriating young woman it's ever been my misfortune to meet."

And, oh yes, John Travis could be eloquent too, Carrie thought, seconds before she rose to the bait as usual.

"What do you mean by that?" she said indignantly.

He laughed, and the tension between them eased.

"Just that I want to marry you for the best and only reason I would marry anybody, that's all, and you won't give me a straight answer. So do it now. Give me a date to dream about, Carrie Stuckey, or I swear I'll go out of here and propose to the first old biddy that I see."

"You wouldn't!" she said, the laughing lights dancing in her blue eyes now.

"I would," he said, and got to his feet. She stood up, both of them breathing heavily, tea and pie forgotten in the exhilaration of flirting.

"Pa always said he'd never let me wed until I was eighteen, but that after that, he couldn't stop me," she said in a rush.

"So when will you be eighteen?"

"On the twenty-eighth of June."

He gave a low groan. "So far away. But all right. I formally ask you, Miss Caroline Stuckey, to marry me on the twenty-eighth of June next. *Please?*"

The teasing ended, and she swayed into his arms. There was only one answer she could give, and knowing John, it had to be given in words.

"Yes," she said. "I will."

They didn't announce the news to Ma at once. These days it seemed necessary to test the atmosphere inside the house before anything new was broached. Ma and Billy were the only ones at home, and once Ma had assured them that she was getting on tolerably well, they had to hear Billy's excited chatter about the last letter they'd got from Frank, and to examine the map of Spain that Frank had sent especially for him.

They waited until Billy had got all this news out of the way, spreading out his map on the big family table as he tried to pronounce some of the Spanish names, and showing his delight when John was able to help him with them. They asked after all the family, and were glad to know that Wilf didn't seem to be faring too badly at his railway job, and was taking on more and more extra work.

And then they told her their own news. Ma looked suitably pleased, though she was becoming so short of breath and irritated by the constant stitch in her side, that she only spoke in brief sentences. It was just to save her having to breathe too deeply, she told them.

"You'll need to speak to Pa. See what he says to it, I mean," she said.

"Pa won't object, Ma, because I'll be eighteen at the end of June, and we're not rushing into anything," Carrie said, hardly able to believe they were actually having this conversation. Discussing her wedding, no less . . . the dazzling prospect almost made her overlook the way Ma moved so slowly about the house now, as if every step was an effort.

"Ma, could we invite John and his uncle here for Christmas Day?" she asked on an impulse. "It would be such a good time for us all to meet, and the extra work would be no problem for me, especially with Elsie to help. I wouldn't want you to do a single thing, mind, except put your feet up and let us young 'uns get on with it all. Billy could help, and I bet John would too, as well as our Wilf."

She hadn't discussed this with John first, and she knew she should have done. Nor did she know how he and Wilf might get on under the same roof for this big day of the year, especially if Elsie began her silly flirting. She really should curb this talking before she thought . . . But John's reaction was instant.

"That's a fine idea, Carrie, and if your mother won't think I'm taking a liberty, my uncle and I would be pleased to contribute our own Christmas fare to the party."

"Pa won't take kindly to it," Ma warned at once.

"You let me deal with that, Mrs Stuckey," John said forcefully. "I'll see him down on the waterfront this evening and get it settled. I'll be tactful, I promise."

He was being tactful now, since Carrie knew very well he was referring to the waterfront inn, where her Pa was such a regular these days. But Ma nodded, too done-in to get into a long discussion about it. Carrie felt real alarm, seeing how much Ma had aged in recent weeks, and she prayed that the babby would come on time, for Ma had clearly almost had enough of the carrying by now.

"Can I walk down the waterfront with you, John?" Billy said hopefully.

"All of you go," Ma huffed. "I'll rest while you've gone. Go on now. You weary me with your talk."

It was obviously what she wanted, and it gave Carrie a chance to pump Billy over her mother's health.

"Is she always like this, Billy?" she demanded to know, the minute they were outside the house and striking down the hill.

"Like what?" he said.

"Like – is Ma always so tired, ninny? She hardly seemed able to drag herself around the house today."

Billy gave the uncaring shrug of an eight-year-old.

"I dunno. Ma's just Ma. She don't say much about herself. But she boxes my ears more'n she used to," he added as an afterthought.

Carrie glanced at John. "Sometimes I wonder if it was such a good idea for me to be working at the Barclay house," she muttered. "Ma's still doing bits of washing and ironing at home, and there's not so much need with me and our Wilf earning money now. But if I was still home, I could see that she got proper rest and didn't tire herself out."

"You can't live her life for her, sweetheart," John said reasonably. "And nor can your family be dependent on you for ever. When we're married – "

She stopped walking so suddenly that Billy cannoned into her with a howl of rage. She was too full of anxiety about her mother to see his words as anything but censure.

"*When* we're married, my family will still be my family, and if I feel the need to help them, then I will," she snapped. "Being married to you don't mean I'm going to be shackled every single second, John Travis!"

"For God's sake, I never thought it was! I was only offering suggestions, so come down off your high horse. Bloody hell, I might fight with my fists, but you have the edge on me when it comes to words!"

She glared at him. "And you don't intend to give any of that up when we're married, of course."

"Did you think I would? It pays well, and I'd be a fool not to make use of my skills."

She didn't miss the arrogance in his voice, or the implication. A man with any pride at all didn't give up his pastimes for a woman. But she had always thought that to be working-class mentality, and that John was a cut above that.

"I'm not sure I want to live my life wondering if my husband will come home with his head knocked about until he's half senseless."

"That's something you'll have to think about then, isn't it?" John said distantly.

They strode on down the waterfront, together and yet not together, with Billy trailing along behind. They were in danger of forgetting their real purpose, Carrie thought, which was to alert Pa tactfully that the Travis men were invited for Christmas Day. It all seemed farcical now.

They found him in the midst of a crowd of gamblers playing shove ha'penny in one of the smoky taverns. Carrie recognised his triumphant shout as he picked up his meagre winnings even before she saw him. Sam Stuckey had a fine pair of lungs on him when he chose to use them. He saw the trio coming towards him, and his eyes narrowed at once as he pushed his way through the loungers in the tap-room.

"What's all this then? Has your Ma taken a turn for the worse?" he said at once.

It was on the tip of Carrie's tongue to say he'd do better to stay at home and help her than to play pointless games with the waterfront riff-raff, but she knew it would only aggravate him if she did so. He was already swaying slightly on his feet, even in the middle of the afternoon. He was unshaven too, and Carrie felt a stab of sorrow for the fine figure of a man he'd been not so long ago when he was in work and more than just the nominal head of his family.

"Ma's no more weary than usual, I daresay," she said pointedly. "Though she don't look at all well, Pa."

"The doctor says that once the babby's here, she'll get her strength back, so I suppose he knows what he's talking about." Sarcastically, he passed the responsibility back to the doctor with the ease of a man who chose not to see trouble until it was pushed under his nose.

He sat down heavily on one of the wooden settles by the window, and the other three did the same. Sam called for more ale for himself, but didn't offer to buy one for John, Carrie thought indignantly. He never used to be so uncouth, before his mind became twisted with resentment at being thrown on the scrap heap as he called it, while others seemed to prosper.

"We want to talk to you about Christmas Day, Mr Stuckey," John said.

Sam's eyes widened mockingly. "Is that so? What's up with it, then? Are they thinking of moving it? Has Jesus decided he'd rather have His birthday in the summer or summat? It's too cold for they skimpy robes, mebbe."

"*Pa!* That's blasphemous talk!" Carrie said appalled, not missing the sniggers going on all around them at Sam Stuckey's heavy-handed humour.

"What's there to talk about then?" Sam's mood quickly changed. "Christmas Day's just another day this year. We ain't got money to splash about like your fancy rich folk, miss!"

Carrie's heart thumped sickeningly. Pa was in a foul mood, and they shouldn't have come here to find him. She was ashamed of hearing such talk in front of John too.

"Mr Stuckey, hear me out, please," she heard John say. "Carrie and I have decided to be married on her eighteenth birthday – "

It was clear that Sam couldn't immediately take in the connection of a wedding at the end of the following June, and the imminence of Christmas Day. His eyes went blank and he belched noisily. Then he let out a stream of abuse.

"You mean to tell me you've interrupted my game to tell me summat I don't care to know, man? You'll marry my daughter when I give my say-so, and not before! And what the bloody hell has Christmas Day got to do with it, anyway?"

"Pa, stop it!" Carrie leapt to her feet, her palms flat on the table in front of them. "If I choose to marry John on my eighteenth birthday, you can't stop me. And since Ma looks so poorly, I'm taking over the cooking on Christmas

258

Day. The Barclays are giving us a goose, so we won't starve. Elsie's coming to help, and I've invited John and his uncle for the day, and Ma's agreed to it. *That*'s what we've come to tell you, and to get your approval."

She was breathing so fast by the time she finished that she thought she was going to explode. It had all gone wrong, of course. John was supposed to be saying all this in a tactful manner, and instead of that, she had burst out with everything in one fell swoop. But perhaps she knew her Pa better than he did. Perhaps it was better to bombard him with everything at once, rather than tip-toeing all around him.

She heard his fist bang on the table in a fury as he lurched to his feet to lean towards her. His eyes glared redly into hers, and she almost reeled from the strong smell of drink on his breath.

"Well, that's that then. My say-so don't matter a damn in nothing no more, by all accounts. All right!" He waved his arms about him in the melodramatic way of the very drunk. "Bring your sluttish friend and your fancy man and his whole bloody family if you like. Fill the bloody house with strangers, but just don't expect me to speak to 'em, that's all. Now let me get back to me game before me luck runs cold."

He pushed past them and rejoined his mates. Carrie could have wept with shame and fury, and even Billy stayed silent, too afraid of his Pa's wrath to ask him for a copper or two for a pie.

"Let's get out of here," John said.

The atmosphere was so thick with smoke, ale and body odours that it was a relief to be outside and to breathe in great gulps of the cold December air. The worst of the river whiffs were muted at this time of year, and they turned quickly back towards the city.

"I'm sorry, John," Carrie muttered. "I know I did it all wrong, but at least he's agreed. He won't forget,

259

or go back on his word about Christmas Day. You'll all be – "

She nearly said "welcome", but she knew none of the outsiders would be really welcome. They'd be tolerated because the Stuckey womenfolk had somehow manoeuvred it that way. It didn't bode well for the festive occasion.

Chapter 15

Wilf walked home with a jaunty step. With a week to go before Christmas, he'd managed to do some legitimate overtime on the railway, so he had a bit of extra money jingling in his pockets. He was glad. He'd never liked deceiving his family on the overtime lark. He'd told them about working on the doll's house for the foreman's daughter, but nobody knew about the other bit of extra work – about the exquisite little replica of the Woolley house that he'd been making for Nora.

Wilf was pleased with the result. He knew Nora would be thrilled with it, and didn't dare give too much thought as to how she would explain its presence to her parents. Though he doubted that Gaffer Woolley would ever see it, since Nora would undoubtedly keep it in her bedroom. He already knew that Gaffer was so strict with his daughter that her mother compensated for it by being extra soft, so he just prayed that Mrs Woolley wouldn't give the game away.

He'd be seeing Nora tomorrow evening, and that was the last chance he would get before Christmas. The Woolleys were entertaining guests for a week, and returning to London with them for the New Year celebrations. It would be a long lonely fortnight without seeing her, but there was nothing to be done about it. It also meant that tomorrow morning he had to sneak Ma's bread bin out of the house, so he could place the little wooden house carefully inside it to protect it, and take it from the railway works into the city.

He was rubbing his hands thankfully by the time he went inside the house on Jacob's Wells Road that evening. The nights were frosty now, with the temperature dropping fast, and some said there would be snow by Christmas. He hoped not. Clearing the stuff off the rails would be a thankless and freezing task.

His thoughts stopped abruptly when he heard the uproar going on inside. Pa was obviously in one of his moods. Young Billy was sitting halfway up the stairs well out of the way of any cuffing, but near enough to eavesdrop.

"What's to do then?" he said, to nobody in particular. Ma was sitting tight-lipped with her hands protectively over the huge lump of the babby, and Pa was red-faced and ranting. There was a sound of rattling crockery from the scullery, so he assumed Carrie must be there.

"Only those two, that's all!" Pa bellowed. "Scheming behind my back the way women do, and filling the bloody house with strangers, as if we ain't got enough with our own."

At that moment Elsie Miller came through from the scullery with a tray of tea and egg-toasts in her hands. She dumped it down on the parlour table and stood with hands on hips, glaring at Sam Stuckey.

"If you're including me in all that, Mr Stuckey, then I might as well go right now."

"Sam's not including you, Elsie," Ma said quickly. "You know you're welcome here, and I'm grateful for your help. It was good of you to call in on your way home from work and get the meal ready for me, duck."

"No, I ain't including you in my grumblings, girl," Pa managed to say with a mite of graciousness. "'Tis t'other lot. *Strangers*, who'll expect to be entertained and want to see me done up like a dog's dinner on me one day of rest."

262

Ma's hoot of laughter at that showed a spark of her old spirit.

"Your whole life is one long day of rest nowadays, Sam Stuckey, so don't go chafing at having to act a bit more like a gentleman for once. Anyway, it'll please our Carrie, and I've agreed, so there's an end to it."

"Is somebody going to tell me what you're all going on about, or am I supposed to play guessing games?" Wilf said.

It didn't please him too much to see Elsie Miller so firmly ensconced in the house, even if it was only temporary. If she'd helped Ma get the meal, then that was something in her favour. But he didn't like the girl, and never would, especially those great flirtatious eyes of hers that seemed to almost strip a man down to his underpinnings. Such frankness of manner didn't go well with Wilf. To him, Nora's refinement was far more alluring than all Elsie's flouncings and poutings.

"Your Ma's intending to fill the house on Christmas Day," Sam began again.

"Will you stop it, Sam?" Ma snapped. "The house will not be filled. It will be a large happy gathering, I hope and pray, and you're not to spoil everything for Carrie and her young man."

Wilf's indulgent smile vanished as he stared at his mother. "You're not saying the Travis fellow is coming here for Christmas Day?"

"And his uncle, and Elsie, of course. The girls will do all the cooking to relieve me of the chores, and you men will no doubt find your own pleasure in playing cards in the afternoon when you've slept off the effects of the goose."

She spoke quickly, anticipating trouble from her eldest son. It exasperated her that in planning for this most special day of the year, there had to be such problems. People needed to be together to celebrate Christ's birth. Families needed to be together. And if you believed in Christ's teachings, then those who had families should welcome into their homes those who had no-one, like young Elsie here. And since the Travis men were eventually to be related to the Stuckeys by marriage, it was only right and proper, and good manners, that they should all be together too.

"I've no wish to play cards or sit at table with John Travis," Wilf snapped. The smarting humiliation of being beaten in a fist fight with the man was still too vivid in his mind for him to be so readily forgiving.

"You can sit beside me then, Wilf," Elsie said quickly. "I'll look after you."

He grunted something in reply beneath his breath, and Ma wished the girl wouldn't be so blatant. Not that Wilf took the slightest notice of her attempts to flirt, thank goodness. She was considerate for Elsie's welfare, but she had no wish to have her as a daughter-in-law. She glanced at Wilf and sighed, thinking how cheerful he had looked a few minutes ago, and how black he looked now.

"What possessed you to ask them?" he said curtly.

"Carrie and John intend to be married on her birthday, and it's only right that we should all get acquainted," Ma said patiently as if she was talking to a child. Sometimes she thought Billy had more sense than some of the older ones. Life was less complicated when you were only eight, and at least Billy was excited at the prospect of having people in the house. He missed Frank, and John was his hero.

Sam spoke up again. "You won't change her, boy. I've tried, but her mind is fixed. Bloody women. They rule us all. You mark my words and steer clear of them as long as you can." It was a rare censure of his wife in public. Ma got stiffly to her feet and moved to the table.

"You two can argue all you like, but the thing's done and there's no changing it now. And Elsie's taken the trouble to make us all egg-toasts for supper, so I'm eating mine before it gets cold. Billy, you come down and eat some food too, and stop gawping up there."

Wilf sat down heavily at the table, glowering all around. "So our Carrie's still set on marrying him then, is she? I thought perhaps she'd have found some other attraction while she was working at her posh Clifton mansion."

"Why don't you like John?" Billy put in belligerently. "He's more fun than you, our Wilf."

He got a mild cuff around the ear from his brother for that, and he howled in protest.

"Yes, why don't you like him, Wilf?" Elsie said sweetly. "I reckon most girls would think him a real swell. They all give him the eye when he's working the ferry boat."

"Most girls are welcome to him then. Does our Carrie know he's such a favourite?" Wilf said.

"I don't know. I never asked her," Elsie said innocently, when to her surprise she felt Ma's hand move over hers in a surprisingly firm grip.

"Then don't. We want no mischief-making between Carrie and her young man, Elsie. And that goes for the rest of you. Our Carrie's made her choice, and 'tis up to her to make a go of it."

A spasm of pain took her breath away at that moment, and she hid the discomfort by pretending to drop a fork and asking Billy to go foraging about on the floor for it to save her bending. The spasm passed off quickly enough, but left May thinking briefly that once this babby made his appearance, he'd best pull his weight in the family, or she'd know the reason why. A body shouldn't have to go through all this for nothing.

"We must think about decking up the house a bit to make it look festive," she said, when she felt more able to speak easily again. Without realising it, she gave Wilf his chance.

"There's some fine holly bushes along the railway line, Ma. They don't like us taking the holly, really, but if

265

I take your old bread bin to work with me tomorrow, they'll think I'm just carrying tools or eats or summat. Then I can put some sprigs inside it, and nobody will be any the wiser."

"That sounds like a good idea," Ma said in surprise. Wilf never normally bothered about such things, but at least it made her think he wasn't totally against their unusual Christmas Day.

He was as nervous as a kitten when he handed over the bread bin to Nora inside the Woolley carriage the next evening. He was still trying to figure out how he'd explain the non-arrival of the holly to Ma later on, but he'd put that right another time. This was of prime importance to him.

"What's this?" Nora said in puzzlement. "I've never been given a bread bin as a gift before, Wilf."

"Open it," he instructed. "And I promise you won't find a cottage loaf inside."

It was a play on words that as yet she didn't follow. She lifted the lid curiously, and then gasped as she took out the perfect miniature of her own home. It was complete in every detail, with windows that opened and closed, and tiny wrought iron lamps attached to each of the doors. Wilf had fashioned it with the wood that he loved, and painted it in faithful colourings.

Nora said nothing for a few minutes, and then she looked at him with shining eyes.

"Oh Wilf, it's so beautiful! And you're so clever, and so – so *dear*."

She swayed into his arms, and hugged him close. She hated the thought of being away from him for a minute, but her father's wretched cousins who were coming for Christmas the very next day, had insisted they spend the New Year with them in London. She hated the very thought, but there was nothing she could do about it.

"Oh, I'm going to miss you so much," she said against his shoulder.

"No more than I shall miss you. And with such company as I shall have on Christmas Day too," he said, unable to resist a scowl.

Nora put on a prim face. "Now Wilf, please promise me you won't be unpleasant to your sister's young man. Try to like him for Carrie's sake. I only wish I could take you home and announce to all my family that you're the man I love, but Father's so unpredictable, I daren't even think about it. He's still so scratchy whenever the name Stuckey is mentioned."

"I know, sweetheart, and I'll try to behave with the Travis fellow, but only because you asked it of me. Now, do you think you can get the doll's house home safely?"

"Oh yes. Our driver is very loyal and discreet, and will assist me, I'm sure. I'll wrap it in the carriage blanket, and if anyone questions me, I'll say I've been buying Christmas gifts, and that no-one must spoil the surprise."

Wilf laughed. "How clever we're becoming at subterfuge these days. And how dreary that we have to resort to it!"

In answer, she pressed her soft mouth to his. At that moment, he would have given her the earth if he could.

By the time he left her it was growing dark, and he strode home with the bread bin beneath his arm, already missing her. He paused as he saw the light from the open church door where Mr Pritchard, the minister, preached. Almost at once, the door closed again, and the minister was on his way home. But not before, like a gift from God, Wilf had seen the holly bush in the churchyard, ablaze with berries. With one bound, he was over the hedge, and had filled the bread bin with sprigs, content with his night's work.

*   *   *

Two days later, the Honourable Rupert Egerton presented himself at the Barclay mansion at precisely four o'clock in the afternoon. He was not such a stickler for time-keeping as Helen's father, but he knew he had better not be late for this important meeting. He had known Helen for some years, and they had always got on well, but of late he'd taken to observing her secretly. The young lady herself wasn't aware of his intentions yet, but he'd noted her mannerisms and admired her qualities many times. He was convinced, by her beauty and her background, that she would make him an admirable wife.

Although the Barclays had been invited to Egerton Hall for their annual Christmas dinner and evening entertainment, Rupert was a man who liked to put plans into action the minute he had decided on them. And he had definitely decided on Miss Helen Barclay as a fine match for himself. The gel had a good pedigree, she was fiery in spirit, and she was also well-proportioned. He couldn't abide the string-bean type of woman. Helen Barclay would do very well for him, he ruminated. And it would put a sparkle to the festive celebrations if their engagement could be announced to each family's satisfaction.

The girl of his calculations manifested herself into his vision at that moment. She came towards him with both hands outstretched as he waited in the hall for the maid to announce him to her parents.

"Rupert, what on earth are you doing here? I thought you'd be at home running the estate, or whatever it is you landowners do," she said, having known him long enough to tease. "Don't you have a lot of planning to do for the Boxing Day hunt or something, or do you leave that all to your gamekeepers, or whatever they're called?"

"Something like that," he grinned back, liking this easy manner of hers more and more, despite the vagueness on country affairs. "Actually, I'm here to speak with your parents on a personal matter of some importance. But since I've got you to myself for a moment, I trust you're going to join us in the hunt on Boxing Day?"

"Well, yes, it might be fun, though I didn't know we were invited for Boxing Day too," she said, smiling, and liking the idea more and more.

"Our festivities go on until the New Year, so why not stay for the entire week?" Rupert said casually. "This is one of the reasons I'm here, Helen. I know it's appallingly short notice, but we've been having extended renovations done to the house, and weren't sure if the workmen would be finished in time, but it's in splendid shape now, and I'd love you to see it. My mother always says she never sees enough of you to get to know you properly, so I hope your parents will agree to the extended visit."

Her eyes widened a little. He was really a most personable young man, and an Honourable too. He was the sole heir to a vast country estate of deer parks and farms, and the old family seat of Egerton Hall itself was so exquisite . . . and after all, she *was* able to ride, and had been complimented on her seat on a horse . . . all Helen's old notions of boredom in the depths of the country underwent a swift radical change.

"Why, that might be very enjoyable," she said. "It all depends on my parents' agreement, of course."

"Of course," Rupert said, smiling, sure that once he had presented himself and his fortune to the Barclay parents there would be no opposition at all. He could sweep this delightful girl off her feet here and now if he wanted to . . . and almost to his surprise, he wasn't exactly averse to the idea either.

He'd planned this offer for her hand rather cold-bloodedly, after sifting through an array of eligible young ladies. He was careless enough to settle for a marriage of mutual convenience, since any personable young gentleman could find his dalliances outside the marriage bed whenever he wanted them.

But the more he saw of Helen's soft skin and melting eyes, the more he realised that this was a marriage that could become something far more. It gave Rupert a piquant feeling, because so many landowners married just for convenience, and many of his acquaintances weren't blessed with love matches . . . how extraordinary if this one turned out to be one of the exceptions after all.

"Rupert, you'll make me blush if you stare at me so long and so hard," he heard her say in a breathless manner that was quite unlike the forthright young woman he knew her to be. But he didn't object to that either. He liked her soft and feminine and breathless, every bit as much as he liked her strong, and perfectly capable of being mistress of his estate. And perhaps of his heart too, Rupert thought, with a rare burst of sentimentality.

"That's because you remind me of a beautiful painting, and all men like to stand and admire beautiful paintings until they've taken their fill," he told her now.

They had known one another too long for him to be lavish with such compliments, and he saw her mouth open slightly in astonishment at this one. And then the butler opened the door to the drawing-room and announced that the lady and gentleman of the house were ready to receive him. On an impulse, he took Helen's hand in his, and raised it to his lips. Above her fingers their eyes met, and she fell instantly, and irrevocably, in love.

When she reached her own room, she gazed at herself in her dressing-table mirror for long moments, before she rang imperiously for Carrie to come running.

"What's happened?" Carrie said at once, still too worried at her mother's appearance to mince words while she awaited instructions. And for once, Helen didn't chastise her.

"The Honourable Rupert Egerton has come to see my father," she said, and then she couldn't say any more

270

as the dazzling realisation that Rupert's father was a Lord surged into her mind. Rupert's wife would one day be Lady Egerton . . . for a young lady who had always known wealth and a comfortable life, Helen was completely bewitched by the thought of love and money going hand in hand . . .

"Is he the gent whose house you're going to on Christmas evening?" Carrie asked. "It ain't cancelled, is it?"

She hoped it was, if it meant she could spend more of the evening at home. It was tiring to keep running back and forth, especially when the hills were slippery with frost, and besides, Ma needed her far more than Miss Barclay.

Helen laughed, twirling around on her dressing-stool. "No, it's not cancelled! I have a strong suspicion that he's going to ask my father for my hand, and if he does, I've decided I shall accept!"

"Good God almighty!" Carrie exclaimed without thinking. "Bit sudden, isn't it? I mean – well, you ain't exactly been falling over yourself to get wed, have you, miss? It's not for me to say, of course, and I should be begging your pardon for my impertinence – "

"Yes, you should, but I forgive you today, Carrie," Helen said gaily. "Rupert is also inviting us all to stay over Christmas and for the New Year celebrations, and naturally I shall expect you to accompany me to the country."

Carrie felt the blood drain out of her face. "But I *can't*! It's the very time that Ma will need me most. The babby could come any time now, and I can't go off and leave her, 'specially the state she's in."

Her heart began to thud as she saw Helen's face darken, and the tight-lipped look she remembered so well spoiled the pretty features.

"Don't be ridiculous, Carrie. While you work for me, you'll do exactly as I wish," Helen snapped. "You take far too many liberties as it is, and I've given you endless time off in the last few months. I'll certainly hear no excuses this time. If I say you will accompany me to Egerton Hall on Christmas evening and stay for the duration of our visit, then that is exactly what you will do."

"And if I won't?" Carrie said through dry lips.

Helen got to her feet in a fury. "You insolent baggage! After all the kindness you've been shown in this house, feeding your wretched family half the time, and encouraging you to see that young prize-fighter whenever you liked, you have the audacity to question my wishes?"

Tears threatened to fill Carrie's eyes, but she'd be damned if she'd cry in front of this haughty madam. She dashed them back angrily, her voice tight.

"You've no right to speak of my family in that way. They're good folk, and Ma's had a rough time all these months with the babby. And John ain't primarily a prize-fighter neither."

"People like you shouldn't be filling the world with babies they can ill afford to keep," Helen said. "They should have more control over themselves."

She was impossible, Carrie raged. She had no idea of how other folk lived, or loved, or tried desperately to keep their dignity when times were bad. She tried to hold on to her temper.

"Well, I'm not going to the country with you, and that's flat," she heard herself say tremulously. "Ma needs me, and it's my duty to look after her."

"Then you may leave this house immediately," Helen said. "Pack your things and go, for I'm sick of the sight of you. I'll see that your wages are sent on to you."

Carrie stared at her dumbly. She hadn't meant to be so defiant, or to give such an ultimatum, but neither would her pride allow her to plead with this spoilt, pampered miss. And it was easy to see there was to be no compromise from Helen.

Carrie turned on her heel and walked stiffly from the room, and it was only when she was outside it that she leaned against the door, feeling as if every bone in her body was turning to water.

What a fool she had been! Even though she had good reasons for not wanting to go away at this time, and would have felt like a rat deserting a sinking ship if she wasn't around when Ma had the babby, Helen Barclay had her rights too. Helen was her employer and could dictate whatever she wished to her. And until all this tirade had started, she had looked so ecstatic about this new beau of hers.

Carrie's momentary stab of guilt at dashing such happiness from her employer's eyes, vanished just as quickly, and her mouth twisted. The Hon. Rupert Egerton was welcome to her, she thought savagely, wondering if he knew just how quickly his beloved's moods could change when she didn't get her own way.

Well, it was no longer any concern of hers. She'd been given her marching orders, and the sooner she was away from here, the better. Though how she was going to face Pa and tell him she'd lost her job, with all the little extras that went with it, she didn't know.

The oddments from the kitchen . . . the fruit that was so good for Ma . . . the Christmas goose . . . at the thought of the table bird they'd all looked forward to so much, her face finally crumpled, and she fled from Miss Barclay's room with her hands over her face to the sanctuary of her own chilly room, where she could sob in peace.

"You just let me say whether or not you get that Christmas goose," Cook told her indignantly, once the story became common news below stairs. "There ain't a body who's worked harder'n you for that young madam, what with the washing and pressing, and being at her beck and call every minute of the day and night."

"She had a right to expect me to go with her though, Cook," Carrie said, between sniffs.

The kindness she had met below stairs was almost more than she could bear, after the scratchy scene above with Helen. The skivvies had been openly admiring of anyone daring to answer the young lady back, and especially to refuse point blank to do as she wished. But a fat lot of good it had done her, Carrie thought.

"The gentry don't have no right to think they can control folks' thoughts and feelings," Cook went on, "and of course your Ma needs you. Mebbe once the babby's here, safe and sound, Miss Helen will reconsider your position with her."

Carrie shook her head vehemently. "I could never work for her again. Besides, if she goes off to Egerton Hall to live, I'd never see Ma at all."

"Nor your young man," Cook reminded her.

She gave a start. She'd hardly given John a thought in the last hour. Aside from her fury at hearing him referred to as a prize-fighter, all her worries had been about Ma, and how she was going to tell Pa she'd thrown away a good position. She began to wonder if she really was in love with John Travis after all, or if she had just had her head turned by having a young man so interested in her. It was one more sobering thought among a day of gloom and one she didn't want to dwell on for too long.

"Anyway, you just leave the Christmas bird to me," Cook said again. "There'll be plenty of tid-bits from the pantry too. The rich folk have no idea what comes in and out of their kitchens, and you ain't going to go short, my duck."

"Thank you," Carrie said, too choked to say any more.

There was nothing else to do then, once she'd drunk the cup of steaming tea Cook had insisted on, but to take her bag of belongings and go home. Everyone here had work

274

to do, while her hands were suddenly idle. It was a very odd sensation.

She felt more than a mild panic, wondering how she was going to fill her days . . . and then her common sense took over. Wasn't this the ideal time to ease Ma's load, and to take over the running of the Stuckey house? And there were still many rich Clifton clients who would welcome the skill of the washer-girl who took such care of their precious silks and laces in her own home.

If it all seemed very much like a backward step, Carrie refused to see it that way. She lifted her chin and left the Barclay mansion with a firm step, and only her white knuckles on the grip of her bag betrayed a smidgeon of the turbulent feelings inside.

"Well, that's a fine to do, I must say," Sam Stuckey bellowed, as soon as she had blurted out her news, and dumped her baggage on the parlour table. "I always knew you had a fiery tongue in your head, but I didn't think you were completely stupid as well."

"Leave it, Sam," Ma said quickly. "Can't you see the girl's had enough for one day?"

"We've all had enough," he said. "Enough depending on charity and worrying about where the next penny's coming from, but we don't all throw in a good job when we find one."

Carrie burst out at him. "And when did you last find a good job? As far as I can see, you don't even look for work any more. You just leave it to Wilf and me, and you've driven Frank away."

She ducked as his hand lashed out, missing her by inches, and she wished she could bite the words back, because at least that wasn't true. Nothing had driven Frank away from Bristol except his own desire to see a bit of the world.

Before she knew what he was about, Sam grabbed hold

of her shoulder, and yanked her through the house to the back yard. In the little shed he used as a workshop now, she could see the rough fashioning of a child's coffin.

"You're right, girl. I don't look for work, because there's ain't nothing about for a skilled man to do except for this. And God knows there's plenty enough going hungry who are glad of my work, whether or not I get paid a fair price for it. Would you have me charge above the odds to a man whose babby has died in his arms?"

She felt a swift shame then, combined with something else. She didn't recognise it for a moment, and then she knew. It was a premonition as real as if a cold hand had reached out and touched her. This coffin was for some unknown person's baby, but it could so easily be for Ma's.

Without thinking, she put her arms around her father, in a way she hadn't done for years. He was still a proud man, and she was nothing if not his daughter.

"I'm sorry, Pa. But you wouldn't have me kow-towing any longer to that rich little madam, would you. I can still work in the house. I'll take in washing like I used to. We won't starve, and besides, I want to look after Ma until the babby comes, Pa. She needs looking after."

And he hadn't done much of that lately, she added silently. But she felt his rough hands on her hair, and knew she was forgiven. She breathed a little more easily, even though there were only three days to go before Christmas now, and nothing was turning out the way any of them had expected.

By the time Wilf got home from work that evening, the aroma of hot spicy mutton stew greeted his nostrils, and he gave a surprised smile to see his sister working in the scullery, with the house looking tidy and ship-shape. Not that he blamed Ma for not attending to her duties as throroughly as of old, he thought

276

quickly. But the place certainly looked more cared-for tonight.

"Something smells good," he said.

He was feeling good too. If it weren't for the fact that Nora was going away for Christmas, the way so many rich folk did, he'd feel even better. Not that he particularly wanted to be on the move at such a time. He'd seen enough of railways, and felt enough stinging smuts in the eyes as the great lumbering engines steamed into Temple Meads Station with all their comings and goings, to settle any wanderlust.

"Our Carrie's come home to stay," Billy came hurtling down the stairs to impart the news. "She told that Miss Barclay what to do with her job, and she's come home to look after us all instead."

"Is that right?" Wilf said, staring, as Carrie came into the parlour with two plates of steaming food in her hands and dumped them on the table.

"More or less," she said over her shoulder as she went to get the other meals. She sounded more breezy than she felt. It had been such a big step to take, and she'd taken it without due thought. But she was here now, and Ma's appreciative eyes were all the reward she needed. All the same, she had thrown away a good job.

"What happened? Did she upset you, our Carrie?" Wilf said. "I always thought she acted too big for her boots."

"You don't think I'm daft then?" Carrie said, her face flushed from the cooking, and the fact that he didn't rail at her the way Pa had done earlier.

"Not if you stood up for yourself the way a Stuckey should," he said. "There's no cause for hitting folk when they're down, and you'll be more appreciated here if this stew's anything to go by."

"Sit down and eat it then," Ma said, as briskly as in the old days. "And call your Pa, Billy. He's been out in that old shed for long enough tonight."

277

As they all sat down at the table, Carrie's throat was full. It was just like the old days, when they all sat together for their evening meal. The days before their glorious ship was finished, and Gaffer Woolley had to lay off all his best carpenters, and things got bad. Before Carrie had met John Travis and had had to leave the nest and work at the big house. There was only one thing missing. Frank's place at the table was empty, and they had no idea whether or not he would be home for Christmas.

She could see that Ma ate very little, though she was determinedly bright that evening, and clearly thankful that Carrie was taking over all of her chores. It was obvious that the baby was still lying awkwardly, from the many times Ma would pause and catch her breath or press her hand to her side.

Carrie sent up a frequent little prayer that everything was going to be all right when Ma's time came. But, try as she might, she was unable to get rid the spectre of a cold still child lying in the tiny coffin her Pa had almost finished. She wished he'd never taken her outside to see it. It seemed like too much of an omen, and Carrie had always believed in omens.

When the hammering came on the front door later that evening, she almost jumped out of her skin, as if she had conjured up the devil himself with her dire prophesies.

Her next thought was that it surely couldn't be someone sent from Miss Helen Barclay, insisting that she return . . . that farcical idea was just as instantly swept out of her mind as Pa went frowning to the door, clearly annoyed at this disturbance, and threw it open to reveal the familiar face of the man standing there.

"Now then, Sam Stuckey, are you going to ask me in, or do I have to stand here stamping my feet in the cold all night?" came Gaffer Woolley's belligerent voice.

278

Chapter 16

"I suppose you'd best come inside," Pa growled. "Though unless you're going to offer me work, I've nothing to say to you."

Aaron Woolley came inside the house, followed by a stocky man with rather similar features, but a more affluent air. The two of them seemed to fill the remaining space, and as Pa seemed disinclined to offer them a seat, Carrie felt obliged to do so.

"They don't need seats, since they won't be stopping," Pa said at once.

"Since when were the Stuckeys so discourteous to visitors?" Ma suddenly said with surprising vigour in her voice. "Sit you down and welcome, Mr Woolley and sir, and our Carrie will fetch you each a glass of cordial, if you've mind to drink with us."

"That will be very welcome, missus," Gaffer said. "It's a cold night, and we could do with a little warming."

Carrie went to fetch the drinks at once, aware that Billy seemed tongue-tied by the magnificence of the two men. Gaffer Woolley was dressed up in weskit and overcoat and top hat instead of his working clobber which was normally dusty and covered in sawdust. He might be a gaffer, but he was always prominent in his warehouse and knew exactly what went on there. It was the mark of a successful businessman, Pa used to say, in the days before he had nothing good at all to say about the man.

Wilf was also saying nothing. There was nothing unusual

in that, since he rarely wasted words, but there was something about him that puzzled Carrie . . . he had a kind of defiant unease about him, almost as if he was waiting for something.

The gentlemen made small talk with Ma, enquiring about her health, and commenting on the state of the weather, until the drinks were handed around, and then Pa could clearly stand the suspense no longer.

"So what's this deputation all about, man?" he said impatiently. "Is it a charity visit, or what? If 'tis, you can sling your hooks, the pair of you. Or are you just inspecting the poor, mebbe? As you see, we live plainly, and plainer still in recent months, but if we'd known we was expectin' royalty, we might have managed a crust or two."

"Sam Stuckey, you always had the most pig-headed pride of any man I ever knew," Gaffer said sharply. "But rest easy. I've not come here offering charity, nor to bandy words with you. It's your young 'un I came to see."

"Our Billy? What's he been up to? I've warned him not to go near your warehouse for sticks."

"Not the sprog. The other one."

He looked directly at Wilf now, and Carrie was surprised to see her brother's face go a dull, angry red. His hands were clenched as he faced Gaffer Woolley.

"Whatever you have to say to me, I'd prefer it said in private. This has nothing to do with my folks."

"I'd say it has a lot to do with 'em, if you intend to go on seeing my daughter – "

"*What!*" Sam roared. He rounded on Wilf at once. "Have you been sniffing around the Woolley girl's skirts, you numbskull, and got her in the family way? I'll thrash you to within an inch of your life if you have!" He had to pause for breath, and Wilf snapped back at him, livid with rage and embarrassment.

"Don't shame me, Pa, and don't talk about summat you know nothing about."

"I know well enough what it means when a man starts bleating on about a boy seein' his daughter."

"Sam, will you listen a minute?" Gaffer thundered above the din. Carrie saw Billy go helter-skelter up the stairs to his favourite spot between the banister rails. "I've not come here to censure your son, though that was my first intention, I'll admit, until my womenfolk got at me."

He scowled for a moment, then went on briskly. "Anyways, this here gent is my cousin from London, here on a pleasure visit as well as a business one, and he's got a proposal to make to your Wilf, if you'd shut your trap and listen a minute, instead of going off half-cocked as usual. God damn it, but you'd try the patience of a saint, man."

"Perhaps you'd care to let me interpose, Aaron," the other man said, speaking up for the first time. Carrie didn't recognise the accent, which was much quicker and more rounded than their slower West Country one, but even without it, she'd have guessed the man didn't come from around here. He was altogether more genteel than Gaffer Woolley too.

"What kind of proposal?" Pa said, looking from one to the other suspiciously.

"I think that's for me to find out, Pa," Wilf said. "It's me they've come to see, if you'd be obliged. Though I'm as muddled as you as to why that might be."

Because as sure as eggs were eggs, they didn't intend proposing that Wilf Stuckey married Gaffer Woolley's daughter! The sweetest and best thought in all the world was so unlikely and so laughable it had the effect of calming him down totally after all the ructions in the house. He folded his arms across his chest and looked directly at the two visitors, while his Pa sat down heavily beside Ma, outfoxed for once.

Sitting there close together, the two of them looked so *old*, Carrie thought. And with all the other troubles lately, Ma shouldn't have to be coping with carrying another babby, when she'd thought all that was behind her. It was well known that the older a woman got, the more the risks in childbearing, and Ma had never found it easy.

Carrie realised it was the first time she had ever really thought of her as mortal. Children always thought their parents would live for ever. But now it occurred to her that in giving birth to this child, Ma could even die. Nor could she quite rid herself of the haunting thoughts of a newborn babby fitting as tidily as a hand in a glove inside the tiny coffin in Pa's shed, and she felt a sliver of fear run through her, as sharp as a blade.

She forced herself to shake off all the disquieting thoughts, as Gaffer Woolley formally introduced his companion.

"This is Mr Cedric Woolley, my cousin from London," he repeated, more grandly. "And he was so impressed with this young feller's handiwork that he wants to instal him in a business venture he's been trying to set up here in Bristol. Now then, what do you say to that, young Wilf?"

Nobody said anything for a moment, and the two most prominent sounds in the room were the monotonous ticking of the clock on the mantel and Ma's sharp intake of breath. But all eyes were on Wilf then, and his own narrowed.

"What handiwork would that be, sir?" he said carefully. Surely Nora hadn't been so reckless as to show her family the doll's house he'd made her? But if she had, and it had produced . . . *what* had the man said? Installing Wilf Stuckey in a business venture here in Bristol? His heart suddenly leapt, and his hands were so clammy he'd never have been able to whittle the simplest stick at that moment, let alone perfect his craftmanship.

"What's all this about, Gaffer?" Pa wouldn't be silent any longer. "Has your cousin been taken over the *Great Britain* to see some of the wood carvings me and my boys did, perhaps?"

Mr Cedric gave a short laugh. "I have not, sir. Though I'm to have the honour of being shown around the great ship while I'm here. No. I refer to the exquisite replica of my cousin's house that your son made for my niece."

He ignored the varying exclamations and shocked Stuckey faces at this information.

"It's truly remarkable workmanship, and since the fashion for wooden toys has become so much the rage in London, it will soon appear in the provinces also. I am in the retail toy business, and although I haven't yet opened a shop in Bristol, the time would seem to be ripe for it. I hadn't thought to have a local craftsman in a workshop on the premises who can make things to order for my customers until I saw your son's work. Now that I have, I foresee even greater fortunes to be made, since local skills always enhance profits. So this is the proposition I'm offering you, Mr Stuckey."

His words were directed at Wilf, while the rest of them sat in stunned silence as they tried to take in too many separate pieces of news at once. The family knew Wilf had been making a doll's house for the railway foreman's child, and how much he had enjoyed doing it. But none of them knew of the extra overtime he'd put in at the railway workshop, nor of the wooden house he'd made with such loving care for Nora. Nobody knew of his association with Nora . . . he realised his mouth had dried. How the hell had Gaffer Woolley reconciled himself to *that*, let alone anything else?

"Well, boy?" Mr Cedric was saying now. "Does the idea appeal to you? I need an answer before I go back to London, since I shall need to put things in motion right after the New Year. I've already seen some premises in the Queens Road here that will be admirable, and I'd say the business could be in operation by early March. My cousin here will allow you the use of a disused shed alongside his warehouse in the meantime to make a start on some toys. You'll be drawing a salary from the first of January, and I pay well for quality work. We shall want the place stocked for the grand opening before Easter. So what do you say?"

The shocks didn't stop coming. Wilf was so dazzled with all he was hearing, he could hardly take it all in. His fortunes were changing spectacularly, and all because of the little house he'd made for Nora. He glanced at Gaffer Woolley, wondering if he dared say what was uppermost in his mind. But his pride was returning in leaps and bounds. If this Mr Cedric Woolley thought his skills were so highly valued, then he could dare anything.

"All this is like a dream come true, sir, and I won't deny it," he said, trying to remain as calm as possible. "But there's a condition attached to my accepting."

"Wilf, don't be foolish," he heard Ma say in a strangled voice, but Mr Cedric merely looked amused.

"Name it, young sir."

"Don't you go asking for jobs for me, our Wilf," Sam warned, anticipating what was to come.

"I wasn't going to. I'm asking permission to court Gaffer Woolley's daughter," Wilf retorted. "If I'm good enough for her uncle to employ as a craftsman, then I reckon I'm good enough for Nora's father to consider me a suitor."

He fully expected a tirade from Gaffer, but instead, the other gave a irritated grunt.

"You're too late, boy. I've already had storms and tears from my daughter, and I'm told if I don't allow you to see her, she's never going to speak to me again. And I can't be doing with tearful females in the house, so I suppose I'll have to give in. You'd better come to supper on Boxing

Day if you've a mind to it. A man should know when he's beaten."

He looked hard at Sam as he spoke, clearly expecting him to ask if there was any work going at the warehouse for himself, but Sam remained obstinately silent. And Gaffer had no intention of humbling himself any further in this devilishly proud family.

"Then I accept your offer, Mr Woolley," Wilf said, and his hand was clasped firmly by the London cousin. The details would all be sorted out later, and Mr Cedric would clearly need to frequent Bristol often in the next few months. But Wilf could now leave the hated railway navvying, and do the job he loved best of all.

He managed to hold in his elation until the two gentlemen had left, and then he gave out a whoop of joy. He clasped Carrie around the waist and swung her around the parlour until she begged for mercy.

"I can't believe it! When I saw Gaffer at the door, I thought I was in for it," he said, when he finally flopped down on the rag rug, running his fingers through his hair in disbelief. "And invited to Boxing Day supper as well. There is a God up there after all."

"Wilf, there's no cause for that kind of talk," Ma said sharply. "But I'm pleased for you, son, even though you shouldn't have been seeing the Woolley girl behind her father's back."

"Just how long has that been going on?" Sam said, not willing to give an inch, even now.

"Long enough for me to know I want to marry her, Pa. I love her and she loves me, but we ain't done nothing to be ashamed of, and don't intend to," he whipped back. He was a man and proud of it, and as he stared his father out, Sam just as silently backed down.

"Oh Wilf, I'm so happy for you," Carrie said. "If only our Frank was home now, everything would be wonderful this Christmas. And I'm *glad* Miss Barclay sent me packing, if only so I could hear all your news when it happened!"

"And if only the babby would hurry up and make his appearance, I'd be happy too," Ma said, needing to shift her weight on the settle as the stitch in her side caught her out with a gasp again.

"Can I rub your back for you, Ma?" Carrie said at once, knowing this sometimes eased things.

"I think I'd be better lying flat, so I'm taking to my bed after all this excitement, Carrie. You'd best go too, our Billy, and the rest of you can chew over the fat as long as you like."

She bundled the protesting Billy up the stairs in front of her, while Carrie began wondering just how soon she'd be able to tell John what was happening in the Stuckey family. She hadn't seen him for a few days, and hardly at all since the end of the Christmas fair on the Downs. He didn't even know about her leaving her job yet, let alone Wilf's more exciting news. But at last she had something of family interest to tell him and his uncle, instead of her usual second-hand stories of the way other folk lived.

"I'm not sorry you've left the Barclay girl's employ, Carrie, and naturally I'm glad for Wilf. It's good and right for a man to do what he has his heart set on," John said, when she had toiled up Bedminster Hill the next afternoon and blurted out everything at once. He had greeted her with pleasure, pulling her into his arms and kissing her hard, and she had felt warmed by his reaction to the unexpected visit.

But she felt oddly let-down by his flat response. He used all the right words, but they weren't said with any enthusiasm. And she had been so bubbling over when she'd gone to tell him. She hadn't had the satisfaction of relating it all to his uncle, since the old man was fast asleep in his room. It was a pity, since she was sure Uncle Oswald would have enjoyed the telling.

"You don't sound as if it's wonderful," she complained. "Or perhaps you think I was stupid to say I wouldn't spend so long away with Miss Barclay at this country estate with her new beau?"

"Why should I think that?" he said, showing his irritation.

"I don't know. But you didn't mind making up to her that day on the Downs, did you? Perhaps you fancy her yourself! Perhaps you'd have liked me to keep an eye on her to see how things were going," she said wildly.

"I think you're going mad," John said shortly. "What Miss Barclay does is of no interest to me, and if you want to throw up a perfectly good job, then that's your business."

"Don't you think it might be your business too?" she said in frustration. "After all, we are supposed to be more or less engaged, aren't we?"

"More – or less? Which is it, Carrie?"

She felt suddenly frightened. "John, I didn't come here to quarrel with you. I don't know why we always seem to be arguing lately, either."

"Everybody argues."

"But not all the time," she muttered. "And not with the person they intend spending the rest of their life with."

"Is this a roundabout way of saying you don't want to spend the rest of your life with me?"

The fright became a hurt in her chest. To her vivid imagination it seemed certain he was the one who wanted to get out of their engagement, but he was waiting for her to say it, rather than say it himself. That was it, of course, Carrie thought bitterly. A woman could get back at a man for breach of promise, but if she threw in the towel herself . . . but God knew she didn't want to end it, and so should John . . .

"Of course not. I just wish we didn't argue so much," she finally said. To her own ears she sounded feeble. She cursed herself for being so spineless, but she didn't dare risk losing him. She loved him, and she thought desperately that her pithiness must surely be due to the trauma of the last weeks with Helen Barclay.

Not for the first time, she breathed a great sigh of relief that she didn't have to pander to that young lady's whims any more. John mistook the reason for her sigh, and put his arms around her.

"Don't ever doubt that I love you, Carrie, but I do have something on my mind, and I was going to keep it from you until after Christmas. I have news of my own."

"What news?" she said, alert at once. She was still in the circle of his arms, but she could feel his tension, and she knew she wasn't going to hear anything pleasant. "It's not your uncle, is it? Is he worse?"

John shook his head. "He does well enough, and he's improving all the time. No, it's an opportunity that's come my way. It's hardly in the same class of skill as Wilf's, but it seems too good to miss."

Somehow she didn't need to ask. She felt her face flush with anger. "You're not going to tell me it's to do with fighting, are you? You *know* I hate it, John."

"Don't take on so," he said, keeping her firmly in his embrace as she would have wriggled away. "But you're on the right track. I did well against BIG LOUIE for the rest of the week at the Downs fair. I beat him twice more, and twice more it was called a draw, and the promoter was well pleased at the outcome with all the crowds it drew."

"How nice for you," she snapped. "I'm sure having it twice called a draw was better than having your brains knocked out completely."

And now that she had time to draw breath properly, she could see the dark smudgy evidence of where the skin on his cheeks had been bruised and battered, and there was a small cut on his forehead. It was obvious to her now that fighting was in John's blood, and that she wasn't going to be the one to rid him of it.

She managed to shake free of his embrace, or maybe it was because he simply let her go, so that she almost fell.

"So who will your next opponent be?" she cried out. "Some giant of a man who will really finish you off? You surely don't expect me to stand by and watch such a thing happening, and to keep praying that someday you won't be brought home on a slab?"

She felt near to crying as the prospect took hold of her. His face was tight with anger, but she could see the stubborn look in his eyes. And dear God, if she was stubborn, then so was he . . . she felt him shaking her arms as she ranted on, and she lapsed into a stony silence.

"Will you just listen to me? You know my dream is to buy a boat large enough not just to take folk up and down the river, but out into the Channel and along the coast on day trips. It's the coming thing, Carrie, and from the pittance I get from ferrying folk across the river in the winter months, it would take me for ever to save enough. I want to offer my wife a good life and a good future, and the offer I've had from Garfield Pond is too good to miss."

"Garfield Pond? What's that? Some boating firm or other?" she said stupidly, too mesmerised by the sudden enthusiasm in his voice to say anything else.

"It's the name of BIG LOUIE'S fight promoter. You saw him that day on the Downs, introducing the fights. They get regular engagements in various towns in the west, not just at the travelling fairs. BIG LOUIE always travelled with the regular sparring partner you saw that day, before the other contestants were invited into the ring, but now the sparring partner's ill, so they've offered me the job."

"What?" She could hardly take all this in. Wilf's new

prospect had been a thrill – this news was anything but. "How can you even think of such a thing? You once told me those travelling fairs go all over the country."

"Not all over. But I'll be travelling through Somerset and Devon, and maybe even as far as Cornwall in the next four months," he said warily.

Four months . . . her mouth dropped open, but before she could question him more, he went on quickly.

"I've said I won't do more than four months, Carrie, and I've done my calculations. Uncle Oswald's agreed that I can put our present boat up for sale when I'm ready, and with putting the proceeds to what I'll earn, I can save enough to put down most of the money on the bigger boat in that time. I've seen the plans for one I want already."

"And if it's not what I want?" she said slowly. "Oh, I don't mean the boat. That sounds wonderful – but don't expect me to approve of the means of getting it."

"I don't," he said in a clipped voice. "But fighting is a skill I have, and I intend to use it. Garfield Pond reckons I'll draw the crowds, and that there'll be a bonus in it for me every time we get above a certain number. But if you're not prepared to wait four months, Carrie – "

"It's not that, and you know it, though I don't relish the thought of you going all over the country, but what about your uncle? Do you intend leaving him here to fend for himself?"

Her mind surged on, thinking of all the objections she could, while knowing full well that John intended going ahead with this. She could see it by the lights in his eyes. He was a man who would never back down for a woman. She began to wonder if she really knew him at all, and more importantly, if she still liked what she saw.

"Uncle Oswald's all in favour of my plan. He has a sister up Keynsham way who wants to buy a property near the coast some time, so she's going to sell up and live here while I'm away, until she can find a little place for herself. I've been to see Aunt Vi, and she's more than happy about the arrangements."

"I see. It seems as if it's all cut and dried then, and everyone knew but me," she said, more hurt by this than anything else so far.

"I didn't want to tell you until we'd had our Christmas together, Carrie. I thought you'd still be working at Clifton, and that the day would be busy with your family. I didn't want to upset you."

"And of course you knew it would upset me."

He gave a heavy sigh. "Of course I knew. But this is man's business, Carrie, and if you don't like it, then I'm sorry. All I can tell you is that it won't last for ever."

"You can guarantee that, can you? Or will this kind of thing happen every time a travelling fair comes to town, and somebody dangles the bait?"

He looked at her steadily, and dropped her hands.

"That's something we'll just have to wait and see, isn't it?" he said.

She knew she had goaded him into the reply, but it didn't help. Her stomach had turned more today than she had believed possible. Good news or bad news was stomach-churning, she thought, and there had been more than enough of both lately. She had arrived here full of excitement, and she was leaving in a fit of depression. And apart from John's fisticuffs job, which she hated, he would be gone for four months. The wry thought surged into her head that if their wedding was to go ahead, at least it would give him time for his cuts and bruises to heal before they walked down the aisle . . . *if* their wedding was to go ahead . . .

"I think I had better go," she said in a tight voice. "I want to see Elsie before it gets dark, to arrange about Christmas Day."

"I'll walk with you."

"No, don't. There's no need for it, and I think I'd rather be alone."

They were a step apart, when without warning John gave a low oath and pulled her back into his arms. She could smell the freshness of his skin against her own, and her eyes stung with tears as his voice roughened.

"Don't take on so, Carrie sweet. I'm doing this for us both. This time next year, you'll wonder what all the fuss was about. We'll be well set up by then, and I promise there'll be no more fighting once I've got the new boat."

She wanted to believe him so much. And with his mouth seeking hers, it was so easy to be swayed into thinking that professional fighting was only a job after all. Plenty of others did it, and didn't end up with half their brains bashed in . . . but she would miss him so badly.

Everything was changing, she thought, and nothing ever stayed the same. They all moved on, except for Carrie herself, who seemed to be moving backwards.

It was one more depressing thought to accompany her down the hill towards the river when she'd finally said good-bye to John, promising to be in a better humour by Christmas Day, and belatedly sending her regards to his uncle.

She knew Elsie would be glad to see her. She could pour out all her irritation into Elsie's ears, and get the usual cheerful no-nonsense response that would probably have them arguing in five minutes flat, but wouldn't be half as emotional as her arguments with John.

That was the worst of it when you argued with a lover. The emotions were far too involved to keep things on a level keel. Whereas an argument with Elsie was a good old ping-pong affair to clear the air, with neither of them taking any permanent offence.

She had to go a bit cautiously, though. She had forgotten Elsie's infatuation with Wilf, and she wasn't sure how she was going to take it once she knew that he was officially walking out with Nora Woolley. She decided to tell Elsie this news first, and she eyed her uneasily as she did so. But she was surprised and relieved by Elsie's matter-of-fact attitude that if a thing was settled, then you just looked around for something else.

"Well, that's that, then," Elsie said airily, when she was told the news. "I s'pose I always knew he weren't for me, and I daresay they'll make a good pair. He don't ever speak much, do he? And from what I recall of the namby-pamby miss, she never had much to say for herself neither."

"That's right," Carrie agreed, preferring to let Elsie think what she would, as long as she didn't go all po-faced over losing Wilf to another girl. And as long as she didn't brood over it once she was left here in the cottage alone.

Carrie glanced around while they were talking. Elsie never thought to offer drinks. She had little idea of homemaking, and how her old granpa had survived as long as he did was a mystery to Carrie. The place was shabby and rarely cleaned. The windows were so grimy you could hardly see through them, but as far as Elsie was concerned, it was just a place to eat and sleep in. She fussed over herself, but not the cottage.

Carrie certainly wouldn't have wanted to live here alone, so close to the waterfront, with all the human flotsam in the vicinity. But Elsie didn't seem to have many nerves in her body, and had simply refused to move away after her granpa died, and since the rent was minimal it served her purpose. She never seemed to need anybody, Carrie thought, half in admiration, and half in annoyance.

"So what else has been happening lately? You're still at the beck and call of your fancy piece, I s'pose?" Elsie said brightly, when the silence between them became awkward.

"Not any more. That was summat else I was going to tell you," Carrie said, and saw Elsie's eyes widen.

"What happened, then?" she taunted. "Did my lady suspect you of dipping your fingers in her jewel-box, like the one before you?"

"Of course not! She's got this new Honourable making up to her now, and she wanted me in attendance when she went off to his country estate for Christmas until the New Year. I refused to go, so I was told to leave." It didn't sound quite so brave, said so baldly, and Elsie clearly thought the same.

"Are you completely dippy or summat?" she demanded. "You'd have been well set up there, girl, if her ladyship ends up married to an Honourable. What in hell's name possessed you to refuse?"

"Ma, of course. Ma's babby's due at the turn of the year, and she looks so poorly now, and so heavy, that I'm sure it could happen any time. And besides – " she hadn't yet put her fears into words, but suddenly they all came pouring out. "I've got a real bad feeling about this birthing, Elsie. I keep thinking we ain't never going to see it laugh or hear it cry, and the only time we'll spend with it is seeing it laid out in one of the little coffins Pa makes."

There. She had said it all now, and she wasn't even aware of how her shoulders seemed to be shaking so badly, or how Elsie's rough hands with the whiff of fish on them were shaking them even more. Her head spun for a minute, and she saw Elsie's eyes glaring into hers.

"Good God almighty! You must be going dafter'n I thought to get such stupid ideas! Your Ma don't know you feel like this, do she? And she ain't expecting nothing bad to happen, is she?"

"*No*. And you're not to breathe a word of this to anyone, mind," Carrie said sharply. "It's just me. It's just – oh, everything happening at once, I suppose. I'm happy for Wilf, and I'm glad and sorry all at the same time about leaving Miss Barclay. It wasn't all bad, Elsie, and at least Cook was always kind to me. But now there's John's news."

She gave a great shuddering sniff, feeling truly as if the weight of the world was on her shoulders, and despising herself for such weakness. It was not the stuff of the Stuckey family. Ma would never give in to such weakness, not even when she was aching all over and weary of carrying the babby.

"So what's he done then? It surely can't be too bad. Not your wonderful John!" Elsie said, trying to tease her out of the doldrums.

Carrie told her quickly, unable to bear this mockery, however well-meant. And Elsie, as ever, was more practical about the news.

"Well, that ain't so bad. At least he ain't going for ever, and he still means to marry you, don't he?"

"Yes, but – "

"Well then, stop bleating, and just be glad you've got a good man to look after you," Elsie said, in sudden irritation.

"He won't be here to look after me – "

"He will when he gets that new boat of his." Elsie's eyes took on a faraway look. "Do you think he'll take me on one of these trips if I ask him? Maybe he'll even take his boat across to Wales. I wouldn't mind seeing some of these towns my boyos keep telling me about."

As if the words were a trigger, there was a sudden shifting in her attitude, and Carrie had the distinct feeling that she wanted to get her out of the cottage. She had glanced at the old clock in the corner of the room, as if she was expecting somebody. There was no reason why Elsie shouldn't have other friends, though Carrie had never heard her mention another girl's name in friendship. But it was time to go, anyway. She had been away from home too long, and she wanted to be sure Ma wasn't taxing herself with any of the household chores.

"I'll see you on Christmas morning then," she said, when there didn't seem to be anything else to say.

"I'll be there bright and early and ready for anything," Elsie said cheerfully. "And you just be in a better humour by then, or I'll wish I'd stayed home by meself."

Carrie nodded, knowing it was time she calmed down. There was no point in fretting over things that couldn't be changed, and if John had made up his mind to take the travelling job, then that was that. She would surely get used to it.

She hurried back along the waterfront with her head down against the biting December wind, and cannoned straight into somebody coming the other way. She muttered an apology, and heard a cheery male voice say it didn't matter at all, *cariad*, before the figure moved on.

Carrie frowned for a moment, thinking about the odd word. She had no idea what it meant, although there was something about the lilting accent that was vaguely familiar. Maybe he was one of the foreign sailors who were always hereabouts . . . though he hadn't sounded foreign.

It was a minor puzzle that served to divert her mind from her own problems for a moment. She glanced behind her to take a brief stock of the jaunty young fellow, and was just in time to see him disappear inside Elsie Miller's cottage.

Chapter 17

Early on Christmas morning, the little house on Jacob's Wells Road was warm and steamy with the tantalising aroma of cooking. The goose had been slowly roasting all night, and the juices that ran out of it and into the pan below for the potatoes and parsnips to cook in later, were enough to get every mouth watering.

The goose and other Christmas fare had been duly sent down from the Barclay mansion, along with Carrie's wages, together with a brief note written in Mr Barclay's own hand to say he wished the girl and her family well. Ma had exclaimed in surprise when she saw it.

"You must have done summat to please the family, then, if he took the trouble to do this, Carrie."

"I never saw much of him, but he always passed the time of day with me if we met on the stairs," she said, startled herself by the magnanimous gesture.

"You're sure you weren't too rash in leaving a good employer?" Ma said, eycing her keenly.

Carrie shook her head. "I know I did right. My place is here, and now that our Wilf's going to be bringing in a regular wage every week, he's said there's no need for me to be thinking of finding outside work until you get your strength back after the babby, Ma."

She crossed her fingers behind her back as she spoke, praying that this house wasn't going to be plunged into a place of mourning once the birthing was done. Try as she might, she still couldn't rid herself of the premonition of death, but she was determined that such bad thoughts were not going to spoil Christmas Day.

She turned from basting the goose with a smile, just as Billy came hurtling down the stairs to seek out his Christmas stocking.

For a while, they had thought there would be nothing to go into it, but now everybody had one containing an apple and an orange and some nuts. There were also a few small playthings in Billy's, that Pa, as well as Wilf, had been fashioning in secret. It had amused both men to discover that each had thought of the same thing.

"Perhaps I should take you into partnership with me, Pa," Wilf had said cautiously, when he'd seen the spinning top Pa had made with such perfect symmetry.

Sam had grunted, and told him not to be so daft, and he'd see hell freeze before he worked for Gaffer Woolley again – unless the man came and begged him, of course.

Pa always liked to give himself an option, Carrie realised, but it wasn't a bad thing to do. It wasn't like backing down if you had a compromise to think about. It still let you keep hold of some of your pride.

"Oh Ma, this is lovely," she said now, revealing the beautifully worked hanky in her own stocking. There was an intricate letter C thickly embroidered in satin stitch in one corner, and the hanky gave out a sweet scent of fresh laundering and pressing.

"As long as it pleases you," Ma said. "'Tain't much, love, but 'tis personal."

"And I love it," Carrie gave her a quick hug, knowing only too well that even a small square of fabric like this one could take many hours to transform it into a lace-edged thing of beauty.

They all gave each other small gifts, all promising that next year would be better. Even Elsie arrived with a small basket of fruit from the market, a bit overripe in places,

298

and probably the leftovers when the day's business was done, but a gift nonetheless.

The Travis men weren't arriving until mid-day, and the Stuckeys were going to church as usual on Christmas morning. Elsie wasn't a church-goer, and volunteered to stay behind and keep an eye on the cooking. It wasn't really necessary, especially as Ma decided at the last minute that she didn't think she could toil up the hills after all.

At this, they began fidgeting and wondering if none of them should go, but in the end they were all shooed out of the house, leaving Elsie and Ma behind.

Carrie held onto Billy's hand, her heart starting to lift with a feeling of happiness as they set out on that crisp, bright morning. Snow was in the air, and they could smell it, but it hadn't come yet. And she loved this. The walk to church, dressed in their Sunday best, and nodding to acquaintances and friends.

The only people about on Christmas morning were churchgoers like themselves, and even Pa had tidied himself, and resembled the old Pa today, more than at any other time lately. Wilf, of course, was already in his seventh heaven, with thoughts of Nora and his settled future filling his head, and once the service had begun inside the ancient building, they all sang the old hymns lustily.

"Give my best regards to your lady wife, and the season's greetings to you all," the minister told Pa when he was bidding them all farewell after the service. "I'll be down to see her at the house some time during the week, Mr Stuckey."

"Thank you, sir," Sam said, awkward as always at the thought of having a gentleman come to the house, and a clerical one at that.

Billy ran on ahead, like a child let out of school, and Carrie had to admit that the minister did go on a bit, even on Christmas Day. But the crib had been lovely, as was the church, all decorated with holly and evergreens, and the baby Jesus doll had reminded her of their own coming baby. She had sent up a special little prayer for it, and for Ma too.

They reached home just as a hire carriage was drawing up outside, and for a moment Carrie's heart stopped. Anxiety for Ma dominated her thoughts these days, and she breathed a sigh of relief as she saw the driver alight to open the door, and then John jumped down to help his uncle stiffly out of the carriage.

"Christ, but we're grand today, aren't we?" Wilf muttered in an aside to Carrie.

"Keep your voice down," she hissed. "The minister's just been telling us all to be loving to one another, and if you can't be generous-hearted today, then when can you be, our Wilf? Don't go spoiling things for Ma, neither."

Nor for me, she added silently, her face breaking into a smile as she saw the pleasure on Uncle Oswald's face as he recognised her. She ran to greet them, pressing a light kiss on his old creased cheek.

"It's lovely to see you both, and such good timing too. We've just come from church, so we can all go inside and get warm together."

She drew them all into the family circle with her words, and once inside the house, introductions were quickly made, and then the men sat stiffly around making small talk, while the womenfolk attended to the cooking.

"How do you think it's going, Ma?" Carrie whispered, when she heard Pa give a short laugh a while later. "I don't hear our Wilf saying much."

"Nor you will," Ma said dryly.

The girls had insisted that she sit on a stool in the scullery, directing things, while they warmed plates and made the gravy from the oozing juices from the goose, and tipped the steaming vegetables into the huge serving dishes.

"Perhaps when they've had their fill, they'll relax a bit more," Carrie said hopefully. "John can converse with anyone, but if our Wilf stays so starchy, he's going to spoil things."

They heard Pa laugh again, followed by Uncle Oswald's chortle, and Carrie felt cheered by the sound. It had been a clever idea to get John's uncle here as well, she realised, since they could jaw together over old times, and cover any awkwardness between Wilf and John.

"Did I hear you say you usually play charades during the afternoon?" Elsie said, flushed from being in the midst of this large family, and the enormity of preparing so many meals at one time.

Carrie nodded. "Or any other kind of party game, for those who aren't sleeping off the effects of the meal," she said with a grin.

"I think you can leave me out of it this time," Ma said. "I may do some of the guessing, but I'll leave the acting to you young 'uns."

"Frank was always the best at guessing," Carrie said wistfully. "Still, we've got Elsie and John and his uncle to make up the teams today."

Elsie smiled dutifully, though she'd never been much of a one for party games. Come to think of it, she'd never really bccn in any large enough gathering to indulge in them. But she supposed a game of charades would liven up the day, and at least it would stop her guiltily wishing that she could have spent the day with Dewi Griffiths instead.

She knew she should be grateful for the largesse of the Stuckeys, and so she was, but since she had spent all those hectic hours in the lustful arms of Dewi Griffiths, she had been unable to think of much else. Even Wilf had finally lost his charm, as far as Elsie was concerned.

301

Carrie didn't know about Dewi yet though, and perhaps it was just as well, since Carrie's association with young men, even John, didn't seem to be anywhere near as hot-blooded as Elsie's. It gave her a delicious shiver, just thinking about Dewi.

"You're not feeling faint, are you, Elsie?" Ma said. "You gave quite a shudder then. Sometimes the heat in the scullery gets a bit too much for me too."

"I'm all right, Mrs Stuckey, thanks for asking," Elsie said quickly, thankful that this fine upright woman could have no idea of the lurid images going around in Elsie Miller's head at that moment.

Images of herself and Dewi Griffiths making hay in what used to be old Granpa Miller's bedroom, and his rich deep Welsh voice whispering in her ear and telling her she was the *cariad* of his heart . . .

"Wake up then, Elsie, or have you gone into a trance now?" she heard Carrie say. "That's twice I've asked you to get our Billy to set the table, and check that Pa's sharpened the carving knife for the goose."

Elsie blinked. God, but she'd been quite carried away there . . . and it was a good thing the place was so hot and steamy and that they all had faces as red as turkey-cocks, or somebody would surely have wondered at her own.

Ma had decided on the table places, and Billy had made out little cards for them all, writing their names in his large childish hand-writing to show off his skill. In the middle of the table was the small Christmas crib Pa had made a long time ago when Carrie was a small girl. It always came out on Christmas Day, with its tiny wooden animals that Frank and Wilf had made when they were still learning their craft at Pa's knee. It was a symbol, Carrie thought now. A symbol of continuity, of faith and family love, and everything that was good. It was a thought to cherish.

She raised her eyes from the centrepiece, to meet John's

steady gaze, seated opposite her. And she caught her breath. There was such a look of love in his eyes that it brought a lump to her throat, and a throb to her heart. His love was blatant for all who cared to look, and she knew it must be reflected in her own tremulous smile.

But by now everyone else was busily exclaiming at the sight of the fine goose Pa was triumphantly bringing to the table, ready to carve. And the special look of love was a small, private moment between Carrie and John, as sometimes happens in the midst of a roomful of people. It was too poignant to last, and it was John himself who broke the spell.

"I'd almost forgotten something," he exclaimed. "Please excuse me for a moment."

He left the table to fetch a package he'd deposited inside the little front door porch, and he handed it across the table to Wilf.

"Perhaps you'd care to deal with this," he said.

The package revealed two bottles of finest port wine, and Wilf thanked him stiffly. Pa had bought a large jug of ale for the day that was already quite depleted, but nobody had thought to buy wine. Carrie said at once that she'd fetch glasses so they could all celebrate Christ's birth with their meal. She looked hard at Wilf as she said it, reminding him that this was a good day, and not one to be ruined by personality clashes.

"I thank you, John, and Oswald too," Pa said, clearly now on first name terms with the older man. "We'm coming up in the world with our new relatives, what with the Travises at our table, and our Wilf getting himself attached to young Nora Woolley and all. It'll be your turn next, I daresay, miss," he added jovially to Elsie.

She had passed up her plate for the meat, and had a great slice of goose slapped onto it. She didn't give him one of her pert answers, Carrie thought thankfully, and merely let the moment pass.

Sam's usual carving precision was not quite as clever today, and he was hacking at the goose with some relish. Ma raised her eyebrows at him, but nobody else seemed to notice, and by the time the plates were loaded with Christmas fare, enjoying the meal was of more importance than heeding Pa's occasional belch.

The port wine was an extra they hadn't expected. They toasted everyone and everything, especially the Lord Jesus Christ. And then their absent Frank, and Ma's coming babby, and Carrie and John, and Wilf and Nora. And since nobody should be left out of anything on Christmas Day, they toasted the rest of the household too, and the Barclays for sending them the goose.

Pa's words were becoming decidedly slurred by the time the meal ended. But he declared that it was the finest meal they had had in ages, and complimented the womenfolk profusely. Carrie was becoming increasingly mortified at such a show in front of guests, though Ma seemed to be finding it quite funny now, and so did John and his uncle. She hoped they weren't laughing *at* Pa, and was mightily thankful when he decided to take himself off to bed for an hour to sleep it off.

"Thank goodness," Ma said with a grin. "He wouldn't have been able to play charades in that state, anyway. Lord knows what antics he'd have got up to. Now then, Billy and you girls, help me clear all this out of the parlour. I might even go up and join your Pa for a sleep later."

"Why don't you go now, Ma?" Carrie said. "Me and Elsie and Billy can do the washing-up."

"I'll help you," John said at once.

Wilf gave a derisive snort. "That's women's work, man. You don't catch me skivvying."

"It never diminished a man to carry out plates and dishes he helped to empty, neither," John retorted.

Carrie could see the battle brewing. "Nobody asked you to help, our Wilf," she said quickly. "Nor you, John."

"It's no trouble, love. You forget that my uncle and I have fared for ourselves for many years, so I'm quite familiar with dishrags and plate-washing."

He wouldn't be dissuaded, and Wilf and Uncle Oswald were left in the parlour together, with nothing to say, and nowhere to go to avoid each other. Oswald solved the problem by simply closing his eyes and snoring gently, while Wilf folded his arms and stared at nothing. He was being uncouth and he knew it, and it was not the way Nora Woolley would expect her gentleman to behave.

Nora was a lady, and if Wilf intended being a match for her, he grudgingly knew he had best mend his ways. Even if it meant being sociable for the rest of this day to his sister's fellow, he thought with a scowl.

He didn't really know why he'd taken such an instant dislike to John Travis, except that Wilf always mistrusted folk who seemed to be as working-class as himself, and turned out to be better-educated and more silver-tongued, and better-looking too.

He scowled again, for if that wasn't reason enough for disliking a fellow who could also beat him hollow at the fisticuffs, then he didn't know what was.

The object of his dislike was suddenly standing in front of him and rolling down his sleeves before he sat down in Pa's chair. Wilf bristled at the presumption, and then he felt his lip curl. A fellow who picked up a dishrag to help the women in the scullery, except in the direst of circumstances, wasn't much of a man at all, in his opinion.

"We're going to play charades, I understand. I suggest that you and I play our own charade, and pretend to like one another, for this day, at least," John said. "Is it agreed?"

Wilf felt his eyes narrow. That was another thing. The fellow came straight out with it, leaving you no margin for getting out of things if you wanted to. And a charade it would be, he thought irritably. But it made sense too. And that was *another* bloody mark against him . . . he had the gift of the gab and could always make sense.

"Well?" John persisted. "Do we shake on it?"

"Good God, do you want blood, man?" Wilf said explosively. "I'll agree, and that's enough."

"Good. So tell me about this new venture of yours. It sounds a great opportunity, and I haven't had the chance to congratulate you on it yet."

Wilf's eyes narrowed even more. But the fellow looked and sounded sincere, and he could hardly be churlish enough to go on snubbing him. He even looked interested . . . and before he knew it, Wilf was expounding on the golden chance Mr Cedric Woolley had put his way.

"I'm glad for you, Wilf. A man has to have a dream." John looked down at his hands, and then glanced towards the scullery where sounds of mirth were coming from the girls and young Billy. "Has Carrie told you of my plans?"

"We don't discuss you," Wilf began stiffly.

"Then I'll tell you myself. I'm leaving Bristol soon for a travelling job, and I'll be gone about four months."

"What kind of a travelling job?" Wilf's interest was caught now. "I thought your life was on the river."

"So it is, and that's where I want to be eventually, in a fine new boat big enough to take paying folk out for picnics and days out. But a boat like that costs money."

"So how are you thinking of getting this money then?"

John gave a slight smile. Perhaps it hadn't been such a good idea to start this conversation with Wilf after all, since the two of them had managed to bloody each other's noses almost the first time they'd met.

"With my fists. I'm going as a sparring partner for a fighting promotor."

"Christ, our Carrie won't like that!" Wilf forgot his own antagonism to this man, imagining his sister's fury.

She was no wilting daisy herself, and she could be as vinegary as the next one with her tongue, but when it came to fisticuffs, she was dead against it.

"She doesn't like it, but she sees the sense in it," John went on. "We want to be wed on her birthday next June, and if all goes well, I aim to be naming my new boat after her as a wedding gift."

Wilf stared at him. Other men's dreams weren't the same as his, and he'd never had anything as grand in mind as owning a boat, but he could respect another's dreams.

"Then I wish you luck," he said now.

"And you too," John said briefly.

They had little in common, and he had the feeling they would never really be friends, but a mutual respect was better than nothing. And it was going to be far more comfortable in the family circle for them to tolerate one another, than to always be at one another's throats.

It was worth it, too, to see the delight in Carrie's face when she saw them apparently conversing amicably. She didn't even notice that each of them turned to the idea of playing the party game of charades with some relief.

Hours later, Carrie reflected that all in all it had been a good day. By then, she was snug in her bed in her old room, and Elsie sleeping on a mattress in the corner, having been persuaded to stay the night. Billy slept in Wilf's room now, in Frank's old bed, which gave Carrie some privacy.

John and his uncle had arranged for the hire carriage to take them back up Bedminster Hill at about eight o'clock, and she and John had at last managed to have some time alone together in the scullery while Uncle Oswald was saying his thanks to her parents.

"Am I allowed a Christmas kiss at last?" John said softly. "I've spent the entire day wanting to hold you in my arms, instead of playing the gentleman and trying to be pleasant to your brother."

"Was it such an effort?" she teased. "I thought the two of you carried it off splendidly, if you want to know."

"I don't, and nor do I want to waste this time alone with you talking about Wilf," he said. "All I want is to hold you close to me."

He held out his arms, and she went into them willingly, wanting him every bit as much as he wanted her. She had already discovered that the waiting time of courtship could be as frustrating as it was sweet.

"Then if you don't hurry up and kiss me, I shall want to know the reason why," she whispered back.

His mouth sought and found hers, and there was no more need for talking. The love that flowed between them was powerful and strong, and when she was in his arms she could forget everything else. Even the parting that was to come . . . resolutely, Carrie blotted it out of her mind, refusing to let it spoil these precious moments together.

She leaned her head against him, feeling the steady beat of his heart against her body, and revelling in the warmth of his arms around her.

"I wish it could always be like this," she murmured. "I wish we could always be together." She stopped, blushing, wondering if she had been too forward, but she felt him hold her tighter, and knew that his feelings matched hers.

"And I wish I need never let you out of my arms for a single second," he said, his voice roughened with desire. "I wish I could watch you go to sleep in my arms every night, and waken you every morning with my kisses. I love you so much, Carrie."

She felt the sweet thrill of passion run through her veins at his words.

"Oh John, I love you too," she whispered, winding her arms around his neck to hold him closer.

The door handle rattled, alerting them that there was only a thin layer of wood between them and the parlour, and they broke apart reluctantly. As an engaged couple, they were allowed a certain amount of leeway and time to be alone, but not too much. And Sam Stuckey could make a fine old noise of clearing his throat when he decided young Travis had been alone with his daughter for long enough.

"Your uncle's waiting, boy," Sam said pointedly, when the door opened, "and it's starting to snow. You won't want to be about too late if the weather sets in."

"That we won't," John said briskly. They were already paying the hire carriage driver over the odds for coming out on Christmas Day, but they had had no choice. Uncle Oswald could never have got to Jacob's Wells Road on foot, and John couldn't have come without him. And the cost of hiring a carriage was a small price to pay for this best Christmas Day he had spent in years.

Now, in the darkness of her bedroom, Carrie closed her eyes blissfully, remembering how John had held her so close and told her he loved her. She was in that lovely half-state of warmth, imagining a hazy future married to the love of her life, when she heard Elsie call her name.

"Carrie, are you awake?" the other girl said in a loud stage whisper.

"I am now," Carrie said. "I was almost asleep."

"Well, I can't sleep," Elsie stated. "Me mind's too full of stuff, and me head's going round and round."

"You shouldn't have eaten and drunk so much then," Carrie retorted. "And Ma's plum pudding's not the best thing to go to bed on, neither."

"It ain't that," Elsie said. "I was thinking about summat else."

"Tell me in the morning," Carrie said, but Elsie was wide awake now. In the end, Carrie could stand the noisy stage whispers no longer.

"Look, you're going to waken the whole house in a minute," she said crossly. "You'd better come over here and tell me what's on your mind, then perhaps we can both get some sleep."

Elsie padded across the small bedroom and slid beneath Carrie's quilt with a shiver, trying to snuggle up to her friend. The bed was much too small for them both, and Carrie wriggled in annoyance to get as far away from her as possible.

"My God, but you're touchy, ain't you?" Elsie said in amusement. "I hope you ain't going to be this standoffish when you share a bed every night with your lusty John!"

Carrie was thankful for the darkness of the night then, sure that her cheeks must be scarlet at hearing the careless remark. It might be just a casual thing for Elsie to say in her usual unthinking way, but it had intruded into her dream and ruined it. John had made it all sound so beautiful, watching her fall asleep, and awakening her with a kiss . . . and Elsie had the knack of making it all sound so ugly.

"If that's all you wanted to say – "

"It ain't. God, what's up with you, Carrie? Ain't we had a nice day? I was on me best behaviour, and I never made up to your Wilf for a minute, did I?" she said indignantly.

"You were very well behaved," Carrie said, mellowing at the hurt in Elsie's voice. Just as swiftly, she reminded herself that her friend was entirely alone in the world, while she, Carrie, had everything. A good home, a loving family, and John. She was the lucky one.

"So do you want to hear about Dewi or not then?" Elsie whispered, unable to keep the great secret to herself for one minute longer.

"What's Dewi? Is it a dog or something?" Carrie said, starting to giggle. She'd had a glass or two of port wine as well, and her own head wasn't as steady as usual.

"Oh, thanks very much!" Elsie said, with mock annoyance. "*No*, ninny, Dewi's me little Welsh fellow. A real grand boyo he is too, with dark flashing eyes and a real swagger to his walk."

A vague memory came into Carrie's mind at that moment, but she couldn't quite capture it. Besides, she'd heard too many of Elsie's sudden fancies before. She'd be mad about this Dewi fellow for a week or so, and then he'd be history, and there'd be some other strange name cropping up in her conversation.

"It's the real thing this time, Carrie," Elsie was whispering excitedly now. "Dewi's better than all the others put together, and he makes me feel good."

"Oh yes. Until the next one comes along, I suppose," Carrie said, feeling her head begin to swim, and only half listening now. "I've heard it all before, Elsie. Go back to bed and go to sleep."

There was a small silence, and she felt Elsie sit up in bed. She guessed the girl was staring down at her, even though she couldn't see much in the darkness. If it wasn't for the snow clouds lightening the sky a mite through the bedroom window, the room would be in its usual inky blackness. Carrie tugged the quilt back around herself, wondering how much more pointed she could be that she wanted to be left alone and to get some sleep.

"You ain't heard that I've *done* it before though," Elsie said quietly.

For a second, Carrie wondered if she was dreaming, or if Elsie had really said what she thought she'd said. She twisted round in the bed at once, staring through the gloom. Elsie lay back in satisfaction, and folded her arms across her chest, sure that she'd got Carrie's full attention now.

"What do you mean – you've *done* it?" she said. Though she knew full well what Elsie meant. Of course she knew. She hadn't been born yesterday. What she

311

didn't understand was why Elsie was making such a show of telling her. She'd hinted so many times before that she knew all about laying with a boy, and that it was a fine old pastime . . . not that Carrie had really believed her goings-on for one minute. She'd never really known if it had all been said for show, to shock . . . but she was saying it now as if it was the first time . . .

"Me and Dewi," Elsie said. "Dewi and me."

It seemed as if she couldn't say anything else for the moment, and Carrie sat up now, wrapping the quilt around her shoulders and snapping out a question.

"Do you mean to tell me that all this time you've been play-acting with me, and that you and Dewi – " God, she was doing it now, splicing them together like bookends – "that it's the first time you've ever actually *done* it, with this Dewi?"

"I do," Elsie said, as solemnly as taking an oath. And then her voice suddenly dissolved into sheer delight and awe. "And Carrie, I can tell you it's even better than I ever imagined it could be! It needs to be done with someone you really like, see? So I reckon you'll be all right with your John," she ended up in her more usual style.

"So you've been lying to me all this time? You've been as – as – " indignantly, Carrie had no intention of letting this go.

"*Virginal*, that's the word, duck, though when the minister says it he makes it sound as wicked as fornicating, don't he?" Elsie said with a snort of laughter. "But I never really meant to deceive you, Carrie. It was just too easy, I suppose, and people have always thought the worst of me, anyway, so why not let 'em, I say?"

There was a sudden loud banging on the wall between Carrie's room and her parents' bedroom, and they both jumped with alarm.

"If you two girls ain't going to go to sleep tonight, then

312

go downstairs to do your talking, and let those that want to sleep get some," Pa bawled out.

"Sorry Pa," Carrie called back.

She glared into the dimness to where she could see Elsie hunched up on the bed, and hugging her knees. Her hair was spilling all around her in its usual disarray. And if there was ever a moment when she could believe that Elsie Miller had been – had been – *fornicating* – it was now, when she looked so wanton and so brazen.

"I don't want to hear any more," she said. "I just want to go to sleep, so I'd be obliged if you'd go back to your mattress and give me some room."

She yanked the quilt away from Elsie as she spoke. There was no logical reason why she should feel so upset, or so betrayed. Elsie had played the flirt often enough . . . but all the time, Carrie supposed she really had believed that it was all a game, or she had simply *wanted* to believe it. But now, everything was different between them.

Elsie had had carnal knowledge of a man, as Mr Pritchard would say in his direst sermon voice, and that was a sin. Carrie shivered as her friend almost flounced out of her bed and curled up on the mattress on the floor, tugging her blankets around her.

"I might have known you'd go all po-faced about it," she snapped. "God help your John when he tries to lay a finger on you, that's all. You'll probably go screaming for the constables."

The hammering on the bedroom wall effectively shut her up at last, but Carrie lay sleepless and restless for a long while afterwards. She felt a soft trickle of dampness on her cheeks and dashed it away angrily.

When she and John were married, everything between them would be beautiful. They would have waited for intimacy between a man and a woman, the way God intended folk to wait, until they had the Church's blessing on their union, and their families had come together to witness it all. Making love should be a celebration and an avowal of love, not like Elsie and Dewi's hole and corner affair.

Carrie's own grand thoughts began to annoy her. She wasn't grand, or pompous . . . but this was the way Ma always spoke of such things – if she ever talked about them at all. It was the way Mr Pritchard referred to them in sermons – if he ever referred to them at all. And she knew full well she risked the wrath of Pa if ever she did anything so wicked as lying with a man before she was wed . . . or if she was found out, she could almost hear Elsie say mockingly . . .

And it was true. By now she knew she was as capable of passion as anyone else, and there were times when she ached to feel John's arms around her, and discover the last great mystery of two joining as one. And it was probably getting caught out and fearing the sting of Pa's leather belt, that stopped her more than anything else. So much for noble thoughts.

Chapter 18

On Boxing Day afternoon, there would be the annual small boat races on the river to look forward to, when boats of all descriptions vied for the honour of monetary prizes donated by local boatbuilding firms.

By morning, the ground was blanketed with a moderate covering of snow, though the wind had begun to blow much of it into swirling drifts. The Stuckeys shivered in the sharpness of late December, their breaths blowing great plumes of air into the cold, as they opened doors a fraction to inspect the day.

"For God's sake, close that door," Sam roared at Billy, as the boy lingered with the toe of one boot delightedly kicking up the snow.

"I've got to see if it's deep enough to get me tray out to slide down to the wharf," he complained. "Can I, Pa?"

"Depends if there's enough snow left for it by the time this wind's done. If there ain't, you'll end up bumping your backside from top to bottom, and be all the sorrier for it. Don't come crying to me if you can't sit down for a week."

"I won't, Pa," Billy said. "I won't go hurting meself, neither."

"Do you know better than your Pa now, then?" Sam growled, suffering with a bellyache from yesterday's over-abundance of ale and goose and port wine.

"Oh, let the boy be," Ma said mildly. "He'll learn the hard way, same as all of us. You go and stoke up that fire

315

for me, Sam, and let me get on with the breakfast. You'll be taking him down to see the races, in any case?"

"I daresay. I sure as hell ain't letting *you* go sliding down there in your condition, woman," he retorted. "I suppose those two girls will be coming as well. Giggling and jabbering halfway through the night, they were. Though, come to think of it, I ain't heard no sound from our Wilf yet," he said suddenly, his grumbles switching to the unusual fact that his eldest son wasn't up and about.

"That's because he was off out early," May said briskly. "He wanted to take a look around this workshop Gaffer Woolley's putting his way."

She leaned against the doorpost for a minute, her hand in the small of her back as the familiar nagging little pains stabbed at her. The babby wasn't due for a week yet, but she knew the signs well enough. A woman's body always made a show of practising the pains before it was quite ready to push the babby out.

May was an old hand at helping other women give birth, and was prepared for the ordeal to come. This time, she'd be the patient, and as soon as she was sure the contractions had properly begun, Carrie would go and fetch the midwife, Mrs Green, to help her with the birthing. The men would be banished from the vicinity, and if it happened at night, as most babbies seemed to do, then young Billy must just bury his head beneath the bedclothes and ignore any small sounds she might make.

May gritted her teeth. She would bear her pain tight-lipped for as long as possible, but she knew the pangs of childbirth only too well. She'd been through them four times already, and she tried not to dwell on the fact that this little lot was coming at a time when her body was settling into middle-age and was nowhere near as supple as of old. But if the Lord hadn't wanted her to have another babby, He wouldn't have sent her one, she affirmed, with her own brand of logic, and there was no going against the Lord's Will.

"Are you all right, Ma?" she heard Carrie say, as the girl came clattering down the stairs with Elsie following.

"Just a twinge, duck." She moved away from the doorpost and gave the girls a brief smile.

"You sit down, and I'll make the porridge and breakfast toast," Carrie said, but May waved her aside.

"I'm not an invalid yet, girl, and I don't aim to be acting the lady until my time. Yesterday was an exception, with so many folk in the house and the heavy lifting and all, but I'm quite capable of managing breakfast."

"I don't want any, Mrs Stuckey," Elsie said quickly. "I'll be on my way now, and thanks for yesterday."

She avoided Carrie's eyes as she spoke. As far as she was concerned, Carrie was in one of her silent, prissy-mouthed moods again, and she couldn't be doing with it. If she did but know it, Carrie was simply too embarrassed to look at her, since she'd had such a night of tossing and turning, unwillingly imagining Elsie lying in some ardent Welsh boyo's arms, and wishing so badly it was herself and John Travis.

"You'll not leave this house on such a cold morning without some food inside you, my girl," Ma said firmly. "And aren't you going to watch the Boxing Day river races today?"

"I really couldn't eat a thing. I'm still full from yesterday, Mrs Stuckey, but I'll see you all down by the river this afternoon," Elsie said. "I want to go home and tidy up the place a bit first. I thought I might put a lick of paint on the walls too, before the landlord starts complaining, seeing as it's got so dingy inside. Me granpa never bothered overmuch about such things."

Neither did Elsie Miller, to Carrie's sure and certain knowledge! She almost laughed out loud at the virtuous look in Elsie's eyes. But if this sudden burst of domesticity was the effect of having a boy come to visit her, then perhaps this Dewi Griffiths was going to turn out to be a good influence after all.

"We'll be around our usual place for the races," Carrie told her casually. "So we'll look out for you."

It was about as far as she could go right now, and in her mother's presence, to reviving a friendship that had somehow gone sour during the night. But Elsie never bore malice, and she merely nodded and grinned, and wrapped her shawl tightly around her body before stepping out into the freezing morning.

Wilf was surprised to find Gaffer Woolley and his cousin at the warehouse that morning. Though he guessed that he shouldn't have been. Gaffer took little time off during the year, except for special days when his womenfolk would have something to say on the matter of his working all hours. He sensed that the two Woolley men were alike in many respects, both being the kind of men who took a pride in their achievements and in showing them off to others. And this London cousin would seem to be a firecracker of a businessman.

"Well now, young Stuckey, it's good to see a man who's as keen as mustard," Mr Cedric greeted him, just when he was wondering awkwardly if he should be here poking around at all.

After all, the last time he had been in this warehouse had been on the bitter day Gaffer had stood him and his father and brother off, and the relationship had gone steadily downhill since then. But everything was changed now, he reminded himself. Now he had the say-so to court Gaffer's daughter, and he was going to the Woolley house later on for Boxing Day supper. He lifted his head a mite higher and after nodding at Mr Cedric, he spoke directly to Gaffer.

"I trust you don't mind. I'm anxious to see the premises I'm to use, Gaffer."

Gaffer shrugged. "As you will, boy. Come inside out of the cold and I'll show you the place I mean."

They had to drag the heavy warehouse doors open against the drifted snow. Already thin shafts of sunlight were glinting on the overnight fall and it was starting to melt. Wilf had passed a dozen small urchins on Jacob's Wells Road, up early and slithering down the hill on their tin trays, and guessed that his brother Billy would be among them by now.

As soon as Wilf was inside the huge warehouse, the familiar smells of sawdust and aromatic timbers rose to his nostrils, as sweet as nectar. Stacks of cut planks were piled high, awaiting despatch or orders for use, and he felt a sudden ache of nostalgia for the old days, when he and Frank and Pa had worked to the music of the saws before the raw cut timbers were passed on to the crafstmen they were, to be fashioned and carved into things of beauty.

It was a far cry from creating fittings and fitments for Brunel's great ship and others of lesser magnificence, to making toys for children.

But beggars couldn't be choosers, and he was grateful for this chance fate had handed him. And he'd make Woolley's Toys the best that could be found anywhere in the West Country, he vowed. Maybe the best from here to London . . .

"Does this suit you then, boy?" he heard Gaffer say shortly. "It's the best I can do for now, but I gather you'll have your own workshop behind the new shop in due course."

He realised they had walked the length of the warehouse and he hadn't even noticed it. He'd been so wrapped up in his love of his creative materials, and the challenge that was opening up to him. But now he stepped into one of

319

the old storerooms at the back of the place, and nodded at once.

"It's perfect," he declared. For a moment, he wondered if he dared ask about sharing the work with Pa, but he decided it could wait a while yet. It was Cedric who was paying him his wages, and he still had the feeling Gaffer was loaning him this storeroom on sufferance. Wilf Stuckey wasn't the man he'd have chosen for his daughter, and he didn't want to push his luck too far too soon.

"Then we'll see you this evening," Gaffer said, clearly not wanting to prolong this meeting any longer than necessary. "My daughter is naturally pleased that you'll be putting in an appearance for supper."

"I look forward to it," Wilf said gravely, and tipped his hat to both gentlemen before turning on his heel and going back through the vast warehouse, with his boots ringing on the cobblestones.

"You've a young man to be proud of there, Aaron," Cedric Woolley said thoughtfully, watching the upright stance of the retreating Wilf.

Gaffer grunted. "Mebbe so, though I wouldn't tell him so. It don't do to be too free with your praises when you've a lot of workers under you. It lets 'em get above themselves, and it pays to keep reminding 'em who's boss."

Cedric laughed. "Them's fine sentiments for ordinary workers, cuz, but you're talking about your future son-in-law now – or ain't you given that much thought yet?"

"Not too much," Gaffer retorted. "Besides, young girls don't always know their own minds. Mebbe when Nora's allowed to see young Stuckey as freely and as often as she likes, her feelings will cool down."

Cedric laughed again. "I reckon you're on a loser there, mate. You've only got to see how your girl's eyes light up every time Wilf's name is mentioned to know it's a true love match. No, she's going to end up changing her name to Stuckey all right, and you'd best get used to it."

He slapped his arm around his cousin's shoulder while they strolled on through the warehouse together, never guessing that Aaron was wondering viciously if the whole damn world was conspiring against him with regard to these Stuckeys. The more he tried to be rid of them, through no fault of his own other than lack of work, the more determined they seemed to be back in his life.

And he could still feel remorse over Sam, whom he'd once been prepared to think of as friend as much as employee. Sam was a good man if ever there was one, but lately . . . well, it was common knowledge he'd taken to drinking more than usual. And Wilf . . . Wilf was as good a craftsman as his father, and it was only the fact of Nora taking up with him behind his back that had got him really riled up.

Good God, he must be mellowing with the goodwill season, he thought sourly. And since there was no backing down now he'd given his word, he had to agree with Cedric. His girl was in love, and she was never going to change her mind about that. Nora could be heard singing about the house nowadays, and for good or ill, it seemed certain that he was going to end up with a Stuckey for a son-in-law.

John was entering his boat in the races that afternoon. If Carrie had been a betting person, she would have backed him against all comers, if only out of love and loyalty. She'd persuaded her Pa to put a few coppers on John's boat, despite the fact that Ma disapproved of gambling, and the money should be put to better use. But not if he won! Carrie had every confidence in John's manoeuvring of his craft, and her persuasive ways had Pa agreeing amiably enough.

"Mind you, if the boy loses, and your Ma gives us

tongue-pie for throwing good money to the fishes, I shall put the blame on you," he told her.

She laughed, hugging his arm. He was suddenly more like her old Pa, teasing and cheerful, and striding out down Jacob's Wells Road as best he could in the snow, made even more slippery by the hurtling tin trays flying past them with small boys astride them.

"He won't lose," she said confidently. "Ma's making some hot punch and baking mincemeat pies while we're down at the races, and I aim to ask John to come back for some later. As long as you don't object, Pa?" she added hastily.

He jumped out of the way as their Billy screeched a warning and went careering past them on his tray, sending flurries of snow everywhere.

"It seems like a good idea," he said tolerantly. "We'll all be glad of summat hot inside us by then, providing these young devils don't cut the legs out from under us before we see the end of the day."

Two more tobogganers slid past them, their faces red and glowing, shouting out a cheeky greeting to Sam Stuckey and his daughter. Carrie felt her heart lift. Everyone seemed to be in a holiday mood today, and all the bad omens she'd felt for Ma and the babby seemed to dwindle away into foolish fancies.

When they reached the waterfront, she saw John almost at once. He was talking to a familiar figure, and as he caught sight of her, he left Elsie's side and came to greet Carrie and Sam. His hands were cold as he took hers inside his own, and she felt an unreasonable burst of jealousy that he'd spent a little more time with Elsie than with herself.

"I thought you'd never get here," he said at once. "The first race is almost due to begin, so I need to get on board. I just wanted to hear you wish me luck," he said, smiling into Carrie's eyes. The jealousy vanished at once, and on

322

impulse she pulled the blue ribbon out of her coppery curls and handed it to him. The wind caught at her hair at once and blew it all about her face, but she didn't heed its sting.

"Take this to bring you luck, the way ladies used to give favours to their knights," she said.

She had done it without thinking, and she hoped John wouldn't think her too sentimental. To her delight he pressed his lips to the ribbon, and just as quickly, pressed a kiss on her cheek, despite the fact that her father was looking on.

"I'll bring my lady back a trophy at the end of the day," he said gallantly.

"And John – you'll come back to the house for hot punch and a warm, won't you? You're invited."

"Thank you, yes," he said, smiling.

Before Carrie could guess what Elsie was about, the other girl had pushed her way forward and handed John a second ribbon from her own unruly dark hair.

"Take this for double luck, John," she said, and to Carrie's furious disbelief she was obviously waiting for a kiss on her cheek as well.

John took the yellow ribbon with a laugh, and clambered back across the sea of waiting boats, the way all the other contestants were doing. They needed to be nimble-footed, but there was little swell in this part of the river, and none of the boatowners took exception to having their crafts invaded by many feet.

"That wasn't necessary!" Carrie said, blazing.

"What wasn't?" Elsie said, all innocent eyes and mouth.

"You know what," Carrie hissed under cover of the jostling and excitement going on all around them. "You've got your own Welsh boyo sniffing round your skirts, so don't go making those cow eyes at mine! Especially not now."

Elsie was full of wickedness, sensing exactly what Carrie

meant. "Why not now, *especially*? You mean because I might have interesting new ideas about every boy I see, now that Dewi's shown me what's what?" she said, crowing.

"You just try it, that's all!"

The two of them hardly heard the starting gun, or the way the mass of boats surged into action for the first of the races. Rowing-boats went first, and later on it would be the turn of the paddle-tugs, of which John's was one, with a young lad crewing for him.

The river was so full of craft, and the waterfront so full of noisy onlookers, it was possible to carry on a heated conversation in almost total privacy. Carrie and Elsie glowered at one another, still caught up in their own contest.

"What you going to do to stop me?" Elsie goaded, clearly with the devil in her that day. "Are you thinking of tying me up so I can't ever look at your fancy man? Or tying him up, more like. I might even think of doing that meself, for a novelty."

It might have all ended in harmless teasing, since Carrie knew how Elsie's tongue ran away with her once she got started. But things were different now, and unreasonable or not, the coupling of Elsie and this Dewi fellow had unsettled Carrie more than she realised.

For some reason, she kept remembering vividly how Miss Helen Barclay had once commented on the kind of woman who was a self-appointed *femme fatale*. In Helen's opinion, such a creature was the lowest of the low, and someone to keep well away from any beaux of one's own. Suddenly, with her hot eyes and pouting mouth and suggestive words, Elsie had become the *femme fatale* who posed a real threat to Carrie's relationship with John.

In answer to her taunting question, Carrie gave the other girl an almighty push that had her staggering almost into the river. She hadn't meant to push so hard, but fury gave her strength, and her eyes flashed blue fire at her so-called friend.

"You stupid bitch!" Elsie yelled, just managing to recover her balance with the aid of a few helping hands to push her good-naturedly back into the crowd.

The next minute, Elsie had pulled hard at Carrie's loosened curls, hard enough to make her squeal with pain. In swift retaliation, Carrie grabbed a handful of Elsie's tousled locks, producing a howl of rage in return. Within seconds, a small crowd had gathered around them, quickly losing interest in the slow start to the boat races, and sensing that a good fight was about to break out between two nubile young females.

Carrie fought off Elsie's grasping hands, slapping at her opponent's face to free herself. Gasping, Elsie returned the slaps, harder and sharper, until Carrie's cheeks were ringing from the blows.

"I don't want your fancy man," Elsie yelled between slaps. "But if I did, I'm damn sure I could get him off you!"

"There's only one way you'd get a boy interested in you, and my John's not likely to be taken in by the likes of a tart!" Carrie yelled back, to the cheers of the onlookers.

"Do you want to put a wager on it?" Elsie bawled.

"I do not!"

"Two to one the dark one wins," a voice yelled out from the surrounding crowd, to Carrie's acute embarrassment.

"Nay. I reckon t'other 'un's got the edge," another added his piece.

The two opponents ignored the banter and cat-calls of encouragement. They were wrestling with one another now, each breathing heavily, and seemingly getting nowhere. The sweat was running down Carrie's back, despite the cold of the day. It was all so stupid and unnecessary, and it became obvious that neither really intended to hurt the other unduly.

The folk surrounding them began sensing an impasse. They started to disperse and find other interests as the shouts from onlookers farther downstream heralded the turnaround of the boats in the first race, with the leaders clearly in sight now.

Out of the corner of her eye Carrie saw her father thrusting his way through the hordes towards them, with Billy on his heels. The little devil had obviously gone to alert their Pa, she thought furiously. And he would have plenty to say about brawling in public . . . Carrie was suddenly aware of what she had done. *Brawling in public*, indeed . . . and she the one who had been so scathing of John fighting with her brother, and of his whole interest in professional bare-knuckle fighting.

She was worse than a person who did it for gain, she thought in horror. She was acting like a guttersnipe and showing herself up badly. If there had been a hole in which to hide, she'd have gladly jumped into it. But there was no hole big enough to hide her away from Sam Stuckey right now.

He hauled her away from Elsie by the scruff of her collar, separating them as if they were no better than two dogs rutting in the street.

"What in God's name has come over you two?" he said murderously. "I thought you was meant to be best friends, though from the screeches that was coming from this quarter, I'm fair ashamed to own that I know either of you. If you can't behave yourselves, then just keep as far away from each other as possible, for I'll have no brawling gossip attached to the Stuckey name."

"It suits me fine to keep away from your daughter," Elsie said in a high shrill voice. "I ain't got time for a friend who looks down her nose at everything I do."

"And good riddance," Carrie yelled after her as she flounced away into the crowd. She felt Pa shake her arm hard, ordering her to stop shouting like a fishwife or go back to the house and stay with her mother for the rest of the day.

Carrie's eyes smarted with unshed tears. All this fuss had blown up in a moment, and now she had lost her best friend and was in disgrace with her Pa. And as far as she could see, her irritating little wretch of a brother was standing there gloating over it all, because she was the one getting the chafing, and not himself.

"What's so funny?" she snapped at him, resisting the urge to rub at her reddened cheek where Elsie had slapped it.

"You are," Billy taunted. "You and Elsie fighting like two tom cats was funny. It weren't much good, either, not like real men fighting."

Carrie glowered at him. "Well, that's something to be proud of, at least. I've no wish to fight like a man, thank you very much."

"Don't you like to watch John fight?" Billy said. "I seen him up on the Downs a coupla weeks ago, and I cheered 'im all the way, so he gave me summat to spend at the end. I might be a fighter when I grow up."

"Don't talk so daft," Carrie snapped again, thoroughly out of sorts on a day that had begun so well. She was duty bound to stay and watch John race, but if it hadn't been for that, she'd have turned tail and marched straight home again.

Instead, she turned away from Billy's too-knowing eyes, and watched the end of the first race, and the line-up of the next. For the next hour or so she clapped and cheered with the best of them, and couldn't have told anyone who'd come in first or second. She was too deep in depression at the sadness of falling out with Elsie.

It had been a serious falling-out too, and one that she sensed couldn't be patched up too readily. They had each said bitter things to one another, and it had been far worse than their usual meaningless squabbles. The threat

327

in Elsie's manner had put a definite unease in Carrie's mind. If she decided she wanted to do so, Elsie would waste no time in trying to prove that she could take John away from her. She'd do it just for sport . . . and for the first time, Carrie was guiltily glad that in a few days' time, John would be far away from Bristol, and Elsie would be unable to get her hot little claws into him.

She was angry with herself for imagining that John would be taken in by Elsie's flirty ways, or that she herself was feeble enough not to keep her own man. But she knew she could never quite trust Elsie again, and she had discovered that the nasty little streak of jealousy inside her was stronger than she'd realised. It was so virulent that she would even put up with the sadness of being apart from John herself, if it meant she could also keep him away from Elsie. She didn't much like the side of herself that she saw, but as she faced it, she knew it for her own personal Lucifer.

She heard Billy's sudden shout, and felt his hands on her arm.

"John's won his race!" he shouted in her ear. "I knew he would. He's the best, ain't he, our Carrie?"

"Yes, he is," she echoed, ashamed to realise she had seen none of it. But as it all came back into focus now, she could see John holding aloft the winner's trophy for his class. Tucked into his belt was the talisman of her own blue hair ribbon. She could see no evident sign of Elsie's, until she caught a glimpse of a bright yellow streamer floating down the river. And she was defiantly glad. She hated herself for being so all-fired petty, but she was triumphantly *glad*!

"So you did well," Ma said placidly, when the tale of the races had been told over and over, by John and Pa, and an exuberant Billy.

"The boat did well," John said modestly, at which Carrie chided him at once.

"A boat's only as good as the man who steers it, John, so don't sell yourself short. You were more skilful than all the rest of them put together."

"Well, thank you, my lady," he said, smiling. "I tried to see where you were, but you seemed to have disappeared among the crowds."

"Our Carrie and Elsie –" Billy began importantly, and then he gave a howl of rage as Carrie trod on his foot and spoke swiftly.

"There were so many folk there, we didn't get the vantage point we wanted, but even when we couldn't see you all the time, the folk at the water's edge passed on the messages of who was winning to them at the back."

She glared at Billy as she spoke, seeing no reason why her shameful escapade should be broadcast to everyone else. She certainly didn't want John to get wind of it, and Pa had already warned Billy not to go telling of it and upsetting Ma.

"Come and help me carry in the mincemeat pies," she said to him now, "while Pa hands round the hot punch. If you're lucky, he might even let you have a drop mixed with water."

She almost pushed him ahead of her into the scullery, where the sweet aroma of mincemeat and pastry wafted into their nostrils.

"You just keep quiet about Elsie and me, you hear?" she told him severely. "Pa told you it'll only upset Ma, and it's no business of yours anyway."

"All right," he said sulkily. "Will you give me a copper to spend if I don't?" he added hopefully.

She gave a grin, seeing the speculation in his eyes. He was obviously destined to end up a businessman, she thought, with his eye always on the main chance.

329

"I'll give you a cuff around the ear if you do," she said smartly.

By the time they went back to the parlour with the tray of mincemeat pies, John was relating his intentions more fully to her parents. And the thought of keeping him away from Elsie receded into the place it belonged, as the enormity of their own separation overtook her.

"I wish you didn't have to take on this job, John," she murmured.

"It will only be for four months, love. I've had that stipulation put into my contract with Garfield Pond."

"What's one of them stip things?" Billy said at once.

"It means a condition," John told him. "It means that once we've both signed the contract, neither one of us can change our minds on anything. We're signing at a lawyer's office in Queen Square tomorrow. My Aunt Vi's arriving from Keynsham the day after, and it's likely the tour will be moving on at the end of the week."

"So soon?" Carrie said, feeling her heart jump at the thought. Of course she had known it must be soon, but to have days and dates all spelled out made it far too definite.

"The sooner it starts, the sooner it will finish," John said, which didn't make her feel any less edgy at all.

She didn't want him to go. Still less, did she want him to risk being injured or disfigured, or even brain-damaged. She had heard tell that some of the more unfortunate victims of vicious opponents could be . . .

Before he left for home, they managed a short time together in the small inner front porch of the house. The family left them discreetly alone now, and Billy was forbidden to interuppt them.

"I hate the thought of you going away to be a fighter," Carrie said, her mind still full of the parting to come. He tipped up her face with one finger, his voice teasing.

330

"It didn't look that way this afternoon, when you and Elsie were scratching at each other like wild-cats."

"I didn't think you saw!" Now she was doubly embarrassed.

"If I hadn't, young Billy would have told me soon enough," he said dryly. "And I gather that neither of you came off the winner."

"We both ended up as losers," Carrie said, knowing the truth of it. "I lost my best friend, and so did Elsie."

"She'll come round. In a couple of days, she'll be knocking on your door again."

Carrie shook her head. "She won't care enough," she said, a lump beginning to fill her throat. "She's tougher than me, and besides, she's got other interests now. I've lost her, and I'm about to lose you too."

"It's not going to be for ever, sweetheart. I'll write to you as often as I can, of course, but you're not to worry if you don't hear too quickly. The mail coach takes its time when the weather's bad."

Everything was conspiring towards change, Carrie thought. It unsettled her so much, even though she wasn't daft enough to think things could always stay the same. People grew up and moved on . . . but not all at once. Not so that it seemed that it was Carrie Stuckey's life that was turned upside down, while all these other folk had good things happening to them.

First Frank, then Wilf, and now John. Even Elsie, who wouldn't care two hoots that she'd lost her best friend, when she could be cosy in the arms of Dewi Griffiths . . . and Miss Helen Barclay was moving on too. There was little doubt in Carrie's mind that this new Honourable Rupert Egerton was going to figure in that young lady's life from now on.

That left Billy, who could be discounted, since he was still a babe in arms compared to the rest of them. Pa, who still wasn't himself and seemed to have lost his direction

331

in life. Ma, who would be glad and thankful when the new babby arrived, but who was still forbidding Pa to bring the old baby carriage into the house because it was bad luck.

And Carrie, who seemed to be going nowhere faster than any of them. She felt a welter of self-pity wash over her, and buried her head against John's thick jacket for a moment as a feeling of fear swept over her.

"You'll visit Uncle Oswald now and then, won't you, love?" She heard his voice, rumbling deep in his chest. "Aunt Vi's dying to meet you, since we've both been singing your praises so much."

"Yes, I'll visit your folks," she said bitterly. "It'll be all I've got left of you, won't it?"

He didn't say anything for a minute, and then he gave her a little shake. "Carrie, I'm not going to pick a fight with you. There's no point in wasting the time we've got left in arguing. What's done is done, and come the spring, you'll be counting the days till I come back."

But there was a long way to go between winter and spring, and try as she might, she couldn't rid herself of feelings of doom.

"Besides, you've got plenty to think about between now and then. There's to be a wedding in June, if I recall. Or have you changed your mind about that?"

"I have not," she whispered swiftly, and felt his mouth seeking hers in the seclusion of the front porch. "Oh, John, I have not!"

"No more have I," he responded just as swiftly to her sudden ardour. He held her so tight she feared for her bones, but she never wanted to let him go. She just wanted to stand like this, and hold him like this, for ever and always . . .

"It's time that young man went home," they both heard Pa call out a few minutes later. "His uncle will be wondering what's become of him."

332

"What your Pa means is, am I ravishing his lovely daughter?" John whispered wickedly in her ear.

He hadn't been doing any such thing, of course, but for a wild sweet moment, Carrie almost wished he had. He would surely never have left her if she was in trouble . . .

But that was the wickedest thought of all, and she was too flustered to face her family while it was still so hot in her mind. Instead, she hurried through to the scullery and began banging pots and pans about in a pretence of clearing up, rather than admit to such wanton longings inside her.

Chapter 19

Elsie hadn't really intended to flounce away in such a huff, but the more she thought about it, the more she intended to let Miss high-and-mighty Carrie Stuckey stew in her own juice for a while. She didn't need to keep running to the Stuckeys for anything. She was quite capable of managing her own affairs, thank you very much. And *affairs* was not a bad word, in the circumstances.

She paused in her haphazard sloshing of beige paint over the walls of the scullery in the waterfront cottage. It didn't improve things much, and the old cooking splashes would soon show through, but since Dewi Griffiths had once mentioned how his Mam was such a dab hand with the cleaning and cooking in their neat little Welsh terraced house, she had decided it wouldn't hurt to give her a bit of competition.

She had never cared a jot about such things before, and nor did she ever expect to meet this wonderful person who went to chapel twice on Sundays and mended Dewi's socks almost before the holes showed through.

Normally, such information would have got her scoffing. She couldn't abide such prissy attention to detail . . . even the regimented daily routine of the Stuckey household soon had her panting for air . . . but all that was before she'd had her head turned by Dewi Griffiths.

Or rather, her *back*, she thought, with a wicked little shiver of pleasure. She paused in her paint splashing, to remember the last time she'd got so all-fired hot and bothered in his arms.

"You do love me, don't you, Dewi?" she'd breathed, as his hands had fumbled everywhere in an attempt to rid her of her clothes in the fastest possible time.

"Of course I do, *cariad*," he'd said thickly. "You don't think I'd be spending so much time with you if I didn't think a lot of you, do you?"

"Say it then," she'd insisted, clamping her knees together as they lay wrestling on the squeaky old bed in what had been Granpa Miller's bedroom. "I'm not letting you do nothing until you say you love me!"

"*Duw*, what a fusspot you are!"

She could see the beads of sweat on his brow, and feel the heat in his body through her remaining under-garments.

"Tell me, then," she insisted.

"All right, I love you, see? Does that satisfy you, witch? Now, for God's sake, stop your teasing, or I swear you'll be doing me untold mischief, *bach*."

She capitulated then, letting her limbs go slack, and hearing his groaning sigh as his hands sought and found their goal. And so did hers . . . Elsie was nothing if not curious, and these new games of forbidden pleasures were to be savoured to the full. And Dewi swore that he'd be careful . . . that nothing was going to happen, except that they'd each feel a damn sight better for it afterwards.

It might not be the most romantic of remarks, but it suited Elsie, and she wasn't the sort to wallow in soft words for too long. Not like Carrie would . . . Carrie would take a month of Sundays extracting vows of everlasting commitment from a fellow before she let him touch her like this . . .

As Dewi's exploring fingers went deeper, and his breathing got heavier, it was easy to forget all about

Carrie's prim little Sunday face, and glory in this new and nerve-tingling experience with this lusty Welsh boyo.

It was only much later that she marvelled at herself for asking if he loved her. And especially for saying that she loved him back! It wasn't Elsie Miller's style. But then, she'd never met anyone like Dewi before, so dark and intense that she was set to shivering just by thinking about him. You never knew how topsy-turvy you were going to feel until it happened. You just never knew.

She smiled now, remembering. And she gave a small impatient sigh, getting bored with the painting, and deciding to leave it for another day. Dewi wouldn't be here to see it until next week, anyway. He came over to Welsh Back Market once a week on the trows, and stayed for two nights before going back to work at the Cardiff markets for the rest of the week. He'd always stayed in lodgings in Bristol before, but from now on, he was going to stay with Elsie.

And that was certainly something she wasn't going to tell Carrie Stuckey about! she thought decisively. She could just imagine the disapproval on her face, and if Carrie ever let her Ma get wind of it, there would be another lecture on the evils of fornicating before marriage . . . the wicked word slipped into Elsie's head without warning, sending a chill down her back for a moment, but only for a moment.

She brushed it aside, thinking instead that it suited her very well for the present that she and Carrie were at loggerheads. The less she saw of her friend, the less Carrie could tell her what a fool she was being, and what risks she was taking . . . she could even smile at how she'd once connived as to how she could get her own back on Wilf Stuckey for snubbing her so badly. Now, she couldn't have cared less about Wilf, because now she had Dewi.

*   *   *

336

A week later, Carrie was far too anxiously watching her mother to be bothered with thoughts of what Elsie Miller might be doing. The baby was due, but it didn't seem at all keen to put in an appearance, though the vague aches and pains Ma kept getting was certainly keeping Carrie's mind off any other topics.

Wilf went off jauntily to his workshop every morning now, and she had said a tearful goodbye to John as he went off on the brightly painted Garfield Pond promotion wagon, along with BIG LOUIE and several other brawny fellows who seemed to be all part and parcel of the set-up. Carrie couldn't help thinking it was all a little like a circus act.

"If you don't stop inspecting me every five minutes, Carrie, I shall begin to feel like a pan of stew being watched," Ma finally said crossly. "There's no hurrying babbies, and this one won't come until he's good and ready. Why don't you find summat to do? There's the beds to be made yet, and I daresay your Pa will be wanting a hot drink soon. He's been hammering away in that yard for this last hour."

They all knew what he was making. A small boy on the other side of the river had died of the measles, and Sam Stuckey's modest fees for turning out a fine coffin at rock-bottom prices were becoming well known. He'd been glad of the work, but after being approached at a tavern by the boy's heartbroken father, his skills weren't giving him any pleasure.

There was also a somewhat shameful thankfulness at knowing the weather was cold enough for folk not to be out and about so much as usual, for measles could spread like wildfire, and it could be a killer. The evidence of that was in the little mite who'd be placed in the narrow wooden box Sam was shaping. He hated these jobs.

Making a coffin for a child was surely a man's saddest occupation. But somebody had to do it, to make a fitting resting-place for the last send-off for a loved child. He gave up a small prayer of thanks that his own family had always been a healthy brood, no matter how they went without.

He remembered to mentally cross his fingers as he thought it, not stopping in his work, and spitting the tacks out of his mouth for the tap-tap fastening together of the coffin-sides, to hold the glueing in place.

"A cup of hot chocolate for you, Pa," he heard Carrie say, and he gave a start. He'd been so engrossed in his task, he hadn't heard her approach.

He eased his back. It was a cold morning for the first day of a new year, but dry and clear for all that. The snow had mostly gone, and it was only the softest of men who'd scorn working outside in a yard.

"That's a welcome sight and no mistake," he told her, taking the mug from her hands. "What about one of Ma's currant cakes to go with it, then, or am I on short rations now?"

Carrie laughed. Maybe Pa was being extra cheerful to keep his mind off the end-result of his task; and maybe she was trying to be extra cheerful to keep from worrying about Ma's confinement. Whatever the reason, she was more than happy to chafe along with him for a few minutes, as she pulled her shawl around her shoulders to keep out the bite of the morning.

"Perhaps you should be," she teased. "You don't look as if you're starving!"

"No more I do, girl," he grinned, patting his stomach. "Though I've a long way to go yet to catch up with the ale drinkers at the waterfront taverns."

"I hope you never do catch up with 'em, Pa! Their bellies must go in their front doors five minutes before the rest of 'em!"

He chuckled at her cheek, but she wasn't altogether bothered that he seemed to be putting on a bit of weight. It suited him. And the leanest months, after the work on the *Great Britain* finished for the Stuckey men, had passed.

They weren't flush with riches, and probably never would be, but Wilf would be bringing in money now, and it seemed as if the bounty from the Barclay kitchens hadn't run out yet. Carrie was no longer the washer-girl of old, at everybody's beck and call, and nor did Ma take in quantities of washing for the rich Clifton folk, but they still did a few bits, and were asked for especially by those who respected their diligence.

And spring wasn't that far away. Everything looked better and brighter in the spring. Father and daughter had similar thoughts at that moment, and Carrie seemed to hear the echo of John's voice in her head as she thought it. And after the spring would come thoughts of a summer wedding. She felt her heart skip a beat, not quite able to think that far ahead, or to believe that it would really happen.

"You'd best go in now, girl," Sam said, seeing her faraway look. "You don't want to take cold, and I aim to get this job finished and delivered today. They're wanting it early tomorrow morning."

It was still a job to him, no matter how distasteful, but Carrie knew he was making the box with skill and love. As far as she was concerned, she wanted it away from the house before Ma's pains began. It was surely bad luck to be making a coffin for one child to leave this world, when another was pushing its way into it.

"I'll go and give Ma her hot drink," she said, turning quickly, before Pa could guess at her fearful thoughts.

If only the babby had come on time, it would all be over now, but there was no sign of it yet, and Ma insisted that the midwife didn't need calling until well after the waters broke or the pains began.

Carrie was apprehensive about her own role in the birthing. Ma had said calmly that now she was a woman, there was no reason why she shouldn't assist in any way she could. The menfolk would be banished from the house, taking Billy with them, no matter what time of day or night. Birthing was women's work, and at such a time only another woman could understand it.

Mrs Green, the midwife, was an efficient woman whom Ma had helped out on many other occasions, and she would instruct Carrie on anything she had to do. The words were so vague that they only made her more nervous, but Ma never volunteered more. And still there was the dire presentiment in Carrie's head that they would never hear this baby cry . . .

She had no rational reason for her fears, and had never voiced them to anyone. Ma was strong and healthy, despite the awkwardness of the baby's lying, and always dismissed any notion that carrying a baby was an illness.

Several times recently, Carrie had dreamed that the birth was all over, and the midwife held the baby aloft in her arms, but when they looked into its face, it was still and dead and grey. The dreams had become nightmares, and she had woken up, cold and sweating with fear, whimpering into the night, and longing for the dawn.

"Are you all right, Ma?" she said now, going back to the parlour, and seeing her mother grimace.

"I'll be a sight better when you stop your fretting. Are you going to bring me some of that hot chocolate or shall I get it myself?"

"I'll do it. Pa wants a currant cake too," she said, smothering the fear. If she went on like this much longer, she was going to be a nervous baggage by the time the baby arrived, and she'd be no use for anything.

"Your Pa's getting fat," Ma said complacently, though it was hardly the truth. "He'll never have the belly that I've got, though, praise God!"

"But you'll be rid of yours soon, Ma."

"The sooner the better." She put her hand against the hard mound of the baby, and spoke softly as if it could hear her. "You just hurry up and get born, my lamb, and let's all have a look at you."

Carrie's eyes prickled as she took the cake out to the yard, before bringing her mother the hot drink. This baby had been a mistake, but now that it was nearly here, she knew how fiercely her parents would welcome it and love it. It was a part of them all, and she too wished it would come soon. She'd heard Ma say that it didn't do for a child to be too long overdue, as it made the delivery that much harder.

A week was long enough. Two weeks was the limit, and longer than that could be a sign of trouble – or else a mix-up in the timing in the first place.

It was the middle of January when Carrie was awoken in the early hours of the morning by the sounds of activity in the house. She was awake at once, pulling a shawl around her nightgown and opening her bedroom door to see Pa, still in his nightshirt and struggling to tuck it into his trousers.

"Her time's come at last," he said briefly. "I'm off to fetch the midwife. Our Billy's still sound asleep, so I ain't going to waken him for a while yet. Wilf's stoking up the fire and putting kettles and saucepans on to boil. You'd best go and sit with her while I'm gone, Carrie."

For a few seconds, her feet wouldn't move at all. She seemed to be transfixed as Pa went clattering down the stairs and out of the house. She wanted to scream that she couldn't do this. She couldn't bear to witness her mother's agony, especially if it all came to nothing . . . she cursed the lurid accounts Ma had told her of other women's labours, and the nightmarish dreams that had this tiny babe dead and gone before he had even been given life.

She heard a soft moan coming from her mother's bedroom, followed by the sound of her name, and she swallowed hard. Ma needed her, and that was the only thought that she must keep in mind. Ma needed her.

She pushed open the door and went inside. The oil lamps threw a soft warm glow around the room, and onto the face of the woman sitting on the bed. She was half bent over, her hair loose about her shoulders, in a way the family rarely saw. She looked younger and more vulnerable despite the fact that pain was creasing her face.

"Shouldn't you be lying down, Ma?" Carrie said, her voice a dry husk.

"Not yet. This gives me some relief," she said. "There's time enough for lying flat when I have to. I don't need the midwife yet, neither, but Pa thought it best."

She gave a twisted smile, catching her breath between her teeth, and making a grab for the bedpost. Carrie felt her hands go clammy.

"What should I do?" she asked in panic. She was already helpless and afraid. Ma was going into a place she didn't know. Childbirth was a time when a woman hovered between life and death. She'd heard Ma say that often enough when she'd been attending some other poor woman. The preacher too, had intoned to them all in one of his lengthy sermons that childbirth was a time of mingled reverence and savagery, and the wrenching of a child from a woman's body was the most mystical happening God had given the world. But He hadn't given it lightly, nor without the need to suffer for such a miracle.

Dear God, but she wished these remembered sayings didn't come back to haunt her now! She ran towards the bed.

"Ma, what should I *do*?" she said again, as her mother breathed shallowly and fast.

"Go downstairs and fetch me a pitcher of water, for my mouth's dust-dry," Ma said shortly. "And I don't need your wailing, Carrie. There's a long way to go yet, and 'twill ease in a minute or two. You'll be no help to me if you're bleating all day."

Carrie turned on her heel, her eyes smarting. This was going to go on *all day*? But she knew very well that it might. Ma had often been away more than twenty-four hours helping Mrs Green, and had come home totally exhausted. She ran down the stairs, bumping into Wilf at the bottom.

"Ma wants a pitcher of water," she said through chattering teeth.

"I'll fetch it," he said. "It's cold outside and there's ice on the top of the well. You go and get dressed, and by the time you're downstairs again, I'll be back."

"Thank you, Wilf."

She turned again. She was like a leaf in the wind, needing to be directed to her tasks. She couldn't seem to think for herself at all. Then she heard Billy's scared little voice as he came clattering downstairs, finally waking up and wondering what all the noise was about. She steeled herself. A fat lot of use she was going to be to Ma if she turned into a shivering jelly.

She hugged Billy to her, feeling him squirm as usual, but not quite as much. She didn't know what to do with him. It was barely light outside, so the men wouldn't be going off somewhere just yet to be well away from the child-bearing process.

"Is summat up with Ma? Is the babby hurting her?" he asked fearfully. "She ain't going to die, is she?"

"Of course she's not going to die," Carrie said. "It just takes a lot of effort for a baby to be born, that's all. That's why they call it labour."

He wasn't convinced, and stood with his arms folded tightly around himself, glaring at her. Billy always took refuge in anger when he was troubled.

"Well, I ain't never going to have a babby if it hurts so much," he said defiantly. Carrie grinned.

"You're never likely to, you goose. It's only mothers who have babies."

"Why do they? And how it did it get into Ma's belly?" he said. "When I asked Pa how to make babbies, he bawled my head off, and said it weren't my business, only his and Ma's. Ain't it going to be my babby as well, Carrie?"

The laughter died on Carrie's lips at the plaintive little question. It had never occurred to her before that a child in the family could feel totally left out, just because nobody spoke about such intimate and personal details.

"It'll belong to all of us," she assured him. "And you'll be told all about how it got there when you're a bit older. I expect Pa thought it was a bit difficult for you to understand it just yet. But the important thing is that we're all here to welcome our baby when it arrives."

Billy didn't look at all satisfied, and Carrie prayed that she wouldn't be pushed into giving more detailed explanations. Especially when her own knowledge of making babies was so scanty. What did she know, after all? She was aware of occasional bumps in the night from Ma and Pa's room, though not lately, of course . . . and she had heard Elsie Miller's garbled reports, which weren't always to be trusted . . . and that was all. She chose not to think about herself and John Travis right now. It didn't seem right, when Ma was struggling upstairs with the pain.

She was as innocent as Billy in knowing all the facts. But she knew her own body, and it was only common sense to suppose that every other woman's body must be fashioned the same as her own. So just how a living breathing baby could emerge from the place it had to, was beyond her comprehension and filled her with terror.

"Here's the water for Ma," Wilf said, coming in from the yard, and bringing a gust of cold air in with him. "Now then, sprog, what are you doing awake?" he said, seeing Billy curled up on the settle.

"The babby's hurting our Ma," he said. "Our Carrie

344

won't tell me nothing, but you'll tell me, won't you, Wilf?"

Above her small brother's head, Carrie caught her brother's glance. What would Wilf know about birthing and making babies! And how would he ever find the words to explain it, even if he did . . .? She started to take the water upstairs and was surprised by the gentleness in Wilf's voice as he answered.

"Maybe it's time you knew a few things, young Billy, and since we've nothing else to do until Pa gets back, I'll try and tell 'em to you."

Carrie would never have believed Wilf could be so forthcoming, though he'd undoubtedly tell things in the simplest terms for Billy to understand. Presumably Nora Woolley had done this for Wilf, she thought with sudden comprehension. Bringing him out of his silent shell, and making him a sight more human than of old. Well, well.

But she soon forgot all about Wilf and Nora when she saw Ma's face. Although it was quickly composed, there was no missing the discomfort written all over it. Deeper lines than usual were etched in her skin, and Carrie quickly poured out the water, slopping it awkwardly and handing her the glass.

"Is it bad, Ma?" she said huskily.

"It's the usual," she answered. "No child ever came into this world without making his presence felt, and this one seems certain to be a large and lusty one."

She caught her breath again and this time she bit hard on a folded towel. Carrie had heard tell about contractions and the time between them, but these pains were giving Ma no time at all to recover. They seemed almost constant. She felt a burst of alarm. Dear God, supposing the baby decided to make a rush into the world, and the midwife hadn't arrived? As if she could read her daughter's mind, and sensed her instinctive backing away, Ma removed the towel from her lips and gave a ragged smile.

"Don't you worry none, my duck. It won't happen for hours yet. I've been this way before, remember."

But she was younger then, and more supple, and Billy's birth was eight years ago. It must surely be like the first time all over again . . . Carrie didn't need to be versed in medicine and midwifery to know that much.

"Was that Billy I heard?" Ma said now, and Carrie nodded, hardly able to speak.

"See that he's dressed warmly for the day. Pa will take him off with him this morning, and then take him to his lessons this afternoon. If this is still going on by nightfall, then we'll think of summat else."

"John's Aunt Vi said he could sleep at their house if need be," Carrie reminded her. "She's a kindly person, and I did tell you how she said she wouldn't mind having him there when your time came, and Billy's always keen to hear Uncle Oswald's stories about the river."

"We'll see what's happening by late afternoon, then," Ma said. "But you'd best ask our Billy what he thinks first. I don't want him thinking he's being pushed out."

She stopped talking then, as another pain assaulted her. Carrie saw how she arched and braced herself, and how the great mountain of the baby seemed to harden beneath the thin nightgown with each new contraction.

To her wild relief, she heard the midwife's voice, and when Mrs Green bustled into the room, Carrie almost fled down the stairs, mumbling that she had to see that Billy got himself dressed properly.

She was all fingers and thumbs as she helped to button him into his trousers and lace his boots, ignoring his prot-estations that he could manage by himself. She mentioned John's aunt and uncle casually to him, preparing the way, and heard his screech of delight.

"Can I go there after my lessons, Pa? When our Carrie took me there before, Aunt Vi said I could go again any time I wanted."

346

"I said I'd do it," Carrie began quickly.

"It's best that you stay here, girl," Pa said. "I'll tell you what, Billy. We'll go up Bedminster Hill this morning and see if it's all right, then if 'tis, when I collect you from your lessons I'll take you back there. Unless things have moved on apace here, o' course."

He avoided Carrie's eyes. A man didn't speak about such things as confinements and labour pains. His job was done in the thrashings of the bedroom, and it was the woman who had the ordeal of producing the babies. Carrie had never thought about it so acutely before, and wondered how she would react when her own time came. As it surely would, when she and John were married, and the babies came along.

A thin trickle of sweat ran down her back as she heard the muted moans from upstairs. Ma was the strongest of women, but there was a limit to how much pain anyone could stand. And seeing her like that . . . suppressing her agony like that . . . Carrie couldn't help wondering about her own ability to bear such torment.

"Come on, young feller," Pa was saying stoutly. "Into the scullery with you for a wash while Carrie gets us some breakfast, then we'll be out of the women's way."

But she didn't miss the worry in Pa's eyes, and guessed he was as anxious as she was. She pressed her hand on his arm.

"Everything will be all right, Pa," she said quietly. "And I'll do all that's asked of me."

He nodded. "I never expected anything less, girl."

It was as far as he could go towards sentimentality, and Carrie understood that. Mrs Green would be brisk and businesslike, and it would do Ma no good to have Carrie frightened and wailing all around her. She had to be strong for Ma's sake, and so she would.

Twelve hours later, it was clear that something was wrong. The pains continued, but they were less intense, as if

347

the baby itself was weary of the push to be born. The midwife was clearly alarmed, and Ma looked exhausted, and so *old*.

"I fear it may be a breech," Mrs Green said briefly. "If so, 'twill need turning, and the sooner the better. Run and fetch Doctor Flowers, Carrie, and tell him exactly what I've said."

"Is Ma going to be all right?" she said in a cracked voice. Dear God, were her worst fears about to come true? Was this agony her mother had suffered all day long to come to naught . . .?

"Don't worry about me, Carrie. Just do as Mrs Green says," came Ma's thin voice.

But what about the baby? In her nightmares it had always been the baby that was lying still and cold in one of Pa's tiny coffins . . . terror sent Carrie flying up the hill without bothering to put on a coat or even to pull a shawl around her shoulders. Slipping and sliding on the frosty ground, she hammered at the doctor's door, praying that he wouldn't be out on one of his calls. To her relief, he answered at once, and she clutched at his arms.

"Oh, Doctor Flowers, please come quick. Ma's been labouring all day, and Mrs Green says the baby might be breeched and will need turning. She says to hurry."

"All right, don't fret. I'll just get my bag."

She didn't listen to any more. She was already winging her way back down towards Jacob's Wells Road. She was terrified of witnessing the birth, but just as terrified of not being there when Ma needed her.

She rushed inside the house and then stopped dead. It was too quiet. She couldn't hear anything, save for her own laboured breathing, and she felt a real sense of dread. Then she saw Mrs Green come swishing through from the scullery, with a tray of tea in her hands. It was such a homely, ordinary little scene that Carrie

348

almost burst out crying. For a moment, she had been so very afraid.

"Now then, Carrie, you can take this upstairs for me while I fetch some towels and hot water for Doctor. Your Ma's fair parched and begging for a cup of tea. You got hold of him, I hope?"

"Yes. He's coming right away," Carrie stammered. She took the tray without thinking, nearly dropping it in her relief. Ma was still all right then, and asking for tea . . .

She took the tray upstairs to the bedroom. Her mother looked very pale, and her hair lay lankly around her face, but she managed a weak smile.

"This is a fine carry-on and no mistake," she said conversationally, just as if it was no more dramatic than dropping a stitch in her knitting. "The sooner Doctor gets the little 'un turned about, the sooner I can get on with my work."

Carrie stared at her, pouring out the tea with shaking hands and handing her the mug.

"Aren't you scared, Ma?" she said faintly.

Her mother shrugged. "It happened with our Frank, so I might have guessed at summat like this. It'll be a bit of a trial, but there's one thing for sure. The bab can't stay where he is, so there's no help for it."

She is so brave, Carrie thought. So very brave . . . and all this while Pa was out somewhere, keeping well out of the way, when he could be here wiping her brow and holding her hand . . . even as she said it, she knew it had been Ma who ordered him away. She always said there was no dignity in birthing, and the only menfolk capable of witnessing it without fainting right away, were the medical men who were trained to it.

The doctor came bounding up the stairs a short while later, and told Carrie to make herself scarce while he took a look to see what was happening. They would call her if it was necessary. Mrs Green was hovering behind him then, and Carrie fled thankfully back down the stairs. She had never felt so useless, nor so guiltily glad to be so.

The day grew dark. Wilf returned from his work and was sent up Bedminster Hill to meet Pa and inform him that there was no news yet. Carrie had no doubt the men would be staying up there awhile, at least until Billy was put to bed in his strange room.

She guessed that the jovial Aunt Vi would provide them with a meal. All would be normal and everyday, while down here it seemed that all she could do was to wait helplessly and wish she could close her ears to Ma's frequent anguished cries. God only knew what was happening now, and she didn't want to know.

She discovered that her finger-nails were digging grooves in the palms of her hands where she was clenching them so tightly. The time dragged on, and Wilf came home again.

"I don't know what's happening. They've sent me out of the room – " Carrie began. Without warning, she was sobbing and held fast in her brother's arms. Childbirth was terrifying, and surely Ma would never be the same again after this . . .

Suddenly, she jerked up her head. A strange, thin squawking was coming from upstairs, followed by a sharp slapping sound that increased the squawking to a lusty and healthy bawl. The bawl of a child who was drawing good, deep, protesting breaths to announce his arrival into the outside world . . . there was a lot of activity up above, but nobody summoned her for a good five minutes.

"Carrie!" At last she heard Mrs Green call her name. "You can come upstairs now, to see the finest specimen of boy bab produced this century."

She raced up the stairs then, followed by Wilf. He hovered at the door until Ma nodded and waved him inside. The doctor was packing away his things, and there seemed to be a number of blood-stained towels strewn about the room. But the most important thing of all was the sight of Ma in the bed.

For a moment Carrie just stared at her. Ma looked quite beautiful now, she thought in awe, as if she had never gone through the ordeal of a day and a night at all. And in her arms, still wrapped in the cloths that had had been prepared to hold him, was her red-faced infant, already with a definite angry look of Billy about him.

"Oh, Ma," Carrie breathed, moving closer to the bed. "He's just beautiful."

The baby opened his eyes a fraction, blinking in the smoky glow of the lamplight. His eyes were a deep blue, the same as all the Stuckeys.

"He's a fine boy all right," Wilf said gruffly.

"Fine and healthy and a credit to you all," Doctor Flowers was brisk. "I'll be on my way now, Mrs Stuckey, and Mrs Green will see to the rest of it."

"I'll see you out," Wilf said at once, clearly not wanting to stay too long. "Then I'll go and find Pa."

"Yes, get you gone, Wilf. There's still some tidying up to do here," Mrs Green said delicately. "Carrie, I'd like you to take the child while I see to the mother."

Carrie moved forward to take the baby from her mother's arms. He felt weighty and strong, and all her foolish fears fell away as she gazed down into the wizened little face. Her heart was full, and as she met her mother's relaxed smile, freed from all stress, she knew the fundamental truth that women had always known. No pain was too great to bear, when this miracle was the result.

The baby gave a slight belch in her arms. It seemed to release his anger, and just for a second his mouth crooked into an involuntary, lopsided smile. To Carrie, the smile seemed to be directed straight at her, and she adored him from that moment.

351

Chapter 20

The baby thrived, and so did Ma. They decided to call him Henry, after Sam's father. On a blustery morning at the end of February, he was baptised by Mr Pritchard, who declared him to be the loudest and lustiest child he had ever poured holy water over. Carrie wasn't surprised. The minister had a very free hand with the freezing water, and little Henry had a fine pair of lungs.

Henry also had piercing navy-blue eyes and a ready smile, even at little more than a month old. His father insisted it was merely the colic, but Carrie and Billy swore that the baby knew them already.

Billy worshipped his little brother. There was no jealousy, to everyone's relief, and on Sunday afternoons, providing the weather wasn't too cold, Carrie and Billy pushed Henry in his baby carriage down the hill and along the waterfront, as proud as peacocks.

On one such occasion, they had bumped straight into Elsie Miller. They hadn't seen one another since Boxing Day, when they had nearly torn one another's hair out by the roots, and for a minute, Carrie had thought her one-time friend wasn't going to speak at all. Then Elsie stopped abruptly, peering into the carriage.

"It's come then. What is it?" she said, her voice uncompromising.

"It's a boy. We're calling him Henry," Carrie said, just as stiffly.

"How's your Ma doing?"

"She's well enough, thank you."

"Remember me to her, then." And with no more than a sniff and a toss of her head, Elsie had gone swishing off up Hotwells Road, leaving the others staring after her.

"I don't like her," Billy said darkly. "She don't smell of fish no more, but I still don't like her. And she didn't even give our Henry a proper look."

This was clearly the biggest insult of all to him. Carrie gave a short laugh, though she was sorely put out and still upset by the fact that two old friends could be so distant and hostile to one another. She knew she hadn't helped at all, but it took two to make up, just as it took two to break up . . .

"Never mind about that. We know he's beautiful, don't we?" she cajoled her small brother.

"Boys ain't beautiful," Billy retaliated at once. "Boys are just – well, *boys*."

"Babies are beautiful, whatever they are," Carrie insisted, as they strode along the waterfront. It was more silent than usual today, being Sunday, and some of the larger ships in dock seemed like majestic castles, awaiting their princes . . .

She grinned at her own thoughts. Some princes, those foul-mouthed sailors who swarmed about the taverns to start up drunken fights with any takers. But they weren't all like that, she amended. Frank wouldn't be like that . . .

As Mr Pritchard's voice rang more sharply in her ears, Carrie realised her thoughts had still been wandering far away from the occasion they were all attending in their Sunday best. Young Henry Stuckey had now been formally introduced into the Church, and Ma was wrapping his sturdy little body up in his shawls again after the minister's vigorous dousing.

But for a moment, Carrie had felt a real pang of

sadness, and wondered if Ma felt it too. Here they were, all gathered around the font for the small service, but the family circle wasn't complete. There were her parents, with Pa more than a mite awkward and out of his environment, but blessedly sober since before Henry's birth; Wilf, accompanied by Nora Woolley now that their relationship was all official and above-board; herself and Billy and the baby.

But something was missing. Frank should be among them, and so should John. And no amount of letters from either of them could replace their physical presence. Not that either was a great letter writer; Frank rarely wrote, because he was simply having too exciting a time on board ship and seeing all these foreign places that had been only names to him before now; and John, because it was difficult to snatch a moment's peace in his touring, or to get the letters sent forward. There had only been two, so far, but the most important bits in each were imprinted on Carrie's heart . . .

". . . remember that you always have my undying love, sweet Carrie, and I count the days until we're together again. Don't ever forget that, love, and when you think of me, remember that I shall be thinking of you. When you look at the moon at night, I shall look at that same bright moon and send you all my love. When you look at the stars, assume that each one is a kiss from me to you . . ."

She had treasured the words, and she kept the letters beneath her pillow, kissing them every night before she went to sleep. John was educated enough to have a fine turn of phrase, and to be unafraid to say what was in his heart. It comforted her in the lonely nights when she missed him so dreadfully.

"Well, thank goodness that's over," Pa said, when they finally spilled out into the daylight from the gloom of the church. "The old boy goes on a fair stretch, don't he?"

He looked around him at his family, and felt a stab of pride that was reminiscent of the old days when there was plenty of work to be had. Not that he suffered too badly now, he had to admit. Coffin-making hadn't been a trade he'd ever have chosen, but there was a certain satisfaction in giving a body the best send-off he could, in as much comfort as possible. He smiled faintly at his own pun.

He realised that Wilf's young lady was approaching him shyly. He liked the little maid, and Wilf could have done a lot worse for himself, despite her bumptious parentage . . . but Nora couldn't help her father being the way he was, and Sam knew he couldn't have wished for a more pleasant future daughter-in-law.

"Well, Nora, what do you think of our young off-spring?" he said, as proud as any new father, despite this one being a tag-end child.

"He's a truly lovely boy, Mr Stuckey, and my parents send you their best wishes on this occasion."

"Do they now? Well, that's mighty generous of them," Sam said, unable to keep the sarcasm out of his voice.

Providing him with work during the last difficult months would have been a sight more acceptable than best wishes, but at Ma's frowning look, he let that pass.

"My father says he'd like to see you some time, Mr Stuckey," she went on in her soft little voice.

"Well, he knows where I live, don't he?" Sam stated, marching on down the road with the family trailing behind. She glanced at Wilf, who quickly strode after him.

"Pa, don't go off in a huff. Gaffer Woolley might have something of interest to say to you."

Sam stopped. "Do you know summat I don't, boy?"

"No more than Nora's told you. Gaffer says he'll have no objection if you go to the house this evening, though."

For a minute, Carrie thought Pa was going to explode. This suggestion had obviously been decided beforehand, but Wilf had put it clumsily, making it sound like a command, rather than a request. She knew he was about to round on his son. If it hadn't been Sunday, and other folk were taking the air and passing the time of day, he surely would have done.

"Please, Mr Stuckey, don't be cross," Nora pleaded now. She put one small hand on his arm, and looked up into his face. Sam hesitated a moment, but one look into her melting hazel eyes beneath the pert little bonnet she wore, and he could see exactly why Wilf had been so bowled over by her. He gave a grunt.

"I ain't cross with you, my duck, and never could be."

"Well then, won't you please go and listen to what Father has to say, if only for my sake?"

Sam gave a sigh of resignation. Womenfolk! They had their own soft ways of getting around a man, and sometimes it was simpler just to give in.

"Well, all right, since you ask it of me. I'll go and see him this evening, but just for ten minutes, mind, and just to hear him out," he warned her. "And I ain't saying no more than that."

Wilf smiled at Ma and gave her a small wink. Gaffer had given him a small hint of what it was all about, but he wasn't going to say a single word to anyone and spoil the surprise. Besides, there was never any knowing how Pa would react these days. He was just as likely to bawl and shout and tell Gaffer what to do with his proposal. Wilf hoped it wouldn't end like that, though. He felt so secure with his own life now, and he wanted everyone else to feel the same.

The storehouse at the back of Woolley's warehouse where he made his toys was not ideal for his purpose, but any day now, the spacious workshop behind the new premises would be available, and he could move in there.

356

In a month's time, the fittings and fitments should all be in place, and there would be a grand opening, with posters all around the town advertising the event.

It irked him slightly that the shop-fitting work hadn't been offered to Pa, but Mr Cedric Woolley had his own regular London contractors that he brought down with him, and there had been no arguing with that. He was already discovering that Mr Cedric Woolley was a canny businessman, with ventures all over the place, and that they inevitably succeeded. It boded well for the future.

Sam presented himself at the Woolley house in Ashton Way that evening, telling himself that whatever Gaffer had to say to him, he wasn't going to give an inch. He had his pride, and he wanted no warehouse plank shifting work, just because there was a vague family connection now that his eldest son's future was assured by Gaffer's cousin, and he was courting Gaffer's daughter.

Sam's pride had come very much to the fore again, now that he had a new young son to raise. He had stopped drinking, and he was becoming known as a reliable coffin-maker. Wilf was bringing money into the house as well, and Ma didn't need to take in washing any more, though she seemed to enjoy the bits that she did, he thought vaguely. Carrie had taken on the task of dealing with young Henry most of the time, leaving Ma to the wash-tub, which seemed to suit them both. He shook his head slightly, unable to fathom the ways of women.

But one thing he did know. He was no longer prepared to take a pittance wage for warehouse stacking, if that was what Gaffer Woolley had in mind. No, sir . . .

He was shown into the library at the Woolley house by a servant. Uneasily, he'd never realised before that Gaffer lived so fine. Nor had he realised that a private house boasted such a room as this, and he gazed in amazement at the rows and rows of books on the shelves around the room. It smelled of old leather, a comfortable, masculine smell, and the chairs reflected that too. Solid, deep, and inviting a man to sit and browse at leisure.

Sam's mouth twisted. It just showed the difference between them who had, and them who had not, he thought sourly. When did a man like himself have any time for leisure, except when he was thrown out of work by the likes of the Woolleys? And even then, all his spare time would be taken up with scratching a living for his family.

He turned, full of renewed aggression, as his host entered the room, dressed in elegant style, and swathed in cigar smoke.

"Ah, Sam, it's good to see you," Gaffer said genially. "I thought we'd be more comfortable in here, away from the rest of the household. Would you care for some brandy?"

Before Sam could open his mouth, Gaffer had moved to a side table where a decanter and glasses stood ready. A glass containing a liberal amount of the golden nectar was put into his hand, and without thinking, he took a great gulp, which produced an immediate coughing fit.

"Steady, man," Gaffer said, by the time he'd done spluttering and watering. "I don't want you expiring on me before you hear what I've got to say."

"Then say it and be done with it," Sam growled, furious at being shown up by the attack.

Gaffer wouldn't be ruffled. He blew a large smoke ring into the air and looked at Sam through the lingering haze.

"I understand you've been doing a fine line in cheap coffins of late, Sam."

"What of it? Poor folk have a right to be buried decently, same as the toffs."

"Good God, man, I'm not arguing with that. And if you're going to leap down my throat at every sentence, we're not going to get anywhere."

Sam clamped his lips together, not knowing where the man's thoughts were going, anyway. He took a more cautious sip of his brandy, feeling the stinging liquid warm his vitals.

"So how would you feel about making a coffin for me?" Aaron Woolley said calmly.

The question startled Sam so much he almost spilled his drink. He stared at the complacent bull of a man seated opposite him.

"You ain't telling me you're about to snuff it, are you?" he said, unable to think of anything else.

He heard the other man laugh and saw him shake his head. "Not for a long while, I hope, but it does my heart good to see a touch of alarm in your face at the thought, Sam. Perhaps there's some hope for our friendship yet."

Sam glared at him. He didn't like being sent up for a fool, nor taken unawares like that. There had been too many shocks lately, and too many of them were coming from this man's doorstep. He drained his glass and stood up.

"I doubt that. And if all you wanted me here for was to bait me – "

"Sit down and shut up, man," Gaffer said sharply. "And perhaps some more brandy will mellow you a bit."

Before Sam could argue, Gaffer was tipping up the decanter into his glass, and he sat down again heavily, his head already spinning from drinking too much, too fast.

"Now then, when I asked if you could make a coffin for me, I wasn't meaning anything quite so personal."

"'Twas a pretty daft request, then, and not in the best of taste," Sam said with a scowl.

"What I meant was this," Gaffer went on patiently. "If you were supplied with the best materials and a place to make 'em, could you turn out expensive and elaborate coffins to special order, that the toffs would pay a bundle for?"

Sam stared at him now, as the workings of Gaffer Woolley's brain began to turn over in his mind. He took another swig of brandy before he answered.

"You know my work well enough, Gaffer. You know very well I could turn out the best damn coffins in Christendom, given the materials. Fit enough and fancy enough for a prince, if need be."

"Yes, well, let's hope such a one won't be needed for many years yet. And have you any idea what the demand for such work might be if it was advertised discreetly enough?"

Sam gave a short laugh.

"I know that death don't make no distinction between rich folk and paupers. We all go the same way in the end, and we all need a box to carry us off in – "

His eyes narrowed. It was true enough, and he'd never even considered it before. He'd made his coffins for paltry sums, and been glad to do so to help those worse off than himself. But there must be folk willing to pay handsomely for as fine a piece of furniture for burying as ever graced an elegant drawing-room

"I see that you're beginning to see daylight," Gaffer said now, leaning back in his chair.

"No, I ain't," Sam said shortly. "Where would I ever have the wherewithal to start up such a workshop or have the know-how to contact clients? It ain't like shopping for turnips."

"That would be my job," Gaffer said. "It was my cousin who put the idea into my head, and once he did, it became obvious. I would provide you with premises and supply the materials, and I'd see to the advertising, and contacting the undertaking firms. We wouldn't want no truck with that side of it, o' course," he added quickly. "Ours would just be a supply business."

"And what would be in all this for you?" Sam said, still suspicious of everything the man was saying. It sounded too good to be true, but it was well known that Gaffer Woolley never gave anything away for nothing, and he wasn't likely to be starting now.

"A fifty per cent share of the profits," Gaffer said calmly. "You'd be doing all the manual work, but I'd be supplying all the materials, the business know-how and the premises. What do you say to it, Sam? Do we strike a bargain?"

"I don't rightly know what to say! I never aimed to end up as a coffin-maker, though I don't deny there's as much skill in turning a piece of wood into a fitting resting-place for the relatives to admire, as in any other task."

"And there ain't never likely to be a shortage of such work, is there?" Gaffer reminded him.

"I'd want me own sign above the workshop," Sam said suddenly. "'Sam Stuckey, coffin-maker' sounds about right. It needn't be nothing fancy, just enough so folk 'ould know the name of the craftsman."

"I think I could agree to that," Gaffer said, smiling, and he held out his hand. Sam stared at it thoughtfully for a moment more, before spitting on his own, then slapping Aaron's hand squarely in the middle. They had made a deal.

By the time Sam rolled back down Jacob's Wells Road late that night, he was awash with brandy and high spirits. If neither he nor Gaffer Woolley had precisely referred to their association as a partnership, each of them knew damn well that was what it amounted to. And since Gaffer was going to have some papers drawn up to the effect that they'd each be taking fifty per cent of whatever the new venture earned, Sam was more than satisfied with this night's work.

He'd always known Aaron Woolley was really a stout-hearted fellow, he thought expansively, conveniently forgetting all the past antagonisms. The man had even pressed an advance of cash on him, to tide him over until the business was under way and the orders came flowing in, as Aaron was confident that they would.

Sam had money jingling in his pockets, and he'd be buggered if he was going to squander it all on ale. He was a Somebody now, and he could hold up his head as high as anybody. And he wasn't so stewed that he couldn't recognise the fact that Gaffer Woolley knew a good thing when he saw it. Gaffer Woolley would never consider going into a fifty-fifty partnership with Sam Stuckey without being pretty damn sure it was going to be a money-making arrangement.

He managed to stumble inside the house, well pleased with the night's business, and grimacing that for the present he'd do better to mind where he put his unstable feet than to keep his head stuck up in the air.

It was all dark and silent indoors. The rest of the family had obviously gone to bed long ago, and he crept up the stairs as quietly as he could, swearing every time he stubbed his toe. He was itching to tell Ma about the change in their fortunes, but his head was fair muddled with it all, and he supposed the morning would do just as well.

He fell across the bed, fully dressed, and was asleep in seconds, snoring as loudly as a train at full steam, while May tried in vain to push him away from her side of the bed and was obliged to cling to the edge in vexation.

Sam awoke with the grandaddy of a headache, and a screeching sound going right through one of his ears and out the other. He resisted opening his eyes, sure that the raising of even one lid would send his nerves jangling with pain. Slowly he recognised that the noise came from his youngest son, Henry, bawling and caterwauling fit to raise a church roof. As he managed to let one eye flicker a little, wincing as he ascertained that it was daylight, he vaguely glimpsed Ma sitting up in the bed and offering one blue-veined breast to the hungry infant. Thank God, Sam thought feelingly. He was enormously proud of his new son, but he could do without his yelling this morning, thanks very much.

"Don't pretend you're not awake, Sam Stuckey," he heard May say severely. "And if you're not, then you ought to be. Coming home here at all hours and sprawling all over me like that! What did you and Gaffer Woolley get up to last night, for pity's sake, or shouldn't I ask?"

His one wakeful eye opened a fraction wider. If only his head didn't throb so much . . . if only he felt as buoyant as he knew he should, with all that he had to tell her . . .

"We're going to be rich, Ma," he said hoarsely. "I wanted to tell you last night – "

"Oh ah, and my name's Mrs Gullible," she said sarcastically, biting her lip as Henry sucked more forcefully. His tiny fingers dug into her breast, and she cuddled him in close to keep him warm, glowering at her man. "What kind of romancing have you been doing now?"

"'Tain't no romancing, woman. I tell you me and Gaffer's going into partnership."

May stared for a minute, then burst out laughing.

"What? You ain't had a good word to say about the man these past six months or more, and now you come home with these daft tales."

Sam sat up in bed, discovering to his shame that he was still wearing his clothes. But God damn the woman, he'd show her. He thrust his hand in his pocket, and felt the coins there. It weren't no dream, then, as he'd almost feared himself when May had got so scathing. It was all true. He spilled out the money on the bed, saying nothing, and watched her eyes grow round.

"What have you been doing?" she whispered. "Sam, you ain't done nothing wrong, have you?"

That did it. He swung his legs off the bed, feeling them buckle as he did so. But he'd be buggered if he was going to stay here and be accused of being a thief, when he'd never done a dishonest thing in his life.

"No, I ain't, woman," he shouted. Henry flinched, pulling away from the nipple and bawling in fright, until May coaxed him back on again. "And if you want to know any more, you can damn well come downstairs and ask. And make haste there, for the sprog's not the only one wanting breakfast."

He stumped down the stairs, aware that the rest of the household was stirring. He wasn't surprised. He hadn't meant to snap and snarl, especially when he was so full of good cheer . . . too bloody full, he groaned, feeling the bile in his gut after the lashings of brandy Gaffer had swilled into him. He turned as Wilf came downstairs, a grin on his face.

"Did the meeting go well then, Pa?"

"I suppose you knew all about it," he said curtly.

"Does it matter? I'd have thought what matters was whether or not you accepted Gaffer's offer. So what did you say to it, Pa?"

For a minute Sam looked at him resentfully. The boy was getting far too big for his boots lately. But a man with a secure job and a bride-to-be had every right to look big. As did a man with a new opportunity landing slap bang in his lap. He gave a hooting laugh.

"I said yes, boy! What else do you think a sane man would have bloody well said?"

"Is somebody going to tell me what this is all about?" Ma said a short while later, when Henry had been fed and changed, and was belching happily in his carriage in the corner of the room. In answer, Sam caught her around the waist and danced her between the table and chairs until she begged for mercy. But her eyes were like stars all the same, and even without knowing what had happened, she didn't need telling that it was something wonderful.

*   *   *

364

"So my Pa's going to be a fully fledged coffin-maker,"
Carrie told John's aunt and uncle, when she took the
baby to visit them a week later. "I don't like saying it,
really, but he's as pleased as ninepence about it."

"It's an honest job, and a very necessary one," Aunt
Vi said. "Don't ever be ashamed of what your father
does, Carrie. And I doubt that he'll ever be out of work
again."

"Mebbe I should order my box from him in advance.
Do you think he'd give me a discount, being almost
family?" Uncle Oswald teased, and Carrie protested
at once.

"Don't even talk about such things, Uncle Oswald. I'm
sure it's bad luck!"

He chuckled. "It's only you young folk who think
death's summat to be feared and not talked about. But
I reckon a man has as much right to overseeing his own
coffin as buying his marriage bed. He'll be spending a
sight longer in it too."

She hated this kind of talk, and she bounced Henry on
her knees to encourage Aunt Vi to coo over him and tickle
him to make him laugh.

"Have you heard from John lately?" she said, wishing
she'd never mentioned her Pa's new prospects. "I had a
letter this week, and I thought he sounded as if he was
getting tired of the constant moving around."

She couldn't help hoping that it was so. In his last letter
he'd said how much he was looking forward to staying in
one place again, and that there was no place like home.
And the other, more personal messages, had told her that
his love was still strong, and that he was impatient for their
wedding.

"We had a letter too," Oswald nodded. "You can read
it if you like, since there's summat of interest to you in
it. Then Vi can dandle that young bab, like she's bursting
to do."

He handed her the letter from the sideboard. Carrie recognised John's firm handwriting, and opened the pages. It said much the same general information as her own letter, save for a few added bits.

"If you see Carrie, tell her this tour will be the last time I enter the ring on any account. Perhaps you can convince her, that all I want now is to come home and lead a settled life, with Carrie by my side. I've done what I wanted to do, and the money's being safely put by in a bank account. All the same, I've nearly had enough of this life, and some of the wagers that go around the arena are enough to sicken anyone. Roll on the spring and summer, when I can put it all behind me."

There was more of the same, but since her eyes were so blurred, Carrie could hardly read it. Why did she find it so difficult to believe what her heart should have told her? And why didn't John open his heart to her, the way he did to his uncle? But she knew the answer to that one. He still had his pride, and perhaps she had never been intended to read these words. If so, she vowed she would never let him know she had seen them. She handed Oswald back the letter.

"I think this is meant for your eyes, and not for mine, but I thank you for letting me see it," she said quietly.

"Take this charmer back, Carrie, while I get us some tea. It's all ready in the kitchen, and just needs bringing in," Aunt Vi said.

"You enjoy holding him, and I'll do it," Carrie said quickly. She needed to escape for a moment, anyway. And besides . . . she looked around her slowly. One day this would be her domain. It was John's plan that they should live here with Uncle Oswald after their marriage, and Aunt Vi would have found her own little place near the sea that she wanted so much. And Carrie had no objection to any of it.

She put the plate of cakes and the tea things on the tray

and carried it through, imagining for a moment that she was dispensing tea and graciousness in her own home. Being the hostess when Ma and Pa came to tea, perhaps, enjoying an afternoon with them all, then waving them off to Jacob's Wells Road, while she and John closed the door behind them and went back to their own private world of happiness . . .

"Are you all right, Carrie?" Vi said, when she put down the tray. "I told that old duffer not to upset you by showing you John's letter."

"It didn't upset me. It made me think, though. I was beginning to realise it didn't matter what John did, as long as we were going to be together eventually, and now here he is, saying he's going to be done with it after all. Maybe everything's done for a purpose."

She bent to her task of pouring tea, embarrassed at baring her feelings like that. She missed the way Vi glanced at her brother, and saw him nod.

"We've been doing some thinking too, Carrie," Vi said. "As you know, I've had a hankering for a long while to get me a small place by the sea, and I reckon the little fishing village of Clevedon will just suit me fine. As soon as John comes home, I'm going to ask him to take me down there to look around for a place."

"But not on our account, Aunt Vi! There'll be a couple of months to go before we plan to be wed, so you musn't think you have to leave here right away. This is your home now – " she stopped, for none of this was really her business, and she felt as if she was putting her foot in it more and more. But Vi laughed comfortably.

"Don't take on so, love. Me and Oswald have been having a long hard talk about the future, what's left of it, and we've decided that we'd like to spend the rest of our time together. So we shall both be looking for that seaside cottage, and leave this place to you and John, with our blessing."

"Is this what you both want?" Carrie said.

Oswald nodded firmly. "It is, girl. Newly-weds should start off life on their own, and me and Vi are comfortable together now. Besides, when John gets his fine new boat, we shall expect you to come down the coast to visit us."

She ran to him and put her arms around his frail neck. She hoped that her Pa wouldn't have to make a coffin for this lovely old man for years and years yet.

"I love you both," she said, her eyes shining, and as Henry gave a healthy belch, they all laughed. "And Henry loves you too!"

She couldn't wait to relate the news to the family. She felt happier than she had in a long time. Wilf and Pa were in work, Ma looked well, and so did the young 'uns. And John didn't want to stay away a minute longer than he had to, and was never going to do any fighting again . . . she crossed her fingers as she thought it, but somehow she felt she was mature enough now, to know that if he was tempted to take up a challenge now and then, she could accept it. She wouldn't want to tie a strong man like John Travis to her apron-strings.

When she left the house on Bedminster Hill, she pushed Henry's carriage at a fair rate down the hill towards the river, and along the road to the crossing-bridge.

"You're going to see your Uncle John very soon," she told the baby gleefully, "and you're going to adore him."

Henry chuckled, far too young to understand the words or their meaning, but bright enough to respond to her mood.

She was out of breath by the time she had pushed him up Jacob's Wells Road, and hadn't objected to stopping half a dozen times for folk to admire the baby and ask after her Ma. It was late afternoon by then, and although the days were starting to lengthen now in the first gusty days of March, the sky had begun to turn to indigo by the

368

time she pushed open their own front door and called out that they were home.

Wilf wouldn't be home from the workshop yet, and Pa was busy organising his new work premises with Gaffer, and showing a surprising aptitude for business, but there was no sign of Ma or Billy. Then she saw them in the back yard. They were feeding the chickens, and Billy was collecting the eggs for tea, and jabbering excitedly to someone there with them.

Someone who was tall and dark, and broader now than before he went away. Carrie's heart seemed to jump in her chest. She left the baby carriage exactly where it was, and rushed out into the yard with her arms held wide.

"Frank!" she said, her voice suddenly choked. "Oh Frank, you're home!"

Chapter 21

Carrie's first euphoric moments were quickly followed by the arrival of her father and Wilf. The gladness on Wilf's face was clear to see, but Carrie held her breath as Pa came into the house, wondering if old hurts would be forgotten and forgiven. But she had reckoned without Pa's new status now he was in work, and Frank's new maturity. Once Pa had expressed his surprise at the visitor home from the sea, it was the son who went straight to the father and put his arms around him.

"It's good to see you, Pa, and to make the acquaintance of this little 'un before he gets too big to handle," he added, as Carrie lifted Henry out of his carriage and brought him to meet his brother for the first time.

"Oh ah, he's a proper Stuckey and no mistake, and quite a handful already," Pa agreed, and any awkwardness between them quickly passed with the attention everyone gave to the baby.

"So how goes it with you, Frank?" Wilf asked, once the excitement had died down a little, and Ma had brought a steaming pot of mutton stew to the table for the evening meal.

"Very well," Frank said. "And you too, I hear. Ma tells me you've landed yourself a good situation and a fair companion to go with it," he grinned. "You can't keep anything from me now, bruth. I've heard most of the gossip in the hour I've been here."

Carrie bounced the infant Henry on her knee a moment

370

longer before returning him to his carriage while they ate their meal. Ma would have given Frank all the news in her usual terse manner, summing them all up in a few short phrases. She could just imagine the way it went.

"Wilf's got himself a steady job now, making toys for a shop and taking special orders, and he's as good as engaged to Gaffer Woolley's daughter. Your Pa's gone into partnership with Gaffer Woolley and become a reg'lar coffin-maker – and before you turn up your nose, that's not a job that's likely to go out of fashion! Our Carrie's helping me now, while she waits for that young man of hers to come back from his prize-fighting shenanigans, touring about the counties. The two young 'uns and myself do well enough, and that's about the size of it."

Oh yes, Ma would have put them all in their neat little compartments, Carrie thought, with a smile.

"What of you, Frank? Have you got some exciting tales of foreign parts to tell us about?"

He laughed easily. "One place is very like another when you see little more of it than the deck or the hold of a ship, Carrie. Sometimes the turnarounds are so quick, you hardly have time to set your feet on dry land before you're back on the briny again."

"Come on, you're not leaving it like that, boy," Sam said. "Ain't you been ashore and seen none of they fancy French mam'selles I've heard tell about?"

"*Sam*," Ma said disapprovingly, while Billy pricked up his ears at once.

"What's a French mam'selle?" he asked curiously.

"Never you mind, and get on and eat your supper," Ma said smartly. "I daresay our Frank will tell you a thing or two about the different places he's seen when he's had time to draw breath. There'll be plenty of time for that when he's settled down again."

In the small silence that followed, Ma looked at Frank sharply. Carrie didn't miss the way his jaw tightened, the way it always used to when he felt awkward at having to tell them something unpleasant.

"How long are you home for, Frank?" she asked him, when nobody else seemed to have the courage. It stood to reason that this was only a temporary visit, even though she sensed that all of them had simply assumed he'd come home for good, having got the wanderlust out of his system.

"About a week," he said carefully. "That's what I wanted to tell you about, but it can wait until after supper."

Sam put down his knife and fork with a clatter.

"Tell us now, boy," he said.

It was one of those moments when a tiny presentiment shivered through Carrie. It wasn't a feeling that something dire was about to happen, but more like a ripple of sadness for a change of circumstances it was impossible to avoid.

"I'm not satisfied with what I'm doing, Pa," Frank told him. "Oh, I can't deny that my urge to see foreign places is as strong as ever. But loading cargo at the docks here in Bristol, and unloading 'em again in France or Spain is hardly an adventurous life – "

"It is for they who ain't never travelled farther than their own back street," Sam grunted.

"But I've done more than that now, and it's given me a taste for it," Frank said, and none of them could miss the renewed enthusiasm in his voice.

"What have you got in mind, Frank?" Carrie said.

He glanced at her, smiling. "I seem to remember that friend of yours, Elsie, asking if you'd ever like to travel to America on the *Great Britain*. Do you recall it?"

She nodded. "On the day of the launch. Some chance! Anyway, the ship can't even be moved now, until the Cumberland Basin locks are widened to let her out!"

"Yes, but I don't mean to travel on anything so grand as the *Great Britain*," Frank said quickly, "but I do mean to go to America, and try to make a life for myself there."

Carrie heard her mother give a little cry. It was rare for May Stuckey to betray her emotions so openly, but she couldn't help it now.

"Frank, *no*. America's on the other side of the world. If you go so far away from us, we'll never see you again."

He left his place and went around the table to kneel by her side and take hold of her hands in his.

"I know that's likely, Ma," he said gently. "America's three thousand miles away, but it's the land of opportunity, and a man can make a name for himself there. I can use all my skills, and in a new young country where fortunes are made, and great mansions fill the towns, there will always be a need for craftsman-made furniture."

"You seem to have thought it all out pretty well," Sam said slowly.

But Carrie noted that he eyed his second son with more respect than of old. Sam had always dismissed Frank in favour of Wilf, but since standing on his own feet for six months and more, Frank had clearly found the strength of purpose he'd always lacked before.

He stood up and returned to his own seat at the table.

"Not only that, but I've got my passage booked," he stated. "I've been saving my wages all this time, and aside from bringing home a few gifts for you all, I've sunk it all into this new venture."

"Then good luck to you, bruth," Wilf spoke up before his father could start making objections. But it seemed as if Sam was silenced as much by the authoritative note in Frank's voice than his actual words.

"What did you bring me, Frank?" Billy's voice broke in eagerly. "Can I see it now? And can I come to America with you?"

Frank laughed as the boy's eagerness broke the tension.

"No, you can't come to America with me, Billy-boy. And the gifts must come later, Master Impatience! It's been a long while since I ate some of Ma's mutton stew, and I don't aim to let it get any colder."

He smiled at Ma, encouraging her to smile back at him, and to get some colour back into the cheeks that had gone so pale at his news.

"But you won't be here for my wedding!" Carrie said suddenly. "Oh, Frank – "

"What wedding is this? Don't tell me you've got that poor young boatman leg-shackled already, even though he's out of town for a while," he gave a mock groan. "Ma didn't tell me that bit of news."

"I thought Carrie would want to tell you herself," Ma murmured, clearly having no more appetite for food, and pushing it around her plate.

Carrie spoke quickly. "We're getting married on my birthday, and I know John would have wanted both you and Wilf to stand up for him on the day."

She avoided looking at Wilf, not sure how he was going to take this. John hadn't even mentioned it, but she was sure he would have done, when the time came. And surely Wilf wouldn't refuse.

"You'll have to make do with young Billy here in my place," Frank said. "And I must have had a sixth sense when I bought your gift. You can use it for your wedding, and it will remind you of me on the day."

"Well, now I can't eat anything else, either," Carrie exclaimed. "You've got to show us now, Frank!"

Those that were hungry finished their meal, while those who were too impatient to eat, had permission to leave the table and wait while Frank rummaged through his baggage for the paper parcels he handed to each of them. There was a fine embroidered Spanish shawl for Ma, and a bottle of best French brandy for Pa; a Spanish whittling knife for Wilf, and a French ball and hoop game for Billy. He

374

hadn't forgotten the baby, and there was an outfit made of fine French lace that would fit the brawny Henry. And for Carrie . . .

She opened her parcel with excited hands. Out spilled a bolt of the loveliest cream watered silk she had ever seen. It would make a perfect wedding-gown, and her throat tightened with pleasure at the sensual texture of the exquisite material, imagining John's face when he turned around from the altar, and saw her coming towards him on Pa's arm, wearing such a gown . . .

"Well? Does it suit?" Frank said, when she seemed too stunned to say anything.

"Oh, Frank. It's beautiful!" She rushed at him, nearly knocking him over with her hugs and kisses. "Ma will help me make a wedding-gown out of it, I'm sure, and it will be almost as if you're there on the day."

"Except that he won't be," Ma said sadly. She took a deep breath, and gave them both a small nod. "But you've made your decision, son, and 'tis like Carrie says. You'll be in our thoughts all the while we're making the dress, and while your sister's wearing it."

And they all knew Ma couldn't go farther than that in giving Frank her blessing.

It seemed that Frank was no sooner home than he was preparing to leave again, but he was there long enough to see the new toy shop in Park Street open.

All of them, except Billy, who was too innocent to see anything unlikely in his hopes, felt certain they would never see Frank again. Billy, with all the optimism of an eight-year-old, was just as confident that one day, he too would cross the Atlantic, and become as rich Frank was going to be.

But they all tried not to dwell on the sadness of Frank's approaching departure. True to his word, Cedric Woolley had done a fine job of advertising the shop-opening event, with posters all around the town, and announcements in the local newspapers. There was to be free lemonade and balloons for all the children bringing their parents to the shop, and Wilf was beginning to realise what a shrewd businessman he was.

A stout, middle-aged lady was installed in the shop as manageress, with a young boy to assist her. Wilf's part in the business was confined to the workshop at the back, but Cedric had also been canny enough to insist that all the advertising matter included the name of the skilled craftsman responsible for the hand-crafted toys.

"Made to exclusive order" was one of the advertising slogans blazoned out on posters everywhere, and by the end of the first week, Wilf's name was becoming as well-known as the toy shop's, and he had enough orders to keep him busy for the next few months. It was clearly going to be a huge success, and Wilf was already hinting that Carrie's might not be the only wedding on the horizon in the forseeable future.

The day before Frank was due to leave Bristol, brother and sister took a last long walk up to Clifton Downs, the way they used to when they were children.

"Our fortunes seem to have taken a turn for the better at last, Frank," Carrie said.

Frank nodded. "Our Wilf certainly looks well set up now, though I never thought Pa would settle for being a coffin-maker. Not that there's ought wrong with it," he added hastily, at her look. "But it's not as creative as making different pieces of furniture, is it? There's ain't much you can do to alter a coffin shape!"

"I suppose not. But it don't mean to say Pa's going to do the job for ever, does it? He may find different work later on. And he's promised to make a settle for me and John as a wedding-gift, so he'll be kept busy."

They took a breather and sat down on one of the grassy slopes overlooking the river. The day was just warm enough for the dampness not to seep through, as long as they didn't sit for too long. The seasons had moved on, and spring was almost upon them. Carrie gazed down at the tall-masted ships jostling for space far below in the glassy river.

For those of a fanciful nature, she thought suddenly, the river reflected all their lives. So often it was stormy and turbulent, full of upheavals and hidden currents . . . and at other times it was as smooth and unruffled as silk. And if it wasn't tempting fate too much, she could hope that the river's calm appearance today was a good omen for all of them.

Frank glanced at the perfect profile of the girl sitting so deep in thought beside him now. He realised, with surprise, that she was quite a beauty.

He'd always known she was pretty, but now she could be called quite stunning, with those coppery curls tumbling about her face, and her cheeks all flushed and dewy-fresh from the exertion of the climb up to the Downs. He hoped John Travis appreciated what a pearl he was getting for a bride.

"Have I got a smut on me nose or summat?" Carrie grinned, aware of this sudden scrutiny, and lapsing into the old familiar way of talking.

Frank shook his head with a smile. "I was just wondering if John Travis knows how lucky he is, and what a fool he must be to go away for months and leave a girl like you. If I'd had a girl of my own, I doubt that I'd ever have gone to sea."

Carrie felt her face flush even more. You didn't expect to hear such compliments from a brother, but this one was slightly more removed from the close-knit family circle now, and saw things from a distance.

"John had good reasons, and in the end I respected

them," she said, quickly defending him. "But in a few weeks' time he'll be home to stay."

She drew in her breath as she spoke, almost as if, by putting the wishes into words, they would disappear.

"Are you happy, our kiddley?" Frank said abruptly. It was so long since he'd called her anything so familiar that the tears stung her eyes for a minute, and she nodded vigorously.

"As happy as it's possible to be when John's not around. I miss him so much – but I suppose I'd best not go on about that too much, or you may start feeling guilty about your own plans."

"As soon as I get settled, I'll write and tell you all about America," Frank said, so resolutely that she knew nothing would ever make him reconsider his future. And why should it? He was young and fancy-free, and had a good head on his shoulders . . . a shadow suddenly fell across her vision, and as she looked up quickly, her heart jolted.

She jumped to her feet without thinking. Frank stood up in a far more leisurely manner, clearly seeing no reason whatever to kow-tow to the likes of Miss Helen Barclay and her companion in these green open spaces where the air was free for all to share.

"Good afternoon, Carrie," Helen said graciously.

"Good afternoon, miss," she stammered, wishing to God she had all the social graces at her command right now.

"I trust all is well with your family?"

Eyeing the handsome gent beside her, Carrie immediately guessed that Helen was out to impress, and doing her best to appear civil to the most irritating of persons she had ever had in her employ.

"Yes, thank you, miss," she said, resisting the need to bob. "We've got a new baby boy in the family now," she added, doubting that kitchen gossip about the event would have reached these aristocratic ears.

"Well done," Helen said vaguely. "Then my fiancé and I shall send your parents our felicitations. And how go your own affairs? Is this your new young man?"

Carrie almost laughed out loud, though Frank was handsome enough to be anyone's beau, of course.

"Good God, no, begging your pardon, Miss Helen. This here's my brother Frank, who's shortly to be leaving for America to seek his fortune."

"Good gracious me!" Helen said, as Frank made her an elaborate bow. The gentleman with her wished him well in his venture, and told his lady-love they had better walk on, or she would be getting cold from standing about.

Carrie watched them go, mimicking her mincing steps for a moment before Frank told her laughingly to stop it.

"*Well!* Who does she think she is? I don't owe her nothing now, and fancy thinking I could forget my John so quickly and be walking out with somebody else. It just reminds me how often she chopped and changed her mind over her own gentlemen callers."

"I take it you're glad to be out of her employ then?" Frank said mildly.

Carrie laughed out loud. "I should just say I am!"

He tucked her arm inside his as they strolled on across the Downs. "When I think of settling down, I shall look for a girl just like you, our Carrie."

"Will you? What do you suppose American girls are like, then?"

"It may not be a truly American girl. So many folk are going there now, it's just as likely to be an Irish girl or a Londoner, or even a German or Dutch, by all accounts."

"I hope you'll be able to understand 'em then, or you might find yourself hitched to one of 'em before you know it!"

She'd never thought much about America before, nor of the people who lived there. It gave her a funny feeling to think of Frank starting up a whole new life with an unknown girl of a different nationality, and in time producing American children.

"What are you thinking about?"

"Just ghosts," Carrie said. "Nice ones, though."

The days dragged once Frank had gone, and Ma moped about for a couple of days, and then put on her usual brave face, saying there was no use crying over things that couldn't be changed.

Wilf and Sam were so busy about their work that they hardly had time to mope, and Billy already had his head filled with dreams of growing up as fast as he could and joining Frank in America. His sole reason for flying off to his school lessons more eagerly than of old in the afternoons, was to beg his teacher to tell him all she could about this strange big country across the sea.

The baby grew fat and contented, and Carrie counted the days until John came home. She had no idea when it would be, but it must surely be any day now. She was kept busy looking after young Henry, since Ma still refused to leave off doing the washing for her special ladies. She had no need of the work any more, but she insisted it was a way of keeping her mind off all else, and it gave her enormous pride to see the lace collars and cuffs and broderie underpinnings come up white and sparkling under her expert care.

Carrie took Henry down to the waterfront for an airing every afternoon to watch the busy little tugs moving up and down the river. The baby was propped up against a cushion in his carriage now, and starting to take an interest in it all.

"You see that boat, lamb?" she said to him, directing his carriage to where the ferry was working its way across from the other side. "That's what your Uncle John used to do, but soon he's going to get a fine big boat and

380

take folk right out to sea. Maybe he'll take you and me one day."

"I wouldn't be surprised at that."

The voice she knew and loved so well spoke right behind her. Carrie spun round, staring in disbelief for one glorious instant, before she was enveloped in John's arms. And the feel of him, and the smell of him, and the taste of him, was everything and all that she remembered. Her heart thudded loudly against him, matching his exactly. And her tears of joy were damp on his cheeks when they finally broke apart, hardly noticing that they were in a public place.

"You're back!" she gasped unnecessarily.

"I do believe I am," he grinned. "Unless I'm some figment of your imagination, my dearest. And my God, but I've waited too long for this moment."

He looked away from her then, afraid to show so much love so openly.

"And I suppose this is Henry. He's a fine young bruiser if I ever saw one!"

It was almost impossible to think that John had never seen Henry until now. But his words reminded her of the reason John had been away, and she was quick to notice the lingering dark swellings on his face, and the scar below one eye. His time away hadn't been all honey then, despite the way he had rarely mentioned the fights in his letters.

"Come back to the house with me, John. Ma will be that pleased to see you. Our Frank has been and gone lately – and oh, there's so much to tell you!"

"Aunt Vi's already told me some of it," he said. "I went home first, to let them know I'm safely back, but I couldn't wait to see you. I want to pay my respects to your mother, but what I really want is to be alone with you, sweetheart. God, it's been so long since I've held you in my arms properly!"

She felt the hot colour run up her cheeks, knowing

exactly what he meant. And she wanted that too. She wanted him to hold her and thrill her, and love her . . .

"We only have two months to wait until we're wed, John," she murmured, "and then we're going to be together for always. Aren't we?"

For a moment, she allowed a doubt to come into her mind. Supposing he'd got such a taste for the performances he'd given in the ring, and the acclaim that went with it, that he couldn't give it up after all?

"We are, my love," he said softly. "I never want to leave you or this town again, and as for the fighting, I've had enough of that to last me a lifetime. Unless some wag wants taking down a peg or two, of course, like a certain someone's brother I could mention."

But he was only teasing, and Carrie relaxed, telling him it was unlikely he'd have any more trouble from Wilf now that he was such a respectable up-and-coming toymaker.

"And Pa's set up too," she said thoughtfully. "All our lives have changed in so short a time, John. To think that this time last year we hadn't even met."

"And every day I thank God for hurling that young scamp of a brother of yours into the river. But for him, we might never have met at all."

"Yes we would," Carrie said. "Somehow, some time, we would have met, John. I know it."

She felt his hand close over hers as she pushed the baby carriage back towards Jacob's Wells Road.

"That old destiny you believe in would have assured it, would it?" he said with a smile.

"Of course," she said positively.

But now there were plans to be made, and the most immediate one of all was to take Aunt Vi and Uncle Oswald down to Clevedon to look around for a suitable cottage. Now that John was home again, they were anxious to get everything settled, and to be moving out of the house on Bedminster Hill on the day of Carrie and John's wedding, leaving the house to the newly-weds.

The four of them planned a whole day out in the middle of April for the jaunt, and by then John had already found out the name of a good estate agent with suitable properties on his books, and knew just where to find him.

A carriage was hired for the day by Aunt Vi and the journey was something of a holiday. Only Uncle Oswald had been to the small fishing-village before, and that was many years earlier. But he insisted that he well recalled the natural pebble and shingle coastline. Some said that the hilly outlines of the town resembled the seven hills of Rome. And since none of them had ever been to Rome, nor were ever likely to go there, it was something that couldn't be disputed.

They alighted in the middle of the day, stiff and in need of refreshment, and very thankful that the driver could recommend an inn to serve them food and ale. But once replete, they resumed their ride around the village to look the place over, and Aunt Vi declared at once that this was where she wanted to end her days.

From the top of the hill above the cluster of dwellings that made up the small town, there was a fine view right down the Bristol Channel. An old church stood on another not-too-distant hill, inviting folk for worship. The islands in the middle of the Channel were those of Flatholm and Steepholm, of which Carrie had heard John tell, and across the water was the hazy outline of the coast of Wales.

This information immediately reminded Carrie of her friend Elsie, whom she hadn't seen for weeks now, and she wondered briefly how her association with the lusty Dewi was progressing.

"Well, it's all just perfect, and I've no hesitation in saying I want to live here, and I know I don't need to ask Oswald for his approval," Aunt Vi declared. "So the sooner we see the estate agent and find out what properties are available, the better."

The estate agent's offices weren't far away from the Beach Road, and he was only too happy to show them the details of various cottages. It was a welcome surprise to the old couple to see that the prices were far more modest than those of city dwellings, and it was an added incentive for them to retire to the seaside.

"May we see these properties?" John said, when the couple had selected two or three cosy-looking places, and couldn't decide between them.

"Of course," the man said at once. "I shall escort you there myself, though I think I would advise against the Zig-Zag property in view of the accessibility," he said delicately. "The views are magnificent, of course, but the narrow lane leading to the cottage is very steep and winding, and in bad weather can cause quite a hazard."

"Then we had best decide against that one," Aunt Vi said at once. "There's no use being tied to a place we can't leave for fear of breaking our legs."

That left two cottages along the Beach Road. Either would do admirably, Carrie thought, and each had a view of the Channel and the Welsh coastline. It was a lovely setting, and the estate agent informed them that the sunsets on the water in this particular area were glorious. Hearing his eloquent, persuasive manner, and seeing this quaint little village in all its pristine spring glory, Carrie thought she could easily move down here too.

But John needed the river for his summer trippers and would never want to move out of the city. He'd made that clear already. Besides that, Carrie's family was in Bristol, and her brief moment of envy vanished. Clevedon was an ideal place for the older Travises, and she and John could always visit.

They finally settled on April Cottage, on the Beach

Road, which was appropriate to the month in which they were buying it. It had two bedrooms upstairs, a large parlour and reasonable size scullery downstairs, and the privy outside the back door in the narrow strip of garden.

"You've made a very wise choice, sir and madam, if I may say so," the estate agent said gushingly. "Now, if you would care to come back to the office and sign some papers, I will set things in motion for you. The cottage has only been empty for a while, and would surely have been snapped up very soon."

"It's a good thing we happened to view it then," Uncle Oswald said dryly, recognising the sales spiel.

"When were you thinking of taking possession?"

"On the twenty-eighth of June," Oswald and John said together, and they both laughed at the womenfolk.

"So definite!" said the estate agent. "Most folk have no more than a vague idea until we discuss it with them."

"Well, we have a very definite idea," John assured him. "Of course, if the dealings can't be done by then – "

"My dear sir, there's no question of that! Everything will be in order as soon as we go through the formalities."

Above his bent head, Carrie and John smiled at one another. The formalities were signing the deed of sale and for Uncle Oswald and Aunt Vi to hand over the money orders they had collected from the bank. Not for them the hazards of long repayments. This was cash, and as such, commanded respect from this pompous gent.

The formalities also included the date when the cottage would belong to the old couple, and the house on Bedminster Hill would belong to Carrie and John, with all its implications. The twenty-eighth of June was her birthday, and it promised to be the happiest birthday ever. She would attain the magical age of eighteen years, and she would acquire a husband.

She shivered in the cloying warmth of the office. Not just *a husband*, the thought ran around her head, but her own, beloved, beautiful John, whom she would promise to love and honour and obey for the rest of her life . . .

She realised he was still looking at her, and that Uncle Oswald was clearing his throat. She blushed, looking down at her gloved hands, and praying that the love and longing in her eyes hadn't been too plain for all to see. It wasn't seemly . . . at least, not until they were married, and in the privacy of their own dear little home . . .

They had decided to stay overnight in Clevedon, to save journeying on the bumpy road back to Bristol, and they applied for lodgings at a hotel perched on a rocky outcrop at the end of Beach Road. The two ladies would share one room, and the gentlemen another. Aunt Vi had previously called on Carrie's mother and assured her that all would be above-board.

"I never doubted it," Ma had said, a mite tartly. "The girl's been brought up to respect herself, and I'd hope that your nephew had too."

"Have no fear of that, Mrs Stuckey," Aunt Vi soothed. "Now, I wonder, while I'm here, if I'm to be permitted to take a small peep at this lovely wedding-gown Carrie's been telling me about? You're so nimble with your fingers, I hear, and I do envy you that skill."

"Just a peep, then," May said, unable to resist such blatant flattery. "And if you don't mind keeping an eye on Henry while I bring it down."

"It'll be a pleasure," Vi said, knowing there was no way she'd be invited upstairs. There were limits to how far visitors were allowed into the intimacy of other folks' lives, and she and May Stuckey weren't family yet.

But she gave whole-hearted admiration to the gown May had fashioned out of the bolt of silk fabric Frank had bought. She thanked God he hadn't stinted on the amount, for it had taken a great deal to make Carrie a gown fit for a princess. And that was what May was determined her girl would have.

"It's really beautiful, Mrs Stuckey," Vi said sincerely. "And Carrie will look beautiful in it."

But respectability aside, Vi wasn't beyond seeing the romanticism of the occasion when the two young lovebirds were together and away from home, and on the brink of marriage. And when she and Oswald were more than ready to retire for the night, she told Carrie that if she and John wanted to take an evening stroll in that glorious sunset she'd been told about, she wouldn't disturb her when she came to bed.

"I was going to suggest the very same," John said, even though it was long past sunset now. They had watched it through the windows of the inn though, and Carrie had thought she had never seen anything more beautiful than the sun's dying rays spreading across the water in all their brilliant shades of crimson and orange and gold.

Carrie fetched her shawl from her room and the two of them slipped out of the inn, to stroll with arms entwined along the short undulating stretch of Beach Road. By now, a huge yellow moon had risen in the sky, its golden sheen across the rippling water replacing the blood-red of sunset, and only serving to enhance the romance of the balmy evening.

They paused by a rickety fence to gaze outwards, to where the dim, hazy shape of Wales could no longer be seen. They seemed to be bathed in the moon's golden glow, and they might have been the only two people alive in the world. As John pulled Carrie into his arms, he held her close enough for her to imagine that their hearts had ceased their individual beating, and had merged into one, and his kiss was sweetly sensual on her lips.

"I want you to know how much I love you, my Carrie,"

he said softly against her mouth, "and nothing is ever going to separate us again."

He held her even closer, and she wound her arms around him tightly, as if she would never let him go. Her shawl slipped away from her slightly, and a small breeze prickled on her skin for a brief moment and made her shiver. She told herself it meant nothing. And for once she wouldn't let herself believe in omens.

Chapter 22

By the beginning of June, they were planning for the wedding the end of the month, and Ma's fingers were constantly pricked from long hours of sewing the wedding-gown. But it was a labour of love, and as such, she disregarded the discomfort of the nicks.

But as well as arranging with Mr Pritchard to perform the ceremony, there were other things taking shape as well. John requested that Carrie accompanied him to the yard of one of the prominent boat-builders in the city.

"So what do you think of her?" John said, with as much pride as if he displayed a new-born babe to the world.

Carrie looked, and felt a stab of disappointment. John hadn't said much about the new boat that was being prepared for him, except that it was due to be completed by the first day of July, just in time for the main summer tripping trade. It couldn't be finished before, because not all the funds were available yet, and he would still owe some on account when he took delivery. He skimmed over that particular fact, not wanting to alarm Carrie too much, or get her worried as to whether he'd be tempted to go into the ring again.

But she had expected to see something more than this. Sitting securely in its cradle, the boat was certainly a recognisable shape, but the paddle-wheels were stacked forlornly at the side, there was no paint on it, and nor did anyone seem to be working on it on that particular day. John saw her face, and squeezed her waist.

389

"Don't worry, sweetheart, it will all be done in time. I just wanted you to see that the work has begun, that's all. If you'll come into the gaffer's office, he'll let you see the blueprint, so you can see just how it will look when it goes into the water."

She wasn't too impressed. She had seen boats before, and although this one was obviously going to be much larger than John's old one, and fulfil his dream, she felt as far removed from it as ever. But she followed him dutifully into the gaffer's dusty little office, and allowed John to introduce her.

"I know your father's work, miss," he commented. "And I hear he's doing well these days."

Carrie nodded stiffly. He might have done even better, she thought sourly, if one of these boat-building gaffers had given Pa and her brothers work when it was so sorely needed. But to be fair, she knew that hard times had hit them all once the *Great Britain*'s teams of carpenters had been made redundant.

"May we see the blueprint for my new boat, please, Mr Cummings?"

The man took down several rolled-up plans and spread them out on his hotch-potch of a desk. They were no more than sketchy outlines, with a mass of figures and measurements that meant nothing to Carrie. The man started to explain the finer points of balance and draught and water-displacement, all of which went above her head, while she tried hard to look interested. After all, this was her future too . . .

And then he pulled out the final drawing from beneath all the others and spread it out in front of them. And Carrie stared, bemused and enchanted at the sleek, beautiful lines of the boat, with the paddle-wheels so symmetrical and graceful at either side. And proudly emblazoned along the side of the boat, prominent for everyone to see, was the name Caroline.

She caught her breath, and turned sharply to John with shimmering, luminous eyes.

"It's my wedding gift to you, sweetheart," he said softly. "Wherever I am, at home or on the river, my Caroline will always be with me."

He drew her towards him and pressed a light kiss on her mouth. She responded with fervour, too full of love to speak. The boatyard owner cleared his throat noisily at this unlikely exhibition of affection in a boatyard office. John smiled, unperturbed as ever.

"You'll forgive this little display, sir. The lady had no idea of my choice of name, and as you can see, it has delighted her."

"Quite so," Mr Cummings said. "Then, if there's nothing more, sir?" He was clearly wanting to get on with his business and not waste time with these two, despite the fact that one was a paying customer – or would be, eventually.

"Good-day to you, sir," John said at once, shaking the man's hand. Carrie gave the man a nod, still too stunned to say anything else. They walked out into the sunlight, and she gave a little skip of pure pleasure.

"Why didn't you tell me what you planned?" she squealed, hugging his arm.

"And spoil my surprise? Never! I didn't even mean to tell you now. I wanted you to wait until you saw the boat in the water, but in the end I couldn't resist showing you the plans."

"I'm so glad you did. Oh John, it's the most beautiful thing anyone has ever done for me."

He laughed, sliding his arm around her waist and squeezing her tight.

"If it takes so little to please my lady, then I think I can safely promise you a lifetime of far greater pleasures, my darling," he said teasingly.

They had walked as far as Welsh Back, where the

Wednesday market was in full swing and crowded with people. They were in the midst of them almost before they knew it.

"I'm supposed to buy some fruit for Ma," Carrie remembered. "I'd best not go home without it."

Her heart suddenly leapt as the person standing behind the fruit stall glared at them. She hadn't seen Elsie for several months now, though she had heard rumours that a dark-haired boy was often seen leaving her cottage in the early hours of the morning.

"If you want fruit, you can ask some other stall-holder, for I'll not serve you," Elsie said rudely.

"Don't be stupid, Elsie," Carrie muttered. "You can't refuse to serve a customer."

"I can do what I bloody well like, and the likes of you ain't going to stop me!" Elsie yelled.

"There's no need for that, girl," John said in annoyance. Elsie rounded on him at once.

"And I don't want no lip from you, neither. I mighta fancied you once, but I don't no more. You buggers are all the same when it comes to leaving a girl in the lurch, and if Carrie don't know it by now, then more's the pity."

"What do you mean?" Carrie demanded. "Nobody left you in the lurch, and if you'd wanted my friendship, you knew where to come."

"Oh ah! But you Stuckeys have gone up in the world now, ain't you?" Elsie sneered. "Your Ma wouldn't have wanted the likes of me hanging around, looking all pious and disapproving at me."

She paused for breath, and some of the interested onlookers were beginning to tut-tut at this outburst, while others were crowing with amusement.

"I don't know what you're talking about, Elsie, and I'm not going to stop and listen to your nonsense. Come on, John, we'll get the fruit elsewhere."

Elsie whipped around the front of the stall as fast as

lightning, knocking over a basket of oranges, and sending them rolling everywhere. She banged her hand against her belly in a fury.

"This is what I'm on about, my fine lady," she shouted. "Not that you'd care if I'm up the spout, would you? You and your fine young man. Maybe he'd like to take the blame for it, seeing as nobody else is owning up to it?"

"That's enough, girl," John snapped, incensed now as several eavesdroppers began muttering. Elsie glanced around at them, seizing the moment.

"That's right, folks. Deserted in me hour of need, I was, and who's to say that this 'ere gent ain't to blame for it? I gave 'im my favour, so I did, and then he went off and left me!"

"Elsie, for pity's sake, stop it!" Carrie screeched. "You'll have folk believing you in a minute."

The rumpus was beginning to get out of hand. Other baskets of fruit were being tossed to the ground, and several ragged urchins took the opportunity of scrabbling for apples and oranges. In minutes a loud-pitched whistle rang out as a constable came running to see what it was all about.

"It's this young tart," someone shouted. "Accusing this 'ere gent of puttin' her in the family way, by all accounts."

"It's all a mistake," Carrie gasped, as the policeman fought his way through the crowd towards her and John. "Elsie, for God's sake, tell them it's all a mistake!"

Elsie's face had gone the colour of chalk. The sight of the constable and the realisation of bringing the law into the affray had the effect of reducing her to jelly.

"I ain't saying no more," she stuttered.

"Take him in custody, Constable," a guttural voice shouted. "The poor maid's done in, by the looks of her, and the gent should be made to pay for his sins."

"It ain't a hanging offence, sir," the constable snapped, "and girls like these ain't exactly saints neither."

Elsie found her voice at that. "What do you mean? I never encouraged 'im, if that's what you think!"

"Are you saying he raped you, miss?"

As the constable's voice took on a sharper tone, Carrie felt as if she was living through a nightmare. Why in God's name didn't Elsie put a stop to all this here and now? John was trying to protest that he'd had no part in this, but the crowd was shouting him down, clearly enjoying the unexpected bit of excitement and wanting blood.

To her horror, they caught the word, and even though Elsie hadn't answered, new anger rippled around the crowd.

"We're getting out of here," John said fiercely in her ear. "She can sort this mess out by herself."

Even as he spoke, the constable's hand shot out and grabbed John's shoulder. Without a second thought, John turned and gave him a double punch that sent him to his knees. One knuckle caught him squarely under the chin, and the other winded him in the gut. The women in the crowd screamed, and pandemonium broke out. Several rough male hands held John fast until police reinforcements arrived, and before Carrie could really comprehend what was happening, John was being hauled off to the cells in the Bridewell.

The crowds slowly dispersed once all the excitement was over, and Carrie stood motionless for a moment, watching in disbelief as Elsie began picking up fruit and righting the baskets on the stall. Customers were obviously deciding to give the fruit stall a wide berth now, and no wonder.

Then Carrie moved into action, and she rushed forward, shaking Elsie by the hair until she howled with rage.

"How could you do this? What in God's name are you playing at? You *know* John's not responsible for your condition, Elsie. You know it, and I know it."

Elsie yanked herself away, rubbing at her sore scalp, but Carrie was almost overcome by emotion now. This was her friend, and she had betrayed Carrie in the worst possible way.

Her face crumpled. "How could you do this to us, Elsie? Are you so very jealous of John and me?"

Elsie tossed her head, and her eyes flashed. "I don't give a damn about John and you," she mimicked. "All I cared about was – was – "

"My God, was it that Welsh fellow? That Dewi something or other?" Carrie said suddenly.

"Of course it was Dewi! He said he loved me, and I ain't been with nobody else, and now he's disappeared off the face of the earth. I ain't seen him in two months, and nobody knows what's happened to 'im," Elsie said, all in a rush.

"Oh, Elsie," Carrie said sadly.

"Is that all you can say? *Oh, Elsie?*"

Carrie went round the back of the stall and put her arms around her.

"You should have come to Ma. She'd have helped you."

"Oh ah? What would she have done? Offered me the needle to be rid of it or summat?"

"Of course not. But she'd have understood. You're to come home with me today – as soon as we've got all this sorted out."

"All what?" Elsie said uneasily.

"You've got to go to the Bridewell with me and tell the truth. John's been accused of something dreadful, Elsie. Rape is a very serious offence."

"I can't! They'll sling me in the cells instead."

"Of course they won't. But if you don't want to lose my friendship for ever, you'll come with me right now, and tell them."

She couldn't even be angry with her any more. Elsie

395

looked such a pathetic figure now, and so far removed from the brash, flouncy girl of old. But she was severely anxious on John's behalf, and the sooner they got it all cleared up, the better. Then they'd go home to Jacob's Wells Road. Ma would know what to do.

"You'd better go and get this sorted out, *bach*," one of the Welsh boyos said quietly. "Tell you what. I'll make enquiries over in Cardiff during the week, and see what I can find out about Dewi before next week, is it?"

"Do you promise, Ivor?" Elsie begged, so pathetic it made Carrie wince. "You never listened to me before."

"Aye well, perhaps it's time somebody did, *cariad*," he said uncomfortably. "You leave it to me, girl."

The two girls made their way to the Bridewell in fear and trembling. Neither had been in a police station before, and had an unspoken wish to keep as far away from men in blue uniforms as possible. They went up diffidently to the front desk.

"Yes? What do you two want?" the sergeant said uncompromisingly.

"My fiancé was brought in a short time ago," Carrie spoke up as confidently as she could "There was a complete misunderstanding, and he shouldn't be here at all."

"That's what they all say, miss. What's the name?"

"Travis. John Travis."

"Travis, eh? You mean the ruffian who struck one of my constables? Any member of the public who commits such a felony is certainly entitled to be detained at Her Majesty's pleasure," he said pompously.

"But you don't understand! He didn't mean to strike anyone. It was done on impulse because he was being accused of something he hadn't done, and my friend here will vouch for that. You must listen – please!"

The man shook his head. "Can't be done. The charge

is common assault, and unless he's got a good lawyer to deal with the matter, he'll stay in the cells until the case comes up in court – or until he rots."

Carrie felt her face blanch. "But we're getting married in less than a month. You can't keep him here!"

The sergeant's eyes narrowed. It was clear he didn't expect such argument from two young girls who looked pretty dishevelled themselves by now.

"I can do whatever I choose, miss. Now, if you'll excuse me, I've got work to do."

"We ain't leaving here until somebody listens to me," Elsie said flatly. "It's my fault John Travis is in the cells, and at least I can set one thing straight. He never raped me, nor even touched me, and this lump in my belly ain't no more due to him than the man in the moon."

She might not have the most eloquent way of speaking, Carrie thought faintly, but she had the desired effect.

"Would you swear to that on oath?" the sergeant snapped.

"'Course I would, if I had to," Elsie snapped back. "The feller belongs to my friend here, not to me, and I've got me own boy. I never said John Travis raped me anyway. It was the crowd who got it all wrong, and then your constable come along and grabbed John, and he turned without thinking and caught him one."

The sergeant leaned on the deak. "That's where you're wrong, young woman. If he'd just caught him one, as you put it, it might have been a different matter. But he struck him twice, and that constitutes a pre-meditated attack."

"Nothing of this was pre-meditated," Carrie almost wept at the man's implacable face. "It was all an unfortunate incident."

"You tell that to my constable, who's needing attention from a physician," he said sourly.

Out of the corner of her eye, Carrie saw a man she

recognised emerge from a side door. She turned to him with relief.

"Doctor Flowers, thank goodness," she gasped.

"Carrie, what on earth are you doing here?" he said in astonishment. At the concern in his voice, she burst into tears, and was guided to a bench alongside, while Elsie stood in silent guilt at having caused all this furore. Carrie burst out the whole sad story in little gasping sentences. He patted her hand.

"Sergeant Sullivan has his duty to do, and there's nothing to be done here tonight. The constable's not badly hurt, and may be persuaded not to press charges, since you've explained it all. It'll need to be properly recorded and written down though. Has that been done yet?"

Carrie looked blank. "No. We just told the story."

Doctor Flowers went to the desk and they heard him speak tersely. The two girls sat together on the bench, their hands held tightly together. The doctor then went with them into a little office, where another constable wrote down all that they had to say.

"I'd like to see Mr Travis for a moment," the doctor said next.

"He ain't leaving here tonight, Doctor," Sergeant Sullivan said.

"I didn't ask if he was leaving. I said I'd like to see him. I have a right to see if he needs any treatment," the doctor said. He told the girls to wait until he came back.

"What good do you think he can do?" Elsie muttered.

"I don't know, but thank God somebody's trying to do something."

It seemed a long while until he came back, but he offered to give the girls a ride home by way of Greenwood Street. It seemed a very long way round, and Carrie said they could just as well walk.

"As you will, but I'm going to Greenwood Street to alert Mr Thomas Venn, Mr Travis's lawyer, and to request that he calls on the old uncle at Bedminster Hill this evening to let him know what's happening. With luck, Venn will get this whole thing sorted out in the morning."

"Thank you, Doctor," Carrie said, with a flood of relief. "I don't know why you're doing all this for me, but thank you all the same."

"It's because of my respect for your mother, girl, and also because I believe your talk of a misunderstanding. I don't like to see injustice. And I'm no legal man, but I don't reckon any real harm's been done, except to the constable's pride. I don't expect he'll relish appearing in court on such a flimsy case, since Venn would just wipe the floor with him. My guess is that he'll agree to drop the whole thing."

They went out into the daylight, feeling drained and ragged. To Carrie, it hardly seemed possible that people were still hurrying about the city, going about their business in the ordinary way, when theirs had been such a traumatic afternoon. They thanked the doctor again, and after a few brief words to Elsie to go and see him as soon as she felt the need, they parted company from him.

It was the first time the two girls had been properly alone for months, and they were both awkward and tongue-tied, and very aware of the great gulf that had been put between them. Yet it was a gulf that could be breached, and one that both wanted breached. Their friendship had lasted too long to be lost for ever.

"Carrie, you know damn well I never meant things to happen like they did," Elsie muttered as they made their way back through the city. "I never meant to accuse your John, only you know how my tongue runs away with me sometimes."

"You should try harder not to let it," Carrie retorted. "You hurt people, Elsie. You always have."

"I know," she said contritely. "Me granpa used to say the same thing. I've been better lately, honest I have, leastways, until Dewi went missing. I really love him, see, Carrie. I know you think I'm flighty and don't know what love means, and I never did, 'til I met Dewi. He said he loved me too, and now I just don't know what to think."

"So he don't know about the babby then?" It shocked her to even think about it, but it was a living, breathing child in Elsie's belly, and there was no getting away from the fact, even though it hardly showed as yet.

Elsie shook her head. "I was going to tell him the last time he came over on the trow, but he didn't turn up. None of the other Welshies live near him, see, so they don't know what's happened, neither."

"Do you think he'd have married you, Elsie?" Lord knew what would happen to her if he didn't.

"I dunno. It's what I want, Carrie. I do love him, see?" She couldn't seem to think any farther than that, and Carrie made up her mind.

"You're coming back home with me tonight. I'll have to tell Ma what's happened, and – "

"I can't!" Elsie said in a fright. "They'll blame me for having your John put in jail!"

"No they won't, not if we say what a stupid fuss the crowd made and got the wrong end of the stick. That's what really happened anyway, isn't it? If the constable hadn't asked if you were raped, the crowd wouldn't have got it all wrong, would they? And John wouldn't have hit the constable, and landed in the cells."

She listened to herself, making all the excuses for this fair-weather friend, when her dearest John was languishing in the cells at the Bridewell. But the truth was, Elsie looked so desperate now, that she feared for her safety if she was once left alone. The river near the cottage was deep, and full of hidden currents that could sweep a body into the undertow and out into the Channel before anyone was missed. And who would miss Elsie Miller, anyway? She had no-one.

And if anyone was understanding, it would surely be Ma . . . but the nearer home she got, the more uneasy Carrie felt. Elsie had sinned in so many ways, and her Pa wasn't much of a one for forgiveness. And Wilf would be sure to imply that it was no less than he'd always expected from Elsie Miller.

Carrie's stomach was beginning to feel tight long before they reached the house, and Elsie had fallen silent. They opened the front door, and went inside, calling out Ma's name. She came into the parlour from the steamy scullery, where the aroma of fresh baking wafted towards them and made their mouths water.

"Why Elsie, this is a nice surprise," Ma said, at which Elsie promptly burst into noisy tears.

The telling didn't take long, because Elsie was suddenly blubbing it all out on May Stuckey's comforting shoulder while Carrie stood helplessly by.

"I know I did wrong, Mrs Stuckey," she wailed at last. "I've been wicked and now I'm paying for it. But I didn't mean to make your Carrie and her John pay as well, and I'm fair ashamed of it all."

May didn't say anything for a few minutes, and then she spoke briskly. "Well, you ain't the first girl to pay for being too free with her favours, and I daresay you won't be the last. And once that lusty young Welsh feller's brought home to roost and does right by you, you can put all this behind you. That there lawyer fellow will sort John's problems out, since it's what they're trained to do, so there's no use fretting over it tonight. And I'm sure our Carrie won't bear a grudge for blaming her young man, however unintentionally."

But had she known it, Carrie was beset by all kinds of doubts now. She didn't believe for a moment that John

401

had ever been dallying with Elsie. But uglier thoughts had been put inside her head now, and they wouldn't go away.

For all those early months of the year, John had been travelling around the western counties, cheered and adored by all the female admirers who flocked to see the bare-knuckle fighting and thought the participants so glamorous . . . and how was she to know whether or not he had been tempted . . .?

It was all to do with something called trust, a small voice inside her head insisted. And so it was. And she did trust him . . . she did . . . but still the thought festered and nagged at her, and in her heart she wished Elsie to Kingdom Come for unwittingly putting the doubts in her mind.

She caught sight of the girl's tear-stained face, and put the devilish thoughts away. Elsie had crumpled like a deflated paper bag, and needed all her compassion now. And she was being a selfish pig for letting Ma in for this and seeming to stand by so stiff and awkward . . .

"You're to stay here for a day or two," Ma was saying firmly now.

"I can't! What will Mr Stuckey – and Wilf – have to say to me!" For about the first time ever, Elsie had the grace to look ashamed and embarrassed at the thought of seeing the Stuckey menfolk. Billy was in the habit of calling in on his Pa at the coffin-maker's workshop every afternoon now, and they came home together. Billy would be another hurdle to face.

Henry began bawling for his tea, and Ma picked him calmly out of the carriage in the corner and dumped him on Elsie's lap.

"Here. You may as well get used to bouncing a babby while I make us all a hot cup of tea. And don't give me no more nonsense about not staying. You look fair done in, girl. You'll stay in our Carrie's room for a coupla days, and there's an end to it."

"Yes, missus," Elsie said meekly, and stared down into the encouraging blue eyes of young Henry Stuckey.

The men took it all surprisingly well. Billy was hushed up when he began asking too many questions. And as for Wilf . . .

"So your man hit out at a bobby, did he?" he grinned at Carrie. She was about to rise indignantly to his defence, when she realised Wilf wasn't exactly censuring the act. "Many's the time I've itched to do likewise, but never had the opportunity – nor the nerve for it."

"'Tain't nothing so clever if he's going to be banged up in the cells for a month, though," Sam grunted.

Carrie felt her heart turn over. "They couldn't do that, Pa! The wedding's in less than four weeks now."

"You'll just have to leave all that to the lawyer, girl, and there's no use fretting over it until you know what's what," Sam told her.

"I hope he let Uncle Oswald and Aunt Vi know," she went on. "They'll be so upset. I should have gone myself."

"I'll take you there later if you like," Wilf said suddenly. "You won't stop worrying over it until you see 'em for yourself, if I know you."

It was the first time he'd put himself out on John's behalf, however obliquely, and also the first time he'd ever taken any interest in going to the house on Bedminster Hill. Carrie was startled and touched.

"Oh, would you, Wilf? I'd consider it a great kindness."

"Ah well, don't get carried away. I'm as anxious to see he gets out of the Bridewell as you, I suppose. I've no more wish to have a jailbird for a brother-in-law than the next man," he said dryly.

But she knew by the softness in his eyes that he was mellowing towards John and the unfortunate circumstances that had sent him to the cells. How extraordinary,

403

she couldn't help thinking. It was fighting that had made them so hostile to one another, and it was fighting that might just be bringing them together. But she wasn't going to count her chickens too fast, and she still had the elderly Travises to face tonight. She prayed the shock wasn't going to be too much for them.

She discovered they were more resilient than she thought. By the time she and Wilf had toiled up the hill to the house, Venn, the lawyer, had been and gone, and they were already acquainted with the happenings of the afternoon.

"I'm so sorry, Uncle Oswald," Carrie said awkwardly.

"It weren't your fault, my lamb," he said, "so there's no cause for you to feel guilty."

"But if I hadn't got into an argument with my friend, and caused such a rumpus at the market, none of this would have happened, and John wouldn't be in the cells now."

"What did Mr Venn have to say about his chances?" Wilf asked practically.

Aunt Vi came into the parlour at that moment, with her pot of tea to soothe all ills. Just like Ma, Carrie thought fleetingly. At this rate, she would be awash with tea.

"He thinks he can smooth things over without it ever going to court," she said. "The only thing is – "

"The only thing is, he'll have to pay up to get his freedom," Oswald finished for her.

"But that's not right!" Carrie said.

Oswald gave a shrug. "The lawyer never went into the rights and wrongs of it, love. If John's able to pay a fine straight to the Bridewell, and settle things to everybody's satisfaction, I reckon they'll let him go in a day or so."

She felt close to tears now. She had no idea how much of a fine it was likely to be, and somehow she couldn't ask. It all sounded like devious undercover dealings to her, but maybe that was the way of lawyers and officials.

But all she could see was that John's precious savings would be dwindling away because of that stupid fight, and the brand new boat would sit for ever on that cradle in the boatyard.

"It's all Elsie's fault," she muttered bitterly. "Why did she have to go and get herself – "

She bit her lip, embarrassed to be discussing such things with these good people. And what must they think of her and her family and friends now, when they had been the cause of John being locked away? She smothered a sob.

"Now, you just listen to me, Carrie," she heard Aunt Vi say. "These things happen, and your friend needs a bit of sympathy, I reckon, until that young Welsh fellow of hers is found. You've a big heart, Carrie, so don't let her down now."

"Don't you blame me too?" she said huskily. "Don't you hate me, for being a part of all this?"

"Of course we don't hate you," Uncle Oswald said. "You're still our sweet Carrie, same as you always were, so don't go letting such nonsense enter your head and spoil things for you and John, do you hear?"

She nodded, and took a sip of Vi's strong sweet brew. When she had drained the cup, she said they had better go. Lord knew how Elsie was getting on at home with her family and she needed to be a buffer, just in case . . . she smiled faintly. Already she was being protective of Elsie again . . . perhaps true friendship never really died, no matter how many hurdles life threw at you.

"I'll call at the Bridewell tomorrow, and Carrie and I will come and see you again tomorrow evening to let you know what's happening," Wilf said. The others looked at him gratefully, and none more so than Carrie. As they went back home again, she tried to thank him properly.

"I want no thanks," he said roughly. "I want to see you happy though, and if John's the one for you, it's right by me. I may have been a bit slow to see it, that's all."

Yes, it was a funny old world all right, Carrie thought, too full of emotion to answer. And with Elsie installed in the house for a couple of days as well, it was almost like old times . . . almost.

As it happened, Elsie was installed in Jacob's Wells Road for a bit longer than that. During the night, she became ill with stomach pains and the doctor had to be called out. After a brief examination, he looked at her shrewdly.

"Unless you rest up for at least a week with your feet higher than your head, you're in danger of losing this baby, young woman. You've had my advice, now it's up to you what you do with it."

Elsie looked at Carrie after the doctor had gone off into the night again, and Carrie knew she was thinking about the choices. It would be so easy not to rest, to rush about until the inevitable happened, and she was rid of this baby for ever, and for life to go on as it was before.

"I want this babby, Carrie," Elsie whispered, a note of wonderment in her voice, as if she'd never even considered it before. "It's summat of Dewi, and if he never comes back, at least I'll have that much of him."

"Then you must really love him," Carrie said slowly.

Elsie gave a cracked laugh, and the ghost of the old Elsie was in her impatient voice. "Ain't I been telling you that all this time, ninny? 'Course I love 'im, and I love this babby too, and nobody's taking it away from me!"

"Shut up and go to sleep, you young girls!" came Sam Stuckey's roaring voice through the wall.

Carrie snuggled down beneath the coverlet with a wry smile. Some things never changed, no matter what. It was an oddly comforting thought in this turbulent day.

Chapter 23

Dewi Griffiths opened the door of his Mam's cottage and stared in surprise at the older man standing there. He recognised Ivor Jones at once, though he'd never been more than one of the casual acquaintances he met on the market at Bristol's Welsh Back. He'd never expected to see him here in Cardiff, seeming to recall that he lived over Newport way.

"Can I come in then, Dewi?" Ivor said, when the boy seemed too bemused to speak.

"Oh aye, come in, of course, Ivor. Forgetting my manners now, I am," Dewi said, flustered. "Things have a got a bit like that round 'ere lately, what with one thing and another."

"Have you got troubles, then, boy?" Ivor said at once. He eyed the spick and span cottage with approval, but thinking that the boy would have a few more troubles by the time he told him his news.

Dewi spoke tersely. "I have that. My Mam took sick a few months back, and there was nobody else to look after her, see? So I stayed home here most of the time, just working the local markets when she seemed well enough to leave for a few hours at a stretch. She died a few weeks back, and I'm not rightly over it yet, see?"

"There's sorry I am to hear that, boy," Ivor said, taken aback by this sorry tale, and knowing he should tread carefully in view of the boy's bereavement. "We was all wondering what had happened to you, see? It seems quite a while now since you was on the trows going over to Bristol."

"Aye, and I missed going there, man, but there was no help for it while Mam was so bad. Now, o' course, things are different again."

"So you'll be thinking of coming back to Bristol some time, will you?"

Dewi gave a small shrug. "Well, I know it's no use dwelling on things that can't be changed. Mam's gone now, and I daresay I'll have to be thinking of what to do about the cottage. It's my home, and I don't want to leave it, but it's not the same without a woman in it."

"You keep it tidy enough though, boy," Ivor said, knowing he must find the words to tell him about the girl's trouble, and reluctant to add to Dewi's already heavy load.

"There's not much tidying to do for one," he replied, and then gave a sigh. "But I'm glad to see you, Ivor *bach*, for you've reminded me there's still work to be done, and I should be getting over to Bristol soon, anyway. There's somebody I've got to see, or she'll be thinking I've deserted her."

Ivor breathed a small sigh of relief. "It's her that I've come about, Dewi," he said carefully, thankful to him for giving him the lead.

A week later, Elsie was languishing on the bed in Carrie's room, thinking that if this was the life of a lady, then they could keep it. It was boring and dull, just lying still, but the doctor said she could get up this afternoon, and that the danger to the babby seemed to be over at last.

Until she was in danger of losing it, Elsie hadn't realised how much she wanted it. It had staggered her to know how much she wanted the child, since she'd never been maternal in the slightest way. But even if she never saw Dewi again, this babby would always

408

be a part of him and of the glorious times they had shared.

She wasn't the romantic sort either, but she could still feel the thrill of it. And she *did* love him, she thought, with a catch in her throat. That much hadn't been play-acting, whatever Carrie might have thought about it all in the beginning.

She wished Carrie was here to chat with her. But Carrie had plenty to think about. Her wedding-day was only three weeks away, and Elsie felt a real pang of envy, thinking how lovely her friend was going to look in that creamy dress hanging up against the wall closet. Ma Stuckey had finished sewing it now, and Carrie was going to look a real picture.

Elsie's belly was starting to bulge, and she didn't even dare try it on to preen herself in it in secret, she thought with a grin. Her chest was expanding rapidly too, and starting to feel tight against her old working dress, though she knew Dewi wouldn't have objected to *that* . . .

She felt the weak tears start to her eyes again, and switched her thoughts hurriedly away from the images of herself and Dewi, locked in their wild and wanton embraces. And she reminded herself fiercely that she *never* cried except in times of dire emergency.

Thank God that fancy lawyer had managed to get John Travis off, she thought instead. God knows what she would have done if she'd ruined Carrie's wedding by her antics at the market.

Guiltily, she knew very well there had been a price to pay for his liberty, but nobody was letting on how much of John's savings it had been. Carrie had merely said that if the boat wasn't ready for the bulk of the summer trippers, they'd just have to wait a little longer for it.

Anyway, there was obviously enough for her and John to go shopping for some present or other they were buying for the Travis old folk, as a kind of house-warming present. They had gone into the city that afternoon to look for something suitable, while Elsie lay here, feeling fat and frustrated, and gloomily contemplating that the boyos from Wales would be over on their trows today, and wondering if she would ever see Dewi Griffiths again.

She didn't even bother to turn her head when she heard voices downstairs. It would probably be one of the maids from the posh Clifton houses, bringing Mrs Stuckey some more fine laundry work to do. Having scratched out her own living all her life, it didn't seem odd to Elsie that May still wanted to keep her hands busy. It was odder to be lying here, bored out of her mind with nothing to do.

She heard the creak of the wooden stairs, and noted that the footsteps accompanying Mrs Stuckey's were heavier than a woman's. She groaned, wondering if it was the doctor, coming to check up on her. He'd instructed that she was to stay put until late in the afternoon, and that she was not to get out of that bed one minute sooner.

"Elsie, there's someone here to see you," May said. "In the circumstances, I'm allowing him to come upstairs and into the bedroom, but I shall be leaving the door open, and if you need me, you're to call out at once. I shall be just below in the parlour."

As if she was going to get up to anything with the elderly doctor or even the dashing Prince Albert himself! Elsie thought fleetingly . . . and then all such daft thoughts flew out of her head. She gave a little cry of joy and disbelief as Dewi Griffiths came into the room and was across the bedroom and at her side in seconds.

"Oh, *Dewi*," was all she could manage to croak at that moment. But he was hugging her so tightly, she hardly had breath for anything else. He smelled of the river and the trows, but it was an old and familiar smell, and as sweet and dear to her as Dewi himself.

"*Duw*, but I've missed you so much, *cariad*, and there's so much I've got to tell you, but first of all I want you to

410

know that I'm never going to leave you again. That is, if you want me to stay!"

Hovering outside on the stairs, May Stuckey heard his voice, hoarse and sincere and full of Welsh passion. It was an intrusion to be listening to such passion, and she turned abruptly, clattering down the stairs to the parlour. And praying that this time, Elsie had found her right road in life at last.

Carrie and John took a breather as they walked up Christmas Steps, having looked in more than a dozen little antique and curio shops for something suitable for Vi and Oswald as a house-warming gift. There were many shops of a similar type in the area, and they had exhausted most of them by the time they had reached this particular one.

They wanted to buy something the old couple would always remember them by, though John was well aware that something even moderately good was going to make a hole in their finances now.

The lawyer had got him out of the cells all right, but they'd had to pay a fine, which Venn had privately considered little more than a bribe – and they'd had to pay the lawyer's fees as well. It had all come to a pretty penny, and having a large debt still to pay on the new boat was no way to begin married life, John thought grimly.

But one thing he was sure about. That last encounter with the constable, and all its repercussions, had decided him once and for all that fighting was best confined to the ring for those who wanted to make it a profession. He knew he wasn't one of them. It had been no more than a fairly lucrative sideline, and a means to an end. It was just unfortunate that the means had come to such a sorry end in his bank account.

"I think a pair of vases would be nice, John," Carrie was saying, as they looked around one of the little antique shops. "They're both keen on gardening, and they like to bring flowers into the house – " she stopped abruptly.

"What is it? I'm sorry if I wasn't paying proper attention," John said. "A pair of vases sounds ideal. Have you seen something you like?"

She wasn't listening to him. All her attention was fixed on a group of objects at the back of the shelf. They were all lumped together as a job lot, with the legend "once belonging to a lady of note" written alongside the box. There was a pair of jade ear-rings, an opal brooch and a silver cigarette box. There were several more small pieces in the collection, with the assumption that they had all come from the same source. Carrie seemed to have lost her voice for a moment, and merely pointed to the shelf as her thoughts whirled. John saw the objects and gave a derisive smile, not understanding her interest.

"'Belonging to a lady of note' indeed. That's just sales talk, Carrie, and I doubt that Vi or Oswald would be bothered about such trinkets."

She shook her head quickly. "It's not that," she whispered urgently, as if there were ears listening at every corner. "I'm sure these are some of the things that were stolen from the Barclay house by that maid who was dismissed before me. You know how servants gossip, and long before I left the house Cook had a full list of the stolen items. I'm quite sure these were some of them, John!"

They were so intent on looking at the contents of the box that they didn't notice the proprietor come up behind them to see what was taking their interest, and sensing a sale.

"Is there something I can show you, sir and madam? I think you will agree that I have a unique selection of fine objects – " he began in an oily voice.

"Those things in the box that once belonged to a lady of note," Carrie said, before she stopped to think. "Can you tell me something more about them, please?"

412

The man gave a small frown. He was used to making a quick assessment of clients, and what they could afford to pay, and this girl didn't look like a person of quality. Never in a month of wet Mondays could she pay any of the fancy prices he was putting on the jewellery and other fine pieces in the collection.

"Those are very expensive items, madam," he said delicately. "Perhaps I could show you something of a less, well, flamboyant nature?"

"If the lady wishes to know more about those particular items, then I'd be obliged if you'd be good enough to tell her, sir," John said with authority.

"Of course, sir, and I assure you I meant to cause no offence," the man said, backing down at once. "If you'd care to come inside my office, I'll look up the transaction in my record books. Many of my ladies are interested in knowing the origins of their purchases."

Carrie felt her heart thump as they followed him and were invited to sit down. The shop had the usual cloying atmosphere of old merchandise, but she hardly noticed it now. She was too excited by the growing certainty that she had stumbled on the missing Barclay property.

The proprietor brought out a large ledger, and turned the pages until he came to the items, recorded separately under their various headings of jewellery and other goods. He turned the pages back several times, reading and re-reading the notes, and Carrie thanked her stars that at least he seemed to be a diligent book-keeper. But all antique dealers in the city were required to keep such ledgers, due to the large amount of thefts and pilferings that went on, and the goods that changed hands so discreetly under cover of darkness and the pawnbroker.

"It seems that all the items were brought in by a young lady who clearly wasn't aware of their worth. My late assistant paid her a nominal sum for them, which I must admit was far less that it should have been, so perhaps we might come to some amicable arangement."

"We haven't come to purchase, sir," John put in, before the man could put an astronomic sum on the selling price for their benefit, and then miraculously appear to reduce it, as was common practise. "The lady believes she recognises these items as having been stolen, and we merely want to find out how you came by them."

"*Most honestly*, I assure you, sir!"

"Mr Travis didn't mean to doubt you, sir," Carrie said hastily. "But we would be obliged if you would give us the name of the person who brought in the items, if you please."

"It's most irregular. If there's any doubt about the background of any item, it's my duty to call in the police. Apparently my late assistant had no such doubts on this transaction or it would have been called to my attention."

"*Please*," Carrie said quietly.

He looked at her for a long moment, and she stared him out, refusing to let her eyes waver for an instant.

"Oh, very well," he said, capitulating, and running his finger over the ledger notes once more. "It was a Miss Sophie Moss of Farthing Lane, Knowle. I seem to recall that she brought us some business at various other times too, on her client's behalf."

"On her own behalf, more like," Carrie said in triumph. "Thank you for your help, sir. Would you be kind enough to put the items aside until I inform the owner of their whereabouts?"

"Now, look here, young woman – "

"I think it would be advisable, sir," John said. "Unless you want to run the risk of being accused as a receiver of stolen goods."

"This is a respectable establishment," the man began stiffly. "I shall give you one hour, and then the goods go back on sale."

They went out into the daylight, and Carrie's heart was still thudding wildly. She was quite certain of her facts, but she hardly knew what to do next. An hour wasn't long enough to go up to Clifton and find Helen and persuade her to come to the mean little antique shop on Christmas Steps. Even if she would deign to do such a thing on a whim of a former employee.

"We must go to Mr Barclay's office," she told John suddenly. "We'll tell him all we know, and let him deal with it. He'll need to be told, anyway."

She trembled as she spoke. She had had no dealings with high-powered businessmen and their offices, but this was necessary if that miserable Sophie was to get her comeuppance, and the Barclays were to get their property back.

"Where is it?" John said.

"It's not far. I've seen the building down in the centre of the city, though I've never been inside it myself."

Why should she, when she had nothing to do with business deals and money transactions? But presumably John would be worldly enough to deal with it all from now on.

They found the building easily enough. It wasn't difficult to find, with the name *The Gentlemens' Finance Company* blazoned across the front of it, and notices inside the plush interior inviting persons of discernment to receive financial business advice with confidence and trust.

"Cheer up. He won't bite you," John said, when they had stated their wish to see Mr Giles Barclay, and were waiting to be shown into the great man's office.

"I feel just as I did when I was first summoned to the drawing-room on my first day in service," she muttered. "Just as young and stupid, and all fingers and thumbs."

She felt his hand curl around hers. "You're not his servant now, Carrie, and you're soon going to be my wife. You don't have to be frightened of anybody."

After a considerable wait, a clerk came out and told them Mr Barclay was able to see them now. They entered the room, and Carrie tried to remember what John had said about not being frightened of anybody. Though it was hard to take courage from it when her teeth were threatening to chatter and her knees wouldn't stop knocking. If she'd thought the Barclay house was grand, then so was this opulent office, a vast workplace that would have housed a whole family, she thought.

"Sit down, please," Giles Barclay spoke, not bothering to look up. "You want to open an account with us, I presume?"

"No, sir, we do not," John said. "We've come to see you on a private and personal matter."

Giles looked up sharply then at this arrogant young man who had dared to invade his inner sanctum without a prior appointment. His glance moved towards the man's companion, and he gave a frown. The girl looked familiar, and although she was clean and tidy and had a pleasant appearance, especially that richly coloured hair, she was clearly not well-to-do. He let his mind wander a moment, imagining her more soberly dressed in servant's garb, and then he remembered.

"Good God, it's young – young – "

Carrie helped him out. "Carrie Stuckey, sir, and I used to be in your daughter's employ."

"So you did." He frowned again, more impatiently this time. "So what is it you want to see me about? If it's another position, then you should approach Cook in the first instance, and not come bothering me in my office." His hand was already straying to the bell pull to summon his clerk to show these people out, when Carrie stopped him.

"I don't want a job, sir, but me and my young man, Mr John Travis, think we have some information of interest to you."

416

"What kind of information?" His eyes narrowed, and then moved towards the young man who was taking up the tale.

"My young lady believes she has identified some of your wife's missing jewellery and other items that were stolen from your house before she was in your daughter's employ, sir. They are in a small antique shop on Christmas Steps, and we've already ascertained that they were sold by the maid who worked for your daughter previously. We have the girl's name and address, and we have asked the proprietor of the shop to put the items aside until you can come with us to identify them."

"Good God!"

Whatever else he had expected to hear, it was nothing like this. But he couldn't doubt the sincerity in the young man's voice, nor miss the fact that he was better educated than the girl. He had called her his fiancée too, so the young Stuckey girl would seem to have done quite well for herself.

She spoke up quickly now. "Please, Mr Barclay, the man said he'd only keep the goods aside for an hour while we came to fetch you. You should come with us right away, sir, before they get put in the window and maybe sold."

Giles leaned back in his chair, his fingers splayed out as he contemplated her words. He was a cautious man, who'd founded a successful business by weighing up all the possibilities of failure before he acted, and he needed to give himself a few moments to ponder on this sudden piece of information.

"And what guarantee do I have that this is not all a hoax? That the two of you haven't concocted this wild tale in order to kidnap me and demand some ransom money for me, eh? Am I going to be at your mercy once I'm outside this building?"

Carrie stared at him in disbelief for a minute, wondering

417

how anyone could think of anything so stupid. And then she burst out laughing, and all her fear of him evaporated.

"I never heard such a bleeding daft idea in all my life, begging your pardon, Mr Barclay, sir!" She almost gasped out the words, hardly knowing whether to laugh or cry. "We've come dashing down here from Christmas Steps, hoping to save you and yours a packet, and put that Sophie behind bars where she belongs, and all you can do is accuse me and my John of trying to kidnap you! Begging your lordship's pardon again, sir, but if that's all you can say to folk who only want to give you some help, then you ain't worth the snuff up me Pa's nose, as far as I'm concerned."

As she stopped for breath, she was appalled at the way she had let herself down in front of such a grand gentleman. And in front of John too, which was even worse. She wished the ground would open up and swallow her, but of course it didn't. It never did. She closed her eyes for a minute, counting to ten before she let out her breath in a long sigh, meaning to mumble a quick apology and leave quickly.

And then she recognised another sound in the room and her eyes flew open again. Giles Barclay was laughing out loud, holding his side with one hand and wiping his eyes with the other. She glanced at John uncertainly.

"Oh, Carrie Stuckey, now I know why my daughter enjoyed having you around, and was sorry when you left. You have a most refreshing brand of common sense in that pretty little head of yours."

Carrie looked at him suspiciously, not sure if he was patronising or complimenting her. She tossed her head. In for a penny, in for a pound now, she thought recklessly.

"Well then, are you going to come to Christmas Steps

with us or not?" she demanded. "Because me and John have got more important things to do today than to sit around while you find all this so amusing."

"Of course I shall accompany you, my dear young lady," Giles said, still chortling, though Carrie couldn't see what was so all-fired funny. But maybe nobody had ever answered him back before, she thought suddenly. And maybe it was time that someone did.

They stood up stiffly while Giles summoned his clerk and told him he was going out, and wouldn't be back for the rest of the day. The staff would be responsible for locking and securing the building.

"And God help them if there's a ha'penny missing," Carrie breathed to John as the unlikely trio made their way back through the city and up towards the steep narrow stone flight of Christmas Steps.

"What were you two young people doing in the antique shop?" Giles enquired, as if he needed to make conversation.

"We were looking for a house-warming gift for my aunt and uncle who are moving to Clevedon on the twenty-eighth of this month, sir, when Carrie and I are married," John told him, since Carrie seemed to be struck dumb all over again.

"I see. It seems that congratulations are in order then. And do the two of you have somewhere to live?"

John explained about the house on Bedminster Hill, and about the new boat at Cummings boatyard that was taking shape so slowly.

"But it will all come right in time," John said confidently. "We've had a few problems to solve recently, but as long as we're together, we shan't go under."

He smiled into Carrie's eyes as he said the words, and her heart surged with love for him, knowing it was true. As long as they were together, they could survive anything. And the solemn Giles Barclay, intercepting the look, glimpsed the ghost of other days, and envied them their love.

It was interesting to Carrie to see how the professional mind worked. Once Mr Giles Barclay had definitely identified his wife's possessions, he claimed them at once, together with the name and address of the light-fingered maid. The antique dealer, not unnaturally, was reluctant to simply hand over the goods, saying he'd paid for them in all good faith.

"Can you prove this, man?" Giles had said sternly.

He scurried to bring out his ledger once more, and pointed triumphantly to the name and address of Sophie Moss, in Farthing Lane. Unfortunately, the entry also contained the miserable sum he'd paid for the goods, and Giles Barclay informed him that he was legally entitled to pay no more than the price of the first transaction. Whether or not this was true, Carrie had no idea, but it was enough for the proprietor, who obviously wanted nothing to do with legal matters.

"Just think yourself lucky I don't simply seize back the goods as being stolen property, man," Giles went on, "but since I do believe your story that you bought them in good faith, and that you have since been co-operative, I shan't pursue the matter any further."

"Thank you, sir," the man almost gasped, clearly mightily relieved to be rid of these awkward clients. But he wasn't quite rid of them yet, it seemed. Giles paused, with his precious belongings in his hands.

"What was it you and – er – Carrie intended to purchase for your aunt and uncle, Mr Travis?" he enquired.

"A pair of vases, but it's no matter," John said quickly. He and Carrie had already decided that the price was more than they could reasonably afford.

"Point them out to me," Giles said, and when John did so, the proprietor was only too ready to begin enthusing

420

on the fine Chinese design and on how much they would appreciate in value in years to come.

Giles brushed all that aside. "Do you think your relatives would like the vases?" he asked John.

"I know they would, but as I've already said, it's out of the question."

"I would be glad if you would accept them as a gesture of thanks for what you've done today," he said brusquely. He turned to the gaping shopkeeper. The vases were really very fine, and it had been obvious to him that these young folk wouldn't be buying them.

"See that they're carefully wrapped and delivered to the address Mr Travis will give you, and send your account to me." He handed the man a business card. Clearly no vulgar monetary transaction was going to take place now. Talk about how the other half lived, Carrie thought in amazement. But they'd got the vases, and Aunt Vi and Uncle Oswald were going to be delighted with them.

They were thankful when they were finally on their way back to Jacob's Wells Road and had parted from Mr Barclay. He had always made her nervous, and always would, Carrie told John.

"I don't know why he should. He's just a man, same as the rest of us, and we were all made the same way," he said. "You shouldn't let yourself feel inferior to anybody, Carrie, and especially not when you're married to me. I don't want my wife to feel as if she's got to dip her head to anybody."

"No, sir," she said meekly, and as he caught her mischievous glance, he relaxed, laughing.

"All right, not even to me!" he said.

"Anyway, it's different for a man. You speak properly, and you have your own business."

"*Our* own business," he reminded her, as they walked back through the city towards the waterfront area. "Don't forget it's your name that will be on the boat for all to see, Carrie. That makes you very much a part of it all."

It charmed her all over again. Their lives were going to be intertwined in every way, lovingly and professionally, and she couldn't be happier.

"I think the old boy could have rewarded you with some little trinket for yourself for your part in recovering his property," John said.

"The old boy" . . . for a minute, Carrie didn't realise he was referring to Mr Giles Barclay. That was another thing that separated them, she thought wistfully. Giles would always be somewhat god-like to her, while to John, he was simply "the old boy" . . . and then she saw that he was teasing again, and she grinned back.

"What would I want with trinkets?" she protested. "It was good of him to pay for the vases, and I wouldn't have wanted anything more."

"You're so easily satisfied. Will it always be so, I wonder, or will you turn into a petulant wife who wants the world at her feet?" he said, still teasing. She stopped in mid-stride, tugging at his arm.

"I will not! As long as I have you, I'll want for nothing else, ever!"

It was one of those rare moments when their eyes seemed to hold their souls in thrall. The words had begun lightly, and ended up intense, revealing all that was in Carrie's heart. John's voice was filled with barely contained emotion as he answered.

"You'll always have me, my darling, and if I died tomorrow, I would die happy, knowing that you love me."

Carrie shivered, and unconsciously crossed her fingers against such bad luck.

"Well, I would certainly not be happy if you died tomorrow, so don't you dare!" she said, and the fragile moment, too poignant to hold in so public a place, was broken.

They hurried homewards, eager with the tale they had to tell. At the last moment John decided he wouldn't come inside the house, as he wanted to make sure he was there when the antique vases were delivered to the house on Bedminster Hill that evening. If he wasn't, the old couple might well think it all a mistake and turn the man away. Besides, he was quite sure Carrie would be very capable of revelling alone in telling how they'd recovered some of the Barclay fortunes, he said dryly. She'd not be tongue-tied about that!

They parted company at the door, and she went inside, bubbling with news. And then she stared in some shock at the sight of Elsie Miller and a dark-haired stranger, sitting so cosily together on Pa's settle, and with her Ma and young Henry nowhere to be seen.

"This is Dewi Griffiths, Carrie," Elsie burst out, before Carrie had a chance to say a single word. "His Mam's died recently, which is why he ain't been back to Bristol lately. But now he's back, and we're getting wed as soon as it can be arranged, and your Ma's gone off to find your Pa and ask him if he'll go to the church and put in a good word with Mr Pritchard for us, so's he'll see us properly blessed before we go and live in Cardiff in Dewi's house."

She was almost blue in the face by the time she finished, not giving herself a chance to pause for breath. Carrie felt her mouth drop open, and closed it again quickly. The Welshman was quite a personable young man, though he had none of John's finesse, she thought briefly, since he made no attempt to stand up and shake her hand. But that could be because Elsie was clinging on to his so tightly, she conceded. It was easy to see that Elsie was quite besotted with this Dewi, and dazzled by his unexpected appearance.

She sat down heavily on a chair beside them, and let out her own breath explosively.

"Well! This is a surprise and no mistake. But I'm happy for you both, if you're sure it's what you want."

Elsie bridled at once, still the old Elsie at heart, despite her prospective new status as a married woman.

"'Course it's what we want! Dewi wouldn't have come back this way to find me again if his intentions weren't honourable, would he?"

They both looked at Dewi, who cleared his throat in some embarrassment. He didn't have to explain himself to this beautiful, if prim-faced friend of his *cariad*, he thought with faint annoyance, but her approval obviously still meant a lot to Elsie, and what the hell did it matter, anyway? He responded readily enough, with a disarming smile and flashing eyes, still the roguish boyo underneath.

"Me and Elsie always intended being together, see, but when my Mam died I had so much on my mind I couldn't see my way clear to coming back over here too fast. Your Mam's been very understanding, love, and we've all agreed that it's best to wed here before I take Elsie back home. Folk are narrow-minded there, see, and wouldn't understand so well. But we'll get a proper chapel blessing once we get back to Cardiff, that my Mam would approve of."

His Mam and the chapel upbringing still seemed to be very much a part of his life, despite his lusty eyes and even lustier loins, Carrie thought, averting her gaze from the pair of them as the thought entered her head.

Elsie had never been much of a churchgoer, either, but she supposed all that would be forgotten in the joy of being married to her Dewi. And before her own nuptials too. That was a turn-up, all right. She'd never thought Elsie would tie herself to any one man, let alone one who would take her away from Bristol and into such a strictly chapel environment. But as she'd already found out for herself, love could change everything.

Chapter 24

Elsie had been urged to stay at the Stuckey house until the wedding, while Dewi decamped at Elsie's place. Not even though the nuptials were so near could Ma go so far as to allow them to sleep under the same roof, nor sanction Elsie going back with Dewi. And not even Elsie had dared disobey her in that.

The ceremony was arranged with all speed, and three days after Dewi's arrival back in Bristol, the minister had said the marriage vows over the couple, having reluctantly been persuaded into it by Sam Stuckey. At least he wouldn't have to constantly see the sinners in his parish, the pious Mr Pritchard thought thankfully.

The Griffiths fellow was just as anxious to get back to Cardiff and show Elsie the neat little Welsh cottage and her new surroundings. The minister had been mollified to see that once the idea of respectability had sunk into both their heads, they were full of activity to get things organised and go back across the Channel.

Carrie let herself think for a moment that it seemed very convenient for Dewi Griffiths to have a ready-made housekeeper to step into his Mam's shoes. In any case, if he was expecting that, he was in for quite a shock with Elsie's slapdash ways.

But there was no dampening their happiness now. Regardless of the hurried circumstances, it simply shone out of them once the knot had been duly tied. May Stuckey had laid on a small tea for the couple, and then they

425

were to spend the night at Elsie's old waterfront cottage, before handing over the keys to the landlord the following morning and sailing for Cardiff. She had packed up her bits and pieces, and she was all set for her new life.

"I'm going to miss you!" Carrie said, giving Elsie a great bear-hug after the ring had been slid onto Elsie's finger and congratulations were in order.

"I shall miss you too, but you know I ain't no good at talking soft stuff, so I'm not going on about it," Elsie said, her eyes suspiciously moist. "I'm just sorry me and Dewi won't be here for your wedding, Carrie, but we think it's best if we get on with our own lives now, since we've done enough to disrupt yours."

It was about the most perceptive thing that Elsie Miller, now Griffiths, had ever said.

"When John gets his new boat and things are settled for us, maybe we'll be able to come and visit you," Carrie said, "and you be sure to send a message by somebody at the Welsh Market when the baby's born. I shall want to know if it's a boy or a girl, mind."

"I still can't rightly believe I'm going to be a respectable Welsh wife, let alone somebody's mother," Elsie confided with a nervous giggle that told of an underlying uncertainty. "I'm sure I'll be no good at it. I don't have your Ma's knack, Carrie."

"Nobody was born knowing how to be a mother, ninny. It comes by instinct. Just look how our Henry's taken to you these past few days, and he won't normally respond to folk who don't like babies."

They were all back at the small house in Jacob's Wells Road now, and in a party mood. Elsie's small cloud of doubt vanished with a laugh as young Henry Stuckey obligingly put up his fat little arms to her to be cuddled. He'd taken to Elsie with a fervour that almost had Carrie feeling jealous. Elsie bounced him on her knees and cooed to him to make him chuckle.

Wilf and John stood awkwardly on the far side of the parlour, trying hard to make conversation with Dewi Griffiths over their tea and cake, while Sam had merely stumped off out into the back yard with Billy as usual, on the pretext of feeding the chickens. Those chickens were going to be too fat to waddle at this rate, Carrie thought with a smile.

But it was a source of delight to her now, that Wilf and John seemed to have forgotten their differences. She doubted that they'd ever be real friends, but at least they tolerated each other, and when John had asked Wilf to stand by him on his wedding-day, her brother had readily agreed.

It would be so soon now . . . less than three weeks . . . Carrie felt a wild thrill of anticipation every time she thought of it. There would be no more partings, no more sweet good-night kisses that had to be cut short because of Ma's ever-watchful presence, no more ignorance of the final mystery of loving that Elsie had obviously learned so well, and which still lay out of Carrie's reach.

Sometimes, in the quiet of these last few nights, turning restlessly in her bed, and listening to Elsie's snuffling breathing that was so reminiscent of Billy's, she tried to imagine herself three weeks from now. To imagine how it would feel to be lying warm in John's arms, and tingling to his slightest touch on her skin, and coming alive for the first time in her life.

In a way, becoming one with another person was like that, she thought. That first intimate sharing of oneself must be somehow like being reborn. You entered a new dimension of being, no longer the same as you were before, but with a knowledge as old as time, and yet as new as tomorrow . . .

"Are you all right, Carrie?" she heard Ma say sharply. "You've been gazing into space for these last five minutes, and breathing as hard as if you've run a mile.

427

You don't want to get poorly before your own big day."

Carrie flinched, thankful that her sane and sensible Ma couldn't have any inkling of the turbulent imaginings that had been swirling around in her head and filling her loins with a wild and wonderful longing. Or maybe she did. Ma was a married woman too, and therefore would know all about these mysterious happenings inside her own body . . . she looked away from her quickly, not wanting to associate her own sensual feelings with anyone else, least of all Ma!

"I'm all right, Ma," she said hurriedly, "I was just thinking that we seem to be parting from so many people. First it was Frank, now Elsie, and soon John's Aunt Vi and Uncle Oswald will be leaving as well."

"It's the way of the world, lamb," Ma said. "You can't keep folk tied to you for ever, and it's only right that young 'uns should move on. It'll be our Wilf's turn some time, I daresay, but we'll still have our Billy and Henry at home a few years longer yet."

She ruffled Henry's curls as she spoke, and the baby beamed up at her from Elsie's lap, making them all laugh. Days like these were the best of times, Carrie thought, the kind to remember and hold to your heart in the dark days of winter.

The fine June weather was holding up, and John was kept busy for the next two weeks with his tripping excursions in the old boat, with many curious Bristolians and others eager to view the *Great Britain* and the lengthy widening of the Cumberland Basin Locks to allow her free passage out of the floating harbour where she was still marooned.

John had arranged for a bit of astute advertising material to be on hand for clients about his forthcoming new and improved tripping boat, the *Caroline*. As yet, even he still didn't know when that was going to be, but he wasn't going to depress Carrie by telling her.

This old boat was paying its way for now, but it had to be handed over as part of the payment price on the new one as soon as it was ready. It was part of the debt still owing on the *Caroline* that was giving him headaches, and since Vi and Oswald had paid out all their savings for the Clevedon cottage, neither of them had the kind of money to help him out. In any case, his pride wouldn't have let him approach them. It was his worry, and nobody else's. And the actual amount still owing was between himself and Mr Cummings.

He was obliged to make regular visits to the boatyard to pay whatever instalments he could, which kept his pride intact and kept Gaffer Cummings sweet, even if little work was being done of the boat at present.

It was late in the afternoon, a week before his wedding to Carrie Stuckey, that he went with a heavy heart to pay what little he could, thinking that her wedding gift was going to be considerably later than he'd hoped.

To his startled surprise, he discovered that the boatyard was humming with industry, and that it was the *Caroline* that was getting all the attention. Carpenters and painters and fitters swarmed in and out of it, and as far as he could tell, it must surely be completed and fitted out in a very few days from now.

He hurried into the Gaffer's office, his heart thudding hard. If Cummings had merely decided to get on with the work and present him with the bill, there was no way he could pay. It was a common, if unpleasant practice, in a boatyard where work was slack. Then, when the unfortunate client was unable to pay up, the boat was simply claimed as unpaid property, and sold off to the highest bidder. John felt sick to his stomach at the thought of his precious bridal gift ending up in sombody else's hands.

Cummings looked up from his paperwork as John went

into the office without bothering to knock. He put both hands squarely on the man's cluttered desk, and wasted no words.

"What the hell's going on, Cummings? I gave no orders for my boat to be finished, and if you think you're going to sell her off to the highest bidder – "

"Please calm yourself, Mr Travis, and take a seat," the man said sharply. "There's no question of selling off your boat, and my men are working all the hours God made to get her finished for the twenty-eighth of the month as requested."

John sat down heavily on the client's chair without even registering that he did so.

"What request was this? I gave you no such request!"

"I have it here, sir." Cummings rummaged among a sea of papers and orders, and silently handed John a letter on heavily embossed headed notepaper. He read the letter with growing amazement.

"To whom it may concern," he read,

For the boat commissioned to the order of Mr John Travis esq, it is hereby requested that the completion date be set at June the twenty-eighth and not one day later. On the surety of this, you will find the enclosed cheque to cover the remaining and outstanding amount payable on the commission."

It was signed "Giles Barclay".

John stared in disbelief. It couldn't be true. Someone was playing a jape on him. But the sound of the hammering and the smell of fresh paint told him that whoever was playing this jape had certainly fooled Gaffer Cummings to the extent of completing his boat with all speed. And if the cheque bounced . . .

"Are you telling me you believed this letter to be genuine?" he said hoarsely.

"My dear sir," Cummings said with a shrug. "I wasn't born yesterday. The gentleman came here himself, swanked up to the nines, and paid over the cheque and the letter. Naturally, before I did anything else, I took it to the bank and had it verified, though there was hardly any need, with that particular letter heading. The gent's loaded all right, and apparently wanted to make a gift of the boat to you and your young lady for some reason."

"I don't want his damn money," John said, suddenly furious. "I earned every penny that's gone into my boat so far, and that's the way it's going to be. You can stop your men working on it right now."

"Can't do that, I'm afraid, young sir." Cummings shook his head, clearly thinking the other was completely mad. "My men have been told this is a rush job, and they're all expecting to be paid extra for it. If I was to stop 'em now, they'd all go on strike. Besides, where's the sense in it, when the amount's already been paid up in full with a bit to spare for all the haste? You go home and be thankful, lad."

John went straight to see Carrie. She opened the door to his hammering, to find him practically spitting nails, as Pa would say.

"What on earth's wrong?" she began as he pushed past her into the parlour.

"I've been taken for a fool, that's what. I'll be beholden to no man, and if I can't pay my way by my own efforts, then I'll go without."

"John, are you going to tell me what's happened?" she said, stamping her foot.

Billy went careering out to the back yard to tell Ma there was a commotion going on inside, and Henry started crying in his carriage. Carrie heard none of it. All she could see was John's blistering anger, and she was suddenly afraid. Everything had been going so well of late, and in less than a week she would be his bride.

But this hard-faced man was more reminiscent of the bare-knuckle fighter she'd seen pasting the hide out of BIG LOUIE up on Clifton Downs than of the lover she adored.

"It's that bastard Barclay," he snapped. "Thinking he can do whatever he likes with his money, and expecting folk to bow and scrape to him because of it."

"But what's he *done?*" Carrie almost screamed. "You're making no sense at all, John."

"He's gone and paid off the rest of the dues on the boat, and instructed Cummings to get it finished and ready by the twenty-eighth, that's what," he raged at her.

She stared at him. He was practically breathing fire from his nostrils, she thought. She felt a wild urge to laugh, because it was all so comical and unreal, and he was getting so stupidly upset because of a *gift* . . . to someone whose family circumstances had always made them grateful for any small gift, John's reaction seemed nothing less than insulting.

"Isn't that exactly what you wanted?" she said mildly.

"I wanted to do it my way," he shouted, more incensed by her reaction. "It's my boat and my elbow grease that's paying for it, and I don't want some big-time city financier thinking he can control my life in any way."

"Well, that's just where you're wrong, then," Carrie's temper exploded, and she snapped back at him. "It's not your boat. It's our boat, like you said it was. It's got my name on it, and if we're supposed to be sharing everything like you always said we would, then it's half mine. And I'm *grateful* to Mr Barclay for being kind enough to pay for finishing off *my* half of *our* boat!"

She half registered the fact that Ma had come and whisked away the bawling Henry and hustled the two young 'uns into the scullery out of the way of these two warring lovers. She stood and glared into John's furious face, not prepared to give one inch of ground.

432

"That's just what I might have expected – "

"From someone of my mentality and class?" Carrie whipped at him. "That's what you were about to say, isn't it? Let me tell you that someone of my mentality and class has the common sense to see that this is Mr Giles Barclay's way of repaying somebody who'd done him a good turn. I know *his* class better than you do, *sir*. Good turns are always rewarded, and in my opinion he'd done more than enough by paying for the Chinese vases we wanted for Vi and Oswald. But maybe it weren't enough for him. Maybe he was persuaded by his lady wife that since you and me were getting married, it 'ould be nice to give us a very special reward for our wedding, see, and that was when it came into Mr Barclay's mind about the boat. Only I wouldn't expect you to get inside such workings of the gentry's mind, seeing as how you never had to work for 'em and kow-tow to 'em the way I did."

The ranting would have continued, if she hadn't had to stop for breath, her eyes flashing with anger and hurt.

"You said you and me *were* getting married," John said stiffly.

"What?"

"Just now. You said her ladyship might say that since you and me *were* getting married – and all the rest of it. Does this mean you've changed your mind about that?"

Her jewel-bright eyes brimmed over.

"Don't be so bloody daft! It'd take more than that to make me change my mind," she said huskily. "Unless you –? "

The question seemed to hang in the air for a minute, and then she was snatched hard against him, and she could feel his heart thudding against hers as his arms held her fast.

"That's the last thing I want, Carrie! God, why do I let myself act like such a fool?" John groaned against her neck. "It seems that a good education isn't the only teacher, and I could learn a lot from you."

"And I intend spending the rest of my life teaching you," she whispered into his cheek.

Ma's discreet cough made them draw apart quickly.

"If you two have stopped acting like waterfront roughnecks, me and the little 'uns are tired of being in the scullery and would like to come into the parlour. You'll have time enough for squabbling when you're in your own home."

Carrie shook her head. "We'll have more important things to do than waste time squabbling," she said, trying to lighten the atmosphere and hoping she wasn't being too daring.

"Don't you be too sure of that," Ma said dryly. "It's a dreary marriage that don't have its share of ups and downs in it, and the making-up's always a compensation."

It was about the nearest thing to hinting at married passions that May Stuckey had ever said, and she covered the moment by telling Billy to go and wash his hands for tea, or he'd get none. She asked John if he'd be staying but he shook his head, his gaze fixed on Carrie. And what she saw in his eyes was like a banner for the future.

"We have a visit to make, Mrs Stuckey, and it can't wait," he said.

"Do we?" Carrie said.

He looked at her steadily. "Didn't your school of life ever teach you that it's good manners to thank someone for a gift? Or aren't you prepared to call on the Barclays by the front door?"

His voice challenged her, and she tilted her chin high. "Of course I am. I'm not their servant any longer."

All the same, she quaked a little as they went boldly to the front door of the mansion, and heard the bell ringing somewhere inside it. The butler answered, and Carrie saw Jackson's eyes widen as he recognised her, but John addressed him before he had a chance to speak.

"Would you please inform Mr Barclay that Mr John Travis and Miss Caroline Stuckey respectfully request a few moments of his time?"

For a minute, Carrie thought Jackson was going to give his usual stiff response that Mr Barclay was not at home to casual callers, but then he gave a short nod and asked them to wait while he went to see if Mr Barclay could receive them.

"You sounded terribly grand, John," Carrie said, trying to hide her nervousness.

"And you sound terrified. Keep that chin up."

When Jackson came back her hands felt clammy inside her gloves, and she wished she'd thought to change her frock, instead of letting John rush her up here without giving her proper time to think. But it was too late now.

"Mr Barclay will see you in the drawing-room. Follow me, please."

They followed dutifully. Carrie thought how many times she had run up and down the stairs at Miss Helen's bidding, and felt a surge of thankfulness that she would never have to do such a thing again. She may never even see her again.

They were ushered into the drawing-room, where Mr and Mrs Barclay were waiting to receive them. Carrie gulped, wishing she dared slide her hand into John's, but it wasn't done in public, and she couldn't help the feeling that they were getting a very public scrutiny.

"Well, Mr Travis, I daresay I can guess the purpose of this visit," Giles said genially.

"I daresay you can, sir," John said evenly. "My young lady wishes me to thank you formally for the very generous gesture you have made towards us."

Barclay's eyes narrowed imperceptibly, trained as he

435

was to notice any nuance in a voice or an ambiguity of words.

"And is it not your wish to thank me on your own behalf, my dear sir?"

Carrie could sense how John bridled a little. Barclay was a forthright man, but she knew John would hardly have expected to be quizzed on his remark.

"I do thank you, sir, most sincerely, even though it was not necessary, and I would have preferred – "

Carrie nudged him hard enough for it to be noticed. Gertrude Barclay leaned forward and touched her husband's arm.

"I think I understand Mr Travis's unspoken words exactly, my dear. Did I not suggest that you approached Carrie on this matter first of all? A man has his pride, and I would guess that this young man's initial reaction was exactly what yours might have been in similar circumstances."

But she smiled encouragingly at the two of them, and Giles spoke more sharply.

"Is that so, Mr Travis? Would you have preferred to struggle on and make your way by your own efforts?"

"I would indeed, sir," John said promptly, at which Carrie let out her breath impatiently. For two pins, their benefactor might just demand his money back – or claim the *Caroline* as his own, and all because of John's stupid male pride . . . as she opened her mouth to protest and eat humble pie, she heard Giles chuckle again, the way he'd done in his office when she had let rip so appallingly.

"You're a man after my own heart, boy, but there are times in this life when it's better to receive than to give, and to be generous enough to allow others to do the giving. Your girl will know all about that, I'm sure. Now then, we'll hear no more about debts and thanks, and I trust you'll both take a glass of wine with my wife and myself to celebrate this forthcoming wedding of yours?"

436

"Please sit down, both of you," Gertrude said, at once the gracious hostess as her husband moved towards the decanter on the sideboard. "And how thrilled you must be, Carrie, to have a boat named after you."

"I am, ma'am," she murmured, awkward and embarrassed at having to sit in this splendidly appointed room and try to make small talk with her erstwhile employers. And then she noticed that Mrs Barclay was wearing the jade ear-rings, and she couldn't help commenting on the fact.

"They were a special anniversary gift from my husband," the lady confided. "So apart from their considerable value, they had enormous sentimental value for me too. I would have given the earth to get them back, so I can't thank you enough for your sharp eye-sight, my dear."

"Well, that's all right then," Carrie said, relieved. If the lady would have given the earth to get them back, John surely couldn't imagine that his remaining boat debts had been too great a gesture to pay?

"I'm glad you came to call, Carrie," the lady went on, as they were handed their crystal glasses of wine. "I also wanted to give you something personal as a small wedding gift. One of the maids would have delivered it, but now you may have it in person."

"It's not necessary, ma'am," she stammered. "You've both done enough already – "

Giles admonished her lightly, as his wife rang the bell for a maid.

"Remember, girl. It's now my wife's turn to give, and yours to be gracious enough to accept."

Carrie blushed, and almost laughed out loud at the startled face of the maid who arrived to do Mrs Barclay's bidding, guessing at the gossip below stairs that Carrie Stuckey and her young man were sitting like real toffs in the Barclay drawing-room drinking wine.

437

Minutes later, the maid had brought one of the lady's jewel-cases as requested, and Gertrude had removed a small diamond pin brooch from inside.

"This is for you, Carrie," she said. "I hope you'll wear it on your wedding-day, and that you'll both have many years of happiness in your future life."

Carrie could hardly speak as she took the gem. She had no jewellery to speak of, save a few trinkets that Helen had given to her, and she had never thought to own anything as fine as this. She stammered her thanks, and had them waved away.

"Just be happy, my dear. That's the best thing that anyone can wish for you. Now tell me, is everything planned for your wedding-day? Do you have a frosted cake?"

"Oh yes. Ma – my mother's made it, and we're to have a small party at home before we leave for John's house."

"I shall see that Cook sends you down a ham and some cheeses the day before," Gertrude declared. "And now, I don't wish to hurry you both, but we do have guests coming this evening."

Carrie drained her drink, feeling her head spin. But it was more than the wine that was making her feel so delirious. It was the joy of knowing that everything in her world was becoming so gloriously right. The man she adored was at her side, and in a very few days he would become her husband, for richer, for poorer, for better or worse . . . but it could surely only be for the better, she thought fervently, sending up a little prayer of hope.

The morning of Friday the twenty-eighth of June was calm and sunny. The young 'uns had been got ready, and threatened not to soil a scrap of their fine wedding clobber. All the food was laid out on the tables for later, and Billy had been forbidden to touch a single morsel until then. The menfolk were togged up in their Sunday best, with Sam almost busting out of his collar, where he'd put on weight since leading a more affluent life of late. And Ma went upstairs with Carrie to help her into the creamy folds of the wedding-gown.

"You look a fair picture, my lamb," Ma said with a small break in her voice as she looked at the vision in front of her. It wasn't in her nature to gush and praise unnecessarily, and in any case she was nearly tongue-tied at seeing her girl look so beautiful. Just like an angel . . . and she quickly hoped she wasn't blaspheming with the thought.

Carrie looked at her reflection in the square of mirror above Pa's sturdily made dressing-table, wondering if the person looking back at her could really be her. It was someone far removed from reality, a princess . . .

"I do look different, don't I, Ma?" she said huskily. "Do you think John will recognise me, looking so fine?"

"I think perhaps he always sees you this way," Ma said. "A man does, when he looks at his bride, Carrie."

As they looked at one another for a moment, they seemed to be no longer mother and daughter, but two women who were loved and cherished. The one, having known the special kind of married love for many years, and the other, on the brink of that love . . .

Carrie turned and hugged her mother hard for a moment.

"I feel I should say summat to you, Ma, but I can't seem to find the words."

"We don't need words, my lamb. All that's needed is what's here in our hearts, and seeing you so happy and fulfilled today is all the thanks a mother needs."

Carrie nodded, and then the air was filled with the heady scent of roses, as she picked up the small coronet of blooms for her head, and the posy of summer blossoms she was to carry into church. At the neck of her gown was the diamond pin Mrs Barclay had given her. But not even diamonds could outshine the sparkle that was in Carrie's eyes on that special day.

A short while later, the Stuckey family took their places in the church opposite John's aunt and uncle, and a few acquaintances from the boatyards and ferries. Nora Woolley and her parents sat on the bride's side of the church, while Wilf and John stood stiffly to attention at the front, awaiting the arrival of the bride and her father. May prayed they wouldn't delay in starting up the aisle and start Billy fidgeting, and that young Henry wouldn't start making a fuss at having to be held still for too long.

She heard the small buzz of approval from the back of the church from the various onlookers who always flocked to church to see a wedding, and she turned her head slightly. Sam looked so fine, she thought, and so proud to have his girl on his arm as she went to be married.

But Carrie saw only John, turning to watch her walk slowly up the aisle, with such a look of love in his eyes that it took her breath away. She went towards him, as if this was still something in a beautiful dream, hardly seeming to move her feet at all, until she reached his side at last. She had to force herself to pay attention as Mr Pritchard said the words that would bind her to John for ever.

"Do you, Caroline, take John to be your lawful wedded husband . . .?" the words droned on.

"I do," she whispered, and she felt the coolness of the plain gold band slide onto her finger. John held it there for a moment, and she felt the warmth of him and the strength of him flow into her. Her eyes stung, loving him so much, and blessing the good fortune that had sent him into her life.

In no time at all they were walking back towards the house again in a fine procession. A carriage would take the newly married couple back up Bedminster Hill later, but for now, they were making this traditional walk from the church to the reception, with all their supporters walking behind, and many others falling into step for the sheer joy of the occasion. They were cheered and applauded all the way by folk who came out of their cottages especially to see all the finery of a bride and groom.

"I wish I could hold onto this day for ever," Carrie told John, when they had nodded and laughed and thanked a score of strangers who wished them well.

She hugged his arm, and felt him squeeze it to his side.

"We'll always hold onto it, my darling," he said. "Every day will be as wonderful as this one, because from now on we'll always be together to share them."

If Carrie was sensible enough to know it couldn't always be so, none of that mattered, because today was the best day of her life, and no thought of a lesser tomorrow was going to be allowed inside her head.

And when all the pomp and excitement were over, and Billy had been assured that he could come to visit them on Bedminster Hill whenever he liked, they set off in the hired carriage that was to take them to their new home. By then, Vi and Oswald had already gone on their way to Clevedon, and the house was empty, awaiting them.

They walked arm in arm up the garden path, fragrant with summer roses, and John opened the front door and held out his arms to her.

"A bride should always be carried over the threshold to ensure that good luck always follow her," he said softly.

He swept her up in his arms, and the sensual silkiness of her gown rustled over and around them both. His face was close to hers, and she murmured against his cheek.

"I already have all the luck I need right here," she said in a soft sighing whisper.

He kissed her with unrestrained and mounting passion, and she responded with a fervour and longing that delighted him. And he was still kissing her as he kicked the door behind them, and shut out the rest of the world.